ELLERY QUEEN'S BAD SCENES

STORIES FROM ELLERY QUEEN'S MYSTERY MAGAZINE

Also edited by Eleanor Sullivan

Murder On Cue

ELLERY QUEEN'S BAD SCENES

STORIES FROM ELLERY QUEEN'S MYSTERY MAGAZINE

Edited by Eleanor Sullivan

Stories in this collection originally appeared
in *Ellery Queen's Mystery Magazine*,
edited by Ellery Queen

**WALKER AND COMPANY
NEW YORK**

First published in the United States of America in 1989
by Walker Publishing Company, Inc.

Published simultaneously in Canada by Thomas Allen & Son
Canada, Limited, Markham, Ontario

Library of Congress Cataloging-in-Publication Data

Ellery Queen's bad scenes : stories from Ellery Queen's mystery
magazine / edited by Eleanor Sullivan.
p. cm.
ISBN 0-8027-5745-6
1. Detective and mystery stories, American. 2. Detective and
mystery stories, English. I. Sullivan, Eleanor. II. Ellery
Queen's mystery magazine. III. Title: Bad scenes.
PS648.D4E375 1989
813'.087208—dc20   89-35365
CIP

Printed in the United States of America

10 8 6 4 2 1 3 5 7 9

Dedication

Stanley Ellin, whose contribution to mystery/detective fiction in general, and to EQMM *in particular, is both impeccable and immense, died on July 31, 1986, with both a short story and a novel partially finished.*

To have known him personally was a privilege, to have access to his work is another. This anthology is dedicated to him with the deepest affection, gratitude, and respect.

Acknowledgments

Grateful acknowledgment is hereby made for permission to reprint the following:

Déjà Vu by Mary Barrett; Copyright © 1972 by Mary Barrett; reprinted by permission of the author.

Falling Object by William Brittain; Copyright © 1970 by William Brittain; reprinted by permission of the author.

Monday Is a Quiet Place by Marjorie Carleton; Copyright © 1962 by E. J. Carleton; reprinted by permission of Harold Ober Associates, Inc.

The Old Barn on the Pond by Ursula Curtiss; Copyright © 1965 by Ursula Curtiss; Copyright © 1984 by Katherine Reilly; reprinted from THE HOUSE ON PLYMOUTH STREET AND OTHER STORIES by Ursula Curtiss, by permission of Dodd, Mead & Company, Inc., and Brandt & Brandt Literary Agents, Inc.

The Shop That Exchanged Evils by Lord Dunsany; Copyright by Lord Dunsany; reprinted by permission of Curtis Brown, London.

The Question by Stanley Ellin; Copyright © 1962 by Stanley Ellin; reprinted by permission of Curtis Brown, Ltd.

A Question of Neighborliness by David Ely; Copyright © 1963 by David Ely; reprinted by permission of International Creative Management.

In a Country Churchyard by Robert L. Fish; Copyright © 1970 by Davis Publications, Inc.; reprinted by permission of the Estate of Robert L. Fish.

The Missing Mortgagee by R. Austin Freeman; Copyright 1949 by Davis Publications, Inc.; reprinted by permission of Austin Edgar Briant and A. P. Watt, Ltd.

CONTENTS

INTRODUCTION

The Dictionary of American Slang defines a bad scene as "something unpleasant, esp. an unpleasant experience." Without question, the twenty-five stories in this new Ellery Queen anthology meet this qualification.

Speaking of questions, they also raise a good many timeless ones.

In John Mitchell Hayes' screen adaptation, for Alfred Hitchcock, of Cornell Woolrich's "Rear Window," starring James Stewart, Grace Kelly, and Raymond Burr, Boyne became Coyne (played by Wendell Corey) and Sam became Stella (played by Thelma Ritter) and Stella disapproves of Jeff spying on his neighbors as he does. "We've grown to be a race of peeping Toms," she tells him—an observation even truer now than when it was written in 1953. "What people should do," she adds, "is stand outside their own houses and look in once in a while."

An even more chilling indictment is made by the son in Stanley Ellin's lead story, "The Question." This story was Stanley Ellin's own favorite among his impressive, superb, award-winning, much collected, often adapted short fiction. Asked why it was his favorite, he said: "For one thing, its subject—capital punishment—tends to draw from those favoring it or opposing it fervently self-righteous and simplistic argumentation, and in attempting a story on the theme I had to dig very deep into myself to come up with an insight into my own feelings. That kind of self-discovery is intensely gratifying to me.

"For another thing," he continued, "the large mail response, pro and con, to the story on publication indicated that I had certainly touched a nerve here, and touching nerves—which doesn't happen all that often—is what I most hope to achieve in any story."

—Eleanor Sullivan

ELLERY QUEEN'S BAD SCENES

STORIES FROM ELLERY QUEEN'S MYSTERY MAGAZINE

STANLEY ELLIN

THE QUESTION

I am an electrocutioner. I prefer this word to executioner; I think words make a difference. When I was a boy, people who buried the dead were undertakers, and then somewhere along the way they became morticians and are better off for it.

Take the one who used to be the undertaker in my town. He was a decent, respectable man—very friendly if you'd let him be, but hardly anybody would let him be. Today, his son—who now runs the business—is not an undertaker but a mortician, and is welcome everywhere. As a matter of fact, he's an officer in my Lodge and is one of the most popular members we have. And all it took to do that was changing one word to another. The job's the same but the word is different, and people somehow will always go by words rather than meanings.

So, as I said, I am an electrocutioner—which is the proper professional word for it in my state where the electric chair is the means of execution.

Not that this is my profession. Actually, it's a sideline, as it is for most of us who perform executions. My real business is running an electrical supply and repair shop just as my father did before me. When he died, I inherited not only the business from him but also the position of state's electrocutioner.

We established a tradition, my father and I. He was running the shop profitably even before the turn of the century when electricity was a comparatively new thing, and he was the first man to perform a successful electrocution for the state.

It was not the state's first electrocution, however. That one was an experiment and was badly bungled by the engineer who installed the chair in the state prison. My father, who had helped install the chair, was the assistant at the electrocution, and he told me that everything that could go wrong that day did go wrong. The current was eccentric, his boss froze on the switch, and the man in the chair was alive and kicking at the same time

1

he was being burned to a crisp. The next time, my father offered to do the job himself, rewired the chair, and handled the switch so well that he was offered the job of official electrocutioner.

I followed in his footsteps, which is how a tradition is made, but I am afraid this one ends with me. I have a son, and what I said to him and what he said to me is the crux of the matter. He asked me a question—well, in my opinion, it was the kind of question that's at the bottom of most of the world's troubles today. There are some sleeping dogs that should be left to lie; there are some questions that should not be asked.

To understand all this, I think you have to understand me, and nothing could be easier. I'm sixty, just beginning to look my age, a little overweight, suffer sometimes from arthritis when the weather is damp. I'm a good citizen, complain about my taxes but pay them on schedule, vote for the right party, and run my business well enough to make a comfortable living from it.

I've been married thirty-five years and never looked at another woman in all that time. Well, looked maybe, but no more than that. I have a married daughter and a granddaughter almost a year old, and the prettiest, smilingest baby in town. I spoil her and don't apologize for it, because in my opinion that is what grandfathers were made for—to spoil their grandchildren. Let mama and papa attend to the business; grandpa is there for the fun.

And beyond all that I have a son who asks questions. The kind that shouldn't be asked.

Put the picture together, and what you get is someone like yourself. I might be your next-door neighbor, I might be your old friend, I might be the uncle you meet whenever the family gets together at a wedding or a funeral. I'm like you.

Naturally, we all look different on the outside but we can still recognize each other on sight as the same kind of people. Deep down inside where it matters we have the same feelings, and we know that without any questions being asked about them.

"But," you might say, "there is a difference between us. You're the one who performs the executions, and I'm the one who reads about them in the papers, and that's a big difference no matter how you look at it."

Is it? Well, look at it without prejudice, look at it with absolute honesty, and you'll have to admit that you're being unfair.

Let's face the facts, we're all in this together. If an old friend of yours happens to serve on a jury that finds a murderer guilty, you don't lock the door against him, do you? More than that: if you could get an introduction to the judge who sentences that murderer to the electric chair, you'd be proud of it, wouldn't you? You'd be honored to have him sit at your table, and you'd be quick enough to let the world know about it.

And since you're so willing to be friendly with the jury that convicts and the judge that sentences, what about the man who has to pull the switch? He's finished the job you wanted done, he's made the world a better place for it. Why must he go hide away in a dark corner until the next time he's needed?

There's no use denying that nearly everybody feels he should, and there's less use denying that it's a cruel thing for anyone in my position to face. If you don't mind some strong language, it's a damned outrage to hire a man for an unpleasant job, and then despise him for it. Sometimes it's hard to abide such righteousness.

How do I get along in the face of it? The only way possible— by keeping my secret locked up tight and never being tempted to give it away. I don't like it that way, but I'm no fool about it.

The trouble is that I'm naturally easygoing and friendly. I'm the sociable kind. I like people, and I want them to like me. At Lodge meetings or in the clubhouse down at the golf course I'm always the center of the crowd. And I know what would happen if at any such time I ever opened my mouth and let that secret out. A five-minute sensation, and after that the slow chill setting in. It would mean the end of my whole life then and there, the kind of life I want to live, and no man in his right mind throws away sixty years of his life for a five-minute sensation.

You can see I've given the matter a lot of thought. More than that, it hasn't been idle thought. I don't pretend to be an educated man, but I'm willing to read books on any subject that interests me, and execution has been one of my main interests ever since I got into the line. I have the books sent to the shop where nobody takes notice of another piece of mail, and I keep them locked in a bin in my office so that I can read them in private.

There's a nasty smell about having to do it this way—at my age you hate to feel like a kid hiding himself away to read a dirty magazine—but I have no choice. There isn't a soul on earth outside of the warden at state's prison and a couple of picked guards there who know I'm the one pulling the switch at an execution, and I intend it to remain that way.

Oh, yes, my son knows now. Well, he's difficult in some ways, but he's no fool. If I wasn't sure he would keep his mouth shut about what I told him, I wouldn't have told it to him in the first place.

Have I learned anything from those books? At least enough to take a pride in what I'm doing for the state and the way I do it. As far back in history as you want to go, there have always been executioners. The day that men first made laws to help keep peace among themselves was the day the first executioner was born. There have always been lawbreakers; there must always be a way of punishing them. It's as simple as that.

The trouble is that nowadays there are too many people who don't want it to be as simple as that. I'm no hypocrite, I'm not one of those narrow-minded fools who thinks that every time a man comes up with a generous impulse he's some kind of crackpot. But he can be mistaken. I'd put most of the people who are against capital punishment in that class. They are fine, high-minded citizens who've never in their lives been close enough to a murderer or rapist to smell the evil in him. In fact, they're so fine and high minded that they can't imagine anyone in the world not being like themselves. In that case, they say anybody who commits murder or rape is just a plain, ordinary human being who's had a bad spell. He's no criminal, they say, he's just sick. He doesn't need the electric chair; all he needs is a kindly old doctor to examine his head and straighten out the kinks in his brain.

In fact, they say there is no such thing as a criminal at all. There are only well people and sick people, and the ones who deserve all your worry and consideration are the sick ones. If they happen to murder or rape a few of the well ones now and then, why, just run for the doctor.

This is the argument from beginning to end, and I'd be the last one to deny that it's built on honest charity and good intentions. But it's a mistaken argument. It omits the one fact that matters. When anyone commits murder or rape he is no longer in the human race. A man has a human brain and a God-given soul to control his animal nature. When the animal in him takes control he's not a human being any more. Then he has to be exterminated the way any animal must be if it goes wild in the middle of helpless people. And my duty is to be the exterminator.

It could be that people just don't understand the meaning of the word *duty* any more. I don't want to sound old-fashioned, God forbid, but when I was a boy things were more straightforward and clear-cut. You learned to do what had to be done, and you didn't ask questions every step of the way. Or if you had to ask any questions, the ones that mattered were *how* and *when*.

Then along came psychology, along came the professors, and the main question was always *why*. Ask yourself *why, why, why* about everything you do, and you'll end up doing nothing. Let a couple of generations go along that way and you'll finally have a breed of people who sit around in trees like monkeys, scratching their heads.

Does this sound farfetched? Well, it isn't. Life is a complicated thing to live. All his life a man finds himself facing one situation after another, and the way to handle them is to live by the rules. Ask yourself *why* once too often and you can find yourself so tangled up that you go under. The show must go on. Why? Women and children first. Why? My country, right or wrong. Why? Never mind your duty. Just keep asking *why* until it's too late to do anything about it.

Around the time I first started going to school, my father gave me a dog, a collie pup named Rex. A few years after, Rex suddenly became unfriendly, the way a dog will sometimes, and then vicious, and then one day he bit my mother when she reached down to pat him.

The day after that, I saw my father leaving the house with his hunting rifle under his arm and Rex on a leash. It wasn't the

hunting season, so I knew what was going to happen to Rex
and I knew why. But it's forgivable in a boy to ask things that a
man should be smart enough not to ask.

"Where are you taking Rex?" I asked my father. "What are
you going to do with him?"

"I'm taking him out back of town," my father said. "I'm going
to shoot him."

"But why?" I said, and that was when my father let me see
that there is only one answer to such a question.

"Because it has to be done," he said.

I never forgot that lesson. It came hard; for a while I hated
my father for it, but as I grew up I came to see how right he
was. We both knew why the dog had to be killed. Beyond that,
all questions would lead nowhere. Why the dog had become
vicious, why God had put a dog on earth to be killed this way—
these are the questions that you can talk out to the end of time,
and while you're talking about them you still have a vicious dog
on your hands.

It is strange to look back and realize now that when the
business of the dog happened, and long before it and long after
it, my father was an electrocutioner and I never knew it.
Nobody knew it, not even my mother. A few times a year my
father would pack his bag and a few tools and go away for a
couple of days, but that was all any of us knew. If you asked
him where he was going he would simply say he had a job to
do out of town. He was not a man you'd ever suspect of
philandering or going off on a solitary drunk, so nobody gave it
a second thought.

It worked the same way in my case. I found out how well it
worked when I finally told my son what I had been doing on
those jobs out of town and that I had gotten the warden's
permission to take him on as an assistant and train him to
handle the chair himself when I retired.

I could tell from the way he took it that he was as thunder-
struck at this as I had been thirty years before when my father
had taken me into his confidence.

"Electrocutioner?" said my son. "An *electrocutioner*?"

"Well, there's no disgrace to it," I said. "And since it's got to
be done, and somebody has to do it, why not keep it in the

family? If you knew anything about it, you'd know it's a profession that's often passed down in a family from generation to generation. What's wrong with a good, sound tradition? If more people believed in tradition you wouldn't have so many troubles in the world today."

It was the kind of argument that would have been more than enough to convince me when I was his age. What I hadn't taken into account was that my son wasn't like me, much as I wanted him to be. He was a grown man in his own right, but a grown man who had never settled down to his responsibilities. I had always kept closing my eyes to that, I had always seen him the way I wanted to and not the way he was.

When he left college after a year, I said, all right, there are some people who aren't made for college, I never went there, so what difference does it make. When he went out with one girl after another and could never make up his mind to marrying any of them I said, well, he's young, he's sowing his wild oats, the time will come soon enough when he's ready to take care of a home and family. When he sat daydreaming in the shop instead of tending to business I never made a fuss about it. I knew when he put his mind to it he was as good an electrician as you could ask for, and in these soft times people are allowed to do a lot more dreaming and a lot less working than they used to.

The truth was that the only thing that mattered to me was being his friend. For all his faults he was a fine-looking boy with a good mind. He wasn't much for mixing with people, but if he wanted to he could win anyone over. And in the back of my mind all the while he was growing up was the thought that he was the only one who would learn my secret someday, and would share it with me and make it easier to bear. I'm not secretive by nature. A man like me needs a thought like that to sustain him.

So when the time came to tell him, he shook his head and said no. I felt that my legs had been kicked out from under me. I argued with him and he still said no, and I lost my temper.

"Are you against capital punishment?" I asked him. "You don't have to apologize if you are. I'd think all the more of you, if that's your only reason."

"I don't know if it is," he said.

"Well, you ought to make up your mind one way or the other," I told him. "I'd hate to think you were like every other hypocrite around who says it's all right to condemn a man to the electric chair and all wrong to pull the switch."

"Do I have to be the one to pull it?" he said. "Do you?"

"Somebody has to do it. Somebody always has to do the dirty work for the rest of us. It's not like the Old Testament days when everybody did it for himself. Do you know how they executed a man in those days? They laid him on the ground tied hand and foot, and everybody around had to heave rocks on him until he was crushed to death. They didn't invite anybody to stand around and watch. You wouldn't have had much choice then, would you?"

"I don't know," he said.

And then, because he was as smart as they come and knew how to turn your words against you, he said, "After all, I'm not without sin."

"Don't talk like a child," I said. "You're without the sin of murder on you or any kind of sin that calls for electrocution. And if you're so sure the Bible has all the answers, you might remember that you're supposed to render unto Caesar the things that are Caesar's."

"Well," he said, "in this case I'll let you do the rendering."

I knew then and there from the way he said it and the way he looked at me that it was no use trying to argue with him. The worst of it was knowing that we had somehow moved far apart from each other and would never really be close again. I should have had sense enough to let it go at that. I should have just told him to forget the whole thing and keep his mouth shut about it.

Maybe if I had ever considered the possibility of his saying no, I wouldn't have done it. But because I hadn't considered any such possibility I was caught off balance; I was too much upset to think straight. I will admit it now. It was my own fault that I made an issue of things and led him to ask the one question he should never have asked.

"I see," I told him. "It's the same old story, isn't it? Let somebody else do it. But if they pull your number out of a hat and you have to serve on a jury and send a man to the chair, that's all right with you. At least, it's all right as long as there's somebody else to do the job that you and the judge and every decent citizen wants done. Let's face the facts, boy, you don't have the guts. I'd hate to think of you even walking by the death house. The shop is where you belong. You can be nice and cozy there, wiring up fixtures and ringing the cash register. I can handle my duties without you help."

It hurt me to say it. I had never talked like that to him before, and it hurt. The strange thing was that he didn't seem angry about it; he only looked at me puzzled.

"Is that all it is to you?" he said. "A duty?"

"Yes."

"But you get paid for it, don't you."

"I get paid little enough for it."

He kept looking at me that way. "Only a duty?" he said, and never took his eyes off me. "But you enjoy it, don't you?"

That was the question he asked.

You enjoy it, don't you?

You stand there looking through a peephole in the wall at the chair. In thirty years I have stood there more than a hundred times looking at that chair. The guards bring somebody in. Usually he is in a daze; sometimes he screams, throws himself around and fights. Sometimes it is a woman, and a woman can be as hard to handle as a man when she is led to the chair. Sooner or later, whoever it is is strapped down and the black hood is dropped over his head. Now your hand is on the switch.

The warden signals, and you pull the switch. The current hits the body like a tremendous rush of air suddenly filling it. The body leaps out of the chair with only the straps holding it back. The head jerks, and a curl of smoke comes from it. You release the switch and the body falls back again.

You do it once more, do it a third time to make sure. And whenever your hand presses the switch you can see in your mind what the current is doing to that body and what the face under the hood must look like.

Enjoy it?

That was the question my son asked me. That was what he

said to me, as if I didn't have the same feelings deep down in me that we all have.

Enjoy it?

But, my God, how could anyone *not* enjoy it!

URSULA CURTISS

THE OLD BARN ON THE POND

He came back on a raw, darkly glistening day in March, but it was not at all the triumphant return he had planned. It was a hasty, off-balance thing, like being pushed rudely onto a stage before the raised trumpets had blown a single note.

Conlon's letter—the letter that had brought him tumbling up from New York to this inhospitable part of the New England countryside—was still in his pocket. He had never liked Conlon, but the architect was Marian's cousin and it would have looked odd, when he had the old barn remodeled, to have given the job to someone else. And now here was Conlon writing ". . . have been approached by friends about the possibility of renting your property here for the summer, with an option to buy. As they have a young child, they would like to drain the pond, and although I told them I was certain you would not permit this—"

For a moment the typed lines had blurred before Howard Hildreth's eyes—except for that one staring phrase.

Drain the pond.

Not yet, he thought lucidly—not after only six months. Anonymous in the 42nd Street Library, he had read up on the subject and learned that under certain conditions—depth of water, amount of rainfall, and other climatic factors—this kind of soil might have sucked its secret under at the end of a year; provided there was no extensive digging.

But not yet. He had sat down at once to write a brief note of refusal, but another phrase struck up at him from Conlon's letter. ". . . I was certain you would not permit this—"

A deliberate challenge? Bill Conlon was Marian's cousin, remember, and had been away at the time. Better go up there, stay a week or two, establish the impression of keeping the

11

place as a country retreat upon which he might descend at any time. It was only necessary for Conlon; the townspeople, he was sure, accepted his remodeling of the barn as proof of his faith that his missing wife would someday return.

At that thought, alone in his comfortable apartment, Howard Hildreth shuddered . . .

On the station platform there were gratifying little whispers and stirs of recognition—"Isn't that Howard Hildreth, the playwright? I'm sure it is"—and a turning of heads which he pretended not to see.

He could hardly pretend not to see Conlon, striding across the platform toward him with his fair head a little cocked. Conlon had Marian's eyes, light grey with a peculiar curl of lid, but that was the only physical resemblance between them.

Hildreth put out a hand and said with an air of geniality, "Well, this is kind. I hope you haven't been meeting trains all day?"

Conlon sent one of his roving glances around the platform. "Matter of fact, a fellow in our office was supposed to catch this one but he seems to have missed it. Come on, I'll give you a lift."

After his first annoyance at Conlon's balloon-picking, Hildreth was pleased; this would give him a chance to demonstrate his calm. He said as they got into the car, "I can see how you thought I wouldn't be using the place this summer. I'd have been in touch with you sooner about coming up but we've had a little trouble in the cast."

He waited for Conlon to show interest, but the other man only said, "Too bad. Play still going well?"

"Very, thanks."

"I particularly liked"—Conlon turned a sharp corner with care—"the third act. It packs quite a wallop. Are you working on a new play?"

"I am, as a matter of fact, and I thought a little peace and quiet . . . You know New York," said Hildreth resignedly. In his tone were autograph hunters, sheaves of fan mail, a telephone carrying an invitation with each ring.

And part of it was true. *The Far Cry* was the rarest of things, a hit first play, and the playbill's revelation that it had been eight

years in the writing had given an additional fillip. Eight years—
what constancy! No wonder that superb third act expertly
shivered like a diamond. Here was no glib young creature with
a gift for bubbling out dialogue, but a major talent who cut his
work like a precious stone.

So the critics said, and the important hostesses, and Howard
Hildreth, who had been laughed at in this little town, and had
his credit refused and his electric light turned off, found his
champagne all the winier and forgot those few hours of frantic
typing.

". . . not a word," Conlon was saying, and Hildreth wrenched
his attention from his play, his other self. They were out of the
town now, rising into little hills and woodland, puddled and
glinted yellowly by a sky which, having rained earlier, was now
gloating over it.

Hildreth's mind spun back and recaptured the sense of his
companion's words. He said, "Nor I. But I refuse to believe . . .
you knew Marian—"

"I think she's dead," said Conlon bluntly without turning his
head. "I think she was dead all the time the police were out
looking for her."

"But where—?" said Hildreth in a shocked voice.

Conlon waved a hand at the dimming landscape. "There's
almost as much water as there is land around here," he said.
"Lake, marshes, even quicksand. She had such a horror of things
eaten up in the water, remember?"

"Stop!" said Hildreth with genuine violence. "You mustn't
talk about her as though— Besides, Marian was happy, she
would never have—"

"Committed suicide, or disappeared on purpose?" said Conlon when it was apparent that Hildreth was not going to finish.
"Oh, I never thought she had. As you say, I knew Marian— Here
we are."

The car had descended a gentle twisting curve. At the bottom, opposite a stand of birches and set perhaps a hundred feet
in from the road, was the pond, as round and clear as a
wondering eye, lashed by willows that looked lamplit in the
approaching dusk.

On the far side of it, on a slight rise, stood the creamy new structure, the remodeled barn, which six months ago had been weatherbeaten planks and a wobbly brown-painted door. There was no breath of wind; the house and reflection met themselves in a mirror stillness.

Howard Hildreth gazed, and his heart raced with such horror that he wondered if he was about to have a stroke. He wrenched at his horn-rimmed glasses with a trembling hand and heard Conlon say curiously, "Are you all right, Howard?"

"Yes. These damned glasses—the doctor warned me that I needed new ones." Even the effort of speaking calmly seemed to put a nutcracker pressure on his heart. "You've done a beautiful job of remodeling the barn, Bill. The photographs you sent didn't do it justice. Shall we go on in?"

The drive up to the house itself was screened by willows. By the time Conlon had helped him inside with his bags, Hildreth was able to say almost normally, "Well, here we are. You'll have a drink, won't you?"

Conlon shook his head. He said with a hand on the doorknob, "Sarah—Sarah Wilde, you know—ordered a few essentials for the kitchen, so you ought to get through the night without starving. Well—"

Hildreth did not press him to stay. He said, standing in the open doorway, "These friends of yours that I had to disappoint—do I know them? What's their name?"

"Pocock," said Conlon promptly, and it was so unlikely a name that Hildreth had to believe him. Or was it meant to be a shortened version of poppycock?

He did not even look around at the long studio that took up most of the lower front of the house. He waited tensely for the final retreat of Conlon's motor, and when even the echoes were gone he opened the door and walked the length of the driveway in the lonely frog-sounding dusk.

And there was light enough—just enough—to show him the same sickening apparition. On the far side of the pond stood the new barn, radiantly pale, bearing no resemblance to its former weatherbeaten brown. But at his feet, glassily etched on the surface of the water, lay the old barn, with its knotholes and weatherstains and the wide brown-painted door.

Hildreth drew a long uneven breath. There was no one to see

him step squashily to the reed-grown edge of the pond and dip a hand in the icy water. The old barn quaked under the willows, and shook, and was presently still again—but it was still the old barn . . .

He did not drink—Marian had—but he took a tranquilizer and headed for his reviews like a child to its mother's skirts. *The Times, Tribune, Daily News,* the out-of-town papers. "Last night at the Odeon Theatre this critic was refreshingly jolted . . ."

"*The Far Cry* is just that in a season so far noted for its weary offerings . . ." "Let us hope we do not have to wait another eight years for the next Hildreth play . . ."

And presently he knew what had happened to him out there at the pond's edge. Auto-suggestion, hallucination—at any rate, there was an accepted term for it; if beauty lay in the beholder's eye, so did other things. He knew what was under that pleasant and pastoral surface, and at the subconscious tension of his mind, because Conlon had been with him, his retina had produced the appropriate setting.

But not for Conlon, with all his suspicions—and in retrospect, the man had exuded suspicion. Conlon had looked at the pond and seen nothing amiss; for him, the still water had reflected only his personal creation of shored-up beams and plaster and creamy paint and whatever else went into his remodeling of an old structure. The thought gave Hildreth a satisfaction that, keyed up as he was, bordered on triumph.

What a joke on them all, he mused as he broiled the steak Sarah Wilde had left in the refrigerator, if only he, Hildreth, could see this watery witness, gaze at it in their presence, say casually, "Lovely day, isn't it?"—and stand there calmly and casually in the midst of their blindness.

Not that the reflection would be on the pond in the morning. Tonight it had simply been a product of nerves and fatigue, and a good night's sleep would erase it. Still, he was shaken, and he prudently avoided his after-dinner coffee. He darkened the downstairs, flipped on the staircase switch, and went up to his bedroom.

And came face to face with a portrait of Marian which he never knew had been taken.

As the blood came and went from his heart more slowly, he realized that the matted and mounted photograph on the bureau was not a portrait but an enlarged snapshot; on closer inspection it bore a telltale grain and blurriness. It was in color and it showed Marian laughing. There was a halo of sunlight on the close curls that scrambled over her beautifully shaped head, and the same light picked out the comma of mirth beside her mouth although her short, soft, full white throat was in shadow.

Marian laughing . . .

. . . laughing at his play, which she was not supposed to have seen at all until he had written the final word—*Curtain*. Managing to say through the laughter, "My dear playwright, you don't mean to say you've been muddling around with this thing for eight years and missed the whole *point?* It ought to be satire at the end, don't you see, and you fox the audience in the third act instead of this heavy Russian gloom going on and on? It would have such a wonderful, final, crack-the-whip effect, and you could get rid of Anna coming in and saying"—she draggled at her hair, which was much too short and curly for draggling—"whatever that long lugubrious speech is."

Her face was brilliant with excited laughter. "Oh, *wait* till I tell Bill and Sarah we've found a way to finish the Odyssey at last! They'll be so—Howard, for heaven's sake, I'm only—*Howar—*"

For such a full throat, it was as soft and weak as a child's.

In the morning Hildreth looked at the pond, and the old weatherbeaten barn was still there, shaken and distorted under a gently falling rain. Disturbingly, he was not terrified or shocked or even very surprised; it was as though, at some point during his sleep, his brain had accepted this phenomenon as readily as the pond had accepted Marian.

After breakfast he made arrangements for renting a car, and then he called Sarah Wilde.

It was through Sarah, who also had an apartment in the building on East Tenth Street, that he had met Marian Guest. Sarah and Marian were copywriters in the same advertising agency, and although Hildreth had a sober loathing of advertising copy and all the people who wrote it—there was a flippancy about them that appalled him—Sarah was well connected. An aunt of hers was a bestselling novelist, and it had never harmed any hopeful playwright to have even a hearsay acquaintance with a publisher. He had cultivated Sarah in the elevator, lent her an umbrella one day, and ultimately wound up at a party in her apartment.

And there was Marian, sitting on the floor although there were chairs available. She wore black slacks and an expensive-looking white silk shirt with a safety pin where a button should have been, and, profile tilted in the lamplight, she was explaining with zest how she had come by her black eye and scraped cheekbone. She had been walking her dog, George, and had fallen over a sheep on a leash. "The man said it was a Bedlington but he was obviously trying to cover up his own confusion. Poor George bit him, not the man, and I think he's got a hairball."

Although there were two or three other girls present, all with a just-unboxed Madison Avenue attractiveness, the attention seemed to cluster about Marian. She said presently to Howard Hildreth in her boyish and uninhibited voice, "You look terribly broody. What are you hatching?"

"A play", he told her distantly, and it might have been the very distance that attracted her, as it was the attention focused on her that attracted him. At any rate, he ended up taking her home to her apartment on Barrow Street, drinking innumerable cups of black coffee, and telling her about his play. He began challengingly, prepared for amusement when she learned that he had already been working on it for three years; but she listened, her light clear eyes as wide and sober as a child's.

She said, "What do you do—for an income, I mean?"

When he said flatly, "I'm a shoe clerk," she stared past him with a kind of wondering sadness.

"How marvelous," she had said, "to give that much of a damn about anything."

There was Marian, summed up in a single sentence; even after they were married she never told him anything as self-revelatory as that. And under the influence of her respect for his dedication, his work, which had always been his Work to him, was able to come out in the open with its capital letter. Until she had defected—

But Hildreth had learned to discipline his mind, and he did it now.

He said into the telephone, "Sarah? I'm an ingrate for not calling you last night to tell you how much I like the way you've done the place—as well as providing my dinner—but—"

Sarah Wilde cut him off easily.

"Do you like it? I'm glad. It's rather a lot of lavender, but you did specify—"

"Yes," Hildreth gazed, secretly entertained, at the lavender draperies, the lavender cushions, round and square and triangular, piled on the black tweed couch. Lavender—Marian's favorite color. Any doubters close to Marian could not help saying to themselves, "Well, if he can live with that—"

"It's very soothing," he said to Sarah with the defensive air of a husband standing up for his wife's vagaries. "Very restful. I like the picture on my bureau, by the way."

It was as though the telephone cord had been pulled taut between them. "It is a good one, isn't it? I took it—oh, sometime last summer, I think, and I'd forgotten all about it until Bill Conlon happened to see it and thought you'd like an enlargement."

"It was very thoughtful of you both," said Hildreth with perfect evenness. "That's the way I think of her, you know. Laughing. I suppose Bill's told you that I haven't given up hope."

"Of course you haven't," said Sarah, bright and artificial.

Between them, in the small silence that followed, lay the many trips that he and Conlon had taken to view unidentified female bodies which corresponded even roughly with Marian's age and height. It was grim work, which helped; he was always a thoroughly pale and shaken man. And with each fruitless trip, because of the very nature of such an errand, the official belief that Marian Hildreth was dead had grown. Hildreth could tell that Sarah believed it, too—in which, of course, she was quite right.

She was veering quickly away from the subject now, saying something about dinner this week. Hildreth accepted for Thursday evening, adding with a deprecating little laugh that he trusted it wouldn't be an Occasion; he'd come up here to get started on his new play.

"No, just two or three people," Sarah assured him. "I did tell you, didn't I, how much I liked *The Far Cry?* I thought I knew what was coming in the third act, but it was one time I loved being made a fool of."

Hildreth thanked her, a trifle aloofly, and there was not the smallest alarm along his nerves. He suspected that Sarah and Conlon, mere acquaintances six months ago, would be married before the year was out, but the fact that they had undoubtedly seen the play together didn't matter. They could not say, "That last act sounds like Marian," because as far as they knew Marian had never laid eyes on the script—she had said wryly, in fact, two or three days before that last night, "Howard thinks I'll mark his baby, like a gypsy."

(What a very tellable joke it would have been, what an irresistible nugget for gossip columns, because Marian's was not a secret-keeping nature: that Howard Hildreth had toiled unremittingly over his play for eight years, and in the space of a single hour his wife, who had never written anything but tongue-in-cheek praise of vinyl tile and slide fasteners, had offhandedly supplied the satirical twist that made it a success.)

Even at the thought, Hildreth felt a qualm of nausea. Although his portable typewriter stood ready on the desk at the far end of the studio, with a fresh ream of yellow paper beside it, he let himself out the front door into the falling rain and walked to the pond's edge. There was the old barn, shaking dimly under the falling drops, and he knew that in some terrible way he was drawing strength from this private vision, locked under the willows for his eyes, and apparently for his alone.

A notion of incipient madness slid across his mind, but he looked quickly about him and everything else was sane and clear. If Marian thought to retaliate after death.

He drew himself up sharply . . .

In the afternoon he was gracious to the editor of the local newspaper, with the result that his favorite publicity picture appeared in the next morning's issue. He was holding his horn-rimmed glasses with one earpiece casually collapsed, and the three-quarter turn of his head almost concealed the double chin developed since those lean days.

". . . seeking inspiration for his new play," said the account below, proudly, and, "Residents will recall the still-unresolved disappearance of Mrs. Marian Hildreth six months ago. Mrs. Hildreth, 38, told her husband late on the evening of October 4, 1963, that she was going out for a walk. She did not return, and no trace of her has since been found. Mr. Hildreth maintains his staunch belief that his wife is still alive, possibly suffering from a loss of memory . . ."

Hildreth read with calm pleasure the rest of the telling—how the pond on the property had been dragged without result. The police had indeed dragged it over his demurs—"Oh, come now, she wouldn't fall into a pond she's lived beside for five years"—and then came the heavily tactful, "Mr. Hildreth, your wife wasn't—er . . . ?"

Because Marian's more madcap exploits were not unknown to the local police. They viewed her with a tolerant and even an indulgent eye—that was the effect she had on people—but under the circumstances they could not rule out a tragic and alcoholic whim.

"No," Hildreth had said with transparent stoutness. "Oh, she may have had a highball or two after dinner . . ."

He knew, he had known at the moment of her death, that the marital partner was usually Suspect Number One. But that had not actually held true in little Ixton, Connecticut. If there had been any whisper of discord, any suggestion of dalliance by either party, any prospect of inheriting money—or even if Marian's life had been insured—the police might have looked deeper than they did. As it was, they walked past the burlaped yew, the burlaped roses, Marian's burlaped body, and then announced that they would drag the pond.

This procedure netted them two ancient inner tubes, a rotted and hinged object which had once been the hood of a convertible, and a rust-fretted oil drum which seemed to have spawned a great many beer cans. If the police had returned at just after dark, when one particular piece of burlap among the yews had been lifted free of its stiffened secret, and the secret transferred to the now officially blameless water . . . but, predictably, they had not.

They could have no further reason for dragging the pond now—indeed, thought Hildreth, they would need a warrant. And for a warrant they would need evidence.

That was the safety element in a spur-of-the-moment murder. The cleverest planners—Hildreth rejected the word killers— had come to grief over elaborate timetables, unsuspected correspondence, a hint of fear dropped somewhere. There could be none of that in this case. Neither he nor Marian had known what was coming until that moment of her crowing laughter, that intolerable tearing-down of the secrecy and seriousness of his Work.

It was not so much that Marian had burst the bonds of curiosity and somehow contrived to unlock the desk drawer which housed his script, nor even that she had slipped at least temporarily into the ranks of the people who found him clownishly amusing. It was that she was right. Like someone engaged on a painstaking tapestry, he had been following stitch after stitch and lost sight of the pattern, which had leaped at once to Marian's unbothered and mischievous eye.

It was as if—he could not say at the time, because his logic had smoked away like cellophane in a flame. Later, more calmly, he could compare himself to a woman who, after a long and difficult labor, watches the doctor merrily bearing the infant off to his own home.

But there was no evidence, and he would not be tricked or trapped. His visit here—the first since the five weeks or so after he had reported Marian missing—would proclaim his innocence. Not to the police—he wasn't worried about them—but to Bill Conlon and Sarah Wilde, the only people who, close to Marian, might just possibly . . .

Hildreth arranged yellow paper beside his uncovered typewriter in the white-walled lavender-and-black studio, but he did not, that morning or the next or the one after that, commence even the roughest work on a new play.

He told himself defensively that he had spent several months under considerable strain; a man didn't bounce back from that right away. And critical success was paralyzing in itself: there was the inevitable restudying of the first work in search of the magic ingredient, and the equally inevitable fear of comparison with a second.

At no time did he allow it to cross his mind that there were one-play playwrights as there were one-book novelists, and that his one play would still be in various stages of rewriting except for Marian's unruly wit. But there was a moment when, seated blankly at the typewriter, he thought, *Do I look like the pond?* and got up and crossed the room to examine himself in a mirror.

But no; he hadn't changed at all, in spite of his damp little tremor of fright. And if he could see the truth on the pond's surface, surely he could see it on his own? There was the gained weight, granted, but his dark eyes gave back their old serious look, his eyebrows were forbiddingly level, a lock of hair—now pampered by his New York barber—still hung with dedication.

But when he stared long enough and hard enough, moving his face to within an inch or two of the mirror, tiny little Howard Hildreths peeked out of the pupils, and behind them—

Ah, behind *them.*

He developed a kind of triumphant passion for the pond. He watched it balloon with clouds, or covered with nervous little wrinkles under a sudden wind. He saw the weatherbeaten planks and the brown door warp and fly to pieces under the miniature tidal waves caused by water bugs or perhaps frogs. Pretending to enjoy a cigarette in the course of a stroll, he took note of the passing cars that slowed for an admiring view of the clean, creamy little house behind the willowed pond, and no car jerked to a shocked halt, no one screamed.

Hildreth had a Polaroid camera, and one afternoon, in a fascinated test, he took a picture of the pond. Conlon's photographs had shown no abnormality, but this time it was he who was pressing the shutter. The day warranted color film—the willows dripped and candled about the round eye of water, enameled so perfectly that it might have been a brooch. Wouldn't it be odd, thought Hildreth, counting excitedly to sixty, if only the camera and I—?

He was peeling the paper shield away when Sarah Wilde's voice said at his shoulder, "Oh, may I see?"

The print and its fluttering attachment dropped to the ground.

Hildreth got only a swinging glimpse of Sarah's slanted white cheek, caught only the beginning of the rueful, "I'm sorry, I didn't mean—" before he bent, barely circumventing her; if necessary he would have put his shoe on the print.

As it was, he snatched it up and turned away, manufacturing a cough, while he finished stripping the shield. He said a second later, turning back, "Not bad, is it?" and handed the innocent color print to Sarah. No, not the camera and himself—only himself.

Sarah, he thought watchfully, was a remarkably beautiful young woman. Her dropped lashes were a thick unretouched silver-brown, her polished hair a slightly deeper brown; her gaze, when she lifted it, would be grey. With the suave red of her lipstick to counterpoint the water-color effect, she was quietly startling in any gathering.

"Very good indeed," she said, handing the print back by its edges. "The pond's so pretty, isn't it? Especially now."

She glanced at the circle of water and then back at Hildreth, who following her gaze had still seen the placidly mirrored old barn. A tremble of nerves ran along his throat. To control a wild impulse toward laughter, he said in a considering, landownerish way, "It seems quite full, but you've had heavy rains this month, haven't you?" and he slid the print casually into his coat pocket.

"Yes, it is full," said Sarah in his own considering tone, and there was no doubt about it; the eyes that moved from the pond to his face held some kind of—doubt? challenge? Hildreth said coolly, "Well, if you'll excuse me, it's back to the type-writer," and he took a step away.

"Wait, I almost forgot what I came for." Sarah was dipping into her calf handbag. "Here—the mailman put this in my box instead of yours. Wonderful to get fan mail. Don't forget about dinner tonight—cocktails at six-thirty."

It wasn't fan mail which Hildreth opened when the red Volkswagen had disappeared over the hill, but one of the many letters which, the police had told him, always arrived in the wake of a disappearance. This one was from *Someone Who Can Help*, and in exchange for $200 mailed to an enclosed box number in Vermont the writer would put him in touch with his missing wife.

The maddening part of these communications was that they could not be ignored—at least, not by a man in whom hope supposedly sprang eternal. Hildreth, sitting down to write the form reply that thanked the writer and said he was turning the letter over to the officers in charge of the investigation, thought angrily that there ought to be a law.

The afternoon passed slowly. Conlon telephoned to say that there would be a plumber coming over to do something to the downstairs bath, and Hildreth said pettishly, "Really, Bill, forgive me, but I thought all that had been taken care of. One doesn't greet plumbers in the middle of Scene One, you know."

He was mollified a little later by a delegation from the local high-school magazine, asking humbly for a "Best Wishes from Howard Hildreth" to be photostated for the graduation issue. One of the shiny-haired, wide-eyed girls ventured close to his typewriter, in which Hildreth foresightedly kept a typed yellow sheet—the opening scene of *The Far Cry*—and he said at once, austerely, "Please don't—I have a 'thing' about work in progress."

It only added to their awe. But he had had it, thought Hildreth, presently seeing them to the door; he had had all the local adulation he wanted. Imperiously buying delicacies at the only market that carried them, he had seen the fawning face of the manager who only a year ago had told him that if his bill wasn't settled promptly he would find himself in the small-claims court.

He had been pointed out respectfully on the main street, and had declined invitations from the town's reigning hostess. More importantly, he had been accepted everywhere without a trace of suspicion; if there was any sentiment in the air, it was one of embarrassed pity for a man who so courageously continued to hope.

In a day or two he could go back to New York, having established to Bill Conlon and Sarah Wilde and everybody else that there was no question of his selling or even renting the property with its pretty, deadly pond.

He was all the more shocked, in the midst of these comfortable reflections, when at a little after three he had a call from a Sergeant Fisk at the police station. Some little girls looking for pussywillows in a field on the outskirts of the town had discovered a woman's leather handbag and part of a dress with some suggestive stains; would Hildreth please come down and see if he could identify them?

"Certainly," said Hildreth, staring angrily out the window. "Of course, being out in the weather, I imagine they're pretty well—?"

"No, sir, they were stuffed in the remains of an old stone wall and they're still in fair condition. Recognizable, anyway."

"I'll leave right away," said Hildreth, tempering his eagerness with the right amount of dread.

At the police station he was asked to wait—Sergeant Fisk would be right with him.

By four o'clock, Sergeant Fisk still was not with him; at four-thirty, fuming, Hildreth walked up to the uniformed man at the switchboard and said sharply, "I came here at the request of Sergeant Fisk to look at some objects for identification, and I cannot wait any longer. Please leave a message—"

"Just a minute, sir," said the policeman unruffledly, and slipped a plug into its socket and inquired for Sergeant Fisk. "There's a Mr. Hildreth here, been waiting since—okay, I'll tell him to go right in."

But the handbag and dress fragment, when Hildreth reached Sergeant Fisk's office, had been transferred to Lieutenant Martin's office, where there was some question as to their possible connection with the vanishing of a Colorado couple making a cross-country tour four months ago. Hildreth contained his temper as he went with the sergeant to Martin's office; he was, he remembered, a man who would do anything to find a clue to his wife's fate.

He was badly tempted when, at after five o'clock, he surveyed a rotted and mildewed navy-calf handbag, empty, and the sleeve and half the bodice of what had once been a yellow-wool dress.

Why not say, "Yes, they're my wife's," and bury his face in his hands and be done with it?

Because, he thought with a feeling of having stepped back from the edge of a cliff, Marian had never worn yellow—she said it made her look like a two-legged hangover, and there was a suggestion of something on the leather lining of the bag that could easily be a nearly obliterated name or monogram. Hildreth had read what modern police laboratories could do with things like that. So he shook his head and said, "They're not my wife's," and with a shudder at the stains on the rotting yellow wool, "thank God."

Three hours, he thought as he drove home seething in the rainy dusk. Three hours on a fool's errand which he could not have risked refusing. Just barely time to dress for dinner at Sarah Wilde's—and then get out of here tomorrow.

He was restored at the thought, and at the glimpse of the old barn quivering on the pond in the last of the light as he drove to Sarah's. His temper was further improved by Sarah's big, casually gay living room—two rooms thrown together in a very old saltbox—and the contrast between an open fire and a cold rattling rain on the windows.

The other guests were already established with drinks—Conlon, a Mr. and Mrs. Slater, and Mrs. Slater's decorative visiting sister.

Hildreth thawed, physically and temperamentally. He felt a slight jar of recognition when he was introduced to the Slaters, but he had undoubtedly encountered them on the station platform at some forgotten time, or in a local store. He noted with approval that Sarah had obviously got someone in for the evening, because there were sounds of kitchen activity while Sarah sat on the couch, in black and pearls, beside Conlon.

On the rare occasions when he and Marian had entertained, Marian had charged in and out like a demented puppy, crying, "My God, who's been watching the beans? Nobody!" Or, abashedly, "We all like nutmeg instead of pepper in our mashed potatoes, don't we?"

Sarah had turned her head and was gazing at him; somebody had clearly asked a question. Hildreth used a handkerchief on his suddenly damp forehead and temples and said, "I got wetter than I thought—that's really quite a downpour," and he got up to stand by the fire.

And the bad moment was gone, further wiped out by Sarah's "You said you mightn't be here long on this visit, Howard, so we're having your favorite dinner—you know, what you won't eat in restaurants."

"Don't tell me," said Hildreth, delighted, but it was—trout, a crisp, deep-gold outside, succulent white within, delicately enhanced by herbs that only hinted at themselves. He ate with deliberate pleasure, not succumbing until close to the end of dinner to his habit of providing backgrounds for people.

The extraordinarily good-looking sister from New Haven— her name was Vivian Hughes—seemed the kind of young woman who, convinced in her teens that she could have any man she wanted, had ended up with none; there was a kind of forced grace to the frequent turn of her head, and lines of discontent around her really striking green eyes.

Mrs. Slater wasn't a fair test because she had ticketed herself earlier by a reference to the young twins they had left with a babysitter, and by her very casualness she had given herself away. She was the new and on the whole the best breed of mother, thought Hildreth approvingly; slender, amiable, intelligent, she kept her maternal dotings strictly for hearth and home.

Slater? Hildreth gazed obliquely through candlelight at the other man, perhaps a year or two younger than himself. The lean, polished, ruddy face suggested an outdoorsman, but everything else pointed to an executive. He went on gazing, and like an exposed print washed gently back and forth in developer, outlines began to emerge.

A desk, not executive-grain but scarred oak. Two telephones on it. A uniformed man in a far doorway saying, "Yes, sir, right away," then disappearing down one of a warren of corridors.

Yes, Slater was a police officer of some sort, or a detective, glimpsed or perhaps even talked to in the first stages of the investigation six months ago. And Sarah and Conlon hoped that he would be terrified by this recognition and go to pieces. That was the whole point of this friendly little gathering.

How very disappointed they must be. Hildreth stirred his coffee tranquilly, because no motive for murder had existed until sixty seconds before Marian died, and there wasn't a single clue. In an enjoyment of the attention he now knew to be trained on him he said in a well-fed voice, "Marvelous dinner, Sarah. I don't know when I've had trout like that," and Sarah said, "As a matter of fact, you never have."

She was leaning forward a little in the candlelight, her gaze cool and removed. "The trout were from your pond, Howard, and they were caught this afternoon while you were down at the police station. You didn't know that Marian had had the pond stocked for you, as a birthday present, just before she—disappeared—because you love trout but never trust it in restaurants. We didn't know about it, either, until the friend who did it for her stopped by to see Bill a couple of weeks ago."

Hildreth's neck felt caught in one of those high white collars you saw on injured people; he could not turn it even when he heard Conlon's, "Nice fat trout, I thought, but lazy. They bit at anything"—while he had sat in the police station, decoyed there by a telephone call.

"You all ate it," said Hildreth triumphantly, in a candlelight that had begun to tremble and dampen his face. "You all—"

"No. Ours was perch from the Old Town Fish Market," said Sarah, and although she continued to hold his gaze, her forehead had a cold glimmer and her mouth seemed clenched against a scream.

Hildreth lost them all then. He dropped his eyes, but instead of his dessert cup he saw his dinner plate, with the neat spiny bones from which all the succulent white flesh had been forked away. Marian's soft white throat, and the busy, inquisitive, nibbling mouths at the bottom of the pond, and the plump things placed on his plate—

He heard his chair go crashing back, and the gagging cry of horror that issued from his own throat as he plunged blindly for somewhere to be sick, and, from a mist, Slater's voice saying, "Looks like it. Very definitely. We'll get at it first thing in the morning."

MARY McMULLEN
HER HEART'S HOME

At ten o'clock on the sunny morning of that terrible day in March, Miss Rounce felt herself more than justified in taking ten minutes to relax at her desk with a cup of coffee.

Her world was in perfect order. Mr. Caudrey's great teak desktop was immaculately clear of papers, his telephone was serenely silent. He had flown off to his week in the sun in Jamaica—Miss Rounce smiled to herself as she mixed metaphors—on greased rails.

She had not only made all his travel arrangements, managed to get him in at his favorite hotel even though they said at first they were full; she had also, over a quiet lunch, made up Mrs. Caudrey's wavering mind for her. Yes, much wiser to skip Jamaica this time, the sun did such disastrous things to the skin; better a week at that luscious spa in Texas—why, Mrs. Caudrey wouldn't know herself, and certainly Mr. Caudrey wouldn't know her, when they met again.

She had canceled and rebooked dentist's and doctor's appointments, as he had only made up his mind to go away last week. She'd had the lock on his alligator suitcase repaired, tracked down a pale-peach broadcloth shirt to replace the one with the collar just beginning to fray where it rubbed against his tie. She had filled his office flask with Canadian Club from the hidden swinging bar in the teak paneling and tucked it into his attaché case along with four paperbacks by his favorite mystery novelists, titles he hadn't read before. She had checked over his pills, added a big bottle of Vitamin E. And had deliberately not minded, had given him a brave cheerful smile, when he said a peculiar hasty goodbye, hardly even looking at her.

Excuses for this came readily to mind. He was being pressed on all sides. Philip Caudrey was president of Hope & Hayes Pharmaceuticals, still young, mid-forties, handsome, vital, popular. But being pushed, nevertheless, by that blowsy-haired boy

Alec Mortimer, who was making such a big thing of the cosmetics division. And under attack from the board because of business conditions which certainly Mr. *Caudrey* had no control over. No wonder he wanted to get away, rest a bit, and regather his forces.

We'll get through, Miss Rounce thought, sipping her coffee. She had been his secretary for the past thirteen of her twenty-five years with the company. Up with him, from district sales manager to vice president of sales to president, the office he held now for five years.

Perhaps another cup of coffee, and then the boy would be around with the 10:15 mail.

The door of Mr. Caudrey's office opened and two strange men walked in, one dark, one fair, both in Miss Rounce's opinion rather peculiarly dressed. She sat in her own small comfortable room off the big sunswept office. There were folding doors between, but he liked them kept open.

"Can't close the doors on my eyes and ears and memory, Maria, now can I?" he would say.

Feeling a little as if the privacy of her own home had been invaded, she rose from her desk and went over to the men.

"Yes? Can I help you?"

The dark one gave her an abstracted glance and continued in mid-sentence. "—I see a magnificent dark-cave effect, aubergine vinyl walls, no daylight whatever—"

"I *beg* your pardon!" Miss Rounce commanded. She was a compact woman of medium height; her upright stance made her seem taller. Her pink face, going a bit to jowl, was pinker with indignation. "I am Mr. Caudrey's secretary. Will you please tell me what you are doing here?"

"Larrup Design Consultants, ma'am," the fair one said. "Doing over the office. Didn't your boss tell you? And your little room there"—he walked into it and looked over his shoulder at the other man—"all white? Crazy contrast? Think of it as a surprise extension of his office? A mirrored wall maybe with an étagère, tons of gorgeous green stuff, almost a conservatory effect?"

Her office. *Her* office, her place of being, bandied between these two strangers. Something began to beat in Miss Rounce's throat like a misplaced heart. The fair man's eyes, resting on

her horn-rimmed glasses, gleaming little beaked nose, crisp
curly graying hair, no doubt accurately figuring her age as fifty
or thereabouts, thinking, *you* don't go with the mirror and the
étagère.

It was a relief in a way when one of her two assistants,
Minnie-May, who was in charge of the files, poked her lavender-
blonde head in at the door. "Mr. Fenelli would like to see you,
Miss Rounce. At your earliest convenience, he said."

At any other time, Miss Rounce would have said, "Indeed?
Then tell him he knows where to find me." But better, for the
moment, to get away from this upsetting silliness and try to
sort things out. Would Mr. Caudrey have arranged for redeco-
rating without consulting her? Hardly. Fenelli might be able to
enlighten her.

She glanced over her shoulder as she left, a loving look that
stabbed her, at the fine old ivory-and-gold Kirman, the glow of
teak, the soft rose brocade at the windows, the motionless swift
white model under glass of Mr. Caudrey's sloop *Valkyrie*, the
photographs in silver frames, one of them, the youngest girl,
named Elizabeth Rounce Caudrey for her godmother. Was it all,
then, to be violated, her heart's home?

Or maybe—with a delightful secret surge of feeling as she
strode upright down the long bright corridor and around the
corner—maybe he meant it as a great big marvelous surprise
for her.

She knocked at the closed door, studying, during the annoying ten seconds she was kept waiting, the little white-lettered
black label: Ronald Fenelli, Personnel Manager. Ronald indeed.
Rocco more likely. Next thing you knew it would be Ronald
Fennell. Just two more seconds and she would turn and go.

"Come in," Fenelli said, opening the door. "Sit down, Miss
Rounce."

She thought afterward that she must have heard at the time
every word he said to her, from his swift opening: "I have a
most unpleasant duty to perform. I must tell you that effective
immediately you are to be separated from the company . . ."

But, always, only faraway bits and pieces remained, like half-
caught phrases carried by the wind from some distant hill.
"Cutting back . . . long and honorable service . . . our executives

putting themselves on a budget . . . after your position, naturally
you wouldn't want to consider . . . pension on the basis of early
retirement, not the larger sum, but . . ."

In the middle of the floating phrases, the crystal vision
striking. New office like "a magnificent cave," new secretary's
office like a conservatory, new secretary, shining and young, to
match.

". . . as of two weeks from today. Of course, you may come in
if you please and use the office. Not Caudrey's, it's about to be
torn apart, but I'm sure we can find you a cozy cubbyhole
where you can use the phone and so on. On the other hand . . .
embarrassment . . . Minnie-May can pack up everything of yours,
bring it to your place."

A tremor started deep inside Miss Rounce; then, to her
horror, she began to shake. Her head shook. Her cheeks shook.
Her voice shook.

"But, what have I *done?* Twenty-five years—" Not her voice
at all.

Fenelli sighed and then smiled harshly. "Don't make it hard
for me, Miss Rounce. This is off the record, and don't quote me,
and if you do I'll deny it. You're a woman of the world. Youth's
the story today. We must make way. We must make way. You've
had your turn, now haven't you? You said it yourself. Twenty-
five years."

He stood up, warily eyeing her, waiting, she knew, for some
awful, some shaming explosion. One thing that kept her from
it, in addition to a quality of iron in her, was the cold knowledge
that he was thoroughly enjoying himself.

She stood up, turned, walked out of the office, and closed the
door behind her. Around a corner, from the door of the typing
pool, she heard a high young voice cresting on a giggle, "The
Rounce is bounced!"

Shortly before eleven o'clock, Miss Rounce, pale, erect, a
poisonous, dangerous bag of pain and hatred, went out for the
last time through the revolving doors of Hope & Hayes Pharmaceuticals.

She lost the next three days more or less completely out of her
life. She slept a lot, day and night, like someone recovering

from, or contracting, some dreadful disease. She supposed later that she must have eaten and drunk now and then: the teacup in the sink, the soup can at the bottom of the brown paper bag in the little yellow garbage can. Occasionally the telephone rang, unanswered.

There had been flashes of all-too-coherent thought. Of course, that was why Mr. Caudrey had suddenly decided to go to Jamaica. He didn't want to be around when his faithful secretary was dumped, canned, got rid of, fired. That was why he'd hardly looked at her when he said his nasty strange goodbye. He couldn't bear to regard poor doomed Miss Rounce. And it must—bite savagely at the aching tooth—must have been he who said she must go. New offices, new image, new man, to fight back at twenty-nine-year-old Alec Mortimer, the hairy terrier snapping at the heels of his glossy English shoes.

Was it dreaming, was it waking, that the darkness had rushed into her mind? *She would somehow fix Mr. Caudrey, Mr. President Philip Caudrey. She would fix Fenelli, too, his willing, enjoying instrument. How?*

On the morning of the fourth day, she got out of her tossed damp bed. She showered, combed her tangled hair, dressed, and remade the bed with taut immaculate white sheets and a fresh white blanket and a starched white eyelet bedspread. Maidenly, maidenly, she thought. Why did I work so hard all those years? Why did I never sin?

She made herself do an almost impossibly hard thing. It was something she had to know before—

She called Hope & Hayes and asked for Mabel Ross in Accounting, an old trusted friend. She cut across Mabel's where-have-you-been and I've-been-trying-to-reach-you. "I can't talk now, Mabel, I'm on my way out—but tell me, what's my replacement like?"

Concerned, reluctant voice. "Oh, you know, the kind they stamp out by the thousands now. Long straight blonde hair. Ridiculous huge pink sunglasses. Legs like a—like a heron. I tell you, Maria, I'm in such a rage. I found out she'd been hired by *him*, Caudrey, last week and was just sort of waiting in the wings—"

"Call you soon," Miss Rounce said, hanging up. Her face was

expressionless; there could be no further hurt when you hit the bottom of pain.

She found herself responding to a schedule that someone else seemed to have thought out for her. She went out and bought groceries. She bundled up the laundry and left it outside her apartment door. She washed, dried, and put away the few cups and dishes in the kitchen. She made a pot of hot strong tea and took it to the typing table she kept set up in her bedroom.

Often, on weekends, she did typing chores for Mr. Caudrey. Articles for trade newspapers—for which she did all the research—personal letters he didn't want to bother with, his address to the graduating class of Morningtown College. The machine on the table was new, bought only last month, an electric; it wouldn't do to have a comma the least bit out of alignment in anything she typed for Mr. Caudrey. She hadn't as yet, in fact, used the new machine. Good. Not that it could possibly come to that.

She closed her eyes in concentration, to collect the odds and ends. A half-heard telephone call to South Carolina, an order to the florist, an accidental glimpse of two figures ducking through the rain into his Mercedes. She hadn't been jealous when to her all-seeing eye the odds and ends formed themselves into an unmistakable pattern; indeed, she felt a certain vicarious pleasure in the sheer brigandage of it, right under the nose of the chairman of the board, and his second wife at that, only married two years ago.

After pulling on a pair of thin white nylon gloves, she began typing. No formal salutation. Not in a letter like this.

"Dear Phillip [he always misspelled, on memos, Mr. Caudrey's first name]: I will make this brief and to the point. Dossiers, you know, are more or less my business and I have a complete one on you and Cecelia Hayes—or shall we call her Cissie? Do you, for instance, recall a weekend in Charleston, South Carolina, at the Bluebird Motel? Six dozen white roses delivered to her house the day after Holy Joe Hayes left for the conference in the Virgin Islands? And so on, friend, and so on.

"You're feeling the hot breath of Mortimer and I'm feeling the same from Skillington, who questions some of my interviewing practices with young girls—quite unfairly, I may add. But as my tenure here may not be indefinite, I must make plans. I want from you, in exchange for my dossier, $50,000, which will be acceptable in five installments—cash, of course—the first to be placed in my mailbox at home no later than six o'clock on Monday. I'll let you know the dates for the other payments. As you may or may not know, I start my vacation on Monday and will not be at the office, but I do assure you that your offering will be picked up. As ever, Ronnie F."

Miss Rounce did very well with the scrawled signature. She had had to learn to do Mr. Caudrey's, too, so that no one could tell the difference, the time he'd suffered from a pinched nerve and a resulting wrist malfunction. She addressed the envelope to Mr. Phillip Mr. Caudrey, 108 Chancery Road, stamped it, put it in her handbag, and reached thirstily for her now half-warm tea.

She would drop the letter, after business hours on Friday, through the mail slot of the main post office. On examination, it could be seen not to have been typed on Fenelli's own machine in the office, but presumably on his typewriter at home. Not that it would come to that. Not if she knew Mr. Caudrey. The letter would be destroyed instantly. And then—

A man of powerful rages. And sudden, strong, unhesitating action.

In the meantime, there was a little exploratory work to be done. It had been three years since she with most of the executive staff had gone to a large cocktail party at Fenelli's. She got her compact from the parking lot at the rear of the apartment and drove through the pleasant Pennsylvania city-town to a near southern suburb, just now beginning to be developed.

At the bend of a lane lined on both sides with birches was Fenelli's low white-brick ranch house, trim March-drab lawn in front, great shadowy groves of pine trees nodding in the wind on either side of the house and behind it. The lane angled at the house, turned left, and ambled past it to join a main road a quarter of a mile away.

Miss Rounce drove along it slowly, pleased with the anonymity of her sensible black car. That path, through the fir trees—

glancing up it, she could see the wink of glass in a window, the edge of a low roof. A secret, silently pine-needled path.

Fenelli, she knew, kept no servants. A cleaning woman came in once a week—a woman he had got from Mabel Ross, and who enjoyed talking about one employer to another. There was no Mrs. Fenelli in the house among the pines; he was divorced. At the start of his vacation he would, if he followed past habit, spend Monday at home, lazing, packing, and closing up the house, then leave on Tuesday morning for Vail. Fenelli was a dedicated skier.

His reservations were all in order for Tuesday, Miss Rounce learned, when she called to check with the airline.

Mr. Caudrey would be back on Sunday afternoon, late. He would have the house to himself; Mrs. Caudrey was not due back until Monday. He would change his clothes, pour a drink— call Cissie Hayes? Holy Joe Hayes had to go to Memphis for a weekend seminar he was addressing. Yes, call Cissie—then he would go leisurely through his mail.

I'd say between seven and eight, Miss Rounce thought. When it gets dark.

If Fenelli was out somewhere Sunday night, then Monday night.

Waiting for the three days to spend themselves, she felt odd, lightheaded. Torn from the routine of twenty-five years, she didn't quite know what to do with her hands and feet and body. Looking in the mirror, she felt an uncertainty as to who she was. If she was not Maria Rounce, Mr. Caudrey's invaluable executive secretary, the silently purring engine that ran his world, then who was she?

But now, on this thinly raining Sunday as darkness fell, this woman had plans, had things to do.

At six o'clock she made fresh coffee and put a vacuum container of it into her tote bag. She buttoned on a thick sweater under the lined all-weather black poplin coat with its enveloping hood. She pulled on zippered black rubber boots over comfortable shoes that would take a great deal of standing still in one place before her feet began to ache.

She wasn't really in her car, driving cautiously through the rain. She was looking over Mr. Caudrey's shoulder as he ripped open the white envelope—good thick paper, but nothing showy—and glanced at the opening: "Dear Phillip." She saw the slow purple which always seemed to surge down, not up—down from the thick creamy swoop of hair over the square forehead; and the veins, beside his large brilliant blue eyes, beginning to raise themselves ropily.

She saw his hands, with the beautiful long, strong, square-tipped fingers, reaching into the drawer of the bedside table where he kept his Colt .38. A raincoat donned in savage haste, the hand slipping the gun into the pocket. The sound of the Mercedes starting up, so real and near that she looked with panic into the driving mirror.

Not yet—the envelope was still sealed, the gun in the drawer, the raincoat in the closet, the Mercedes in the garage. Nothing at all had happened yet.

And Fenelli—what would he be doing? Waxing his skis, perhaps, sitting by his fire with a drink at his elbow. *(You've had your turn, now haven't you?)* Thinking with relaxed anticipation about his two weeks in Colorado. She had been told that people felt freed, sprung, wonderful on vacation eve; she had always thought how difficult it was to get through the time away from her lovely job.

She approached Fenelli's house from the opposite direction this time, turning off the main road to the west of it into the ambling lane. About an eighth of a mile from the house in the pines was a stark little cottage she had noted on Thursday, empty, a FOR RENT OR SALE sign standing crookedly on its disheveled treeless front lawn. She drove her car behind the cottage and walked the rest of the way down the lane, her eyes adjusting to the wet blue darkness.

Here was the path. She moved along it, branches brushing her softly, rain dripping off the edge of her hood. Lights on in the house. As well as she could remember, his living room was at this end, its side windows looking into the woods, its front ones facing down the lane. Yes, they had gone to the right at the party, to leave their coats in the bedroom. Too soon to move up close to the window.

After a time she began to feel numb all over, with the cold

and wet, and the waiting, and the immobility of her position against the bole of a tree, hiding her under a fall of branches.

The woman inside her, the thinker, the planner, the doer, watched what happened at 7:18 while poor bereft Miss Rounce cowered in the rain, appalled.

The sound of the car coming up the lane, slowly—stopping, at a guess, halfway up. The barest rumor of footsteps. The front doorbell ringing. Fenelli's windows were double-glassed and after he opened the door the two men faced each other, mouths moving, like a scene from a silent movie.

Mr. Caudrey, from a distance of about five feet, shot Fenelli. The other man stood for a moment, rocking a little back and forth as though he were considering some matter of grave importance. But his mouth was wide open. Then he stumbled ungracefully backward and fell across a gold-brocade armchair. He wore a dark suit and Miss Rounce saw no blood. The sound of the shot, muffled by the double-hung windows, seemed to linger in the pines.

Mr. Caudrey stood perfectly still, watching Fenelli. His face was a dangerous purpled red. Oh, do be careful, Mr. Caudrey. Go into the bathroom and take one of your pills.

He finally moved from his frozen stance. Brisk now, he felt Fenelli's pulse, looked for a moment into the open eyes. He scooped up a small portable television set, removed the watch from the dead man's wrist, then began ripping Fenelli's handsome room apart. Desk drawers out, contents in a wild flurry to the floor. A pair of curtains at a front window wrenched down, to lie in a golden heap. He kicked up a corner of the Bokhara rug, took an ornate pansy-painted porcelain clock off the mantelpiece and smashed it on the hearth. Then he went to the front door and let himself out.

The sound of the car starting up again. Not his Mercedes, but the softer sound of Mrs. Caudrey's Chrysler Imperial. Tiremarks—

An odd pride stirred in Miss Rounce. He had done it very well. Mrs. Caudrey wasn't back yet and he could say, if they ever got that close to the matter, that someone had stolen her car while he and she were away. In any case, the police would probably conclude, from the swift staging of it, armed robbery, a scuffle, and yet another sad meaningless death. Money for drugs, maybe.

The newspapers, radio, and television concurred the next morning. Hope & Hayes executive struck down in his home by an unknown assailant. Armed robbery in quiet Morningtown suburb, the third in four months. Police questioning known addicts.

Miss Rounce went again to her typewriter. She had slept badly, tossing and crying out warnings in her sleep, but she awoke feeling cleansed and empty.

She addressed the letter to the Morningtown Chief of Police. In it, she detailed the name, the time, and the circumstances. The Chrysler Imperial, the Colt .38—"As I understand it, you will be able to match the bullet with the marks in the barrel. Don't look for fingerprints because he wore gloves—rough pigskin. But you might find a pigskin imprint here and there, it is a deeply marked leather. It was a wet night and I assume you check for footprints. He wore a pair of Blucher-style shoes, brown, with crepe rubber soles." At the end of the letter she wrote, "I was walking in the woods when I passed close to the house and saw all this happen. Don't trouble to contact me as I am leaving the state as soon as I mail this letter." She typed, for a signature, the name of the only dog she had ever owned, years and years ago when she was young, an Irish terrier, Shandy.

She got into her car and mailed the letter at the main post office a little after noon. They would have it by tomorrow morning. She wanted the confrontation to be, not in the privacy of his house, but in the full glare of day, with people around, people to see and hear.

At ten o'clock on Monday morning her telephone rang. Mabel? To tell her what had happened? I can't, I can't. I must. With shrinking fingers she picked up the cold black plastic.

"Rouncey!" His voice was warm and strong and rich. He only called her that on special, superspecial occasions. "I couldn't get you out of my head down there. My own invaluable, irreplaceable Rouncey."

Liar, she thought. *You're frightened. You want the old, old security of Miss Rounce to guard you from all harm, as she always had.*

But the chilled blood in her veins stirred and rioted.

"To hell with executive budgeting!" he said. "But in any case, the way things have worked out—you've heard about poor Fenelli?"

"Yes."

"There's the job for *you.* You'll make an absolutely magnificent personnel head. I talked to Holy Joe first thing and he thinks it's a great idea. Your tax bracket is going to take an almighty jump, but you can cope with that, Rouncey, right? And you'll be here on the scene, so I can always turn to you for help when my blonde knucklehead—"

There was the sound over the telephone of a door opening, of voices, commotion.

"Oh, God, the police—" His voice became a sort of gasping wail. "Rouncey, *Rouncey*—"

A click. And then there was nothing but silence.

HELEN REILLY

THE PHONOGRAPH MURDER

George Bonfield made up his mind on the night that the maid, Hannah Swenson, came to the door of the bedroom and told him that the thermostatic control on the electric clock on the stove was out of order.

Bonfield and his wife were alone in the first-floor bedroom of the house in West Thirteenth Street, which they owned and in which they had lived for the thirty years since their marriage. At fifty-six, George Bonfield was a slight, wiry man with a gentle face and thinning hair. Louise Bonfield had put on flesh with the years, but she had a shapely head, a fine profile, and rich blue-black hair that she wore fastened in a knot at the nape of her neck.

Louise was getting ready for bed. She had been threatened with an attack of gallstones and was still under the doctor's care. She always went to bed at around nine on the nights when George was going to the office to work.

Louise was sitting on the edge of the bed, taking off her shoes, and George was brushing his hair in front of the bureau. As Louise slipped off her stockings and folded them neatly, she said, "Dr. Seebold's a perfectly wonderful man, George. He says that if I'm careful I'm good for another twenty years."

Twenty years. The words did something to George Bonfield. He stared into the mirror and went on mechanically brushing his hair. Time was done up in bundles. There were fifty-two weeks in a year, seven days in a week, twenty-four hours in a day. And there would be twenty more years of it.

Louise said, "George, no matter how busy you are tomorrow, I want you to see the insurance people. In three months your endowment will mature and we've got to begin to make definite plans about investing the money. I've got some very definite ideas."

George said, "Yes," obediently. Louise always did have definite ideas. She had had ideas about their daughter's first love affair; she had had ideas about not buying the farm in Dutchess County but putting his aunt's bequest into steel; she had had ideas about the serviceable dark wallpaper for the dining room.

Louise's voice flowed smoothly, inexorably. "Steel, perhaps, or aircraft, or maybe—" She went on, devouring his $30,000 endowment to the last crumb. "And, George, there's another thing I want to speak to you about."

She slipped a nightgown over her head. "That Randall account. Don't let it run another week. Either Randall pays or you take the matter to a lawyer. Does he think paper and time and layouts grow on trees? You've been culpably weak with him!"

She got into bed. The springs creaked. She settled herself on her pillows. "My magazine, there on the chair, hand it to me, George. I'm reading a lovely story." She sighed comfortably, and yawned.

"Yes, dear." George Bonfield gave her the magazine. As he did so, his hand came in contact with hers. Her skin was soft and a little moist. He shivered and fought down a sudden sickening, soul-shaking wave of nausea. He turned away, saying to himself with an odd quiver of surprise, "Why—why, I hate her."

There was a knock. The door opened and the maid, Hannah, stuck her head into the room. Hannah was a big rawboned Swedish girl with a dish face and round blue eyes—not bright, and rather excitable, but willing and kind.

Hannah said, "The electric clock on the stove. It won't work."

Louise spoke severely. "You probably didn't set it properly, Hannah. Or you've been fooling with it. It worked all right this morning."

George said dully, "I'll have a look at it, Hannah."

Louise said, from her pillows, "Don't take too long, George— you've got a good night's work to do. Now, Hannah, remember, when you bring me my orange juice at eleven don't wake me, and be careful to see that the front door is bolted before you go to bed. Mr. Bonfield will ring when he gets home and you can let him in."

"Yes, ma'am," the maid said.

George followed her out of the room. The front door was an

old point of issue between himself and Louise. Servants objected, and rightly, to being dragged down from the top of the house in the middle of the night to let him in. The bolt and chain weren't necessary. There was a perfectly good lock on the door. Bolts and bars. He shivered again. Suddenly they surrounded him.

He went downstairs and examined the electric clock. It was then, as he stood beside the stove in the kitchen, that the idea came to him. He fingered the clock. It was an interesting device. He began swinging the dials.

Hannah said, "Will we have to call the stove people, Mr. Bonfield?"

George Bonfield said slowly—and his voice seemed to come from a long distance away—"No, Hannah. I can fix it tomorrow. I'm rather good with my hands."

He stared down at them for a long moment, got his hat, and left the house.

His office was on the second floor of a building on West Forty-second Street. It consisted of a waiting room, another room where Joe Tyler and the two stenographers worked, and George's own room beyond. His advertising agency was small and unpretentious, but it did a good pedestrian business that brought in a steady profit.

As usual on the nights they worked, Joe Tyler was waiting for him. Tyler was a big eager giant with an enormous admiration for his boss. George said hello to Joe, gave him the copy for the radiator folders, went into his office, closed the door, and settled down in the chair behind his desk. He made no attempt to get at the remainder of the outline. George had much more important things to think about.

There was no danger of his being interrupted—Joe wouldn't dream of opening the door while his boss was engaged in creative endeavor. George smiled bitterly. He was about to embark on a creation of another kind.

That was on October the ninth. At the beginning of the following week, George Bonfield bought the clock. It wasn't an electric clock. It was a simple cheap alarm clock with a bell on the top.

He had an appointment that day with a client in Newark. The

client's office was on Broad Street. There were plenty of drugstores on Broad Street, but he didn't buy the clock in any of them. He bought it in Jersey City. Bonfield put the clock in the bottom drawer of the desk in his office. He locked the drawer.

His next purchase, which required more care since it could be traced more easily, was a small portable phonograph. He had to wait to acquire this. Yet he couldn't wait too long. The endowment, the $30,000 to which he had looked forward for so long, was due in less than a month and it was going to take time to get things exactly right.

Five days after he bought the alarm clock, his opportunity came. An old client of his in New England telegraphed from Boston asking George to come up for a promotion conference. Louise grumbled mildly and redoubled her instructions to Hannah about locking the house at night and keeping small boys away from the front steps in the daytime.

George was away two days. It was on the morning of the second day that he stopped on his way to the station at a store he had already located and bought the small phonograph in the neat unobtrusive blue case. He deposited the phonograph, carefully wrapped in brown paper, in the checkroom in Grand Central on his way to the office from the train. Joe Tyler mustn't see it.

Red Lytell sent George tickets for the football game at the stadium on Saturday afternoon. Under the plea of work to be finished, Bonfield gave the tickets to a grateful Joe and, the faithful assistant safely disposed of, George retrieved the phonograph from Grand Central. On the way back to the office he stopped at a crowded five-and-ten and bought four balls of cord of various strengths and thicknesses.

The office was deserted. Once he got a fright when a cleaning woman tried to gain entrance by the door leading from his room directly into the hall, but he remained quiet. As the door was locked from the inside, the woman presently went away. Removing the bell from the alarm clock and placing the phonograph on the desk, Bonfield experimented with all four varieties of cord until five o'clock. There was a queer little thread of exultation running through him as he put the alarm

clock, phonograph, and cord into the bottom drawer. He locked
the drawer and went home.

Louise was more trying than usual that night. She had sent
back the shirts he had chosen for himself and had bought him
others of her own choosing. Over pickles and cold beef, she
said, "Don't pick and choose, my dear. Eat the fat—fat's good
for you. Those other shirts were far too bright, George, and the
material was too thin. What did the insurance people say?"

When he told her that everything was in order as far as the
endowment was concerned, she spent the rest of the evening
calculating percentages until she went to bed at nine. She
required a good deal of sleep.

It was George who tiptoed into the bedroom at eleven that
night with the glass of orange juice she sipped whenever she
happened to wake up during the night. It was Hannah's day off.
Louise insisted that orange juice gave her a wonderful throat,
warded off coughs and colds. He tiptoed out of the room and
examined the windows and the front door before he went to
bed himself.

Twice that week, when Joe was away from the office and the
stenographers had left, George put the experiment into operation again, deciding finally on a thin white string that had the
proper tensile strength. It was a delicate operation: too much
slack wouldn't do, and too little might break the string. That
mustn't happen.

He had two purchases still to make. One, the glass cutter, was
insignificant. He bought it at a hardware store in Brooklyn. The
other purchase, on which success depended, was more difficult.
He must never by any chance be connected with it.

The Rosy Cheek Tomato people supplied him with the opportunity to procure it. Late in the month he went to Philadelphia
to see about some trade-paper displays. That attended to, he
sought a shop that handled radios and phonographs. There was
the usual row of booths where you could try records out. You
could also have your own voice recorded.

George had a record made of his voice. He left the shop with
the small disc in his briefcase.

Nothing remained but the spadework and the question of
getting rid of the various implements safely. That took a good

deal of figuring. The time would be short and the implements mustn't be tied to him in any way. But they were innocent in themselves and, deposited separately, they ought to arouse no suspicion in a city as big as New York.

His endowment was due in two weeks—then in one. The time for action was approaching. He had calculated minutes and distances to a hair, traveling to and fro on the Eighth instead of the Seventh Avenue subway. He had studied the various streets at night, weighing the hazards he might have to encounter.

The time for action came. Everything was in readiness The annuity was due on Saturday. He had a choice of Wednesday, Thursday, or Friday. His client, Frank Morrison, vice-president of Darling Soaps, would have suited equally well on any one of the three.

George chose Thursday on account of the weather. The forecast for Thursday was "cloudy and colder tonight, rain tomorrow."

At two in the afternoon, the sun was still shining. George Bonfield controlled his nervousness. At four the sun went behind the clouds. At six, when he went home on the Seventh Avenue subway, it was raining and he was in despair. Actual rain would be even more fatal than a clear starlit night. To his relief, the rain stopped at around seven.

Louise talked steadily during dinner. Her voice slashed at his ears. He made himself look at her, made himself answer, keeping his voice normal and indifferent. She showed no surprise when he told her he had to go back to the office. He explained that Morrison of Darling Soaps wanted the material for a new campaign by morning and that he might be late.

Louise said, "Don't make noise coming home, and if it's wet out be sure to take off your rubbers before Hannah lets you in."

"Yes, dear." George Bonfield didn't look at his wife. He turned away, picked up his hat, and walked out into the hall.

Back at the office on the second floor of the building in West Forty-second Street, Joe was waiting for him. Bonfield laid out the evening's work. "You'll have to keep at these folders, Joe. Morrison is in a hurry. We've got to get them finished tonight.

I'll be busy with the front material. It's tricky stuff, so don't disturb me and don't let me be disturbed."

Joe said cheerfully, "I'll keep at it, Mr. Bonfield," and Bonfield went into his office and closed the door. He locked it, as he sometimes did when he wanted to remain uninterrupted. He had to run the risk of a question from Joe about the copy, but he had gone over the folders carefully and there should be no questions. He had spent three solid hours the previous night completing the entire Darling Soap campaign to the last dot and dash. He locked the door leading into the hall. That was at 9:20.

The period of waiting was the hardest. He didn't dare walk around because he was supposed to be engrossed in the papers on his desk. Once he heard Joe approach the water cooler, but Joe didn't come near the inner office.

At 9:55 Bonfield opened the bottom drawer of the desk and took out the alarm clock, minus bell, the phonograph in the blue case, and the record. He adjusted the string and set the clock.

At 10:02 he left the inner office silently, by way of the door opening directly on the corridor. He locked the door behind him with his key and glanced quickly up and down the hall. He went down the fire stairs and emerged cautiously into the lower hall. The watchman ought to be in the basement. George Bonfield's heart stood still at the sound of approaching footsteps. Ten feet separated him from the front door. If he was seen now, everything would be ruined. He held his breath. The footsteps receded.

Out in the cold night air, he wiped the sweat from his forehead and pulled the second hat with which he had provided himself lower over his eyes. It was a green hat which some customer had left in his office months before. His own hat and topcoat were in the outer office.

He made his way swiftly to the Eighth Avenue subway, head down, collar turned up around his throat. Pedestrians were scarce. But it wasn't raining. He kept glancing up at the sky anxiously.

He got off the downtown express at Fourteenth Street. The house in which he lived was on the south side of Thirteenth, but there was an alley from Twelfth leading into the bowels of the block. He entered the alley noiselessly.

He paused near the clothes dryer and surveyed the house. It was dark except for a light high up on the roof, the skylight over Hannah's room. He went up the path to the back door. The wind swayed the ailanthus and sent leaves fluttering down. He must be careful afterward about those leaves.

The glass cutter was in his pocket. So was the tape. He put his gloves on and attached the tape to a pane in the rear door. He cut the pane carefully and with the aid of the tape lifted it clear without noise. He put in his gloved hand and turned the key.

He opened the door, stepped into the kitchen, and listened. There wasn't a sound. He crept into the narrow front hall and went to the front door. He took the chain off and unlocked the door. Holding himself tightly, every nerve taut, he tiptoed toward Louise's bedroom.

It was 10:24 when George Bonfield entered his house by the rear door. It was 10:35 when he left the house by the same route. He was back in his office at 10:53 P.M.

He took off the green hat and shook it. There were no leaf fragments clinging to it. There were no leaf fragments on his shoes. He hung the hat in the closet and looked with dull wonder at his face in the mirror. He massaged his eyes and listened. Yes, Joe was at work—the typewriter was clicking along evenly. He rustled a paper on his own desk. A horrible inertia possessed him.

He took the alarm clock, the record and the phonograph from the desk and again left his office. The lavatory was at the back of the building in the middle of a long hall. All the outer offices were dark. He moved as rapidly as he could.

He smashed the record into small pieces and disposed of them through a window in the middle of the corridor. He got rid of the alarm clock through the window at the northern end, waiting until the jangling of a passing truck concealed the noise of its fall. This done, he proceeded to the other end of the hall. Opening the window there, he leaned out. Holding the phonograph well away from the wall, he gave it a swing and let it fall into the deep crevice between the buildings.

For a moment, as the neat blue case disappeared from sight, he wondered whether his disposition of the three things had been wise. He shrugged his doubts away and returned to his office. Assembling the scattered sheets of the Darling Soap campaign already prepared, he settled down to wait.

It was 11:12 P.M. when the call went into the precinct. The call was made by Mr. Gamble, who lived next door to the Bonfields. Promptly at eleven, Mr. Gamble was roused by piercing screams issuing from the red brick house next to his own. He rushed out, a coat thrown hastily over his pajamas, and found Hannah Swenson, the maid, shrieking at the top of her lungs at the Bonfield front door. He pushed her aside and ran along the hall. One glance was enough for Gamble. The police arrived within a few minutes.

They found Louise Bonfield lying on the floor of the bedroom. She had been struck over the head with a heavy brass candle-stick from the mantel. She had also been choked. There were purplish areas on her plump throat. The room was in disorder. The desk drawers had been pulled out and their contents scattered. A beaded purse, empty, had been thrown down on a chair.

The police discovered the pane of glass that had been re-moved from the back door. A brass clock had fallen from the mantel. The glass had smashed, and the hands had stopped at 10:35.

The maid, Hannah Swenson, was interrogated. At best none too bright, she was a wreck, but the police managed to gather, from a story interrupted by moans and shudders and fresh outbursts of weeping, an approximation of what had happened.

Hannah Swenson had discovered her mistress's body at 11:00 P.M. when she entered the room with the glass of orange juice that she prepared for Mrs. Bonfield every night. The maid, coming down the back stairs to get the orange juice ready, must have been heard by the killer after he had done his dreadful work and while he was rifling the desk. His escape through the door at the back of the house was cut off by Hannah. He had fled through the front door.

The medical examiner arrived, took one look at the wildly laughing Hannah, and ordered her to St. Vincent's for the night, where she could receive proper care. The West Side precinct sent detectives around to notify the husband, and the investigation continued . . .

In his inner office on the second floor of the building on Forty-second Street, George Bonfield heard the tramp of approaching feet as two big men came down the corridor. There was a murmur of voices in the other room and Joe Tyler's shocked cry. The door opened.

George Bonfield was not an actor. It was one of the things that had worried him. He found he had no occasion to worry. The blood left his heart and his legs gave way under him at the first sight of the law. But the detectives were considerate, and he recovered himself.

Bonfield returned with the detectives to the house on Thirteenth Street. Hannah Swenson was already gone.

He steeled himself when he was asked to make a formal identification of his wife. The bedroom was full of big men, some in uniform, some not. Flash bulbs went off and there was a lot of noise. Everyone was very nice to Bonfield.

"If you'll step this way, sir?" Two attendants from the morgue were standing at either end of a long wicker basket. George walked slowly toward it. He looked down at Louise. Her eyes were closed. Hair veiled the bruises on her temple and folds of linen obscured her injured throat.

He said in a whisper, "Yes, that's my wife." He stepped back and the basket was borne away.

A tall slender man in loose grey tweeds, with cavernous brown eyes deeply set in the sockets of a fine head, entered the room accompanied by a stenographer. The newcomer was Inspector Christopher McKee of the Manhattan Homicide Squad. The Inspector listened to the precinct men and read the maid's testimony. He spoke only once to George Bonfield. "You were at your office all evening, Mr. Bonfield?"

George Bonfield said, "Yes," and an icy shiver went through him. He waited. The tall man nodded and turned away.

It wasn't until the next morning at nine that Bonfield was questioned in detail. He knew it had to come. Joe Tyler was with him at the time. Joe had come to see if he could be of assistance.

Inspector McKee was there, together with two or three detectives. They asked Bonfield to step into the bedroom with them. Bonfield forced himself to show emotion—but not too much. It was the lieutenant from the local precinct who took charge. He explained the situation.

"The way we figure it, Mr. Bonfield, is that you wife was killed by a burglar who entered this room without realizing it was a bedroom. His intention was evidently to rob. Your wife surprised him. He snatched the candlestick from the mantel, knocking down the clock as he did so. He was searching the desk when the maid surprised him. His retreat by the way he had entered the house was cut off. He made his escape by the front door. Now, about this desk—"

George Bonfield cleared his throat. He said that his wife kept money in the beaded purse. She had no jewelry, and her stock certificates and other valuables were in a safe-deposit box at the bank.

"Now, you yourself, Mr. Bonfield? You'll understand that this is just routine. We will also have to question the maid further when she's well enough. It's simply to get a complete picture of the case. Will you tell us exactly what you did last night?"

It had come, as he knew it must come—a circle of men, eyes fastened on him intently. George Bonfield crossed one knee over the other and began to talk. It was hard to keep his voice level and unhurried. The deadly fatigue which weighed him down was a help. Every time he had tried to fall asleep he had kept on seeing Louise's face.

"My wife and I had dinner at around half past seven and, as usual on the nights I work, I left the house at around half past eight. I had a lot of work to do." He described the campaign for the Darling Soap people. "After I left, I presume Louise did what she generally did—went to bed early."

"Were you alone in your office?"

"My assistant Joe Tyler, was in the next room."

The detective brought Joe Tyler in. Joe corroborated Bonfield's testimony. He said that Mr. Bonfield entered his office at around 8:45 and that he was there until the police arrived. Joe was in the next room every single minute of the time, and he couldn't be mistaken.

The lieutenant said unexpectedly, "There's a door opening directly into the corridor from your office, isn't there, Mr. Bonfield?"

Bonfield knew all about that door, knew what they were thinking about it, and had prepared himself. He said quietly, "Yes, there's a door there. You mean you think I—?"

Joe Tyler sprang to his defense. Joe said excitedly, "Mrs. Bonfield was killed at ten thirty-five, wasn't she, Lieutenant? That's what it said in the paper—on account of the clock." The lieutenant nodded. "Then I can prove that Mr. Bonfield was in his office," Joe said. "I heard him moving around before that and after that, but at ten thirty-five he called Frank Morrison to tell him that the material would be ready in the morning. I heard him."

Bonfield was careful to keep his attitude and posture listless while the lieutenant put Joe through his paces as to memory, exactitude, and further details.

Joe said, "Sure, I remember the time. I remember it because we still had a lot of work to do. I knew Mr. Bonfield was worried about it, too, and I figured when I heard him say to Mr. Morrison, 'It's ten thirty-five now—another two hours and we'll have it licked. I'll have everything ready for you by morning,' that we still had a hell of a lot to do."

Obviously Bonfield couldn't have murdered his wife in the house on Thirteenth Street if he made a telephone call from his office on West Forty-second Street at the same time. The conclusion was written on the faces surrounding him.

After a few purely routine questions about the house, the doors and windows, and the back yard, the police thanked him and took their departure.

An enormous weight fell from George Bonfield's shoulders. They didn't suspect him—couldn't suspect him on the evidence. They were very thorough. They had examined the maid's room, examined the office. They had gone through Bonfield's desk and found everything in order. They had looked into the closet and seen the spare green hat. He had explained that it was a hat some customer had left there months before. They hadn't examined the crevices between the buildings and the phonograph and the alarm clock had remained undiscovered.

Bonfield's nerves steadied. He was safe. For the first time in weeks he permitted himself to relax.

He knew there would be more red tape to be gone through, so he wasn't surprised or worried when he was summoned to the office of the head of the Manhattan Homicide Squad at four o'clock on the following afternoon.

There were half a dozen men in the room. Inspector McKee was seated behind a desk. Bonfield's statement had been taken down in shorthand, and typewritten copies of it were lying in front of the Inspector.

McKee said pleasantly, "Sorry to bring you here, Mr. Bonfield, but there are certain formalities."

The door opened, and a detective came in. He said, "It's okay, Inspector. I just talked to Morrison of Darling Soaps. He said that Mr. Bonfield called him at ten thirty-five. Mr. Bonfield said that he was within two hours of finishing, that he'd have the stuff complete by morning."

A little rustle went through the room. George settled himself in his chair. He felt larger. A new strength flowed through his blood. The world expanded. It was a wide, wide world. There was nothing he had neglected, nothing he hadn't foreseen. He had been very careful.

"Mr. Bonfield, if you'll just sign your name to these?" The Inspector pushed the statements toward him. Bonfield had the pen in his hand when the door opened again. It was only Hannah—big, stupid Hannah. He didn't really need her. All she could do was hammer home the points already established.

He listened idly while the Inspector took her, step by step, over the ground he himself knew so well. Hannah described the preparation of the orange juice at the usual time, her awful discovery when she entered the bedroom.

"And then what did you do?"

"I screamed. I threw open the window, and then I ran to the front door and unlocked it and ran out."

The Inspector looked at her. He said patiently, "But, Hannah, you couldn't have unlocked the front door at eleven o'clock. It was *already* unlocked. The murderer took the chain off and unlocked the door when he fled after killing Mrs. Bonfield at ten thirty-five."

"I don't care," Hannah persisted stolidly. "I did unlock the door after I ran out of the bedroom. It was locked when I found her."

Bonfield swallowed noisily. The crazy idiot! Of course the door was unlocked when she got downstairs at a little before eleven. He had unlocked it with his own hands when he first entered the house at ten twenty-four, so it would seem the way the burglar left the house. Every moment of that interval was burned into his brain. The stupid, blundering fool! Had she lost her mind?

There was a red gauze in front of his eyes. Time and place disappeared and there was only the necessity of getting Hannah to tell the truth. He was on his feet. He heard his own voice shouting. "The door *was* unlocked when you got downstairs. I know because I—"

He stopped. Everything stopped. He was impaled on a bright steel hook in a vacuum of silence. The Inspector was looking at him. So were the other men in the room. The Inspector spoke softly. "You know the door was unlocked because—? Go on, Mr. Bonfield."

Bonfield licked dry lips. He couldn't go on, because there was no place to go. He had been so careful. It was such a little slip—and so utterly damning.

Louise had beaten him in the end. He wasn't really surprised. But it was no use struggling any longer. He was exhausted. Blood pounded in his temples.

He said dully, "Yes, I killed her." He buried his face in his shaking hands.

Later that afternoon, Inspector McKee had a conference with the District Attorney. There was little to explain. George Bonfield had signed a confession.

"This," McKee said, "is what Bonfield did on the night of the killing. He went to his office on Forty-second Street and into his own inner room. His clerk, Joe Tyler, was in the outside room. When the time came, Bonfield arranged his contraption. It consisted of an alarm clock, a phonograph, and a record of his own voice. He set the alarm for ten thirty-five. He attached one end of a string to the clapper and the other end to the lever of the phonograph. Then he left the office, went down to Thirteenth Street, and killed his wife.

"He killed her, not at ten thirty-five—the smashed clock was a blind—but at around ten twenty-five. That done, he staged a fake robbery and then called the soap man, Morrison, over the telephone in his wife's room at about ten thirty-four. Meanwhile, in his empty office, the clapper tripped the phonograph lever, the record revolved, and Joe Tyler heard the identical telephone call, word for word, that Bonfield was then making from the house on Thirteenth Street. It was a perfect alibi."

"I'll say," the District Attorney agreed. "Tell me, McKee, did you suspect Bonfield before he broke?"

The Inspector shrugged. "The absence of fingerprints on the telephone in the Bonfield woman's bedroom looked queer. Someone had wiped it carefully for no apparent reason." He shrugged again. "I don't believe we would ever have got him, except for Mrs. Bonfield—and the wind."

The District Attorney frowned. "Mrs. Bonfield? The wind?"

"Mrs. Bonfield trained Hannah well. The maid was terrified of her. Lying in bed and listening to the wind, Hannah began worrying about the front door—whether or not she had locked it. Finally she couldn't stand it any longer. At not quite ten-thirty Hannah crept down to the lower hall, found the door unlocked, locked it, put the chain on, and went back upstairs.

"She remained there until ten fifty-five, when it was time to get the orange juice ready. While she was in the lower hall locking the door, she didn't hear Bonfield and he didn't hear her. The house is pretty stout, and the wind was high. I guess that ties it up."

The Inspector reached moodily for his hat. "It's all yours, Counselor—and you're welcome to it." And McKee walked out of the room.

McGARRY MORLEY
TESTIMONY OF A WITNESS

"I never used to have any trouble getting to sleep, but lots of nights I just pitch and toss. It was always worse after I'd gone to see Bessie. I tried to get out to the asylum at least once a month, even though she hadn't changed any and still acted like she was walking in her sleep—not seeing or hearing anything and never saying a word. I guess I was the only one that kept on going because everyone else said she wouldn't know them and it would be a wasted trip. The only thing they were ever interested in was, had she said anything about exactly what had happened because that was still a mystery.

"Wasted trip or not I still went, maybe as much for Ben as for Bessie. After all, we had been friends for a long time, clear back to when we were in grammar school together and Bessie was just a little redheaded freckled thing no bigger than a pint of soft soap. We didn't call her Bessie then—it was always Bossy because she was such a hand to take charge.

"If it was a picnic Bessie would be saying, 'Gert, you bring the potato salad,' and 'Floss, you can make the deviled eggs,' and like that. Or if it was some kind of meeting she would be standing up all the time telling what they ought to do and usually she'd end up being president or chairman or whatever.

"Ben was always an agreeable fellow and if someone said, 'Let's go fishing,' he'd go. Or if they said, 'Let's play ball,' why, that was all right, too. He used to just grin when Bessie was ordering everyone around, so I guess he liked her even then.

"In high school they went together, and sometimes folks would tease him and say, 'Watch out, Ben, those redheads are hard to break and she may throw and drag you,' but he wasn't bothered any and after they got out of school they got married and moved to a farm that Ben bought.

"Ben was a good farmer and did all right. After he'd been on the place about seven years and had it all paid for, he figured he could afford some help. So he came to me and said, 'I need a hired hand. How about it?'

"Well, I had just been working around for this farmer and that one, or on a road crew or maybe in the tobacco warehouse during the winter, so I said, 'Sure,' and moved in.

"It had been a considerable time since I'd been with them much and I could see a change. I guess the ones that had said Bessie would be hard to break were right. She didn't interfere with Ben's farming none, but inside the house she certainly ran things. 'Don't go in the Room with your shoes on,' she'd say— the Room was what she called the parlor—'you'll track it up.' Or if he tried to chop some kindling for the range she'd say, 'Here, give me that hatchet and let me do it. You'll litter up the whole place.'

"It was when she was cooking, though, that she was real bossy. If she made pancakes they had to be turned only once. If anyone was helping and turned them again, even while putting them on the plate, she'd say, 'They aren't fit for the dog now.' The potatoes had to be put on the stove in cold water and when a hired girl she had for a short while took some water out of the reservoir to start the potatoes, danged if Bessie didn't grab the pot and throw the potatoes right out.

"She was fussier about the coffee than any other thing. There had to be a heaping tablespoonful for each cup and one for the pot and there had to be eggshells put in to clear it up. Then the pot had to be snatched off the range the very instant the coffee hit the boil.

"Well, I got to admit that she made wonderful coffee that came out of the pot as clear as spring water and you would always want another cup. Ben sat with his back to the stove and he'd reach back and grab the pot and shake it as though he was trying to see if there was any left.

"Then Bessie'd pop out of her chair like a quail taking off and scream, 'Don't shake that pot—you'll ruin my good coffee!' And Ben would look kind of surprised as though he couldn't imagine what was bothering her. This happened time and again, and I could never figure out if he did it just to devil her, or to show her and maybe himself that he was not a doormat in everything. Anyway, he did it every chance he got, and it seemed to make Bessie's voice louder and shriller every time it happened.

"I worked there just over three years and Bessie got more and more fussy, but I didn't complain because she was a wonderful cook and they both treated me fine. A few times I caught myself just in time when I was about to use her old nickname. Lucky for me, because I think if I had ever called her Bossy she'd have grabbed a skillet and run me off the place.

"Along about late in October my Uncle Warren died and as the work was well caught up I went over to Maple Grove for the funeral. I came back on the Monday-morning train and looked around for a ride out to Ben's place and just by luck the sheriff was going out that way. He had a new rifle he wanted to get sighted in before deer season and there was a place near Ben's where he had a hundred yards clear and a bank for a backstop. Of course, the old cuss already had the gun sighted in good enough for the average hunter, but he had to be able to drive tacks with his rifle.

"He drove into Ben's dooryard and just then we heard a noise from the other side of the house and some fellow took off across a plowed field towards the woods. We wondered what on earth and jumped out of the car and went to the door of the kitchen. The sheriff took one quick look, grabbed his gun out of the car, and shouted at the fellow running to halt. He didn't and the sheriff yelled again, 'Halt or I'll fire!' and drew on the man. He must have been two hundred yards away by then and almost to the woods, but when the sheriff pulled the trigger, down he went.

"I walked into the kitchen but I sure wished I hadn't. Bessie was lying on her back on the floor, all covered with blood. Ben was lying half on top of her. He had the little hatchet from the woodbox that they used to split kindling and it was buried right in his head. The table was overturned and the dishes and the coffeepot were all over the floor. The door on the other side of the kitchen that led to the little porch in the back was open and that was lucky because I just made it through before I was sick.

"The sheriff came back and said the fellow that tried to run away would keep. He had got him in the middle of the back and out through the chest, which was darn fine shooting in any man's language, but the sheriff wasn't satisfied.

" 'Bad shot,' he said, shaking his head. 'Aimed to get him in the leg, but the gun shot high. Not sighted in right. Besides, he stumbled and maybe dropped down a bit just when I fired.' It must be tough to have to do everything so perfect.

"I wouldn't go back in but the sheriff did and called Doc Blake. He came out and they took Bessie to the hospital and Ben and the fellow the sheriff had shot to the undertaker. He was just a young fellow.

"On Thursday Old Baldy Briggs, the justice of the peace, held the coroner's inquest. So many people came they had to move to the court house to find room. Old Baldy spread himself, of course, and acted like he was a circuit court judge.

"They had rounded up some people who had seen the young fellow. Aunt Martha Morse said he'd come to her house Sunday and asked if he could do some work for something to eat. He split some wood for her and she gave him a good dinner.

" 'Did you feel uneasy about this man?' Old Baldy says.

" 'Land, no,' Aunt Martha said. 'He was as nice a young fellow as you would want to see. I wasn't a bit worried about him.'

"Then they got Granny Gower and she testified the young fellow had been to her house Sunday evening and asked for something to eat. She claimed she distrusted him from the start and that she was not at all surprised to hear he was a murderer. Of course that just goes to show you about people.

"The sheriff then told about shooting the fellow to stop him from running away. He said they'd sent his fingerprints away, and his prints had not been on file, so apparently the fellow wasn't a regular criminal. Then they got Doc Blake on the stand. He could just about squeeze into the witness chair, and he didn't look natural without his little black bag.

"He said Ben had died from a hatchet blow to the brain, which wasn't exactly news. Bessie he couldn't be sure of, because she had a concussion and hadn't come out of it yet. He couldn't tell if she'd been struck on the head, thrown down by the young fellow who was maybe trying to assault her, or knocked down by Ben when he fell on her—maybe when she had tried to help Ben during the attack.

"The coroner asked him if Bessie would be able to testify soon, to get the actual story.

"Doc looked kind of bothered. 'I just can't say,' he told Old Baldy. 'The bump she got doesn't look too bad, but there must have been some brain damage because she acts like she's in a coma. Of course part of this might be due to shock. All I can say is, I guess we'll just have to wait and see.'

"Well, the coroner's jury talked it over and they decided that the murderer must have been the young fellow, name unknown. Then they adjourned, postponing the final verdict till Bessie could talk.

"The only thing was, Bessie didn't get able to talk. She came to, but her eyes looked stary like she didn't know what was happening and she didn't say a word. They sent her to the state asylum for treatment, but she was back in a couple of months. They hadn't been able to do anything for her. The doctors there thought the trouble was what they called psychic shock, from seeing her husband killed.

"The only other place they had to send her was to the county asylym, where they put her in the kitchen. The cook said she was the best helper she'd ever had and she only wished she could find some sane people that were as steady and hardworking. I'd gone out this day in February, and as usual Bessie didn't show any signs of knowing me, or even seeing me. She didn't even answer when I said hello. It was a real cold day and a fellow named Joe Weber who had just started to work there as an attendant and guard came into the kitchen from outside. He went up to the range to soak in some heat and then he saw the coffeepot on the stove and knew it was just what he needed to thaw out. He picked it up and shook it to see if there was any coffee left in it.

"That was when Bessie said her first words since Ben was killed. 'No, no,' she said. 'No, no.' It wasn't just an ordinary 'no.' It was like someone might say who's just heard some bad news he didn't want to believe.

"Joe said, 'It's all right—there's plenty of coffee here,' and shook the pot again.

"Then Bessie said, 'You are just like my husband. He wouldn't listen either, when I told him.'

"Then she shoved the cook, who was cutting up meat for supper, away from the block and grabbed the cleaver and sunk it four inches deep into Joe's skull.

"Now when I can't sleep nights, thinking about Ben and Bessie, I think about that young fellow the sheriff shot. He must've just stopped to ask for some breakfast and saw what was on the kitchen floor and then heard us and got so scared he'd be blamed that he turned and ran. I lie here and wonder if somewhere somebody is lying awake like I am, and wondering when that young fellow is coming home."

THOMAS WALSH

THE NIGHT CALHOUN WAS OFF DUTY

They couldn't have been in bed more than an hour when Calhoun grew vaguely conscious that Ellen was shaking his arm. Although he heard her words and the labored way her breath was coming he woke slowly, as he always did, with the old odd feeling in his mind that it was scattered in many pieces and that he'd have to reach out for it bit by bit and put it together again before it would work for him. After he had mumbled the cab company's number into the phone and told them where to come, he yawned and rolled his big red head between his hands. Then Ellen gasped again behind him and he sprang up, swearing at himself in an incandescent flare of anger.

He was a fool, Calhoun muttered savagely. He closed the windows, switched on the bureau lamp, and pattered out on bare feet to light the oven of the kitchen stove so that she'd have something warm to dress by. Then he ran back to the bedroom and picked Ellen up as if she were no weight at all, cradling her in his arms.

"How is it?" he asked huskily. "Will I call Dr. Cotter? Will I get him over here?"

Ellen pressed her head against his shoulder. There was a pause in which he felt her body harden like a bar.

"Bring my clothes," she said at last, rather low. "Don't call him yet, John. They'll do that from the hospital. It's all right. It's—I'm glad it's started. I think it will be over soon."

"Sure," Calhoun chattered. "Sure it will." The kitchen light stung his eyes; he saw by the clock over the refrigerator that it was only four minutes past eleven and he stuttered trying to help her, trying to tell her that it wouldn't be bad. They had all kinds of stuff nowadays to give her. She'd probably never know anything about it until it was over.

"Yes," Ellen whispered. "Don't get so excited, John. My bag's in the hall closet, all packed. Put it by the door so we can't forget it as we go out. And go and get dressed—I'll manage fine. We'll have to hurry to be downstairs when the cab comes for us."

Calhoun hurried; he seemed to get his clothes on in a flash. Still, Ellen was ready when he came out—all he had to do was help her on with her coat. "All right," he said breathlessly, "let's go." The shapeless old ulster that he liked better than his other coat because it was big and burly, and he could wear his revolver under it or even carry it in one of the pockets without it being noticed, was on a chair and he snatched it up. His gun and shield were on the bureau but he didn't go inside for them. Calhoun wouldn't be on police duty tonight.

Ellen made him turn back to shut off the kitchen lights and she wouldn't let him carry her down the steps. In the vestibule he glanced at her and saw the desperate trembling fixity of her smile, the small beads of perspiration appearing around the corners of her mouth. He could feel his heart throb like a rubber hammer swung up and down inside his ribs.

Presently the cab came and he had her out on the steps before the driver had a chance to honk. Then they were inside and starting off, but to Calhoun it was even worse than before, for now there was nothing to do until they got there, and her face, white and stiff under the dark rims about her eyes, made his words dry in his mouth.

"Is it bad?" he whispered.

She shook her head as if she didn't want him to talk and then in a moment she seemed fine again. "Who's having this baby?" she asked, smiling at him. "Now I don't want you hanging around the hospital all night. Go home and get some sleep. They'll call you if anything happens. If you're there you'll only worry me."

"I'll wait a little while," Calhoun muttered. It was intolerable that she should think of him even now, when there was nothing he could do to help her. And suddenly he had a frightful thought: that this might be the last time he would ride with her. Women died sometimes.

Not Ellen, he thought after a moment, above the persistent

whisper that ran on in his mind. Why not? that whisper said. Why couldn't she? She just couldn't, Calhoun thought. He wouldn't let her. But he knew he could do nothing, and confused remembrances of the first time he'd ever seen her, the first time they'd gone out together, rose up in him with a chill of terror.

They'd always been happy, Calhoun thought. Then this. It went on for months, but somehow as if it weren't happening to them—as if it concerned someone else. And now—Calhoun swallowed. He thought they must have been crazy. Crazy! All the things in his mind, so ceaseless and so vivid there, seemed to push him with a kind of agony into the future, into a day to come, so that he wasn't really here in the cab holding her hand; he was there, next week, next month, and he was thinking that he'd known then, in the cab, it was the last time they'd ever—

At the hospital a dark little nurse took his name and had them sit down a moment while she saw about the room.

Calhoun put his hat on the floor and tried to be excessively cheerful.

"If it's a girl," he said, "we'll make a policewoman out of her. I'll bet you'd love that."

But that funny look was on Ellen's face again and she didn't answer him. Where was the nurse? It seemed ages before she returned.

"Maternity's on the sixth floor," she said, "and I think we'd better bring Mrs. Calhoun up right away. No, I'll take the bag; you'll have to stay here. There's a waiting-room down the hall."

Ellen kissed his cheek and he touched her shoulder, then stood watching as she followed the nurse to the elevator. Just as she stepped through he had a glimpse of her eyes and he wasn't sure whether she was crying or if it was only a reflection of light. Even if she felt bad she wouldn't let him see it. Ellen was like that. For a while he stood in the hall trying to think of something, of anything he could do to help her; finally he slapped his hat against his side and went into the waiting-room. But he couldn't sit still; he went back to the hall.

A small but very erect young man in an intern's suit was sitting on one corner of Miss Biddle's desk. Once or twice in the last few months Calhoun had met him—the last time in a dingy room where a young girl's body lay quietly on a bed. Young Dr. Minacorn—Windy Minnie to the hospital staff—had a sharp intellectual face and blond hair growing in a spike on his forehead. He greeted Calhoun with a smile.

"Well, well," he said, "a baby! And I didn't even know you were married."

"Cut the cracks," Calhoun said, looking at him levelly from under his brows. "It isn't anything to be wise about."

"Oh, don't take it that way," Dr. Minacorn said. "No offense."

Calhoun went back to the waiting-room without answering him. If only there were something he could do . . .

A fat man in the chair under the lamp was sleepy comfortably and he didn't wake until a husky nurse in a white apron came to the door and called his name.

"Your wife's had a girl," she said, "and they're both fine. In half an hour you can go up to see them."

Yawning, the fat man sat up and thanked her. "But gosh," he told Calhoun conversationally after she'd gone, "I got to get some sleep. Time enough to see them tomorrow. After the first one there's not much difference anyway."

There was, Calhoun thought, no way to describe some guys. He cracked his knuckles and walked over to the window, then back to his chair, then over to the window again. He thought of Ellen and wondered what was happening. Now, when he might lose her, he knew how much he loved her, he knew there was nobody else he could ever love. Three times in half an hour he went out to see Miss Biddle.

"I'm sorry," she always said, "but they haven't called down yet. They will, you know, when they take her to the delivery room. Until then there's nothing I can tell you."

"Okay," Calhoun said, rubbing a hand worriedly through his hair. "Maybe I'm a nuisance to you and I've laughed at stuff like this in the movies myself. Only it isn't so funny when it happens to you."

Dr. Minacorn, coming in from out back after a cigarette, noticed him as he turned into the waiting-room. "How's our policeman holding out?" he asked Miss Biddle. "Any call for a sedative yet?"

"I wish you *would* give him something," Miss Biddle sighed. "Say a nice strong hypo to keep him quiet the rest of the night. He's out here every five minutes, asking."

"Quite understandable. Something like this," he went on, settling himself comfortably on the desk before her, "rather puzzles our friend. What can he do about it? To a man like Calhoun merely sitting about and waiting is an intolerable state of affairs."

Windy Minnie, Miss Biddle thought, was off again. She said only, "Uh huh," not to encourage him, and bent over her paperwork.

But Dr. Minacorn set his glasses more firmly on his nose and went on. Someday S. Kevin Minacorn, M.D., would be lecturing; meanwhile, practice was never out of place even with an audience of one.

"Calhoun, you see, is a man of action—not of thought. Keep his physical being occupied and he won't be overly concerned with the more sensitive side of things. Just now, of course, he's utterly at a loss.

"I daresay," Dr. Minacorn admitted thoughtfully, "he loves his wife. He appears to be extremely worried about her. But there's nothing at all he can do for her now and that preys on his mind. A man like Calhoun, particularly a policeman, is accustomed to action in its crudest manifestations. And if you think of it, the place of the policeman in the modern world is extremely interesting."

This time Miss Biddle made no remark. The hall was empty; there was no relief in sight. She wrote on.

"Extremely interesting," Dr. Minacorn continued, fascinated by his pursuit of an idea. "Take their social background alone and you're struck at the start by a somewhat startling fact—that our criminals and thugs and our, well, protectors, are all from the same social level. Your police today are actually legalized gangsters hired by society to protect it.

"Legalized gangsters," Dr. Minacorn repeated. "Why do you think Calhoun is a policeman? First, naturally, because he's unimaginative and a plodder; and second, because it's a remarkably easy living, with a little authority and no need for the unpleasant job of thinking. Like the rest of his fellows he'll do as little of what he's supposed to do as he can get away with. The problems of society as a whole are meaningless to him."

When he paused for breath, Miss Biddle knew it was now or never. "Who," she asked, "are you going to take to the alumni dance?"

In the waiting-room Calhoun's mouth felt as dry and harsh as an oven. There wasn't a sound either in the hospital or out in the streets. Calhoun thought vaguely of all the people in the world, of life and death and what they meant. He remembered how happy they had been, and suddenly the recollection of that happiness frightened him, because things always struck at the happy ones. Perhaps if he didn't love her so much—and he didn't, really he didn't—nothing would happen to her. Nothing, God, Calhoun whispered. Because she was his wife and he loved her and if she died he'd be dead, too. Panic struck at him again.

In the hall, Miss Biddle muttered something when she saw him come out of the waiting-room and Dr. Minacorn, appearing from the emergency ward in overcoat and hat, stopped by her desk to wait for him.

"Here," he said, struck by a sudden inspiration—the man of action could be given something to do. "How about a ride with me, Calhoun? I've got a call to make."

Calhoun looked at him as if he weren't quite sure who he was, and then down at Miss Biddle.

"Don't worry about your wife," Dr. Minacorn said cheerfully. "She's all right—the first one's always long in coming. Any further word, Miss Biddle?"

Miss Biddle shook her head. "Nothing since the last."

"Then you've got all night," Dr. Minacorn said, gripping his arm. "And we won't be gone ten minutes. Come on, man. It will do you good."

Calhoun knew he couldn't go back to that room and just wait. He'd do something crazy if he had to sit there again. So after a moment he put on his hat dully and followed Minacorn out back where an ambulance was waiting. "Okay," Dr. Minacorn said, getting in. "Let's roll, Eddie."

In the front seat of the car, crowded against Minacorn, it all began again in Calhoun's mind. Suppose now, this very moment, they sent word downstairs and he wasn't there. Suppose Ellen wanted to see him and they had to tell her that he'd gone, that— The four-block ride seemed endless; he was out first, anxious to be through quickly.

"Thirty-three," Minacorn said, looking up at the row of cheap tenements before them. "That's the one over there with the ashcans at the curb. They say what was wrong, Eddie?"

"Not that I heard," the driver said. "I just got the address."

It was a somber street, fretful with shadows. Calhoun followed them around the ashcans, through a dirty hallway, and up a flight of wooden stairs. At the first landing Dr. Minacorn peered about.

"Any apartment number, Eddie? These people never seem to—"

A boy leaned over the railing above them. "It's up here," he said. "One more flight, mister."

Minacorn bounced up that on his quick legs. "Now what's the matter?" he asked. "Who's sick?"

"Pietro," the boy said, staring at them with drawn dark eyes. "He boards with my mother. He's in there."

A grey-haired woman with a shawl around her shoulders spoke to him in rapid Italian. The boy looked up at them.

"She says she don't want him here no more. She's afraid. You'll have to take him away."

"First we'll have a look at him." Minacorn started for the door on the right of the landing. "In here, is he?"

"Watch out," the boy said. The woman spoke, too, in a flow of words that was shrilly urgent. Minacorn said sharply: "Keep quiet, please. We're not going to hurt him, you know," and opened the door.

Over his shoulder Calhoun saw a man facing them from the lighted kitchen—a thin tall man with wild black hair and glittering black eyes that had no sanity or balance in them. There was a rifle in his hands.

"What in hell—" Eddie breathed. He jumped aside and slammed the door just before the man fired. Dr. Minacorn had no chance to get out. He could only jump sideways away from the hole that the bullet had made in the glass upper half of the door, not an inch from his head. Calhoun saw his shadow blur across the light an instant before it was extinguished.

Flattened out against the wall, Eddie stared wide-eyed at Calhoun, across the boy and his mother standing between them. The voice of the black-haired man screamed insanely at them from the darkened kitchen.

"He's crazy," the boy whispered. "He's been acting funny all week, showing me marks on the stoop where he said that the bullets people fired at him hit. Tonight when he took his gun out Mama got scared. She made me call you."

Behind the door, Dr. Minacorn said something but his voice was so low and shaky Calhoun couldn't understand the words. Immediately the other man bore him down with harsh Italian.

"Now he says he's gonna kill him," the boy breathed, holding Calhoun's hand. His young face was white as paper. Calhoun stared down at it for a moment and then looked at the driver. "Somebody's got to go in there," he said.

"Not me." Eddie went backward two steps down the stairs. "Not me. You got a riot squad to handle stuff like this. I saw his gun."

Calhoun rubbed his mouth slowly and looked back along the hall. People were out on the stairs now from the other floors, huddling together in small groups. Inside the kitchen the madman still shouted.

"What's he saying now?" Calhoun asked.

The boy listened, shivering against his mother. "He says he knows who he is and he's going to kill him. He's telling him to get on his knees."

At the end of the hall there was another door. Calhoun saw it would lead into the parlor—there were two apartments on a floor, right and left of the landing, each running through from front to back—and he was moving back toward it before any plan of action cleared in his mind.

"Stay here," he told Eddie. "Make all the noise you can. I'll have to force this door."

Eddie nodded dumbly and, as Calhoun reached the front door, tramped up and down the stairs, shouted, and then banged his body into the wall. In the middle of his yell Calhoun cracked his shoulder against the door in a lunge that burst the flimsy lock like the snapping of a rubber band.

He found himself in a small room with one window opening on the street and a lamp set on a table in the center of the floor, opposite a doorway just right of him that led back into the first bedroom. Calhoun saw that the lamp was going to be a danger—going back through the doorways from room to room he'd be silhouetted clearly against it. He could click it off, of course, but that was something this madman couldn't miss seeing, no matter how dimly it showed in the kitchen. Doing that, he might as well knock on the door and ask if he could come in. No, he couldn't touch it; he'd have to leave it on if he wanted to get out there before this crazy Pietro knew he was coming.

Bent low, he stepped through the doorway, across the line of light that for a prickly instant traced him clearly against itself. But there was no shot; the madman probably was facing Minacorn and the kitchen door. He wouldn't look back. Now, Calhoun thought, if he kept to the darkness left of the doorways, his only points of danger would be the openings themselves—the split seconds when he'd have to slip through them to reach each succeeding room. Even now he could make out nothing of the kitchen but a vague bluish shadow, thinned slightly where the light from the hall filtered through the glass upper half of the door; there was no way of telling where Pietro was standing. Just before he reached the second doorway he paused again to listen. Where was his voice coming from?

If you had asked Calhoun then why he was trying to reach that kitchen, the chances are that he wouldn't have been able to tell you. Someone, he might have said, had to get in there. And who was going to try if he didn't? Eddie? Calhoun knew it was up to him, no one else. He was trying to get into that kitchen just as Dr. Minacorn might have grasped a patient's wrist to feel his pulse. Not entirely because he was a cop, not at all because it was Minacorn who was out there—Calhoun would have gone in if the man had been a stranger. The only thing worrying him now was whether or not this Pietro was playing possum to get him closer. And the one way to answer that was to keep on going.

Calhoun kept on going.

•

He was in the second doorway now and he slipped through it safely. Across the one intervening room he began to distinguish objects in the kitchen: a chair, a table, someone that by the bag in one hand and the white trousers showing under the coat was obviously Dr. Minacorn. From the way his head was set Calhoun got a hint of where the madman was standing—somewhere left of the last doorway, probably against the far wall. There'd be six or seven feet to cover and not much time to get across it. Still, Calhoun thought he could do it. Even Minacorn hadn't noticed him yet; he was standing before the table as stiffly as if he'd been turned to stone.

"Now listen," he was saying in a voice he couldn't steady down, "I've come here to help you. I'm a doctor. Try to understand that, won't you? I'm not your enemy. I don't want to harm you. If you'll just try to see—"

Against those blazing eyes his words beat feebly, without effect. Dr. Minacorn saw that and he was badly frightened; in the shadow his pale cheeks seemed to gleam whiter than the speck of light reflected from his glasses. He had seen death many times before and it had never seemed important or particularly dreadful. If old men whose names he scarcely knew died now and again in a ward, Dr. Minacorn was sorry for them, of course. But what did it have to do with S. Kevin Minacorn, M.D., young and healthy Minacorn, immortal Minacorn? In some far-distant future, of course, he would come to it inevitably, even he. And so what, young Dr. Minacorn had thought, with that comfortable future before him, as solid as eternity—so what?

Just now, when the future was not so distant, it made a lot of difference. Across the dark kitchen he could see the face of the lunatic glaring at him—he could see the shape of it, long and pale, the eyes that glittered even in the blackness. But clearest of all, sharpest of all, he could see the gun.

And young Dr. Minacorn didn't want to die like this— foolishly, stupidly, without any sense to it; there were so many things he had to do first. Sometime, of course, it would have to come. But not now, not now! Trying to speak, thinking desperately that he must make his voice unalarmed, very soothing, he couldn't seem to hear his own words. But he was this man's friend; he wanted to help him.

He dared not move, not even his arms; he knew if he did the madman would shoot him. In a few seconds now he might be dead. No one would help him—not Eddie, not Calhoun, not anyone. Why should they? If he were out there, he wouldn't come in. But damn them—oh, damn them, he thought illogically. He had been the fool; he had walked in first and been trapped, not listening to the boy—

From the last room Calhoun could see him standing there, moving his lips in a confused mumble. What was he trying to say? Calhoun couldn't make it out. Steadying himself for the last rush, Calhoun didn't think of this as something he was paid to do; he readied himself quite slowly and cautiously because of something in him that had been there before he was a cop, something that—it was possible—might have made him become a cop.

Yet something stopped him. It said: why couldn't he stay here where he was until the riot squad came, or the cop on the beat, or someone to give him a hand? Why couldn't he let Minacorn take his chance? What business was it of his? He didn't even like the guy. But the thought never grew serious in his mind. Wasting time was stupid; he had to get back to the hospital. Maybe Ellen had had the kid now—his kid. That seemed odd. Calhoun couldn't understand it as he wet his lips and inched closer to the door. His kid!

Maybe that was the thing that stopped him, but only for a moment. All the time, really, he knew what he had to do. There was a crazy man in there who might kill another man. Calhoun had to stop him.

So he sprang through the doorway and hesitated there for the tiniest breath of time to locate this crazy Pietro exactly. Then Minacorn saw him, and Pietro, too. The rifle swung around to Calhoun as he ran for it low, his arms outspread like a football player about to make a tackle. But the madman had to move the gun only slightly; he pressed the trigger twice as it swung across his belt.

Then Minacorn was on him, knocking him down with a wild

swing of his bag, yanking the rifle from him, and battering it against his head. "Eddie!" he yelled in a voice as shrill as a woman's, after the other man was still. "Eddie! Eddie!"

After a long while Eddie came through the kitchen door carefully. Dr. Minacorn was sitting in a chair, the muscles in his legs jumping and quivering as if they were alive—as if they would never be steady enough to hold him up.

Calhoun lay on the floor, his fine big body still, touched by a last quiet magic that showed no mark in his face, yet that somehow, very deftly, had taken from him reason and emotion, all curiosity.

"Is he—" Eddie asked huskily.

"Gone," Dr. Minacorn said. His voice came out strong now and he knew he'd be all right in a minute. Because it wasn't now, but sometime in the far-distant future, sometime so remote that it would be another Minacorn who would meet it—an old Minacorn, philosophical and tired.

He sat in his chair and stared at Calhoun. Minacorn was so glad to be alive that he couldn't move. Death was remote again, impersonal. Tomorrow he would never have been afraid. Even now he was thinking that this way wasn't so bad. Calhoun could never have felt a thing. Just—

After the husky nurse saw that the waiting-room was deserted, she continued down the hall to Miss Biddle's desk.

"Where's the big fellow?" she asked. "Calhoun?"

Miss Biddle stood up and stretched. It was proving a long night.

"You mean the cop—the legalized gangster? He went out with Windy Minnie."

"So he's a cop," the nurse said. "You know he really looks like one."

"Big and dumb," Miss Biddle yawned, "but kind of nice, though. You should have heard the lecture Minnie gave me about them. I can't remember half of it."

"Who ever could?" the other nurse said. "Any time after three you can send this Calhoun up. His wife's had a boy. I guess he'll want to see it."

"I guess he will," Miss Biddle said.

R. AUSTIN FREEMAN

THE MISSING MORTGAGEE

I. The Story of the Crime

Early in the afternoon of a warm, humid November day Thomas Elton sauntered dejectedly along the Margate esplanade, casting an eye now on the slate-colored sea with its pall of slate-colored sky, and now on the harbor, where the ebb tide was just beginning to expose the mud. It was a dreary prospect, and Elton varied it by observing the few fishermen and fewer promenaders who walked foot to foot with their distorted reflections in the wet pavement; and thus it was that his eye fell on a smartly dressed man who had just stepped into a shelter to light a cigar.

Now, something in the aspect of the broad back that was presented to his view, in that of the curly black hair and the exuberant raiment, suggested to Elton a suspicion of disagreeable familiarity. The man backed out of the shelter, diffusing azure clouds, and, drawing an envelope from his pocket, read something that was written on it. Then he turned quickly—and so did Elton, but not quickly enough. For he was a solitary figure on that bald and empty expanse, and the other had seen him at the first glance. Elton walked away slowly, but he had not gone a dozen paces when he felt the anticipated slap on the shoulder and heard the too well remembered voice.

"Blow me, if I don't believe you were trying to cut me, Tom," it said.

Elton looked round with ill-assumed surprise.

"Hallo, Gordon! Who the deuce would have thought of seeing you here?"

Gordon laughed thickly. "Not you, apparently; and you don't look as pleased as you might now that you have seen me.

75

Whereas I'm delighted to see you, and especially to see that things are going so well with you."

"What do you mean?" asked Elton sullenly.

"Taking your winter holiday by the sea, like a blooming duke."

"I'm not taking a holiday," said Elton. "I was so worn out that I had to have some sort of change; but I've brought my work down with me, and I put in a full eight hours every day."

"That's right," said Gordon. " 'Consider the ant.' Nothing like steady industry. I've brought my work down with me, too; a little slip of paper with a stamp on it. You know the article, Tom."

"I know. But it isn't due till tomorrow, is it?"

"Isn't it, by gum! It's due this very day, the twentieth of the month. That's why I'm here. Knowing your little weakness in the matter of dates, and having a small item to collect in Canterbury, I thought I'd just come on and save you the useless expense that results from forgetfulness."

Elton understood the hint, and his face grew rigid.

"I can't do it, Gordon; I can't, really. Haven't got it, and shan't have it until I'm paid for the batch of drawings I'm working on now."

"Oh, what a pity!" exclaimed Gordon. "Here you are, blueing your capital on seaside jaunts and reducing your income at a stroke by a clear four pounds a year."

"How do you make that out?" demanded Elton.

"Tut, tut," protested Gordon, "what an unbusinesslike chap you are! Here's a little matter of twenty pounds—a quarter's interest. If it's paid now, it's twenty. If it isn't, it goes on to the principal, and there's another four pounds a year to be paid. Why don't you try to be more economical, dear boy?"

Elton looked askance at the vampire by his side; at the plump, blue-shaven cheeks, the thick black eyebrows, and the full red lips that embraced the cigar, and though he was a mild-tempered man he felt that he could have battered that sensual, complacent face out of all human likeness with something uncommonly like enjoyment. But of these thoughts nothing appeared in his reply, for a man cannot afford to say all he would wish to a creditor who could ruin him with a word.

"You mustn't be too hard on me, Gordon," said he. "Give me a little time. I'm doing all I can, you know. I earn every penny that I'm able, and I've kept my insurance paid up regularly. I'll be paid for this work in a week or two and then we can settle up."

Gordon made no immediate reply, and the two men walked slowly eastward, a curiously ill-assorted pair; the one prosperous, jaunty, overdressed; the other pale and dejected, and, with his well-brushed but napless clothes, his patched boots and shiny-brimmed hat, the very type of decent, struggling poverty.

They had just passed the pier and were coming to the base of the jetty when Gordon next spoke.

"Can't we get off this beastly wet pavement?" he asked, looking down at his dainty and highly polished boots. "What's it like down on the sands?"

"Oh, it's very good walking," said Elton, "between here and Foreness, and probably drier than the pavement."

"Then," said Gordon, "I vote we go down"—and accordingly they descended the sloping way beyond the jetty. The stretch of sand left by the retiring tide was as smooth and firm as a sheet of asphalt, and far more pleasant to walk upon.

"We seem to have the place all to ourselves," remarked Gordon, "with the exception of some half-dozen dukes like yourself."

As he spoke, Gordon changed over from one arm to the other the heavy fur-lined overcoat he was carrying. "Needn't have brought this beastly thing," he remarked, "if I'd known it was going to be so warm."

"Shall I carry it for you a little way?" asked the naturally polite Elton.

"If you would, dear boy," replied Gordon. "It's difficult to manage an overcoat, an umbrella, and a cigar all at once."

He handed over the coat with a sigh of relief. Presently their footsteps led them to the margin of the weed-covered rocks, and here, from under a high heap of bladder wrack, a large green shore crab rushed out and menaced them with uplifted claws. Gordon stopped and stared at the creature with Cockney surprise, prodding it with his umbrella and speculating aloud as to whether it was good to eat. The crab, as if alarmed at the suggestion, suddenly darted away and began to scuttle over the green-clad rocks, finally plunging into a large deep pool.

Gordon pursued it, hobbling awkwardly over the slippery rocks until he came to the edge of the pool, over which he stooped, raking inquisitively among the weedy fringe with his umbrella. He was so much interested in his quarry that he failed to allow for the slippery surface on which he stood. The result was disastrous. Of a sudden, one foot began to slide forward and, when he tried to recover his balance, was instantly followed by the other. For a moment he struggled frantically to regain his footing, executing a sort of splashing, stamping dance on the margin. Then, the circling sea birds were startled by a yell of terror, an ivory-handled umbrella flew across the rocks, and Mr. Gordon took a complete header into the deepest part of the pool. What the crab thought of it history does not relate. What Mr. Gordon thought of it is not suitable for publication—he rose looking like an extremely up-to-date merman.

"It's a good job you brought your overcoat, after all," Elton remarked. Gordon made no reply but staggered towards the hospitable overcoat, holding out his dripping arms.

Having inducted him into the garment and buttoned him up, Elton hurried off to recover the umbrella and, having secured it, angled with it for the smart billycock which was floating across the pool.

It was surprising what a change the last minute or two had wrought. The positions of the two men were now quite reversed. Despite his shabby clothing, Elton seemed to walk quite jauntily as compared with his shuddering companion, who trotted by his side with short, miserable steps, shrinking into the uttermost depths of his enveloping coat like an alarmed winkle into its shell, puffing out his cheeks and anathematizing the Universe in general.

They hurried along towards the slope by the jetty when suddenly Elton asked: "What are you going to do, Gordon? You can't travel like that."

"Can't you lend me a change?" asked Gordon.

Elton reflected. He had another suit, his best suit, which he had been careful to preserve in good condition for use on those occasions when a decent appearance was indispensable. He looked askance at the man by his side and something told him that the treasured suit would probably receive less careful treatment than it was accustomed to. Still, the man couldn't be allowed to go about in wet clothes.

"I've got a spare suit," he said. "It isn't quite up to your style, and may not be much of a fit, but I daresay you'll be able to put up with it for an hour or two."

"It'll be dry anyhow," mumbled Gordon, "so we won't trouble about the style. How far is it to your rooms?"

The plural number was superfluous. Elton's room was in a little ancient flint house at the bottom of a narrow close in the old quarter of the town. You reached it without any formal preliminaries of bell or knocker by simply letting yourself in by a street door, crossing a tiny room, opening the door of what looked like a narrow cupboard, and squeezing up a diminutive flight of stairs, which was unexpectedly exposed to view. By following this procedure the two men reached a small bed/sitting-room; that is to say, it was a bedroom, but by sitting down on the bed you converted it into a sitting-room.

Gordon puffed out his cheeks and looked round distastefully. "You might ring for some hot water, old chappie," he said.

Elton laughed aloud. "Ring!" he exclaimed. "Ring what? Your clothes are the only things that are likely to get wrung."

"Well, then, sing out for the servant," said Gordon.

Elton laughed again. "My dear fellow," said he, "we don't go in for servants. I look after my room myself. You'll be all right if you have a good rubdown."

Gordon groaned, and emerged reluctantly from the depths of his overcoat, while Elton brought forth from the chest of drawers the promised suit and the necessary undergarments. One of these latter Gordon held up with a sour smile, as he regarded it with extreme disfavor.

"I shouldn't think," said he, "you need have been at the trouble of marking them so plainly. No one's likely to want to run away with them."

The undergarments certainly contrasted very unfavorably with the delicate garments which he was peeling off, excepting in one respect—they were dry—and that had to console him for the ignominious change.

The clothes fitted quite fairly, notwithstanding the difference between the figures of the two men, for while Gordon was a slender man grown fat, Elton was a broad man grown thin— which, in a way, averaged their superficial area.

Elton watched the process of investment and noted the caution with which Gordon smuggled the various articles from his own pockets into those of the borrowed garments without exposing them to view; heard the jingle of money; saw the sumptuous gold watch and massive chain transplanted; and noted with interest the large leather wallet that came forth from the breast pocket of the wet coat. He got a better view of this from the fact that Gordon himself examined it narrowly, and even opened it to inspect its contents.

"Lucky that wasn't an ordinary pocketbook," he remarked. "If it had been, your receipt would have got wet, and so would one or two other little articles that wouldn't have been improved by salt water. And, talking of the receipt, Tom, shall I hand it over now?"

"You can if you like," said Elton; "but as I told you, I haven't got the money." On which Gordon muttered:

"Pity, pity," and thrust the wallet into his, or rather Elton's, breast pocket.

A few minutes later the two men came out together into the gathering darkness, and as they walked slowly up the close, Elton asked: "Are you going to town tonight, Gordon?"

"How can I?" was the reply. "I can't go without my clothes. No, I shall run over to Broadstairs. A client of mine keeps a boardinghouse there. He'll have to put me up for the night, and if you can get my clothes cleaned and dried I can come over for them tomorrow."

These arrangements having been settled, the two men adjourned, at Gordon's suggestion, for tea at one of the restaurants on the Front; and after that, again at Gordon's suggestion, they set forth together along the cliff path that leads to Broadstairs by way of Kingsgate.

"You may as well walk with me into Broadstairs," said Gordon; "I'll stand you the fare back." And to this Elton agreed, not because he was desirous of the other man's company, but because he still had some lingering hopes of being able to adjust the little difficulty respecting the installment.

"Look here, Gordon," he said at length, "can't you manage to give me a bit more time to pay up this installment? It doesn't seem quite fair to keep sending up the principal like this."

"Well, dear boy," replied Gordon, "it's your own fault, you know. If you would only bear the dates in mind it wouldn't happen."

"But," pleaded Elton, "just consider what I'm paying you. I originally borrowed fifty pounds from you, and I'm now paying you eighty pounds a year in addition to the insurance premium. That's close on a hundred a year, just about half what I manage to earn. If you stick it up any further you won't leave me enough to keep body and soul together; which really means that I shan't be able to pay you at all."

There was a brief pause; then Gordon said dryly:

"You talk about not paying, dear boy, as if you had forgotten about that promissory note."

Elton set his teeth. His temper was rising rapidly. But he restrained himself.

"I should have a pretty good memory if I had," he replied, "considering the number of reminders you've given me."

"You've needed them, Tom," said the other. "I've never met a slacker man in keeping to his engagements."

At this Elton lost his temper completely.

"That's a lie," he exclaimed, "and you know it, you infernal, dirty, bloodsucking parasite!"

Gordon stopped dead.

"Look here, my friend," said he; "none of that. If I've any of your sauce, I'll give you a sound good hammering."

"The deuce you will!" said Elton, whose fingers were itching, not for the first time, to take some recompense for all he had suffered from the insatiable usurer. "Nothing's preventing you now, you know, but I fancy twenty percent is more in your line than fighting."

"Give me any more and you'll see," said Gordon.

"Very well," was the quiet rejoinder. "I have great pleasure in informing you that you are a human mawworm. How does that suit you?"

For reply, Gordon threw down his overcoat and umbrella on the grass at the side of the path and deliberately slapped Elton on the cheek.

The reply followed instantly in the form of a smart left-hander, which took effect on the bridge of Gordon's nose. Thus the battle was fairly started, and it proceeded with all the fury of accumulated hatred on the one side and sharp physical pain on the other. What little science there was appertained to Elton, in spite of which, however, he had to give way to his heavier, better nourished, and more excitable opponent. Regardless of the punishment he received, the infuriated Gordon rushed at him and, by sheer weight of onslaught, drove him backward across the little green.

Suddenly, Elton, who knew the place by daylight, called out in alarm.

"Look out, Gordon! Get back, you fool!"

But Gordon, blind with fury, and taking this as a maneuver to escape, only pressed him harder. Elton's pugnacity died out instantly in mortal terror. He shouted out another warning and, as Gordon still pressed him, battering furiously, he did the only thing that was possible: he dropped to the ground. And then, in the twinkling of an eye, came the catastrophe. Borne forward by his own momentum, Gordon stumbled over Elton's prostrate body, staggered forward a few paces, and fell. Elton heard a muffled groan that faded quickly and mingled with the sound of falling earth and stones. He sprang to his feet and looked round and saw that he was alone.

For some moments he was dazed by the suddenness of the awful thing that had happened. He crept timorously towards the unseen edge of the cliff and listened. But there was no sound save the distant surge of the breakers and the scream of an invisible seabird. It was useless to try to look over. Near as he was, he could not, even now, distinguish the edge of the cliff from the dark beach below.

Suddenly he thought of a narrow cutting that led down from the cliff to the shore. Quickly crossing the green, and mechanically stooping to pick up Gordon's overcoat and umbrella, he made his way to the head of the cutting and ran down the rough chalk roadway. At the bottom he turned to the right.

Soon there loomed up against the murky sky the shadowy form of the little headland on which he and Gordon had stood; and almost at the same moment there grew out of the darkness of the beach a darker spot amid a constellation of smaller spots of white. As he drew nearer, the dark spot took shape: a horrid shape with sprawling limbs and a head strangely awry. He stepped forward, trembling, and spoke the name the thing had borne. He grasped the flabby hand and laid his fingers on the wrist—but it only told him the same tale as did that strangely misplaced head. The body lay face downward, and he had not the courage to turn it over; but that his enemy was dead he had not the faintest doubt. He stood up amidst the litter of fallen chalk and earth and looked down at the horrible, motionless thing, wondering numbly and vaguely what he should do. Should he go and seek assistance? The answer to that came in another question. How came that body to be lying on the beach? And what answer should he give to the inevitable questions?

Little sleep was there that night for Elton in his room in the old flint house. The dead man's clothes, which greeted him on his arrival, hanging limply on the towel-horse where he had left them, haunted him through the night. In the darkness the sour smell of damp cloth assailed him with an endless reminder of their presence, and after each brief doze he would start up in alarm and hastily light his candle, only to throw its flickering light on those dank, drowned-looking vestments. His thoughts, half controlled, as night thoughts are, flitted erratically from the unhappy past to the unstable present, and thence to the incalculable future.

Once he light the candle specially to look at his watch to see if the tide had yet crept up to that solitary figure on the beach; nor could he rest again until the time of highwater was well past. And all through these wanderings of his thoughts there came, recurring like a horrible refrain, the question, what would happen when the body was found? Could he be connected with it and, if so, would he be charged with murder? At last he fell asleep and slumbered on until the landlady thumped at the staircase door to announce that she had brought his breakfast.

As soon as he was dressed he went out. He went straight on down to the beach, with what purpose he could hardly have said—but an irresistible impulse drove him thither to see if it was there. He went down by the jetty and struck out eastward over the smooth sand, looking about him with dreadful expectation for some small crowd or hurrying messenger.

It was less than half an hour later that the fatal headland opened out beyond Whiteness. Not a soul had he met along that solitary beach, and though once or twice he had started at the sight of some mass of driftwood or heap of seaweed, the dreadful thing he was seeking had not yet appeared. He passed the opening of the cutting and approached the headland, breathing fast and looking about him fearfully.

Then, rounding the headland, he came in sight of a black hole at the cliff foot, the entrance to a deep cave. He approached yet more slowly, sweeping his eye round the little bay and looking apprehensively at the cavity before him. Suppose the thing should have washed in there. It was quite possible. Many things did wash into that cave, for he had once visited it and had been astonished at the quantity of seaweed and jetsam that had accumulated within it. But it was an uncomfortable thought. It would be doubly horrible to meet the awful thing in the dim twilight of the cavern. And yet, the black archway seemed to draw him on, step by step, until he stood at the portal and looked in. It was an eerie place, chilly and damp, the clammy walls and roof stained green and purple, and black with encrusting lichens.

At first he could see nothing but the smooth sand near the opening; then, as his eyes grew more accustomed to the gloom, he could make out the great heap of seaweed on the floor of the cave. Insensibly, he crept in, with his eyes riveted on the weedy mass and, as he left the daylight behind him, so did the twilight of the cave grow clearer. His feet left the firm sand and trod the springy mass of weed.

And then, in an instant, he saw it. From a heap of weed a few paces ahead projected a boot: his own boot. He recognized the patch on the sole, and at the sight his heart seemed to stand still. Though he had somehow expected to find it here, its presence seemed to strike him with a greater shock of horror from that very circumstance.

How long would the body lie here undiscovered? And what would happen when it was found? What was there to connect him with it? Of course, there was his name on the clothing, but there was nothing incriminating in that, if he had only had the courage to give information at once. But it was too late to think of that now. Besides, it suddenly flashed upon him, there was the receipt in the wallet. That receipt mentioned him by name and referred to a loan. Obviously, its suggestion was most sinister, coupled with his silence. It was a deadly item of evidence against him. But no sooner had he realized the appalling significance of this document than he also realized that it was still within his reach. Why should he leave it there to be brought in evidence—in false evidence, too—against him?

Slowly he began to lift the slimy tangled weed. As he drew aside the first bunch, he gave a gasp of horror and quickly replaced it. The body was lying on its back and as he lifted the weed he had uncovered—not the face, for the thing had no face. It had struck either the cliff or a stone upon the beach and—but there is no need to go into particulars: it had no face.

When he had recovered a little, Elton groped shudderingly among the weed until he found the breast-pocket, from which he quickly drew out the wallet, now clammy and sodden.

Elton stood up and took a deep breath. He resolved instantly to take out and destroy the receipt and put back the wallet. But this was easier thought of than done. The receipt was soaked with seawater, and refused utterly to light when he applied a match to it. In the end he tore it up into little fragments and deliberately swallowed them, one by one.

But to restore the wallet was more than he was equal to just now. The receipt was gone now, and with it the immediate suggestion of motive. There remained only the clothes with their too legible markings. They certainly connected him with the body, but they offered no proof of his presence at the catastrophe. And then, suddenly, another idea occurred to him. Who could identify the body—the body that had no face? There was the wallet, it was true, but he could take that away with him; and there was a ring on the finger, and some articles in the pockets which might be identified. But these things were removable, too. And if he removed them, what then? Why, then, the body was that of Thomas Elton, a friendless, poverty-stricken artist.

He pondered on this new situation profoundly. It offered him a choice of alternatives. Either he might choose the imminent risk of being hanged for a murder that he had not committed, or he might surrender his identity forever and move away to a new environment.

He smiled faintly. His identity? What might that be worth to barter against his life? Only yesterday he would gladly have surrendered it as the bare piece of emancipation from the vampire who had fastened onto him.

He thrust the wallet into his pocket and buttoned his coat.

"Thomas Elton" was dead.

II. Dr. Thorndyke's Investigation

From various causes, the insurance business that passed through Dr. Thorndyke's hands had, of late, considerably increased. The number of companies which regularly employed him had grown larger, and, since the remarkable case of Percival Bland, the "Griffin" had made it a routine practice to send all inquest cases to us for report.

It was in reference to one of these that Mr. Stalker, a senior member of the staff of that office, called on us one afternoon in December.

"I've brought you another inquest case," said he; "a rather queer one, quite interesting from your point of view. As far as we can see, it has no particular interest for us excepting that it does rather look as if our examining medical officer had been a little casual.

"On the twenty-fourth of last month some men who were collecting seaweed, to use as manure, discovered in a cave at Kingsgate in the Isle of Thanet the body of a man lying under a mass of accumulated weed. As the tide was rising, they put the body into their cart and conveyed it to Margate, where, of course, an inquest was held, and the following facts were elicited.

"The body was that of a man named Thomas Elton. It was identified by the name-marks on the clothing, by the visiting-cards and a couple of letters which were found in the pockets. From the address on the letters, it was seen that Elton had been staying in Margate, and on inquiry at that address it was learned from the old woman who let the lodgings that he had been missing about four days.

"The landlady was taken to the mortuary, and at once identified the body as that of her lodger. It remained only to decide how the body came into the cave—and this did not seem to present much difficulty, for the neck had been broken by a tremendous blow, which had practically destroyed the face, and there were distinct evidences of a breaking away of a portion of the top of the cliff, only a few yards from the position of the cave. There was apparently no doubt that Elton had fallen sheer from the top of the overhanging cliff onto the beach. Now, one would suppose with the evidence of this fall of about a hundred and fifty feet, the smashed face, and broken neck, there was not much room for doubt as to the cause of death. I think you will agree with me, Dr. Jervis?"

"Certainly," I replied; "it must be admitted that a broken neck is a condition that tends to shorten life."

"Quite so," agreed Stalker; "but our friend, the local coroner, is a gentleman who takes nothing for granted—a very Thomas Didymus, who apparently agrees with Dr. Thorndyke that if there is no post-mortem, there is no inquest. So he ordered a post-mortem, which would have appeared to me an absurdly unnecessary proceeding, as I think even you will agree with me, Dr. Thorndyke."

But Thorndyke shook his head.

"Not at all," said he. "It might, for instance, be much easier to push a drugged or poisoned man over a cliff than to put over the same man in his normal state. The appearance of violent accident is an excellent mask for the less obvious forms of murder."

"That's perfectly true," said Stalker; "and I suppose that is what the coroner thought. At any rate, he had the post-mortem made, and the result was most curious; for it was found, on opening the body, that the deceased had suffered from a

smallish thoracic aneurism, which had burst. Now, as the aneurism must obviously have burst during life, it leaves the cause
of death—so I understand—uncertain; at any rate, the medical
witness was unable to say whether the deceased fell over the
cliff in consequence of the bursting of the aneurism or burst
the aneurism in consequence of falling over the cliff. Of course,
it doesn't matter to us which way the thing happened; the only
question which interests us is whether a comparatively recently
insured man ought to have had an aneurism at all."

"Have you paid the claim?" asked Thorndyke.

"No, certainly not. We never pay a claim until we have had
your report. But, as a matter of fact, there is another circumstance that is causing delay. It seems that Elton had mortgaged
his policy to a moneylender named Gordon, and it is by him
that the claim has been made—or rather, by a clerk of his
named Hyams. Now, we have had a good many dealings with
this man, Gordon, and hitherto he has always acted in person;
and as he is a somewhat slippery gentleman, we have thought it
desirable to have the claim actually signed by him. And that is
the difficulty. For it seems that Mr. Gordon is abroad and his
whereabouts unknown to Hyams. So, as we certainly couldn't
take Hyams's receipt for payment, the matter is in abeyance
until Hyams can communicate with his principal. And now I
must be running away. I have brought you, as you will see, all
the papers, including the policy and the mortgage deed."

As soon as he was gone, Thorndyke gathered up the bundle of
papers and sorted them out in what he apparently considered
the order of their importance.

"The medical evidence," he remarked, "is very full and complete. Both the coroner and the doctor seem to know their
business."

"Seeing that the man apparently fell over a cliff," said I, "the
medical evidence would not seem to be of first importance. It
would seem to be more to the point to ascertain how he came
to fall over."

"That's quite true," replied Thorndyke; "and yet this report
contains some rather curious matter. The deceased had an
aneurism of the arch; that was probably rather recent. But he

also had some slight, old-standing aortic disease, with full compensatory hypertrophy. He also had a nearly complete set of false teeth. Now, doesn't it strike you, Jervis, as rather odd that a man who was passed only five years ago as a first-class life should, in that short interval, have become actually uninsurable?"

"It certainly does look," said I, "as if the fellow had had rather bad luck. What does the proposal form say?"

I took the document up and ran my eyes over it. On Thorndyke's advice, medical examiners for the "Griffin" were instructed to make a somewhat fuller report than is usual in some companies. In this case, the ordinary answers set forth that the heart was perfectly healthy and the teeth exceptionally good, and then, in the summary at the end, the examiner remarked: "the proposer seems to be a completely sound and healthy man; he presents no physical defects whatever, with the exception of a bony ankylosis of the first joint of the third finger of the left hand, which he states to have been due to an injury."

Thorndyke looked up quickly. "Which finger, did you say?" he asked.

"The third finger of the left hand," I replied.

Thorndyke looked thoughtfully at the paper that he was reading. "It's very singular," said he, "for I see that the Margate doctor states that the deceased wore a signet ring on the third finger of the left hand. Now, of course, you couldn't get a ring onto a finger with bony ankylosis of the joint."

I admitted that it was very singular indeed, and we then resumed our study of the respective papers. But presently I noticed that Thorndyke had laid the report upon his knee.

"If we take the small and unimpressive items and add them together," he said after a few moments, "you will see that a quite considerable sum of discrepancy results. Thus:

"In 1903 Thomas Elton, aged thirty-one, had a set of sound teeth. In 1908, at the age of thirty-six, he was more than half toothless.

"Again, at the age of thirty-one, his heart was perfectly healthy. At the age of thirty-six he had old aortic disease, with fully established compensation, and an aneurism that was possibly due to it.

"When he was examined he had a noticeable incurable malformation; no such malformation is mentioned in connection with the body.

"He appears to have fallen over a cliff, and he had also burst an aneurism. Now, the bursting of the aneurism must obviously have occurred during life; but it would occasion practically instantaneous death. Therefore, if the fall was accidental, the rupture must have occurred either as he stood at the edge of the cliff, as he was in the act of falling, or on striking the beach.

"At the place where he apparently fell, the footpath is some thirty yards distant from the edge of the cliff.

"It is not known how he came to that spot, or whether he was alone at the time.

"Someone is claiming five hundred pounds as the immediate result of his death.

"There, you see, Jervis, are seven propositions, none of them extremely striking, but rather suggestive when taken together."

"You seem," said I, "to suggest a doubt as to the identity of the body."

"I do," he replied. "The identity was not clearly established."

"And the old woman—" I suggested, but he interrupted me.

"My dear Jervis," he exclaimed, "I'm surprised at you! How many times has it happened within our knowledge that women have identified the bodies of total strangers as those of their husbands, fathers, or brothers. The thing happens almost every year. As to this old woman, she saw a body with an unrecognizable face dressed in the clothes of her missing lodger. Of course, it was the clothes that she identified."

"I suppose it was," I agreed; and then I said: "You seem to suggest the possibility of foul play."

"Well," he replied, "if you consider those seven points, you will agree with me that they present a cumulative discrepancy which it is impossible to ignore.

"Then," he continued, after a pause, "there is this mortgage deed. It looks quite regular and is correctly stamped, but it seems to me that the surface of the paper is slightly altered in one or two places, and if one holds the document up to the light, the paper looks a little more transparent in those places."

He examined the document for a few seconds with his pocket
lens, and then, passing lens and document to me, said: "Have a
look at it, Jervis, and tell me what you think."

I scrutinized the paper closely, taking it over to the window
to get a better light; and to me, also, the paper appeared to be
changed in certain places.

"Are we agreed as to the position of the altered places?"
Thorndyke asked.

"I see only three patches," I answered. "Two correspond to
the name, Thomas Elton, and the third to one of the figures in
the policy number."

"Exactly," said Thorndyke, "and the significance is obvious. If
the paper has really been altered, it means that some other
name has been erased and Elton's substituted; by which arrangement, of course, the correctly dated stamp would be
secured. And this—the alteration of an old document—is the
only form of forgery that is possible with a dated, impressed
stamp."

"Wouldn't it be rather a stroke of luck," I asked, "for a forger
to happen to have in his possession a document needing only
these two alterations?"

"I see nothing remarkable in it," Thorndyke replied. "A
moneylender would have a number of documents of this kind
in hand, and you observe that he was not bound down to any
particular date. Any date within a year or so of the issue of the
policy would answer his purpose. This document is, in fact,
dated, as you see, about six months after the issue of the policy."

"I suppose," said I, "that you will draw Stalker's attention to
this matter."

"He will have to be informed, of course," Thorndyke replied,
"but I think it would be interesting in the first place to call on
Mr. Hyams. You will have noticed that there are some rather
mysterious features in this case, and Mr. Hyams's conduct
suggests that he may have some special information." He
glanced at his watch and after a few moments' reflection added:
"I don't see why we shouldn't make our little ceremonial call at
once."

•

Mr. Hyams was "discovered," as the playwrights have it, in a small office at the top of a high building in Queen Victoria Street. He was a small gentleman, of sallow and greasy aspect, with heavy eyebrows.

"Are you Mr. Gordon?" Thorndyke suavely inquired as we entered.

Mr. Hyams seemed to experience a momentary doubt on the subject, but finally decided that he was not. "But perhaps," he added brightly, "I can help you."

"I daresay you can," Thorndyke agreed significantly; on which we were conducted into an innner den.

"Now," said Mr. Hyams, shutting the door ostentatiously, "what can I do for you?"

"I want you," Thorndyke replied, "to answer one or two questions with reference to the claim made by you on the 'Griffin' Office in respect of Thomas Elton."

Mr. Hyams's manner underwent a sudden change. He began rapidly to turn over papers, and opened and shut the drawers of his desk with an air of restless preoccupation.

"Did the 'Griffin' people send you here?" he demanded brusquely.

Thorndyke produced a card and laid it on the table. Mr. Hyams had apparently seen the name before, for he suddenly grew rather pale and very serious. "What is the nature of the questions you wished to ask?" he inquired.

"They refer to this claim," replied Thorndyke. "The first question is, where is Mr. Gordon?"

"I don't know," said Hyams.

"Where do you think he is?" asked Thorndyke.

"I don't think at all," replied Hyams, turning a shade paler and looking everywhere but at Thorndyke.

"Very well," said the latter, "then the next question is, are you satisfied that this claim is really payable?"

"I shouldn't have made it if I hadn't been," replied Hyams.

"Quite so," said Thorndyke; "and the third question is, are you satisfied that the mortgage deed was executed as it purports to have been?"

"I can't say anything about that," replied Hyams, who was

growing every moment paler and more fidgety. "It was done before my time."

"Thank you," said Thorndyke. "You will, of course, understand why I am making these inquiries."

"I don't," said Hyams.

"Then," said Thorndyke, "perhaps I had better explain. We are dealing, Mr. Hyams, with the case of a man who has met with a violent death under somewhat mysterious circumstances. We are dealing, also, with another man who has disappeared, leaving his affairs to take care of themselves; and with a claim, put forward by a *third* party, on behalf of the one man in respect of the other. When I say that the dead man has been imperfectly identified, and that the document supporting the claim presents certain peculiarities, you will see that the matter certainly calls for further inquiry."

There was an appreciable interval of silence. Mr. Hyams had turned a tallowy white, and looked furtively about the room, as if anxious to avoid the stony gaze of my colleague.

"Can you give us no assistance?" Thorndyke inquired at length. Mr. Hyams chewed a penholder ravenously as he considered the question. At length, he burst out in an agitated voice: "Look here, sir, if I tell you what I know, will you treat the information as confidential?"

"I can't agree to that, Mr. Hyams," replied Thorndyke. "It might amount to compounding a felony. But you will be wiser to tell me what you know. The document is a side issue which my clients may never raise, and my own concern is with the death."

Hyams looked distinctly relieved. "If that's so," said he, "I'll tell you all I know, which is precious little, and which just amounts to this: two days after Elton was killed, someone came to this office in my absence and opened the safe. I discovered the fact the next morning. Someone had rummaged over all the papers. It wasn't Gordon, because he knew where to find everything, and it wasn't an ordinary thief, because no cash or valuables had been taken. In fact, the only thing that I missed was a promissory note, drawn by Elton."

"You didn't miss a mortgage deed?" suggested Thorndyke,

and Hyams, having snatched a little further refreshment from the penholder, said he did not.

"And the policy," suggested Thorndyke, "was apparently not taken?"

"No," replied Hyams, "but it was looked for. Three bundles of policies had been untied, but this one happened to be in a drawer of my desk and I had the only key."

"And what do you infer from this visit?" Thorndyke asked.

"Well," replied Hyams, "the safe was opened with keys, and they were Gordon's keys—or, at any rate, they weren't mine—and the person who opened it wasn't Gordon; and the thing that was taken concerned only Elton. Naturally, I smelled a rat—and when I read of the finding of the body, I smelled a fox."

An exhumation, consequent on Thorndyke's challenge of the identity of the deceased, showed that the body was that of Gordon. A hundred pounds' reward was offered for information as to Elton's whereabouts. But no one ever earned it. A letter, bearing the postmark of Marseilles and addressed by the missing man to Thorndyke, gave a plausible account of Gordon's death, which was represented as having occurred accidentally at the moment when Gordon chanced to be wearing a suit of Elton's clothes.

Of course, this account may have been correct, or again, it may have been false; but whether it was true or false, Elton, from that moment, vanished from our ken and has never since been heard of.

FLORENCE V. MAYBERRY

THE BEAUTY IN THAT HOUSE

So. Willie. And me.

At least, I hope it will turn out that way. Just Willie and me.

William doesn't suit him as a name. But then neither does Willie. But he enjoys the nickname. It sounds affectionate.

Willie has this big beautiful house. Filled with trinkets—at least, that's what he calls them. Like a Chinese lion maybe five thousand years old. Russian icons from the Czar's court. A shaving mug once used by Franz Josef of Austria. Paintings, carvings, illuminated manuscripts. Satin-hung walls. Not wallpaper made to look like satin—real brocaded satin. The candelabrum on Willie's piano doesn't have crystal drops; the drops are jewels. All this is just a start. Those are just the few things I noticed the first night I went to Willie's house for dinner.

Willie gave me the creeps. Oh, he looked good. Too good. His hair had that new fluffy cut, the one achieved when the hair is blown, snipped, then blown and sprayed. It covers any bald spot. Not that Willie was anywhere near bald. Willie had lots of hair, the sandy-blond kind that happens when grey gets mixed in. His eyes were almost as pale. His mouth was well shaped, but when he wasn't talking he held it as if he had just bit in half an hors d'oeuvre about the size of a dime. But when he talked, his mouth opened full and looked fine. His words came out big and round like an elocution teacher's.

His chest was deep. But it didn't look strong and virile. Pouterpigeon. He was tall, with plenty of flesh on him. But it didn't make him look strong. More like a hothouse plant that has been overforced. Like I said, Willie gave me the creeps.

But his house and all the beautiful things in it didn't. Willie knew all about them. Their history. Why they were valuable. How they were made and who made them. I finished high school at night classes—in my twenties, while working in the daytime to support a sick husband. They didn't have anything in those night classes about jewels and paintings and the history of art. So all I knew was that when I looked at Willie's treasures chills went up my spine. And I got a funny crying sensation in the pit of my stomach from the way the soft light of a lamp— alabaster, Willie called it—fell across the painting of a woman whose throat seemed to throb in the glow. I would have sworn, almost, she had a pulse. And the old polished chest with the inlaid design—I felt I had to rub it. When I did, Willie smiled, showing two pointed rat teeth, and he said, yes, rub it, that shows true appreciation, get the feel of the artist in your fingers.

What he said was right. A feeling came into me, as though I had made the chest myself. Then Willie handed me a small jade walnut. A thousand years old, he said. Hold it, he said, rub it; thirty generations more or less of Chinese aristocrats have rubbed that walnut and soothed away their tensions. And now so did he. Well, that did it. The jade had a lovely smooth cool touch. But Willie was all over it. When he turned his back to show me something else I put it down.

So how would it be to touch Willie?

Can you believe it? —Willie's personal bathroom had walls of mother-of-pearl. At least, they looked like that. There was a deep white rug all over the floor and a painting baked in the porcelain of his wash basin. And me with cheap prints in cheap frames on my living-room walls.

Willie's bedroom looked like the pictures in *House Beautiful*—only better because I was actually in the room, my feet sinking into the Chinese rug. The big bed had a black lacquered headboard. On one side was a large lacquered chest, on the other was an inlaid writing cabinet. French, made at the time the wealthy French went all out for Chinese objets d'art. On top of the desk was a figurine of a Chinese lady I could have kissed, she was so elegant and pure and lovely. "Pick her up—touch her," Willie urged.

A man with all that money should have had those rat teeth filed off and capped. "Do you," I asked, "touch her?"

"Indeed I do," Willie said. "She is my darling, my lovely. She's a court lady of China, you know. Oh, what fun I'll have teaching you about my beauties! You'll make an apt student, my dear."

He reached for me. But I slid away as though the sudden sight of a framed Chinese scroll was just too much for me, as though I had to get to it fast and lose myself in it. Just for a minute I wished I could dive into Willie's swimming pool which was just outside his bedroom, beyond sliding glass doors. Only that wouldn't have been possible. Two beautiful boys, maybe twenty or twenty-one, were swimming in it. They were good swimmers, tall, strong, gleaming boys, tanned to a sun-gold. They would have rescued me. Because Willie would tell them to. Not because they wanted to.

Willie came behind me and put his hands on my shoulders. It felt as if little worms were crawling up and down my arms. "You're as lovely as my figurine, Courtney. And how that name suits you, my darling. It's so regal, so aristocratic."

"I'm not an aristocrat," I said. "My people came from the hill country of Kentucky. It's an old family name. I always hated it because it's a boy's name, and I'm a girl."

"Who wants a silly girl's name?" he said. "You're not a silly girl. You're an exquisite, mature woman. You will look so right as hostess of this house. A lovely jewel." He didn't add "in an exquisite setting," but that's what he meant. And he'd make me into that jewel. With his money.

I turned and faced him. "Willie, I have to be honest. To be comfortable with myself. I don't love you. But I love this beauty. I've never had it. Only cheap imitations."

"How wonderful that you can have it now," Willie said. "Now I'll show you the room that will be yours. If you want it redecorated, we'll do it. But it is done in exquisite taste. It was my sister's."

Willie's sister had died, oh, maybe a month before he began asking me out. He'd known me for a year or so before that, but I was only the clerk who usually waited on him at the bookstore.

That same week, after he had shown me my room, Willie and I were married. Willie wanted to make a big thing of it, invite everybody who was anybody for miles around. But I said no. I didn't want to be shown off. So we had a civil ceremony in another state. Nobody we knew—not even the two golden boys, Ferdie and Maurice—was present.

I wonder if anyone who hasn't had yearnings like mine and squelched them all her life could understand the way I felt when I went to live in Willie's house. Even the way the light shone through the thin, thin Irish Belleek china cups at teatime made me shiver. Before I married Willie, I had one cup and saucer nearly that thin. I used it when I wanted to cheer myself up. Finally the cup cracked and then it looked like any other piece of the thrift-store china I was always picking up. Willie's house had two whole sets of Belleek.

I suppose a woman of forty-three ought to have had by that age more of the things she has always wanted. But I was a widow with no training for a job other than selling things. And not anything special at that. Just a low-keyed salesclerk, which is why I fitted well in bookstores. So I satisfied my yearnings by reading books about beauty and looking at beautiful things in stores and museums. I could sew and had a knack for style. Willie noticed that when he came in the store to buy books, usually accompanied by Ferdie or Maurice. But after his sister died, Willie began to come in alone. Next thing I knew I was having dinner at Willie's house, with two Filipino servants waiting on us. Willie was shopping for a woman in his household.

I hated myself for being Willie's front. Not Willie, I didn't hate him—in part I was grateful to him. I just hated me. Ferdie and Maurice helped out with that. They hated me, too—especially Ferdie.

One day when I thought they were all away I decided to take a swim. The swim was more than a luxury, it was therapeutic. But I never used the pool if the boys were around. Their eyes had taken on a veiled laughing look the one time I came out in my bathing suit in front of them. But who could blame them? One leg thin and twisted from the polio I'd had as a teenager. The fact that the rest of me was round and slender and well put together didn't hide that leg.

While I was swimming, Ferdie suddenly came into the pool area. Well, my bad leg couldn't be seen in the water. So I waved at Ferdie and kept on swimming. I figured he would leave. He couldn't stand me. Instead, he came to the pool's edge. "Could I speak with you, Mrs. McKinley?"

I stopped swimming, stood up in the water. "Yes?"

"Please. Come over here, the servants might be listening," he said, beckoning to me. I swam to him. He reached down his beautiful muscled arm and suddenly I was yanked up on the side of the pool. "It will be easier to talk up here," he said, smiling, but his eyes like flames on dark coals.

I was miserable and awkward, knowing how my leg looked. I turned quickly to reach for my robe. Ferdie told Willie later that I slipped. But if I slipped, bent as I was to pick up the robe, the bump would have been on the front of my head, not on the back.

Ferdie said that as I fell, I struck my head on the pool's edge, then sank in the water.

"Ferdie knocked me into the pool. He banged me on the head with something first," I told Willie when I was up to talking. "If you hadn't come home when you did, Ferdie would have left me in the pool to drown." Both Willie's bedroom and mine had two sets of sliding glass doors, one set opening into the pool area, the other set into the patio. Willie came into his bedroom just after I fell, saw Ferdie staring down—shocked, Ferdie explained—rushed out, and ordered Ferdie in after me. "He would have told you I fell in while no one was around. Or that he didn't know anything about it."

Willie's eyes clicked. Like a computer putting things into place. Don't ever think Willie wasn't intelligent. He had a supermind. I don't know what he said to Ferdie, but Ferdie went away for a while. When he came back, he moved out of the main house into the garden guesthouse. There was a kitchenette in it and he even ate his meals there.

After that, Maurice put himself out to be darling to me. Maurice was always a weaker character than Ferdie. Ferdie was sinuous, pantherlike. Maurice was blond, as muscled as Ferdie, but the muscles seemed unused. He was oddly like a gorgeous wax replica of a gorgeous male model—actually handsomer than Ferdie, so handsome that if one didn't spend too much time at it, it was a stark and startling pleasure simply to look at him. But only to look. The boy was cold all the way through.

Willie was fonder of Ferdie than of Maurice. Ferdie was mean, but he wasn't cold. Maurice was a thing of beauty to be displayed like one of the antiques, paintings, or carvings. But there was raw emotion, a kind of flame, in Ferdie. He was dark gold, with large and lambent eyes. He carried a jungle in him.

Perhaps that was why it seemed so natural when Ferdie bought the lion cub. One morning Willie looked out the window of the breakfast room into the patio. He took a deep breath. Then he smiled, "Come here, darling," he said to me. "Look what that Ferdie has done."

Ye gods, what? I thought. Set fire to my bedroom? Dug a pit for me to fall into? I went to the window and saw the cub sniffing at the plants. It was an adorable creature. Big, slappy feet, its head round and furry and innocent-eyed. I love animals. Perhaps better than people. Even if they are vicious there's an honesty about them. Especially I love cats—so graceful, so self-sufficient. But working all the time as I did before I married Willie, I had gotten out of the habit of wishing I had one.

Impulsively, I slid back the glass doors, went into the patio, and touched the cub's head. It was purring, so loud the purr sounded like a growl. It rubbed against my negligee that was trimmed with eider. The cub caught a mouthful of eider and made funny faces as the feathers ticked his nose. I laughed, kneeled, and put my arms around its neck. Ah, the lovely pure thing! It was the loveliest thing in all that house of beauty.

Willie stood over me, his eyebrows peaked, his expression admiring. "Well," he said. "You *are* a constant surprise. Ferdie, aren't you pleased that my wife loves your new pet?"

Ferdie was standing beside the doorway to the garden guesthouse, a leash in his hand. Glowering. He forced a smile and slanted his eyes so their expression couldn't be read. "They make a charming picture," he said tightly. "But I had hoped to have the lion solely attached to me. The animal trainers advised that it should be taught to recognize only one person as its master."

I stood up, staggering a bit as I always do because of my weak leg. Without a word I went in the house, back to my breakfast.

It was difficult to swallow the coffee. For I knew exactly what Ferdie had in mind. Train that cub. Then when it grew up, one day, the end of me. How he'd bring it off I didn't know. Perhaps toss a steak on me. Or grapple me when Willie was away and then toss me to the lion.

Willie joined me. "Darling," he said, "how good Ferdie really is at heart. He has given the cub to you because you were so beautiful together. He said that now he would never be happy owning it just for himself—it was so apparent the cub instinctively loved you."

"I don't want Ferdie's cub."

"It isn't Ferdie's cub," Willie said sleekly. "Ferdie doesn't want it any more. If you don't accept it I'll have to send it back to the animal people."

As I mentioned, Willie is very intelligent. He wanted me in his household. Alive. I went to him and kissed his cheek. Then I hurried back to the patio and my cub. When we were through playing, my robe was stripped of feathers and the cub had a pink-eider moustache.

I had dreamed many times of the gorgeous cats I might own some day—Persians, Siamese, Burmese. But never of a lion. That was the Hailie Selassie, an emperor. Or for a lion tamer. Now I owned one, and with my surroundings I felt royal. The cub, even so young, had strength and a dignified confidence. The way it padded around me, rubbing against me, with a soft show of muscles beneath its loose baby skin, was thrilling. Along with the bold and lovely way it looked into my eyes. All that spring we played, the cub and I. Willie hired an animal trainer to give me pointers, for the cub was growing and becoming rougher in play.

Willie began to spend a great deal of time in the patio with us. Not Ferdie, who sulked in the guesthouse. And certainly not Maurice, who had let out a terrified squeak like an oversized mouse at his first sight of the cub and then fled to the roof above the pool area for one of his interminable sunbaths. Even in that safe place, he shuddered and chittered to himself as he watched us play below.

Willie's reason for staying in the patio was not because he was worried about the cub attacking me. If that had been all,

he would have hired a guard. He stayed because he was fascinated by the pair of us. Sometimes he looked at me as though
he had never seen me before. And sometimes, to tell the truth,
I looked at myself in the mirror as though I had never seen me
before. The reflection was of a woman who should have a lion
for a pet. Tawny-haired as the cub. Sinuous in line when
standing still, when not walking and showing the limp. A woman
that the beauty in that house had rubbed off on.

Willie took up sketching that summer. He had a gift for it. An
amateur's gift, yet with true feeling coupled with delicacy of
line. He liked to catch the cub and me in motion. He grew
better and better at it and his trips to New York, or wherever
he went, became quite rare. He had always kissed me on the
forehead when we said goodnight and I went to my room. Now
he began kissing my lips. One night when a tear trickled down
my cheek he kissed it away. Willie no longer gave me the
creeps.

One cloudy morning in early fall, as I stepped out of my
bedroom onto the shallow brick step leading to the patio, I
tripped and fell over something. My knees struck the bricks and
for a minute I closed my eyes and rocked back and forth, easing
the pain. Then I looked to see what had tripped me. It was the
cub's bloody head.

Yes. Hacked off. My beautiful cat. My darling, soft, purring,
playing love. My pure strong lion.

I just sat there. I never wanted to get up. It was too late to
help the cub. And who wanted to get up and move and live
where hate crouched on the edge of peace and beauty?

Willie found me like that. He helped me into the house and
made me take something—some pill, I didn't know or care
what it was. It wasn't long until I began to fade away into sleep.
And as I did I thought I heard, far away, someone crying.

When I woke, the cub was gone. Ferdie, too. Maurice, of
course, wouldn't have come near enough to the cub to kill it.
Willie and I never discussed it. But he began to pay even more
attention to me than he had before.

Even though no blame fell on Maurice, Willie ignored him.
Maurice often looked like a lost soul—no Ferdie to talk to or

fight with—and he kept wandering from his room into the pool, then up to the roof for his sunbaths. And always smiling and fawning at the dinner table, like a nasty child that people can't bear to pick up and cuddle.

Willie was taking me a great many places. Not like before, which had been only to big events where everyone would see us, but to dinner in some special little restaurant where we knew no one. Or on his New York trips, where he made me do a lot of shopping. He insisted one time in New York on buying me a leopard coat. "You don't know yourself, Courtney," he said. "I do. I'm a connoisseur. You need leopard."

Whoever would have thought that Courtney Aikins, born in southern Indiana, once crippled with polio, who had spent most of her life as a mediocre salesclerk, could look as if the leopard coat had grown out of her. But I did. My grey eyes seemed to turn green and slant catlike as I looked in the long mirror. And my skin from being in the sun so much was tawny and gold to match my hair. How the saleswoman oohed and aahed, while Willie looked sleek and proud, not unlike a cat himself.

Willie finally relented about Ferdie. One morning there Ferdie was, calling from the door of the garden guesthouse to Maurice, who was lying face down on the roof taking his sunbath. Maurice raised up and answered with something sharp—I couldn't make out the words. Ferdie shouted back and Maurice flipped over and dangled his golden legs over the side of the roof as though he would jump into the patio. Willie went out and they both became silent.

After that, every time Ferdie and Maurice spent more than five minutes in each other's company, they had a spat. And from the tense expression on Maurice's face, and the jerky nervous way in which he talked and laughed, it was clear that he was as uptight as I was about Ferdie's return.

One day as Willie and I started out the driveway, headed for lunch at the beach club, I discovered I had forgotten my purse and gloves. While Willie waited, I went back to my room for them.

Ferdie and Maurice were at it again out in the pool, just beyond my partially opened door. Their voices were high and shrill. It was the servants' day off and as far as they knew the house was empty. Ferdie accused Maurice of killing the cub. In a rage Maurice admitted it, saying he had poisoned the beast first, then got the idea about cutting off its head. "Something they would be sure only you would think of!" he shrieked. "You—jealous because she took away your lion! And if you couldn't kill her, like you tried, you'd kill her pet! And that's what they did think. Go ahead and tell on me! They'll never believe you! They'll believe you're making more trouble and you'll get run off again!"

I slipped out.

I could have—maybe I should have—gone right out and told Willie. But that would have left me with Ferdie. Probably for keeps. No doubt Willie would be terribly remorseful and do everything he could to make it up to Ferdie. So I didn't say anything.

That morning, the day of the murder, Maurice and Ferdie chanced to come into the pool area at the same time and saw me swimming. Ferdie turned on his heel and left. Then I heard the bang of the guesthouse door. Maurice smiled, feathered a kiss toward me, and walked up the stairs to the roof. He knew I didn't like anyone else in the pool when I used it.

I never told anyone, not even Willie, that I saw Ferdie go up to the roof. And come back down again. Because I didn't see him. Of course, anyone would know that it would be easy not to see. For I went into the steamroom after swimming. It was a habit of mine. The steam helped my leg. I was still there when I heard screams from the patio. I grabbed my robe and hurried out. There was Maurice, his head smashed against the bricks, the golden face trickled with blood.

The cries were coming from Ferdie, standing over Maurice.

"Have you done it again?" I asked. "Like you killed my cub? Like you tried to kill me!"

He sprang at me, grabbed my throat, and shook me, screaming, "You lie, you lie! I never killed the cub! Maurice killed the cub! You did it, you pushed him off the roof! You'd like both of us dead!"

Which is what he wished, for Maurice and me.

I was half-unconscious by the time the gardener came, the cook jabbering behind him. I could scarcely move my neck for a week.

Willie was in New York at the time. So it had to be me, when I could talk, who called the police. Then I walked over to the sobbing Ferdie and slapped his face hard. "You listen to me," I said. "You're the only one with the strength to pitch Maurice over the edge. I couldn't shove him an inch. The servants had no reason to do it. And you know how I am about stairs, how I avoid stairs. And you hated Maurice. Almost as much as you hate me."

"I didn't, I didn't! I was in my room, listening to my stereo."

"Perhaps," I said. "Between times. I have other ideas. But in this case we have to think of Willie. Accusations and counter-accusations such as we might make in this household will give a poor picture of Willie to the world. I'll phone Willie and have him hurry home. Until then I advise you to say simply that you found Maurice in the patio. And I will say just what happened, that your screams brought me out of the steamroom. It's your problem to think up some explanation for why you choked me."

Willie flew right home. Terribly shaken. Shocked by Maurice's death, and perhaps even more shocked at the thought of any scandal.

Ferdie and I, of course, had to make statements to the police before Willie arrived. So did the gardener and the cook, and the gardener told about having to pull Ferdie off my throat. Ferdie cried and said how sorry he was, that the sight of his friend's dead body had so shaken him that he must have been temporarily out of his senses.

"He's a very high-strung boy," I said. "And he had just come for a visit with Maurice after not seeing him for a long time. It was a shock. Poor Maurice. Perhaps he fell asleep, then turned in his sleep because the sun was getting strong, and simply rolled off. The roof should have a railing."

The reporters attempted to make something out of Maurice's relationship to our family. "He was like a son," I said. "Mr. McKinley is a wealthy man and has endowed several schools. In addition, he has educated quite a few young people on an individual basis."

After that, the newspapers referred to Mr. McKinley's lovely, dignified wife whose "face was pale and set with grief" over the tragic accident.

Willie gave Ferdie a peaked-brow, probing look when he arrived from New York. And they had a private discussion. Ferdie apparently didn't tell him that Maurice had killed the cub, possibly for fear Willie would begin to tie in revenge with Maurice's death. I thought of telling, but then Willie might want to know why I didn't exonerate Ferdie earlier. It might solidify Ferdie's position.

For, after all, I couldn't prove that Ferdie returned to the pool that morning while I was in the steamroom, then slipped up the stairs and pushed Maurice over the edge.

It was chilling to have Ferdie back in the house. Yes, once more in his old room and eating dinner with us every night. Now when Willie was away and the servants not nearby, I moved around like a cat who has suddenly been brought into a house full of dogs.

"Why don't you ever wear your leopard coat? You look so beautiful in it," Willie said one night when we were about to take another trip to New York. It was winter and snowing up north.

"The cleaners did a bad job on it. It looks queer—some of the hair doesn't come up, it's matted and uneven. And it's shedding."

"I'll complain to the furrier," Willie said. "After all, they're the best in New York, they should make good. It cost enough."

"It was probably the cleaner's fault."

"Then the cleaner should make good. People like that oughtn't to be in business."

"All right, Willie," I said. "I'll talk to them. In the meantime, I have the tweed and it's fur-lined."

"You're not the tweed type," he said fussily. "We must get you another coat."

But we were so busy doing other things that we didn't get around to it that trip. Later he asked about the leopard coat, but casually because by then we were planning a trip to Tahiti and fur coats seemed silly.

Some woman in some thrift store certainly found a bargain. Oh, sure, the fur would be matted down here and there, but a little more cleaning in the right spots would put it right. It was just that the coat had stayed too long in the steamroom. I forgot to take it out until after I had gone to my room and dressed. Then when I did get it, I tucked it inside my robe and put it far back in my closet, still wet and steamy. Anyway, I never wanted to see it again. So it dried queer in spots.

The morning Maurice died, Ferdie was in the guesthouse. I heard his stereo playing, in his bedroom on the side away from the patio. The music was loud. Ferdie always played the music so loud when Willie was away that it kept me from concentrating on any music I might want to hear.

I went to my room and got the leopard coat. Then I draped it over one of those silly inflated seahorses we had in the pool, the kind one floats around on. It was difficult for me not to stumble, going up the stairs with that clumsy thing in my arms. My bad leg was trembling, because this was the second time I had gone up those stairs. Just a few minutes before, I had dried off my feet and climbed to the roof. I had seen Maurice lying on his stomach, cheek on his hands, elbows thrust out. He was facing away from the stairs, breathing slowly and deeply. His foot gave an involuntary twitch, as happens when one is asleep.

So then I went down for the leopard coat and the seahorse and came back, quietly, quietly. I knelt down so I couldn't be seen from the patio and thrust the leopard-covered seahorse against Maurice, hard and quick. He woke up, whirled his head to see what it was. His eyes sprung wide, terrified. He must have thought it was another cub, a leopard cub. He let out a choked yip and rolled to get away from it.

"Why, it's only a joke, Maurice," I said. "I was only playing."

I said it as he pitched over the edge. If he had survived that fall I would have said again, "It was only a joke, I was only playing."

Willie has invited Ferdie to go with us to Tahiti. Ferdie hates me. I hate Ferdie. I wonder which one of us will be the first to do something about it?

VINCENT STARRETT
MAN IN HIDING

Dr. B. Edward Loxley (jocularly called "Bedward" by the Chicago gossip columnists), the wife-murderer for whom hundreds of police had been scouring the city for three weeks, sat quietly at his desk in the great Merchandise Exchange reading his morning mail. The frosted glass door of his outer office read simply: *William Drayham, Rare Books. Hours by Appointment.* After three weeks of security he was beginning to feel a little complacent. For three weeks he had not left his hiding place in the huge business complex and he had no intention of leaving it for the time being—except feet first.

It had all been carefully thought out beforehand. The office of "William Drayham" had been rented two months prior to the killing of his wife, and Loxley had quietly taken possession and created his new personality as a dealer in rare books. He had been accepted by all his neighbors in the sixth-floor corridor. The elevator starter was getting to know him. He breakfasted, lunched, and dined at the several restaurants in the building, was shaved by a favorite barber, and was—he had every reason to believe—an accepted fixture. His neighbors were inoffensive and unimaginative workers who did not for a moment question his identity, and the words *Rare Books* on the door were formidable enough to frighten away casual visitors.

Lora Loxley, murdered by suffocation, had been buried for nearly three weeks and even the newspapers were beginning to play down the sensational story. The feeling was growing that Dr. Loxley himself might also have been murdered and a desultory search for his body continued whenever the police had nothing more urgent to occupy them. Since Loxley's office window overlooked the river where, in addition to the normal traffic, police boats occasionally plied, he was able to watch the activities on the river with amused appreciation. He had now spent two lonely Saturdays and Sundays watching the weekend

traffic with a pair of binoculars, waiting for any active renewal
of police attention. He was on excellent terms with the watchmen in his part of the giant building, and they were now
accustomed to seeing him at the most unlikely hours.

The Merchandise Exchange was actually a city within a city.
It contained everything a man in hiding needed—restaurants,
laundries, barber shops, tobacconists, dentists, newsstands,
banking facilities, a gymnasium, even a postal station. He was
already known by name in the restaurants and barber shops. He
bought all the newspapers, morning and evening. Occasionally
he dictated a letter to one of the public stenographers, ordering
or declining rare books. As William Drayham he had a sufficient
banking account downstairs for all his immediate needs. The
rest of his wealth, in cash, was waiting in Paris—as was Gloria.

His principal bogies had been the watchmen and the cleaning
women. But both fears had vanished. The watchmen had proved
friendly, and the cleaning women, a friendly trio who liked
candy, readily agreed to visit his office while he was having a
late dinner. His domestic arrangements were simple. He slept
on a couch in his inner office, which also contained a vault to
which he could retire in an emergency. To date there had been
no emergency.

Dr. Loxley pushed the mail aside impatiently. It was too early
to expect a large response to the small rare-book advertisement
he was running in a Sunday book-review supplement. But it was
not too early for the coffee that Miss Marivole Boggs was willing
to serve at all hours. What luck to have found so admirable a
neighbor in the same corridor, and even, it might be said, in the
same line! Rare books and antiques went very well together.
Miss Boggs had been responsible for most of his infrequent
customers. He glanced at his expensive wristwatch and left
William Drayham's rare books without a pang.

The owner of *M. Boggs, Antiques,* as she described herself on
the show window of her small shop at the end of the corridor,
looked up at his entrance.

"Hello," she said. "I was hoping you'd come in."

"I couldn't resist," he said. His brown eyes took in the familiar
room, resting for a moment on the suit of ancient armor that

dominated one corner of the shop and the old Spanish chest that was Miss Boggs's pride and joy. "Well, I see nobody has bought either of them yet." It was one of their standing jokes that someday, when the rare-book business was better, he would buy them himself.

As Marivole Boggs poured his coffee she said, "The newspaper stories about that doctor are getting shorter every day. I'm beginning to believe he really *was* murdered."

They often discussed the missing Dr. Loxley, as indeed the whole city was doing. At first it had been Miss Boggs's idea that the "society doctor" had murdered his wife in favor of a more glamorous patient who was now living in sin with him somewhere on the French or Italian Riviera.

Dr. Loxley had thought not. "Too romantic, Miss Boggs. I still think his body is in the river or floating on its way to the Gulf of Mexico. That scarf they found on the river bank looks like it."

"Anyway, the police seem to have stopped looking," said Miss Boggs.

"Anyway, this is good coffee, my dear. I hope you'll give me your special recipe. Do you still plan to leave this month?"

"At once," she said. "I'm flying to New York tomorrow, if I can get away. I want to be in London for the Exhibition; then on to Paris, Rome, and Zurich. I'm enormously relieved that you'll be here to keep an eye on things, Bill. Coffee at all hours, eh?"

"Morning, noon, and night," he agreed, rising to leave. Her change of plan had startled him for a moment; but he was quick to see a distinct advantage in it for himself. "Never fear, I'll be here waiting for you when you return."

Strolling back to his own shop, humming a jaunty air, he became aware of a man leaving the doorway of the office directly opposite his own. Something about the man's carriage seemed familiar. The man was heading toward the elevators and walking fast. In an instant they would meet.

And suddenly Dr. Loxley realized that the man was indeed familiar. He was his own brother-in-law, Lawrence Bridewell.

Loxley's first instinct was to turn and flee, his second to return to *M. Boggs, Antiques.* His final decision, made in a split

second, was to see the encounter through. His disguise had
fooled better men than Larry Bridewell, although none who
knew him better. With his former neat beard and mustache
now gone, and his blue eyes transformed by brown contact
lenses, Dr. Loxley was, to all appearances, another man. After
that first appalling moment of indecision, he fumbled for a
cigarette, realizing that after three weeks of growingly complacent safety, he was about to face the supreme test.

He tried and failed to light the cigarette. Then the two men
were face to face, glancing at each other as men do in passing—
and suddenly the test was over.

Or was it? Bridewell continued on his way to the elevators,
still walking fast, and Loxley stumbled to his own door.

Did he dare look back? Had Bridewell turned to look back at
him? Moving casually, Loxley stole a glance down the corridor.
There was no doubt about it—Larry *was* looking back. Perhaps
he had merely been troubled by an imagined resemblance.

Dr. Loxley had some difficulty opening his own door, and just
before he closed it the thought occurred to him to look at the
name on the door of the office from which his brother-in-law
had emerged. Actually he knew very well what he would find
there: *Jackson & Fortworth, Attorneys-at-Law*—and, below, the
significant words: *Private Investigations.*

He tried to take himself in hand and was annoyed to find that
he was shaking. Experimentally he ventured a drink to see what
it would do for him. It helped considerably. But the whole
incident haunted him the rest of the day and gave him a bad
night. In the morning, however, his fears had evaporated. He
was his confident self again—until, a few hours later, a second
incident shook his nerve.

Returning from the cigar stand in the lobby, he passed the
DeLuxe Dog Salon in one of the street-level corridors and, as
he had often done before, paused to look into the windows at
the fashionable dogs being barbered and prettified. It had always
been an amusing spectacle, but this time, as he turned away, an
appalling thing happened.

A well dressed woman was approaching the salon with a
haughty French poodle on a leash. The woman looked familiar.
Good Lord, she *was* familiar! She was Mrs. Montgomery Hyde,

an old patient of his! Loxley's heart seemed to stop beating.
Would she recognize him?

It was the dog that recognized him. With a refined little yelp
the poodle jerked the leash from the woman's hand and flung
himself against the doctor's legs.

With an effort, Loxley recovered his balance and somehow
managed to recover his poise. It was his worst moment since
the murder. Automatically he disengaged himself from the
poodle's attentions and pulled the black ears.

"There, there, fellow," he said to the excited animal in a
voice that he hoped was not his own. "I beg your pardon,
Madam. Your dog appears to have made a mistake."

To his intense relief, Mrs. Montgomery Hyde agreed.

"Do forgive Toto's impulsiveness," she begged, snatching up
the leash. "He loves everybody."

Dr. Loxley left the scene in almost a hurry. She had not
recognized him! It seemed to him a miracle; but again he was
annoyed to find himself shaking. And yet, wasn't it really a good
omen? If Mrs. Hyde and his own brother-in-law had failed to
recognize him, was there anything for him to fear?

Immediately he began to feel better. But when he had
returned to his office, William Drayham again treated himself to
a stiff drink.

In a moment of alert intelligence, he realized that for three
weeks he had permitted himself to become too complacent.
His meeting with Mrs. Hyde had taught him something that was
important for him to remember: he had almost spoken her
name! In the first onslaught of panic, he might well have
betrayed himself. If it was important for him not to be recognized, it was equally important that *he* must not recognize
anyone else.

It was clear to him now that this cat-and-mouse existence
could no go on indefinitely. He must remain in hiding only until
it was safe for him to emerge and get out of the country. Then
William Drayham would ostentatiously pack his books and
remove to New York. After that, the world was wide, with his
immediate destination—Paris and Gloria.

For several days the chastened doctor lived cautiously, visiting *M. Boggs, Antiques* at intervals for coffee and to admire the

suit of armor and the Spanish chest, which continued to fasci-
nate him. He had promised Miss Boggs, now on her travels, not
to cut the price on either if a buyer should turn up.

Twice, returning from the antique shop, he again caught a
glimpse of his brother-in-law—both times entering the law
office of Jackson & Fortworth—and had hurried to lock himself
in his own office before Larry could emerge. What the devil did
the fellow want with a firm of private investigators anyway?

The visit of Jackson, the senior lawyer of the firm, to the
bookshop one morning took the doctor completely by surprise,
or he might have locked the door.

"I've been intending to look in on you for some time, Mr.
Drayham," said the lawyer cordially. "I'm Jackson, just across
from you. Rare books have always interested me. Mind if I look
around? I think that browse is the word."

Loxley rose from his chair abruptly, knocking a book from
his desk to the floor. An icy fear had entered his heart. Was this
the showdown at last, he wondered.

He shook hands effusively. "Glad to meet you, Mr. Jackson.
By all means, browse. Is there anything special I can show you?"

But Jackson was already browsing. When he had finished, he
strolled to the window. "Nice view of the river you have," he
said appreciatively. "*My* windows all face an inner court." He
walked to the door. "Just wanted to meet you, Mr. Drayham. I'll
come in again when I have more time."

"Any time at all," said Loxley with warm courtesy.

Dr. Loxley sat down at his desk and reached for the lower
drawer. Another little drink wouldn't hurt. What had the fellow
really wanted? What had he hoped to learn? Or was he really
one of those strange people who collected rare books?

One thing, however, was undeniably clear. Any day now he
might have to leave the building and the city. If he was suspected, the blow would fall swiftly. At any minute the door
might open again, and this time Jackson might not be alone.
Why not get out of this trap immediately? What was there
to stop him? His stock—300-odd volumes of miscellaneous
volumes bought at a storage house—could be left behind if
necessary.

What stopped him was Gloria's cable from Paris: TROUBLE HERE. PHONING FRIDAY NIGHT.

This was Thursday. Whatever else happened, he must wait for Gloria's call. His hand moved toward the lower drawer, then withdrew. Coffee, not whiskey, was what he needed; and after luncheon he spent most of the afternoon with Miss Boggs's weird collection of antiques. There he had an unobstructed view of Jackson's door, and was not himself visible. If Larry Bridewell was among the lawyer's visitors, Loxley did not see him.

Exploring the antique shop he paused, as always, to admire his two star exhibits, the almost frightening suit of armor and the massive Spanish chest. In a pinch, either would do as an emergency hiding place—if there was time enough to hide.

That evening he was startled to find his picture in the newspaper again—the face of Dr. B. Edward Loxley as he had looked with the neat little beard and moustache before he had murdered his wife. It seemed he'd been arrested by an alert Seattle policeman, but had denied his identity.

Dr. Loxley drew a long breath of relief. After all, perhaps he was still safe in this city within a city. But what could Gloria have to say to him that required a call from Paris? Bad news of some kind. Bad for somebody.

In spite of all his new fears, he hated to leave the building that had been his refuge. It had been his hope to live there indefinitely, undetected—never again to venture into the streets until Dr. Loxley was as forgotten as Dr. Crippen.

Again he slept off his fears and spent an uninterrupted forenoon with his view of the river and the morning newspapers. He was beginning to feel almost at ease again—indeed, when the insufferable Jackson knocked on his locked door and called a hearty greeting he almost welcomed having a visitor. But there was somebody with the attorney. Through the frosted pane Loxley could make out the shadowy outline of another man.

"May we come in?" the lawyer called out. "I've got a couple of friends here who want to talk to you."

Loxley rose uncertainly to his feet and moved to the door. So

it had come at last! He had been right about his damned
brother-in-law and this sneaking lawyer. This was the showdown. And suddenly Loxley knew what he had to do.

He unlocked the door and threw it open. "Come in, gentlemen," he said without emotion. "What can I do for you?"

Jackson was beaming. "These are my friends, Sergeants
Coughlin and Ripkin, from headquarters. They hope you will
come quietly." The lawyer laughed heartily at his own witti-
cism.

"Come in, gentlemen, and sit down." Loxley forced a smile—
he was panicking fast. He seated himself at his desk, trembling,
and addressed and stamped an envelope. Then he stood up,
shakily. "I was just going to the mail chute with an important
letter. I'll be back in a few moments."

"Sure," said one of the two cops genially. "Take your time,
Mr. Drayham."

Was there just the slightest emphasis on the name "Drayham"
or was he merely imagining it?

Dr. Loxley closed the outer door behind him and almost ran
for *M. Boggs, Antiques.* As he locked the door of the antique
shop, still shaking, he was relieved to see that the corridor was
empty. They would follow him, of course, in a matter of
minutes. Every office in the building would be searched, every
office in the vast Merchandise Exchange.

It *had* to be the chest!

It stood open as always, and he squeezed inside—an uncomfortable fit—then lowered the heavy lid until only a thin crack
remained for air. Faintly now he thought he could hear footsteps in the corridor. He drew a deep breath and closed the lid.

There was a sharp "click," then only intense darkness.

Ten minutes later, Sergeant Ripkin said to his partner, "Wonder
what's keeping that guy. We've still got about fifty tickets to sell,
Pete."

"Oh, leave some with me," said Jackson. "I'll see that you get
your money. Drayham's a good fellow—he'll buy a batch of
them, I'm sure."

The two policemen, who had been hoping to dispose of all

their remaining tickets for a benefit baseball game, departed leisurely.

The disappearance of William Drayham, a "rare-book dealer" with an office in the Merchandise Exchange, attracted less attention than the disappearance of Dr. B. Edward Loxley, but for a few days it was a mild sensation.

Returning from Europe a month later, Miss Boggs wondered idly when Bill would drop in for a cup of coffee. He had told her he would be here when she returned.

She puttered happily among her treasures. Some fool, she noted, had automatically locked the chest by closing it. One of these days she'd have to unlock it and raise the lid.

ROBERT TWOHY

MRS. KENDALL'S TRUNK

On her second day in San Francisco, Mrs. Kendall succeeded in renting a little frame house on a hilltop, in an area known as Sunlit Heights.

The landlord, Mr. Peet, old and thin, with a dry, disembodied cough, seemed somewhat in a daze as he conducted her through the house.

"Never thought I'd leave this place. I've lived here thirty-five years. Thirty-five years! And now, all of a sudden, this respiration thing—suddenly I can't smell, can't taste, got this palpitation . . ." He put a leaflike hand to his chest. "Almost blacked out last week. Doctor told me, Jake, you got to get out of the fog, and pronto. Got to go where it's warm—otherwise, you'll be a dead man in three months."

She made a vague sound of sympathy. He went on. "I wouldn't rent to a couple with kids. Never." He gave a kind of shudder. "Kids never leave things alone, house'd be a wreck. But you, now you look like a lady leads a quiet life, who'll take care of things. Rather than rent to the wrong kind, I'd rather not rent at all."

Suddenly he looked alarmed. "Though that's bad, too. You leave a house empty and sooner or later vandals are going to start messing around. No, I sure don't want to leave the house vacant."

She was at the front window looking down over the area. On the slopes beneath her were modest little homes of working-men. It was all so different from the old neighborhood in Chicago, with its large homes and expensive, professionally maintained lawns. Paul would never find her here.

But of course he would. She knew it. He would trace her no matter where she went, no matter how she tried to lose herself in unfamiliar settings. A few weeks, a few months, and one day he would be climbing the porch steps, pushing the doorbell.

119

"Mrs. Kane?"

"What?" It took her a few seconds to react to the false name she had used since coming to San Francisco.

"How long would you want the house?"

She said vaguely, "I'm not sure. Perhaps several months."

"That would be good. I might get well in a hurry, and then I'd be wanting to move back."

He broke off to cough into his handkerchief. "Let me show you the cellar. No leak, no seepage—a wonderful storage place."

She said, "I don't have a great deal to store." But he had turned away, and so she followed his bent, shuffling form out the front room to a door next to the kitchen.

Twisting a bolt, he opened the door, flicked on a light switch, and led her down a flight of wooden steps. Like the rest of the house, the cement cellar was clean and shipshape, with an old-style furnace in one corner, and near it some old lumber and bricks, neatly stacked. Against a far wall were three huge trunks, with brass corners, brass padlocks, and metal straps around, one on top of another and the third alongside.

Mrs. Kendall gazed at the trunks, and suddenly again thought of Paul. Relentless Paul . . .

"Look at those cement foundation walls," said Mr. Peet, gazing pridefully. "Look at the bars bolted over that little window. Nobody's going to be breaking into *this* cellar! I built the whole house myself, thirty-five years ago. Picked this hilltop because I like privacy—those days I had the area to myself. 'Course, the neighbors are creeping up the hill now—since the tract went in, three years ago. But there's still some breathing room."

She murmured, "I'd like a trunk like those."

"You would?"

"Yes," she said. "Yes, I have some—some china, quite valuable, an inheritance, that I'd like to store in a good safe place."

"Nothing safer than this cellar. I'd let you use one of mine, but they're full of metal—gears and such. I used to be in the scrapmetal business. But I've got this friend who's a hauler, and he's got a couple of trunks like these. He'd sell you one."

She was quiet a moment, staring at the trunks. Paul was a

man of average height. Stood on end, each of the trunks would be taller than she.

Back in the front room, she sat on the couch, her purse in her lap. "Should I give you the money for the trunk?"

"No, I'll have my friend bring it out and you can pay him. It'll run maybe twenty dollars, somewhere around there."

"Very well." She was indifferent to the cost. Money was the least of her problems—with several thousand dollars in cash in her purse and over $200,000 in banks in Chicago.

He now stood at the window, his seamed face slack, as he gazed down the slope. "Thirty-five years. Seems like a dream, me blacking out, going to the doctor last week, and him telling me that about my health. I don't have any choice, though. I've *got* to go."

She murmured, "You told me."

"Like a dream. Like I'm walking in a dream. Don't know how I'll like apartment life. But the doctor says I've got to get down the Peninsula where there isn't the fog. My oldest girl has this apartment in Menlo Park, so I'll move in with her. Don't know, though. Living alone, you get used to your own way."

Her voice cut briskly through his reminiscence. "I'm sure it's a wrench for you to leave. Well, thank you for everything." She rose and walked with him to the front door.

He paused. "If it's all right with you I'll just stop by every couple of weeks or so. It'll give me something to do, to come back, look over the house, the neighborhood."

She watched from the window as his dusty old sedan cautiously maneuvered down the steep street. Now, she thought, I have a little house, all by itself on a hilltop, with a cellar. And I'm going to have a trunk. A large trunk with brass corners and metal straps and a strong brass lock.

She murmured aloud, "Don't find me, Paul. For your sake, don't find me."

Six months before, a Chicago detective-lieutenant named Broyles had stared at the man slumped in the leather chair in the study that was hung with rifles and pistols, and had felt uneasy. Gun-cleaning accidents involving gentlemen who left rather large sums of money to attractive widows always made Broyles feel uneasy.

The bullet had struck Roger Kendall under the chin and blown off the top of his head.

According to her calm account, the widow had been asleep in the bedroom down the hall when, at precisely five minutes past midnight—a time corroborated by persons in two adjoining homes—she heard the shot, ran to the study, and found her gun-collector husband dead.

The detective's strong hunch was that the lady was a murderess—but hunches were worth nothing. Without a shred of evidence against her, he didn't have a case.

He would have been interested in a conversation which took place one afternoon shortly after the inheritance was settled. The scene was the living room of the Kendall home and the participants were the widow and a young man named Paul Barton, who was her late husband's nephew.

"What are you going to do with all your money, Pam?" Paul was nonchalantly sipping vodka-and-tonic—his sixth or eighth drink of the day. As he cheerfully admitted, he sustained himself on vodka.

She said coldly, "I don't think that question is in very good taste to murder Uncle Roger?"

She whispered, after a long silence, "You're drunk, Paul."

"Granted. But I wasn't drunk when I saw you at a quarter to twelve on the night of the killing. I saw things very clearly then."

He sat, legs sprawled out, relaxed, smiling amiably, cracking ice with his teeth, a sophomoric habit he had never outgrown. "Remember, Pam? I came here that night about eight o'clock. I was loaded. You were about to go out—to the public library, as I remember. You left the house. I sat with Uncle Roger in the study and harangued him into lending me some money—which he did. To get rid of me. Then I passed out."

He sipped his drink. "Collapsed like a drunken hog on the rug at his feet. He got me up. I said, 'Don't bother to see me out.' He didn't. I closed the study door, started toward the front door, and just kept walking down the hall to the guest room. It seemed like a sound idea at the time. I dropped on the bed, had a comfy snooze, woke up feeling my old self again, whatever that is—and then I heard movement in the hall. You. You were home."

"There's no secret about it. I was home by nine."

"Yes. Too bad you didn't know *I* was there in the guest room. If you *had* known, poor Uncle Roger would have lived—for another night, anyhow."

She lit a cigarette, staring at him. "Why should I believe you were in the house at all?"

"Let me go on. I continued to lie there, dozing, and then I dropped off again—and suddenly came awake. I looked at my watch—a quarter to twelve. The night was still young, I had convalesced, I had money in my pocket, there were bright lights to see, bright bottles to conquer. So I opened the door to the hall. I saw you, walking away from me down that long carpeted hall toward the study. Wearing your green negligee, with woolly green slippers —there's your proof I was here.

"I stood in the guest-room door and watched you go down the hall, past the front-door entrance, and then into the study. I watched the study door close. Then I came down the hall. I turned at the front door, quietly opened it, and slipped out into the night."

Pam Kendall said, after a long silence, "So, actually you saw nothing."

"Nothing of the murder, no. What I *did* see, though, was you going into the study twenty minutes before you said you had— twenty minutes before the shot was fired that was supposed to have awakened you. I think, Pam, that it would be enough to put you behind bars for a long, long time."

He cracked ice with his teeth, grinning at her. "What you did, I suppose, was to bring him a nightcap, with some kind of drug slipped into it, so he was passed out in his chair before you returned twenty minutes later. Then it was a simple matter to lift one of the guns from the wall, slide a shell in, put it in position as if he were cleaning it, take the glass away and wash it, do whatever other stage-managing you had to do—then, with due regard for fingerprints, squeeze the trigger."

She got up and paced in front of the fireplace. Staring at the cold logs she said, "Why didn't you tell the police right away?"

"Oh, I thought I'd just wait—until the inheritance was safely in your hands."

She turned and said scornfully, "If you think I'd pay black-mail—"

He smiled. "You'll pay, Pam. You have no choice."

They settled on a sum. But she should have known. He had no income. A matter of a few months, living as he did, and the money would be gone.

He came again. She said, as she drew cash from her desk drawer, "This is the last time, Paul. Don't come again."

But he did. Leaving off the playboy charm he said harshly, "Give me money. I'm broke, some people are pressing me. I'm desperate."

His hands were bunched, his eyes were hard, glazed. She looked at him, then went silently to her desk.

She said, as she paid him, "I'm leaving, Paul. I'm going to close the house and leave Chicago for a while. Don't look for me."

She left a week later after telling her friends and acquaintances a tale of going off on a European vacation. She took the plane to San Francisco. She thought, When he finds me gone he may let it go at that, may look elsewhere for support. I hope so.

But—did she? She smiled slightly. It would have been easy enough to really go to Europe. Instead, she went to San Francisco under a false name—Mrs. Kane. Why? Because she knew that even under the assumed name Paul would eventually find her?

She had no definite plan. But she knew that in San Francisco she would look for a quiet little house, isolated from any neighbors—a house to which a man might come without being observed, to which it need never be known if a man had come or not.

Three days after she had rented Mr. Peet's house, her trunk arrived in the custody of two strong, solemn men who got it off the pickup truck, carried it through the house and down into the cellar.

They gave her a key, took her money, and departed.

Mrs. Kendall turned the key in the lock and pushed back the heavy lid. Standing there, she gazed into the open black trunk.

"Come anytime now, Paul."

A week passed. Then, early one afternoon, there were sudden footsteps on the porch. Quick, light steps—not the shuffling steps of old Mr. Peet. The bell rang.

She opened the door. "I've been expecting you."

Paul smiled his crooked smile. "It's a hot day and I've had a hard plane trip and a long cab ride. Any vodka in the house?"

She watched the cab that had deposited him make a U-turn, then drive away down the slope. Then she led the way to the kitchen. He watched her pour vodka from the bottle, and grapefruit juice from a can she opened, over ice.

He murmured, "Would you be so good as to taste it for me, Pam?"

He watched her take a long swallow of the drink. Then he took the glass from her and walked with her into the front room.

He sat down on the couch, and she sat opposite him. He sipped his drink and said, "This will be the last time, I swear it. Give me ten thousand. I'll leave the country, go to Canada or somewhere, make a new life—"

Her eyes were fixed on him. "Tell me how you found me."

He smiled, and chipped ice with his teeth. "I followed you to the airport the day you left Chicago. I saw you board the San Francisco flight. I have a friend in San Francisco, an insurance investigator, and I asked him to meet the plane at the airport and follow you. I sent him money for his time, of course. He followed you to your hotel, and the next morning he was watching when you went to the real-estate office. It was easy for him to find out the address of the house you rented."

"So you knew from the day I moved in what my address was. Very resourceful, Paul. You had me on tap for whenever you needed me. Does your friend know you came here to see me?"

"What?" His voice was a little slurred. He took a bit of ice from his mouth and dropped it into the glass.

"Didn't you hear me? I asked if your friend knows you came to see me."

"No, no, he doesn't know I'm in town. No business of his."

"Do you know that I bought a trunk?"

He put his hand to his head. "What?"

"A trunk. It's in the cellar."

His face had gone suddenly slack. His eyes were dull. He said thickly, "What's happening? There's a blur—"

She got up and came close to him. He had fallen back on the couch and his knees trembled violently, as if trying to thrust him to his feet. His eyes flickered, and behind them she saw fear, as realization forced itself into his consciousness.

She said, "A sleeping potion, quite strong. In the ice cubes. A special ice tray, Paul, prepared and waiting for you. That was always an annoying habit of yours—biting the ice. You really shouldn't have come. I *did* warn you, Paul."

He said weakly, "Pam—for the love of God!"

She stood there, smiling down at him, and then she said, "You're asleep now. Unfortunately, you'll wake up. Poor Paul."

Pamela Kendall was not big, but she was strong enough. Strong enough to drag his inert form from the couch and across the room to the cellar steps. Then it didn't take strength—only a hard prod with her foot to send him down the steps.

She looked at him, lying at the bottom, blood oozing from his cut forehead. But he wasn't dead. He would still wake up—one more time.

She dragged him to the trunk, and, as if he were a rolled-up rug, lifted him over the edge one part at a time—first head, then shoulders, then torso, then hips. She tumbled his legs in and closed the heavy lid. She turned the key in the padlock and went upstairs.

Passing the mirror in the hall, she saw her dark hair clinging to her glistening cheeks. "I must take a shower," she said softly. "A tepid shower—then I'll be myself again."

She stood under the shower, and in the rush of water imagined she heard, over and over, a thin faint cry.

And now she must think of what to do about the trunk.

But there was really no hurry. Paul was dead, dead in the cellar, above which she slept.

•

She rose suddenly, in the bright sunlight, her heart beating wildly. What was it? Oh, yes—a recollection. Of course. Mr. Peet. He had said he would be coming by every couple of weeks or so.

Well, she would simply pretend not to be home. There were only two doors, front and back, and each had a twist-knob lock. She would turn the knobs and even with his keys he could not get in.

But what about smell?

She got up, put on her robe, and went into the kitchen to make coffee. One always thought more clearly with coffee.

Well, smell then. She did not know. She imagined that in a week or so—but the house was isolated, and on a hilltop. Industrial plants were not far—refineries, meat-packing plants. If anyone should notice a peculiar odor in the air, would he not attribute it to the factories? And why should anyone think of *her* house? It was quite isolated. No one came around—except Mr. Peet, of course, and what had he said? "This respiration thing—I can't smell, can't taste."

She smiled with relief. There was no need even to keep him out. He could go down into the cellar if he wished, he could make himself at home. No, there was no danger at all.

She got up, went to the cellar door, stood there staring down at the mute black trunk. Could he still be alive in there? No, of course not. There wasn't enough air to have lasted an hour.

But she walked down the stairs, turned the key in the lock, and raised the lid—to be sure.

Then she locked it again and returned to the kitchen to her cup of bracing coffee. So there was really no danger. And she would think of a plan for disposing of the trunk—some clever plan that would, perhaps, cause the trunk to be delivered to another state, delivery to be made in such a way that it could never be traced back to her. In the meantime, she could feel peace—for the first time in the months since Paul had first spoken to her of what he had seen.

She heard a car slither up to the house. Mr. Peet, of course—no one else would come. And he was no danger.

But two men in dark suits stood in the doorway.

"Mrs. Kane?"

"Yes?"

"I'm Detective Miles, and this is Sergeant Williams. We have a warrant."

She stared. "A warrant?"

"Yes." He showed her a paper. "To search your cellar."

She whispered, hand at her throat, "What are you talking about?"

"We hear there's a body. A body in a trunk."

She felt she must be going mad.

She heard her own strange voice: "You couldn't have known. There's no way you could have known."

They had followed her into the front room. She felt as if she were crumbling, her body, her face. "Who told you? Who?"

"Mr. Peet."

Clutching her face, she cried, "He was here yesterday? Spying on me? He saw me put Paul in the trunk?"

They were silent, staring. Then Sergeant Williams pushed his hat to the back of his head and said softly, "Holy Mother of God."

Miles took Pamela Kendall's shoulders, not roughly, but firmly, and backed her toward the couch. "You'd better sit down . . .

"The old man has been talking in his sleep. His daughter heard him. She'd suspected anyway. Suspected that Florence Peet—not her mother, her stepmother—hadn't really gone off to Scotland on a visit, as old Peet had told everyone, and died there. He had letters in her handwriting. They looked authentic, but the daughter always thought there was something fishy. Anyway, after she heard what he said in his sleep she persuaded him to come to us and confess."

"Confess? Confess what?"

"That he'd clubbed Florence Peet to death five years ago and put her body in one of the trunks in his cellar."

Mrs. Kendall stared at them.

Then she closed her eyes, and lay back on the couch.

Her strange, wild laughter went on and on.

CHARLES WEST, JR.

FRANZ KAFKA, DETECTIVE: THE BIRD OF ILL OMEN

I stopped by the Workers Insurance Institute in the Porschitsch-erstrasse on Thursday to see my friend Franz Kafka. He did not seem surprised to see me and greeted me casually.

"I was just thinking of you," he said. "How would you like to accompany me on a small excursion to the countryside—to a village called Cheb in northern Bohemia?" he asked, his large grey eyes widening under thick dark eyebrows.

While I considered Franz my friend, I never imagined he would invite me to accompany him to the country for the weekend. I was introduced to Kafka by my father, who knew him through his office. Although I was only a university student, Kafka always treated me as an equal, even among his small group of friends such as Max Brod, Franz Werfel, and Felix Weltsch. I knew he had often traveled with them, especially with Brod, to France and the Italian lakes.

"I have some small business to conduct, but we should have much of the time to ourselves," he said.

I agreed to go instantly. The German industrial areas of northern Bohemia were not exactly my idea of the ideal place for a holiday. However, both Franz and I welcomed the opportunity for a change of scenery, a chance to escape from our work and the city itself.

I let Kafka make the travel arrangements and planned to meet him at the railway station the next morning. I arrived at the agreed-upon time, but Franz was not there. He appeared about fifteen minutes later, looking fatigued and apologizing profusely. "I meant to be on time, but a cinder or something caught in my throat, causing a somewhat violent coughing attack, together with sweating. I had to lean against a wall until the attack passed."

Kafka dismissed the convulsion as nothing of importance. I almost suggested that he consult a doctor, but decided against it. Franz was peculiarly suspicious of doctors and their diagnoses.

Kafka engaged a compartment for the journey to Cheb. The Insurance Institute paid for one-half since Franz was going on business. Kafka paid for the other half despite my protestations.

Having made the trip before, Kafka was known to the conductors and stewards. He spoke in Czech with them. He spoke and wrote Czech better than I, who, having learned it as a spoken language, used it more colloquially. He used both Czech and German in his work, but more German. Although he used both languages interchangeably, both had the accent of the other, so to Germans he was a Czech, and to the Czechs he was a German.

As the legal representative of the Insurance Institute Kafka made frequent business trips. Franz was very good at his job and was respected by colleagues and superiors alike. He worked in several departments at the Institute and many of his reports were published in the professional journals of the field. He was an expert in the areas of accident insurance and industrial safety. He also proposed such measures as compulsory accident insurance and even, of all things, insurance for motor cars.

The people at the Workers Insurance Institute didn't always understand Kafka. My father once told me a story of an old laborer who lost his leg in an industrial accident. The poor man engaged an inept lawyer who seriously bungled the old man's case. At the last moment, however, a prominent Prague lawyer took over the case and redrafted the suit so that the poor fellow won a handsome settlement.

The lawyer, it was learned later, had been instructed and paid by Kafka so that as the lawyer for the Insurance Institute, Kafka could lose honorably and the old laborer could be provided for fairly. Some of his colleagues say he is an incompetent lawyer; others say he is a great man.

●

I brought one book and one magazine with me for the trip. The magazine contained a short story by Franz Kafka.

"Another proof of my weaknesses and foolishness published for the world to see, all because my friends, led by Max Brod, have contrived to pass my scribblings off as literature." Franz said nothing more about the magazine or the story. I must confess, I do not know what to make of his attitudes toward his own writing.

The other book was a detective novel.

"I didn't know you were attracted to such things," he said.

"Do you disapprove?" I asked.

"No, of course not. Dostoevski wrote something of a detective novel in *Crime and Punishment*. And *Hamlet* is, after all, a crime drama. My only point of dissatisfaction with detective stories is that they are always preoccupied with crimes hidden by bizarre circumstances. I wonder how many crimes happen every day that escape detection because they are without those circumstances which cause them to stand out in everyday life."

A few minutes later he added, "Detective stories contribute to the popular delusion that every mystery is solvable and results in a legal and moral conclusion."

"What sort of business is this?" I asked him.

"A lawsuit. A man died of gas inhalation in an apartment building insured by our office. Although the local police report the death as a suicide, the widow has brought an action which, although not in the proper legal form, must be followed through with the correct procedure."

"And the purpose of your visit?"

"To interview those concerned and to inspect the premises and determine if the condition of the building could have contributed to a gas leak."

In his vocation Kafka absorbed a great deal of knowledge about architecture and building safety. His work in accident-prevention measures often involved disputes with factory managers and landlords who refused to install necessary safety devices and to insure their workers and tenants properly.

"Do you remember Goethe's *Sorrows of Young Werther?*" I

asked. "It created a wave of suicides among young people after its publication."

"I'm not so sure it *created* the suicides. Perhaps the suicides were already created, and Goethe merely set them off. Maybe Goethe and *Young Werther* had nothing to do with them and some scholar drew the wrong correlation years later."

"Could this have been an accident?" I asked.

"Accident is what we call the coincidence of events when we do not know the cause. Nothing happens in the world without cause. Accidents happen only in our minds because our perceptions are limited by a lack of knowledge."

"But what of chance?" I asked.

He smiled. "Chance is merely a struggle against ourselves."

"Can we ever win this struggle?"

"Not entirely," he answered, the small smile reappearing.

We arrived in Cheb in the late evening. Rather than pursue his business immediately, we went to the inn and got a room. As we lay awake in the dark waiting to fall asleep I was startled by a sharp shrill noise that seemed to be coming from everywhere. Kafka informed me they were crickets. How was a city dweller like myself to know that?

"You surprise me, my friend. Mere Bohemian crickets scare you?" He was quite amused.

The next morning we walked to the building where the death occurred. It was an old house, possibly the home of a noble or wealthy landowner at one time. Now, poorly maintained, it had been converted into a group of flats.

We went first to the apartment of Frau and Herr Loos, who lived below the flat of the deceased man. The couple were German, probably Bavarian. I wasn't sure, but I'm certain Franz knew. The husband was an owlish, slightly built man who, for the most part, remained silent. His wife glowered at Franz and me while we were there and seemed extremely annoyed at our intrusion. When Franz asked her a question she answered curtly, frowning as she spoke.

"Were you home on the day Herr Fredersohn died?" he asked.

"No, I was working," Frau Loos replied.

"What time did you get home?"

"About five-thirty—no, at six-thirty."

I recalled from earlier conversations with Franz that the body was found about six. I wanted to ask if she smelled gas when she arrived home. I hesitated, as it was not really any of my business, but Kafka asked the question.

"Did you smell gas when you arrived home?" he asked.

"No!" She answered quickly and without comment.

As he was not getting any information from the wife, Kafka turned his attention to the husband, whose silence had almost caused me to forget he was in the room.

"Were you at work that afternoon as well?" he asked the man.

The wife started to answer: "He was—"

"Let him answer, please," Kafka said quickly. His voice was sharp and had the quality of a command. It was a tone of voice I had never heard from Kafka.

The husband answered nervously. I was not sure if he was more intimidated by Kafka or by his wife.

"I work at home," he said, pointing to a writing desk. "I do accounting and bookkeeping."

"Then you were home all that day?"

"Yes, but I didn't smell any gas," he said, anticipating Kafka's next question.

As the husband answered, Kafka began looking about the apartment, at the stove, the walls, and the ceiling. He walked to a window, the bottom half of which was boarded up. The wife explained the window had been broken by a stone thrown by some passing boys. There was a fair-sized birdcage suspended from a beam in the high ceiling, but there was no bird in it.

"Did your bird escape?" Kafka asked.

"No, it died," the man said immediately. His wife shot him a piercing look and he slunk behind her.

"It probably caught a virus," the wife said. "The weather can become rather harsh in this part of the country."

"What kind of bird was it?"

"A jackdaw," the husband interjected. "It's similar to a crow, only smaller."

He received the same look from his wife that he received before and became silent.

"Did you know," Franz said more to me than to the others,

"that the Czech word for jackdaw is *kavka*, which was the original spelling of my family's name? In Czech superstition it is a bird of ill omen, bad fortune." He seemed oddly pleased by this. "I'm a jackdaw," he smiled. "The jackdaw is generally a sturdy animal," he added.

We next went to the apartment of the dead man and his widow, which was directly above. It was originally the attic of the home, now transformed into a small flat by the present owner to squeeze more income from the property. It was smaller than the apartment below and better kept. The furniture was much the same, but this apartment had a bookshelf lining one wall. The majority of the books were on engineering and science.

The widow greeted us cordially, more so than her neighbor despite her grief. It seemed clear to me she was determined to clear up the question of her husband's suicide, not so much for the settlement as for her husband's honor. The local policeman, Inspector Abel, was also there and we introduced ourselves.

Frau Fredersohn was not a particularly beautiful woman. Her face was plain but her skin was fair and her features well defined. I'm sure if she were rich, the proper combination of clothes, hair, and surroundings would have made her quite attractive. Even without those she had the most striking eyes. To call them blue would not be telling the truth. They approached violet in color and seemed to have the ability to look through a person.

I noticed Franz staring at her. The reason occurred to me later. Frau Fredersohn resembled photographs I had seen of Felice Bauer, to whom Franz was engaged to be married a few years ago. Kafka had never spoken of her to me, and it was only through conversations with Max Brod that I knew anything of her at all. Brod remarked that the couple was at once mismatched and well suited to each other. They met at Brod's house and saw each other for five years, but for some reason the romance was doomed to failure. The couple went so far as to rent an apartment in Prague. Max Brod implied that it was Kafka who broke off the engagement. Kafka continued to steal furtive glances at Fredersohn the rest of the time we were there.

The police inspector was in a hurry to leave and gave the official version of the story without being asked.

"The body was found lying near the oven. The door of the oven was open and his hands and forearms were dirty, apparently from the inside of the oven, leading us to believe he had been tampering with the inside of the oven or had his head in there."

"Approximately what time was this?" Kafka asked.

"I arrived at six-ten exactly," the policeman answered. "The time is always the first thing I note when filing a report, especially a death report."

"Thank you." Kafka shook the policeman's hand and Inspector Abel excused himself and left.

"Was the gas on when you discovered the body?" Kafka asked the woman.

"The smell was very strong. When I came in the room, I first ran to the window to open it and then to the stove to shut the gas."

"And you turned the dials to OFF?"

The woman hesitated. "I must have, although I don't remember. I remember going from the window to the stove before I became unconscious, but I do not remember actually shutting off the valves. I'm not sure how long I was unconscious but when I recovered, the gas had dissipated and the valves were off." She paused. "And Jan was dead. But it wasn't suicide. It couldn't be. There was no reason."

Her voice was rising and becoming hysterical. She collected herself and continued, "Jan was always fixing things around here. Something must have been wrong with the gas lines." Her eyes pleaded with Kafka to believe her. His face showed no expression.

"Is this flat difficult to heat?" Kafka asked as he inspected the apartment much as he inspected the one below.

She was confused by the question but nevertheless answered. "No, it is on the top floor of the building. All the heat from the lower floors rises to heat this one. It makes it quite comfortable in the winter, but it can be unpleasant in the summer."

"Thank you for your time, Frau Fredersohn. I shall call

tomorrow to inform you of my decision regarding your lawsuit." Kafka bowed slightly and began to walk toward the door.

Frau Fredersohn looked apprehensive, as though she believed
Kafka had already made up his mind and was merely postponing
the bad news. "Do you think—"

Franz interrupted her before she could say anything else. "I
will return tomorrow. I will say no more at this time."

As we walked down the stairs Franz spoke about the building.
"This building is old, possibly over sixty years. As with many
old buildings, additions were made to modernize. The plumbing
is an example of that. The gas lines and ventilation are other
examples. The building was not designed to accommodate
these facilities. The owner, in order to make these *improve-
ments,* neglected the maintenance of the rest of the building.
The floors, ceilings, and walls are all badly in need of repair."
He pointed out cracks in the walls near the baseboards and
several loose floorboards.

Kafka was unusually silent for the rest of the walk back to the
inn.

Late that night I awoke to find him sitting in a chair, fully
clothed.

"What's the matter?" I asked. "Is this inquiry keeping you
awake?"

"No, actually I'm an insomniac."

I remarked that insomnia is a common illness.

"Or, perhaps, a sin," he said without explanation. I remember
that he once said that many people considered sleep a symbol
of death. Perhaps insomnia is a symptom of the fear of death. "I
often have sleepless nights. I usually spend the time writing or
thinking."

"What were you thinking about just now?"

"Suicide," he answered.

"Franz!"

He interpreted my thoughts and laughed. "Not my own
suicide, my friend. Suicide in general." He laughed for several
moments at this.

"What are your thoughts?" I asked.

He was silent for what seemed like a long time and then

spoke without preface. "Suicide is a form of egotism combined with hate. The suicide believes his loss will inflict the greatest injury on the person or persons he wishes to hurt. It is an act of frustration and impotence. He feels he cannot do anything else. He rationalizes the act as the last and only logical course of action open to him. The act requires no courage, only despair."

I began to ask him a question, but changed my mind. I was not really sure of what to say, or even if I should say anything at all. Nothing more was said between us that night.

The next morning we had a light breakfast of coffee and rolls. Kafka sent a message to Inspector Abel from the inn to meet us at the Loos apartment in an hour.

At breakfast and while walking we talked of many things—the village, literature, anecdotes—all the things friends talk about. He seemed refreshed by the brief stay in the country. The escape from the city was almost therapeutic. I suggested that he make a permanent move to the country.

"It's not the location that refreshes me, but the change. In six months of country life I would become bored and depressed, longing for the excitement and stimulation of Prague. It is not where you live that determines the quality of life but rather what you do with your time. I am quite satisfied with Prague."

When we arrived at the building, Inspector Abel was waiting at the steps. Together we walked to the flat of Frau Loos and her husband. Frau Loos seemed almost shocked to see us, and Herr Loos appeared frightened.

I remained silent as Kafka and Inspector Abel greeted the couple. Kafka apologized for the intrusion.

"I just wished to demonstrate to Inspector Abel the events of Jan Fredersohn's death as they could have occurred," said Franz. "Frau Loos stated she arrived home at six-thirty, after the body upstairs had been discovered." Kafka spoke to Inspector Abel, but his explanation was clearly meant for all of us. "However, Frau Loos also said she was home when the police arrived. I believe you have in your notes that you arrived at the scene at six-ten." The Inspector checked his report and acknowledged that fact. The woman said nothing.

"Frau Loos also said that some passing boys threw a rock through their window earlier in the week.

"Now, observe: there still are fragments of glass on the outside ledge, which indicates that the window was broken from the inside. If it had been broken by a thrown rock, there would be no glass on the outside."

Frau Loos was silent.

The Inspector was confused. "What exactly are you trying to say, Herr Kafka?"

"I'm saying it is possible that, given these discrepancies in Frau Loos's statement, the official police report, although it accurately recorded the facts, may have missed the real cause of Herr Fredersohn's death."

"What do you mean?" asked Inspector Abel.

"It is possible that Frau Loos came home about five-thirty, not six-thirty as she said. As she entered the flat she smelled gas and saw her husband unconscious on the floor. She ran to the stove, shut off the gas valves, then ran to the window where she broke the glass to allow fresh air into the room."

"If that were the case, I should have opened the window," Frau Loos insisted.

"I think not," Kafka said, moving to the window. "The paint is not worn in the sash and the latch has been painted over, suggesting it hasn't been used in some time." Kafka then tried to open the latch and the window for the benefit of the Inspector. He was unable to do so.

"What does this have to do with Fredersohn's suicide?" Frau Loos asked indignantly.

"This building is old and drafty," Franz continued. "If you recall, Frau Fredersohn said her flat is very easy to heat because all the heat from the other floors rises to heat it. Just as heat rises, so does gas. The gas wafted up to the floor above, killing Fredersohn."

"But Fredersohn was found near the oven, after having obviously tampered with it," Inspector Abel objected.

"Herr Fredersohn was an engineering student as well as a handyman. Smelling gas, he went to the stove to see if there was something wrong. As he was inspecting the oven and the gas lines he succumbed to the gas."

Frau Loos looked at Kafka with rage and then at her husband, the look changing to one of revulsion.

Kafka went on, "Someone in this apartment left the gas valves on—the gas originated here." Kafka pointed to the Looses' oven, glancing at Herr Loos. "The gas filtered upstairs, killing first the jackdaw here, then Fredersohn above."

Herr Loos was weeping quietly as Franz finished speaking.

"This is ridiculous," Frau Loos said to the inspector angrily. "Who is this man that he can come in here and make these accusations!"

She began to speak again, but her husband spoke first. "That is enough!" he shouted. "Herr Kafka has described the events quite accurately. I am responsible for the death of Herr Fredersohn. It was entirely my fault."

Inspector Abel arrested Loos, and Kafka promised to mail a deposition on his return to Prague. Franz was in a peculiar hurry to leave the village. On the train I asked him about his haste.

"My work is finished," he said, "and I did not wish to see the widow, Frau Fredersohn." He sensed my confusion. "I do not take compliments or gratitude comfortably," he added. "People make too much of simple competence. I will, however, send her a letter of explanation along with the settlement of her lawsuit. It is my job," he said.

Later, on the train, I asked Kafka about Herr Loos. "Love is always accompanied by a measure of hate. Only the will of the love can divide the love from the hate."

"What a meaningless life," I said. "Herr Loos's."

"The trouble with life," Kafka said, "is that it is so seldom *really* lived. Man merely *exists.*"

"Isn't that the same thing?" I asked.

He smiled, "No, my friend, it is not the same."

WILLIAM BRITTAIN

FALLING OBJECT

Edmund Plummer stood on the roof of the Talmadge Building and peered over the parapet. He could see the flat stainless-steel-and-glass side of the building seeming to become smaller as his gaze traveled downward to the street twenty stories below. There were no setbacks, no architectural gewgaws to break the edifice's severe rectangular lines; it was a triumph of modern efficiency, providing the maximum of office space with the minimum of materials.

But Plummer thought he had discovered something unusual about the building. If true it might make necessary a revision of his original set of equations. He raised his bifocal glasses and bent forward to peer once again through the telescope of the surveyors' transit he had set up on the roof. Then he checked the measurement gauges on the instrument and jotted some figures into a notebook in neat precise columns.

There could be no question about it. Instead of rising at a precise right angle from the pavement below, the sides of the Talmadge Building leaned to the south almost three inches—two and seven-eighths inches, to be exact.

Edmund Plummer wished to be exact.

He looked at his watch, startled that his time on the roof had passed so quickly. Down below, on the fourteenth floor, men and women would be leaving their offices to go home. Then it would be Plummer's job to sweep and mop and carry away the mountainous pile of wastepaper and other debris created each day in order to keep a few of the wheels in that remarkable machine called American Business running properly.

Plummer neither liked nor disliked his job as a cleaning man. He had felt the same way about his previous job as a dishwasher and the one before that when he went from door to door handing out advertising leaflets for a chain of department stores. They were ways to keep alive, that was all. And even in these

menial occupations, sooner or later he would have to quit and
move on. Eventually, no matter where he was or what he did,
someone would recognize him as the man whom the law had
freed but whom everyone knew to be a—

Plummer tried to keep the word out of his mind. But it was
impossible. Besides, it was all down in the official government
records, which were now probably yellowing and gathering
dust in a warehouse somewhere.

He managed to smile to himself, wondering what the secretaries on the fourteenth floor, who were so pleasant and so
condescending to him, would think if they ever found out that
the odd little man who emptied their ashtrays and dusted their
desks and smiled vacantly at them had received his Ph.D. in
physics at the age of twenty-three. Would they still giggle and
call him "Plumsy" if they became aware that during the fall of
1942 and the spring of '43, at the height of World War II, he had
been considered potentially more valuable to the Allies than a
squadron of bombers?

And what would their reaction be if they discovered that
their genial janitor had once stood in the dock of justice
accused of being a traitor?

There was nothing thrilling or sensational about what had
happened to Plummer; the whole grubby business had been a
tragedy of errors from beginning to end. During October of
1942—at about the time that British bombers were stepping
up their incessant pounding of the German industrial cities—
Plummer was hard at work on a device of his own invention. It
was an improved bombsight.

As any bomber pilot of that time could testify, the most
dangerous part of a mission was the "bombing run"—the approach to the target. At that point the plane had to be kept
straight and level for a period of approximately thirty seconds,
allowing the bombardier to adjust his sight, make the correct
allowances for speed, direction, and altitude, then release his
bombs. During that thirty-second period, the plane was a sitting
duck at the not-so-tender mercies of both the cruelly accurate
anti-aircraft batteries on the ground and the best fliers the
German Luftwaffe could put into the air. Men who have been

through it are willing to swear that the thirty seconds over the target really lasted thirty years.

Plummer's new bombsight was designed to reduce that period of time by a full seven seconds. Seven seconds—the entire R.A.F. would have been willing to sell its collective soul to obtain seven seconds of grace on their flights through the shrapnel-filled hell.

But the device was never to reach the men who so desperately needed it.

Near the end of October 1942, certain "bugs" started cropping up in the new bombsight. On several occasions, problems that had seemed near solution proved to be more complicated than was first supposed, forcing not only Plummer but his entire staff to spend valuable time readjusting their theories to fit cold, hard, unyielding facts.

At about the same time Plummer received a visitor at his small apartment near the Baltimore research center. The visitor gave his name as Norman Gant. He had heard of Plummer's work on the bombsight, and he wondered if he might discuss— no, of course not. The government would be keeping close watch on the progress of such an important device. Still, Gant explained, there were those who were interested in seeing that such an invention did not come into use *too* soon. Perhaps certain problems that Plummer was having might delay final production for a year, maybe longer. Those Gant represented would be willing to pay a huge sum for such delay.

Plummer had thrown the man out of the apartment.

But unfortunately he had neglected to report the offer of a bribe. And even more unfortunately the progress on the bombsight came almost to a halt. First, the optical system had to be scraped; then the unit refused to function reliably at any altitude above 100 feet. And the focusing gauge tended to jam in wet weather. Everything that could possibly go wrong seemed to.

And in April of the following year, during a raid on an apartment suspected of harboring German nationals, the man who called himself Gant was picked up by the FBI. He was quickly identified as Josef Schissel, a former guard at one of the Vernichtungslager—the Nazi extermination camps. Having spent several years in the United States as a youth, Schissel spoke English without an accent, and he was familiar with American slang.

The Abwehr, the German Intelligence Bureau, had received word of the device on which Plummer was working and Schissel had been smuggled into the United States by way of Mexico for the sole purpose of rendering the new bombsight project ineffectual. This Schissel proceeded to do—simply by swearing that the young scientist had indeed accepted money from him to slow down work on the bombsight. Schissel's confession, coupled with the almost total lack of progress on the device itself, was enough to make the authorities gravely suspicious that Plummer had sold out his country.

At the ensuing trial Plummer was pitifully unable to refute the circumstantial evidence against him. Why, it was asked, hadn't he reported his meeting with Schissel immediately? His answer—that he considered the man just another anti-war crackpot—was the object of derisive laughter by the prosecuting attorney. Plummer pointed out that his standard of living hadn't changed a bit since the supposed payoff. The prosecution, however, took the position that a man as intelligent as Plummer would be far too clever to begin spending the money immediately. Secret Swiss bank accounts were hinted at. And yet the government could produce no real evidence of anything more serious than poor judgment. Plummer might even have convinced everyone of his innocence—except for Schissel's testimony.

When the small, clean-shaven German was placed on the witness stand he requested and was granted the privilege of making a statement to the court. Everyone present expected him to scream curses at the government holding him captive. The judge held his gavel ready to hammer down any such attempt. But instead, Schissel began by thanking the court as well as his captors for the extreme courtesy they had shown to him, an enemy agent. He commended the judge for his fairness. Under the circumstances, Schissel went on, he was sorry to have placed the judge in such a difficult position. He realized that the judge would find it necessary to declare Plummer innocent because of the value of his brain to the Allies.

"You must find him innocent because the government forces you to do so," Schissel concluded in a low voice. "It is a pity that the law must yield to expediency." Stretching out his hand, Schissel pointed dramatically at Plummer. "Nevertheless, that man is a traitor to his country."

It may have been that Judge Randall Barth felt compelled to prove that in his courtroom the law still reigned supreme; perhaps Schissel's humble manner and his obvious willingness to take the entire punishment on his own shoulders evoked some sympathetic vibration in the judicial conscience. Whatever the reason, the fact remains that the enemy agent's words had an astounding effect.

"That agent really got under Judge Barth's skin," one reporter was overheard to tell another. "The old man's liable to set Schissel free and hang Plummer instead."

In his final summation Judge Barth left no doubt that he considered Plummer to be the lowest form of human scum. He stated that he would personally see to it that the complete testimony of the trial was made available to any prospective employer foolish enough even to consider giving employment to such a person. Nevertheless, on the basis of the evidence alone—

Forcing each word through teeth clenched in anger, the judge pronounced the accused Not Guilty. The reporters rushed from the building to file their stories.

In the court of law Plummer was innocent. But public opinion doesn't operate by rules of evidence. In a world of defense contracts and top-secret information, Plummer found himself an outcast. His fiancée returned his ring. There was no note attached. He learned that while a rising young physicist attracts friends as honey attracts bees, a suspected traitor attracts only curses and looks of scorn and disgust. The two years in which he went without work wiped out his small savings. And then began the series of pointless, dead-end, menial jobs. He didn't live; he merely existed from day to day.

Then one morning in 1956 he found a cast-off newspaper on a park bench. He was about to pass it by when his eye was attracted by a small headline containing a familiar name. After thirteen years of imprisonment, the article stated, Josef Schissel, a spy for the Nazis during World War II, was to be released.

Schissel would be free.

And Plummer resolved to kill him.

There followed for Plummer several years of keeping painstaking records on Schissel's whereabouts. He was returned to Germany. There he was influential in the exposure of three major Nazi war criminals. A general, grateful for Schissel's assistance in rounding up the wanted men, pulled some political strings to obtain a visa to enable the former spy to revisit the United States. The visa was twice renewed. Finally, in 1965, Schissel was granted permission to live permanently in the United States.

Three years later he bought a small delicatessen only a couple of blocks from the Talmadge Building. Within a few months word of his delicious coffee and generously large slices of rich pastries had been passed to several of the secretaries in the building, and Schissel was commissioned to make daily deliveries for the morning coffee breaks.

It was then that Plummer applied for a job in the Talmadge Building as a janitor. He was hired.

At that time Plummer had no idea which method he would use to kill Schissel. It was enough to have finally located the man who had ruined his life.

During his first day on the job Plummer found out that the coffee-break items were delivered by Schissel himself—the Talmadge Building provided the major part of his income and he didn't trust any of his helpers to make the deliveries properly. But try as he might, for the first week on the job, Plummer couldn't catch sight of his intended victim. He began to wonder what changes 25 years had made in Schissel's appearance.

During the second week Plummer was sent to the roof of the building to clean away a pile of debris left by some workmen. It was hard work, and when he finally finished he leaned against the parapet, enjoying the cooling breeze which never reached the sidewalk far below. He saw a panel truck pull up to the curb in the alley next to the building. A man wearing a white apron got out. From where Plummer was standing, the figure was curiously foreshortened. The man, who from that distance resembled a tiny white insect, opened the rear of the truck, took out a small wheeled cart, and began to fill it with coffee urns and trays wrapped in white paper. Then the man wheeled the cart around the corner to the building's front entrance. There the doorman greeted him cordially and even opened the door for him. It was several seconds after the man had entered that Plummer realized who he must be.

Schissel! There below him in the street, the man whose lies had made Plummer's existence a living hell was calmly making his daily delivery. Heart pounding furiously, Plummer raced down the stairs from the roof. He ran to the door of the service elevator and was about to punch the button when he stopped. As he withdrew his hand he smiled grimly.

He knew now how Schissel would die.

A few days later, from his meager savings, Plummer purchased a small but heavy steel strongbox. By going without lunches for several weeks he saved enough money to buy a secondhand surveyors' transit, complete with tripod, from the pawnshop around the corner from the shabby room in which he lived. The following Sunday he carried the transit to several points within two blocks of the Talmadge Building. From each of these spots the entire height of the structure was visible, and at each he took readings with his transit.

Then Plummer began his calculations. They were comparatively simple for a man who had once designed a bombsight. The Talmadge Building was 242 feet high. Five feet eight inches—he guessed that to be Schissel's height—would have to be subtracted from that, making the distance 236⅓ feet. Weight, of course, was not important. It was the mass that counted, barring the negligible effect of the air itself. Wind needed to be taken into consideration, so he would choose a calm day. A rate of acceleration of 32.2 feet per second (approximately) meant a distance of 16 feet the first second (approximately) and—no! Approximations were not good enough. The figures had to be exact. Plummer was trained to be exact.

And he knew that a heavy strongbox, dropped from the roof of the Talmadge Building at precisely the correct instant, would smash into the head of Josef Schissel on the sidewalk below with the velocity of a cannonball. Even if it were to hit only Schissel's shoulder or back it would most certainly kill him.

There was one further aspect of the problem that Plummer found intriguing. Schissel certainly wasn't going to just stand there and wait for the box to hit him. No, Schissel would be moving, too. But this did not disturb Plummer. With the exception of the fact that the target as well as the "bomb" was in motion, these were the same calculations that bombardiers had performed over enemy factories. It was merely necessary to see that the target and the bomb collided at the same place at the same time.

From one of the secretaries on the fourteenth floor Plummer borrowed a stopwatch. Each day, just before the coffee break, he went to the roof and observed Schissel unloading his trays and urns, wheeling them around the corner of the building, and entering through the front door. The time it took Schissel to push the cart from his truck to the front entrance varied only because he was not always able to park his truck in the same place. Plummer began measuring the time from the moment Schissel passed a fire hydrant and he noted that the man could be depended on not to change his pace. His movements were as regular as clockwork.

The strongbox would be released to hit Schissel's head just as the man reached the corner of the building, since at that spot he cut the corner sharply, coming within two feet of the side of the building.

As a final step in his preparations, Plummer managed "accidentally" to spill a blob of white paint on the sidewalk several yards down the alley from the corner. The spot had been chosen after several days of observation and calculations. When Schissel reached the blob of paint, the box would be dropped. Schissel would continue to walk ahead, and at the precise moment he arrived at the corner the plummeting heavy metal box would have reached a point five feet eight inches above the pavement. Finis . . .

And now Plummer had discovered that the Talmadge Building leaned two and seven-eighths inches to the south.

For a moment he wondered if it would be necessary to revise his entire plan. Then he shook his head. No, there was really no need for it. He would merely hold the box a bit farther out from the parapet before dropping it. A larger object than the box would, of course, be desirable in reducing the margin for error, but something heavy and yet small enough to be smuggled up to the roof was essential. The strongbox would do admirably. Besides, Plummer had another use for it.

Before dropping it on Schissel's head Plummer planned to fill the box with all the newspaper clippings he had saved concerning the German so the world might fully understand the reasons why he had to die.

The following day was rainy. The day after that a high wind sprang up early in the morning, and the same evening a grey mass of fog settled in, remaining for 48 hours. Plummer wondered if he would ever be able to put his murder plan into operation.

Friday morning arrived, sunny and cool and without a breath of wind. Looking through the window of his dingy room, Plummer smiled and hummed a happy tune to himself. It was a perfect day for walking with a girl in the park, for lying on the grass and watching the sky, for taking a trip to the country—and for murder.

Now that the time had come to carry out his plan, Plummer found himself curiously at ease. He whistled gaily at his image in the shaving mirror. He decided to skip breakfast, using the time instead to thumb through his thick packet of newspaper clippings for a last time.

The earliest ones, dated April 1943, he handled gingerly. They were brittle with age but still quite readable. SUSPECT GOVERNMENT SCIENTIST OF SELLOUT read the one on the top of the pile.

Replacing the clippings in their envelope, he crammed it into a jacket pocket and left the apartment. As he reached the sidewalk he remembered that he'd forgotten to lock the door. He considered going back and decided against it. He possessed nothing worth stealing.

He was six minutes late getting to work. In the basement of the Talmadge Building he went to his locker and changed into his blue coveralls, his mind on the steel strongbox waiting on a shelf of the broom closet on the fourteenth floor.

At 9:40 Plummer was on a stepladder, busily polishing the globes of the lights in a hallway on the fourteenth floor. Only twenty more minutes, he thought to himself. At 10:00 I'll put away the ladder in the closet, take the box, and go to the roof. Schissel will drive his truck up to the curb at 10:15 as he always does. But he'll never make it to the front door. All these years I've spent waiting for this chance, and now there's just a few more minutes to—

"Plummer?"

It was Ed Malenski, who worked on the floor above. He must have come down the stairs—Plummer hadn't seen anyone get out of the service elevator. "Yeah, Ed?" he answered.

"Dandridge wants to see you in his office right away. He couldn't reach you on the phone, so he called me and told me to let you know."

Jerome Dandridge was the head of the maintenance department of the Talmadge Building. Plummer supposed he was going to be reprimanded for being late. He didn't mind. Just as long as it didn't take too long. He rode the service elevator to the basement, got out, and knocked softly on the door of Dandridge's office.

"Come in." Plummer opened the door. Dandridge was sitting at his desk, and another man, conservatively dressed, stood beside him. The second man was a stranger to Plummer and Dandridge made no attempt to introduce him.

"Mr. Dandridge, I'm sorry about being late, but—"

"That's not why I wanted to see you," Dandridge rumbled. "How long you been with us, Plummer?"

"About four months."

"And before that? What did you do before that?"

"Dishwasher—other things," Plummer replied. "It's all in my application. Why?"

Without answering, Dandridge turned to the other man and picked up a paper from his desk. "Says here he never completed high school," he muttered. "What d'ya think, Mr. Ross?"

"Hard to tell," was the answer. "A long time has gone by since then. People change.

The man called Ross turned to Plummer. He reached into a pocket and pulled out a leather folder. "Mr. Plummer," he began, "I'm Joseph Ross. I'm with the FBI and—

Plummer was only half listening. Something had fallen from Ross's pocket when the agent had produced his identification. It was a small yellowed piece of paper with print on it. Automatically Plummer bent down to pick it up. His eyes widened. The black print screamed at him from the newspaper clipping.

SUSPECT GOVERNMENT SCIENTIST OF SELLOUT.

They knew who he was! It wasn't fair! Not today! Not after all these weeks of planning!

"No! Not now!" he shouted. Running to the office door he dashed through it, slamming it behind him. Across the hall was the service elevator, its door open. He scurried inside and punched the button for the top floor. As the doors slid shut he had just time to see Ross and Dandridge burst out of the office in a vain attempt to halt the elevator.

The car rose swiftly to the twentieth floor. Plummer stepped into the corridor and looked around. It was empty. They were probably waiting in the basement for the indicator to show which floor he had stopped at. He had only a few seconds before—

Behind him the elevator doors closed and he could hear the car starting downward.

He ran to the stairway leading to the roof and pounded up the steps. Opening the thick door with his passkey, he moved out into the sunlight. Inserting the key into the outer lock he turned it hard in the wrong direction. The key snapped off. Perhaps that would be enough to jam the lock. To make doubly sure, he inserted some small pieces of wood at the edges of the door, forcing them into place with the heel of his hand.

How much time? He glanced at his watch. Three minutes ten seconds before Schissel was scheduled to arrive. Please, please let the door to the roof hold for a few minutes. Just until he had enough time to drop—

The steel box! He had forgotten to take the box! It was still on the fourteenth floor, in the broom closet.

There had to be something else. A brick. That was it, a brick. He scanned the entire roof.

There was nothing but tiny scraps of wood which the slightest movement of air would blow off-course. Even if they were to fall perfectly straight, Schissel would hardly feel them when they struck. He had to find something heavy.

There was nothing.

Plummer heard a pounding on the door to the roof. The lock rattled, but the thick iron door remained closed. "Plummer! Open up!" called a muffled voice.

Far below he could see the sunlight glinting off the top of a panel truck as it moved up the alley at the side of the building. A tiny antlike figure got out and opened the rear doors. The cart was piled high with trays. The coffee urns were put into place.

And in that instant Plummer found the weapon that would kill Schissel. It was one he should have thought of long ago—so much better than the strongbox. He removed the packet of clippings from his pocket and grasped them tightly in his hand.

Behind Plummer, Ross and Dandridge had managed to open the door a scant two inches before a wooden wedge at its base again jammed it. "Plummer, listen!" shouted Ross through the opening. "The army just located a report that Schissel sent to his superiors back in '43. That's why I'm here. It only landed on my desk two days ago and—"

But Plummer, deep in concentration, didn't hear. Down below, Josef Schissel closed the doors of his truck and gripped the handle of his cart. He took a step forward—two—three—

"Open up, Plummer! The government's willing to do anything in its power to make amends! You're cleared! You're inno—"

The front wheels of Schissel's cart glided over a white paint stain on the sidewalk. The rear wheels followed. And then Schissel's right foot came down on the white spot.

With the soles of his heavy work shoes poised on the parapet 236⅓ feet above Schissel's head, Edmund Plummer folded his arms tightly across his chest, smiled through the tears streaming down his cheeks, and stepped off the parapet and out into space.

BARONESS ORCZY

THE MYSTERIOUS DEATH IN PERCY STREET

Miss Polly Burton had had many an argument with Mr. Richard Frobisher about that old man in the corner, who seemed far more interesting and deucedly more mysterious than any of the crimes over which he philosophized.

Dick thought, moreover, that Miss Polly spent more of her leisure time now in that A.B.C. shop than she had done in his own company before, and told her so, with that delightful air of sheepish sulkiness which the male creature invariably wears when he feels jealous and will not admit it.

Polly liked Dick to be jealous, but she liked that old scarecrow in the A.B.C. shop very much, too, and though she made sundry vague promises from time to time to Mr. Richard Frobisher, she nevertheless drifted back instinctively day after day to the tea shop in Norfolk Street, Strand, and stayed there sipping coffee for as long as the man in the corner chose to talk.

On this particular afternoon she went to the A.B.C. shop with a fixed purpose, that of making him give her his views of Mrs. Owen's mysterious death in Percy Street.

The facts had interested and puzzled her. She had had countless arguments with Mr. Richard Frobisher as to the three great possible solutions of the puzzle—"Accident, Suicide, Murder?"

"Undoubtedly neither accident nor suicide," the old man said drily.

Polly was not aware that she had spoken. What an uncanny habit that creature had of reading her thoughts!

"You incline to the idea, then, that Mrs. Owen was murdered. Do you know by whom?"

He laughed, and drew forth the piece of string he always figeted with when unraveling some mystery.

153

"You would like to know who murdered that old woman?" he asked at last.

"I would like to hear your views on the subject," Polly replied.

"I have no views," he said. "No one can know who murdered the woman, since no one ever saw the person who did it. No one can give the faintest description of the mysterious man who alone could have committed that clever deed, and the police are playing a game of blind man's bluff."

"But you must have formed some theory of your own," she persisted.

It annoyed her that the funny creature was obstinate about this point, and she tried to nettle his vanity.

"I suppose that as a matter of fact your original remark that 'there are no such things as mysteries' does not apply universally. There is a mystery—that of the death in Percy Street—and you, like the police, are unable to fathom it."

He pulled up his eyebrows and looked at her for a minute or two.

"Confess that that murder was one of the cleverest bits of work accomplished outside Russian diplomacy," he said with a nervous laugh. "I must say that were I the judge, called upon to pronounce sentence of death on the man who conceived that murder, I could not bring myself to do it. I would politely request the gentleman to enter our Foreign Office—we have need of such men. The whole *mise en scène* was truly artistic, worthy of its milieu—the Rubens Studios in Percy Street, Tottenham Court Road.

"Have you ever noticed them? They are only studios by name, and are merely a set of rooms in a corner house, with the windows slightly enlarged, and the rents charged accordingly in consideration of that additional five inches of smoky daylight filtering through dusty windows. On the ground floor there is the order office of some stained-glass works, with a workshop in the rear, and on the first-floor landing a small room allotted to the caretaker, with gas, coal, and fifteen shillings a week, for which princely income she is deputed to keep tidy and clean the general aspect of the house.

"Mrs. Owen, who was the caretaker there, was a quiet,

respectable woman who eked out her scanty wages by sundry—mostly very meager—tips doled out to her by impecunious artists in exchange for promiscuous domestic services in and about the respective studios.

"But if Mrs. Owen's earnings were not large, they were very regular, and she had no fastidious tastes. She and her cockatoo lived on her wages, and all the tips added up and never spent year after year went to swell a very comfortable little account at interest in the Birkbeck Bank. This little account had mounted up to a very tidy sum and the thrifty widow, or old maid—no one ever knew which she was—was generally referred to by the young artists of the Rubens Studios as a 'lady of means.' But this is a digression.

"No one slept on the premises except Mrs. Owen and her cockatoo. The rule was that one by one as the tenants left their rooms in the evening, they took their respective keys to the caretaker's room. She would then, in the early morning, tidy and dust the studios and the office downstairs, lay the fire, and carry up coals.

"The foreman of the glass works was the first to arrive in the morning. He had a latchkey and let himself in, after which it was the custom of the house that he should leave the street door open for the benefit of the other tenants and their visitors.

"Usually when he came at about nine o'clock, he found Mrs. Owen busy about the house doing her work and he often had a brief chat with her about the weather, but on this particular morning of February second he neither saw nor heard her. However, as the shop had been tidied and the fire laid, he surmised that Mrs. Owen had finished her work earlier than usual and thought no more about it. One by one, the tenants of the studios turned up, and the day sped on without anyone's attention being drawn noticeably to the fact that the caretaker had not appeared upon the scene.

"It had been a bitterly cold night, and the day was even worse; a cutting northeasterly gale was blowing, there had been a great deal of snow during the night which lay quite thick on the ground, and at five o'clock in the afternoon, when the last glimmer of the pale winter daylight had disappeared, the confraternity of the brush put palette and easel aside and prepared to go home. The first to leave was Mr. Charles Pitt. He locked up his studio and, as usual, took his key into the caretaker's room.

"He had just opened the door when an icy blast literally struck him in the face; both the windows were wide open, and the snow and sleet were beating thickly into the room, forming already a white carpet upon the floor.

"The room was in semi-obscurity, and at first Mr. Pitt saw nothing, but instinctively realizing that something was wrong, he lit a match—and saw before him the spectacle of that awful and mysterious tragedy which has ever since puzzled both police and public. On the floor, already half covered by the drifting snow, lay the body of Mrs. Owen, face downward, in a nightgown, with feet and ankles bare, and these and her hands were of a deep purple color, while in a corner of the room, hunched up with the cold, the body of the cockatoo lay stark and stiff.

"At first there was only talk of a terrible accident, the result of some inexplicable carelessness which perhaps the evidence at the inquest would help to elucidate.

"Medical assistance came too late. The unfortunate woman was indeed dead, frozen to death, inside her own room. Further examination showed that she had received a severe blow at the back of the head, which must have stunned her and caused her to fall, helpless, beside the open window. Temperature at five degrees below zero had done the rest. Detective-Inspector Howell discovered close to the window a wrought-iron gas bracket, the height of which corresponded exactly with the bruise which was at the back of Mrs. Owen's head.

"Hardly, however, had a couple of days elapsed when public curiosity was whetted by a few startling headlines, such as the halfpenny evening papers alone know how to concoct.

" 'The mysterious death in Percy Street.' 'Is it Suicide or Murder?' 'Thrilling details—Strange developments.' 'Sensational Arrest.'

"What had happened was simply this:

"At the inquest, a few very curious facts connected with Mrs. Owen's life had come to light, and this had led to the apprehension of a young man of very respectable parentage on a charge of being concerned in the tragic death of the unfortunate caretaker.

"To begin with, it happened that her life, which in an ordinary way should have been very monotonous and regular, seemed, at any rate latterly, to have been more than usually checkered and excited. Every witness who had known her in the past concurred in the statement that since October last a great change had come over the worthy and honest woman.

"I happen to have a photo of Mrs. Owen as she was before this great change occurred in her quiet and uneventful life, and which led, as far as the poor soul was concerned, to such disastrous results.

"Here she is to the life," added the funny creature, placing the photo before Polly—"as respectable, as stodgy, as uninteresting as it is possible for a member of your charming sex to be; not a face, you will admit, to lead any youngster to temptation or to induce him to commit a crime.

"Nevertheless, one day all the tenants of the Rubens Studios were surprised and shocked to see Mrs. Owen, quiet, respectable Mrs. Owen, sallying forth at six o'clock in the afternoon, attired in an extravagant bonnet and a cloak trimmed with imitation astrakhan which—slightly open in front—displayed a gold locket and chain of astonishing proportions.

"Many were the comments, the hints, the bits of sarcasm leveled at the worthy woman by the frivolous confraternity of the brush.

"The plot thickened when from that day forth a complete change came over the worthy caretaker of the Rubens Studios. While she appeared day after day before the astonished gaze of the tenants and the scandalized looks of the neighbors, attired in new and extravagant dresses, her work was hopelessly neglected, and she was always 'out' when wanted.

"There was, of course, much talk and comment in various parts of the Rubens Studios on the subject of Mrs. Owen's 'dissipations.' The tenants began to put two and two together, and after a very little while the general consensus became firmly established that the honest caretaker's demoralization coincided week for week, almost day for day, with young Greenhill's establishment in Number Eight Studio.

"Everyone had remarked that he stayed much later in the evening than anyone else, and yet no one presumed that he stayed for purposes of work. Suspicions soon rose to certainty when Mrs. Owen and Arthur Greenhill were seen by one of the glass workmen dining together at Gambia's Restaurant in Tottenham Court Road.

"The workman, who was having a cup of tea at the counter, noticed particularly that when the bill was paid the money came out of Mrs. Owen's purse. The dinner had been sumptuous—veal cutlets, a cut from the joint, dessert, coffee, and liqueurs. Finally the pair left the restaurant, apparently very gay, young Greenhill smoking a choice cigar.

"Irregularities such as these were bound sooner or later to come to the ears and eyes of Mr. Allman, the landlord of the Rubens Studios, and a month after the New Year, without further warning, he gave her a week's notice to quit his house.

" 'Mrs. Owen did not seem the least bit upset when I gave her notice,' Mr. Allman declared in his evidence at the inquest; 'on the contrary, she told me that she had ample means, and had only worked recently for the sake of something to do. She added that she had plenty of friends who would look after her, for she had a nice little pile to leave to anyone who would know how to get the right side of her.'

"Nevertheless, in spite of this cheerful interview, Miss Bedford, the tenant of Number Six Studio, had stated that when she took her key to the caretaker's room at six-thirty that afternoon she found Mrs. Owen in tears. The caretaker refused to be comforted, nor would she speak of her trouble to Miss Bedford.

"Twenty-four hours later, she was found dead.

"The coroner's jury returned an open verdict, and Detective-Inspector Jones was charged by the police to make some inquiries about young Mr. Greenhill, whose intimacy with the unfortunate woman had been universally commented upon.

"The detective, however, pushed his investigations as far as the Birkbeck Bank. There he discovered that after her interview with Mr. Allman, Mrs. Owen had withdrawn what money she had on deposit, some eight hundred pounds, the result of twenty-five years' saving and thrift.

"But the immediate result of Detective-Inspector Jones's

labors was that Mr. Arthur Greenhill, lithographer, was brought before the magistrate at Bow Street on the charge of being concerned in the death of Mrs. Owen.

"Now, you know as well as I do how the attitude of the young prisoner impressed the magistrate and police so unfavorably that, with every new witness brought forward, his position became more and more unfortunate. Yet he was a good-looking, rather coarsely built young fellow, with one of those awful Cockney accents which literally make one jump. But he looked painfully nervous, stammered at every word spoken, and repeatedly gave answers entirely at random.

"His father acted as lawyer for him, a rough-looking elderly man, who had the appearance of a country attorney rather than of a London solicitor.

"The police had built up a fairly strong case against the lithographer. Medical evidence revealed nothing new: Mrs. Owen had died from exposure, the blow at the back of the head not being sufficiently serious to cause anything but temporary disablement. When the medical officer had been called in, death had intervened for some time; it was quite impossible to say how long, whether one hour or five or twelve.

"The appearance and state of the room, when the unfortunate woman was found by Mr. Charles Pitt, were again gone over in minute detail. Mrs. Owen's clothes, which she had worn during the day, were folded neatly on a chair. The key of her cupboard was in the pocket of her dress. The door had been slightly ajar, but both the windows were wide open. One of them, which had the sash-line broken, had been fastened up most scientifically with a piece of rope.

"Mrs. Owen had obviously undressed preparatory to going to bed and the magistrate very naturally soon made the remark how untenable the theory of an accident must be. No one in their five senses would undress with a temperature below zero and the windows wide open.

"After these preliminary statements, the cashier of the Birkbeck was called and he related the caretaker's visit at the bank.

" 'It was then about one o'clock,' he stated. 'Mrs. Owen called me and presented a check to self for eight hundred and twenty-seven pounds, the amount of her balance. She seemed exceed-

ingly happy and cheerful, and talked about needing plenty of
cash, as she was going abroad to join her nephew, for whom
she would in future keep house. I warned her about being
sufficiently careful with so large a sum and parting from it
injudiciously, as women of her class are very apt to do. She
laughingly declared that not only was she careful of it in the
present but meant to be so for the far-off future, for she
intended to go that very day to a lawyer's office and to make a
will.'

"The cashier's evidence was certainly startling in the extreme, since in the widow's room no trace of any kind was
found of any money. Against that, two of the notes handed over
by the bank to Mrs. Owen on that day were cashed by young
Greenhill on the very morning of her mysterious death. One
was handed in by him to the West End Clothiers Company in
payment for a suit of clothes and the other he changed at the
post office in Oxford Street.

"After that, all the evidence had of necessity to be gone
through again on the subject of young Greenhill's intimacy with
Mrs. Owen. He listened to it all with an air of the most painful
nervousness. His cheeks were positively green, his lips seemed
dry and parched, for he repeatedly passed his tongue over
them, and when Constable E 18 deposed that at two A.M. on the
morning of February second he had seen the accused and
spoken to him at the corner of Percy Street and Tottenham
Court Road, young Greenhill all but fainted.

"The contention of the police was that the caretaker had
been murdered and robbed during that night before she went
to bed, that young Greenhill had done the murder, seeing that
he was the only person known to have been intimate with the
woman, and that it was, moreover, proved unquestionably that
he was in the immediate neighborhood of the Rubens Studios
at an extraordinarily late hour of the night.

"His own account of himself, and of that same night, could
certainly not be called very satisfactory. Mrs. Owen was a
relative of his late brother, he declared. He himself was a
lithographer by trade, with a good deal of time and leisure on
his hands. He certainly had employed some of that time in
taking the old woman to various places of amusement. He had

on more than one occasion suggested that she should give up menial work and come and live with him, but unfortunately she was a great deal imposed upon by her nephew, a man of the name of Owen, who exploited the good-natured woman in every possible way and who had on more than one occasion made severe attacks upon her savings at the Birkbeck Bank.

"Severely cross-examined by the prosecuting counsel about this supposed relative of Mrs. Owen, Greenhill admitted that he did not know him—had, in fact, never seen him. He knew that his name was Owen, and that was all. His chief occupation consisted in sponging on the kind-hearted old woman, but he only went to see her in the evenings, when he presumably knew that she would be alone, and invariably after all the tenants of the Rubens Studios had left for the day.

"I don't know whether at this point it strikes you at all, as it did both magistrate and counsel, that there was a direct contradiction in this statement and the one made by the cashier of the Birbeck on the subject of his last conversation with Mrs. Owen. 'I am going abroad to join my nephew, for whom I am going to keep house' was what the unfortunate woman had said.

"Now Greenhill, in spite of his nervousness and at times contradictory answers, strictly adhered to his point, that there was a nephew in London who came frequently to see his aunt.

"Anyway, the savings of the murdered woman could not be taken as evidence in law. Mr. Greenhill senior put the objection, adding: 'There may have been two nephews,' which the magistrate and the prosecution were bound to admit.

"With regard to the night immediately preceding Mrs. Owen's death, Greenhill stated that he had been with her to the theater. Before he left her, at two A.M., she had of her own accord made him a present of ten pounds, saying: "I am a sort of aunt to you, Arthur, and if you don't have it, Bill is sure to get it.'

"She had seemed rather worried in the early part of the evening, but later on she cheered up.

" 'Did she speak at all about this nephew of hers or about her money affairs?' asked the magistrate.

"Again the young man hesitated, but said, 'No, she did not mention either Owen or her money affairs.'

"If I remember rightly," added the old man in the corner, "for recollect I was not present, the case was here adjourned. But the magistrate would not grant bail. Greenhill was removed looking more dead than alive—though everyone remarked that Mr. Greenhill senior looked determined and not the least worried. In the course of his examination on behalf of his son, of the medical officer and one or two other witnesses, he had very ably tried to confuse them on the subject of the hour at which Mrs. Owen was last known to be alive.

"He made a very great point of the fact that the usual morning's work was done throughout the house when the inmates arrived. Was it conceivable, he argued, that a woman would do that kind of work overnight, especially as she was going to the theater and therefore would wish to dress in her smarter clothes? It certainly was a very nice point leveled against the prosecution, who promptly retorted: Just as conceivable as that a woman in those circumstances of life should, having done her work, undress beside an open window at nine o'clock in the morning with the snow beating into the room.

"Now it seems that Mr. Greenhill senior could produce any amount of witnesses who could help to prove a conclusive alibi on behalf of his son, if only sometime subsequent to that fatal two A.M. the murdered woman had been seen alive by some chance passerby. Mr. Greenhill senior was an able man and an earnest one, and I fancy the magistrate felt some sympathy for his strenuous endeavors on his son's behalf. He granted a week's adjournment, which seemed to satisfy Mr. Greenhill completely.

"In the meanwhile, the papers had talked of and almost exhausted the subject of the mystery in Percy Street. There had been, as you no doubt know from personal experience, innumerable arguments on the puzzling alternatives:

"Accident?

"Suicide?

"Murder?

"A week went by, and then the case against young Greenhill was resumed. Of course the court was crowded. It needed no great penetration to remark at once that the prisoner looked more hopeful and his father quite elated.

"Again, a great deal of minor evidence was taken. And then came the turn of the defense. Mr. Greenhill called Mrs. Hall, confectioner, of Percy Street, opposite the Rubens Studios. She deposed that at eight o'clock in the morning of February second, while she was tidying her shop window she saw the caretaker of the Studios opposite, as usual, on her knees, her head and body wrapped in a shawl, cleaning her front steps. Her husband also saw Mrs. Owen, and Mrs. Hall remarked to her husband how thankful she was that her own shop had tiled steps, which did not need scrubbing on so cold a morning.

"Mr. Hall, confectioner, of the same address, corroborated this statement, and Mr. Greenhill, with absolute triumph, produced a third witness, Mrs. Martin, of Percy Street, who from her window on the second floor had at seven-thirty A.M. seen the caretaker shaking mats outside her front door. The description this witness gave of Mrs. Owen's getup, with the shawl around her head, coincided point by point with that given by Mr. and Mrs. Hall.

"After that, Mr. Greenhill's task became an easy one. His son was at home having his breakfast at eight o'clock that morning—not only himself but his servants would testify to that.

"The weather had been so bitter that the whole of that day young Greenhill had not stirred from his own fireside. Mrs. Owen was murdered after eight A.M. on that day, since she was seen alive by three people at that hour. Therefore his son could not have murdered Mrs. Owen. The police must find the criminal elsewhere, or else bow to the opinion originally expressed by the public that Mrs. Owen had met with a terrible untoward accident or that perhaps she may have wilfully sought her own death in that extraordinary and tragic fashion.

"Before young Greenhill was finally discharged one or two witnesses were again examined, chief among these being the foreman of the glassworks. He had turned up at Rubens Studios at nine o'clock and been in business all day. He averred positively that he did not especially notice any suspicious-looking individual crossing the hall that day. 'But,' he remarked with a smile, 'I don't sit and watch everyone who goes up and down the stairs. I am too busy for that. The street door is always left open. Anyone can walk in, up or down, who knows the way.'

"That there was a mystery in connection with Mrs. Owen's death, of that the police have remained perfectly convinced. Whether young Greenhill held the key of that mystery or not, they have never found out to this day.

"I could enlighten them as to the cause of the young lithographer's anxiety at the magisterial inquiry, but I assure you I do not care to do the work of the police for them. Why should I? Greenhill will never suffer from unjust suspicions. He and his father alone—besides myself—know in what a terribly tight corner he all but found himself.

"The young man did not reach home till nearly five o'clock that morning. His last train had gone. He had to walk, lost his way, and wandered about Hampstead for hours. Think what his position would have been if the worthy confectioners of Percy Street had not seen Mrs. Owen wrapped up in a shawl, on her knees, doing the front steps.

"Moreover, Mr. Greenhill senior is a solicitor who has a small office in John Street, Bedford Row. The afternoon before her death, Mrs. Owen had been to that office and had there made a will by which she left all her savings to young Arthur Greenhill, lithographer. Had that will been in other than paternal hands it would have been proved, in the natural course of such things, and one other link would have been added to the chain which nearly dragged Arthur Greenhill to the gallows—the link of a very strong motive.

"Can you wonder that the young man turned livid, until such time as it was proved beyond a doubt that the murdered woman was alive hours after he had reached the safe shelter of his home?

"I saw you smile when I used the word 'murdered,' " continued the old man in the corner, growing quite excited now that he was approaching the dénouement of his story. "I know that the public, satisfied to think that the mystery in Percy Street was a case of accident—or suicide."

"No," replied Polly, "there could be no question of suicide for two very distinct reasons."

He looked at her with some degree of astonishment. She

supposed that he was amazed at her venturing to form an opinion of her own.

"And may I ask what, in your opinion, these reasons are?" he asked very sarcastically.

"To begin with, the question of money," she said. "Has any more of it been traced so far?"

"Not another five-pound note," he said with a chuckle. "They were all cashed in Paris during the Exhibition, and you have no conception how easy a thing that is to do at any of the hotels or smaller agents de change."

"That nephew was a clever blackguard," she commented.

"You believe, then, in the existence of that nephew?"

"Why should I doubt it? Someone must have existed who was sufficiently familiar with the house to go about in it in the middle of the day without attracting anyone's attention."

"In the middle of the day?" he said with a chuckle.

"Any time after eight-thirty in the morning."

"So you, too, believe in the 'caretaker, wrapped up in a shawl,' cleaning her front steps?" he queried.

"But—"

"It never struck you, in spite of the training your interviews with me must have given you, that the person who carefully did all the work in the Rubens Studios, laid the fires, and carried up the coals merely did it in order to gain time—in order that the bitter frost might really and effectually do its work and Mrs. Owen not be missed until she was truly dead?"

"But—" suggested Polly again.

"It never struck you that one of the greatest secrets of successful crime is to lead the police astray with regard to the *time* when the crime was committed.

"In this case the 'nephew,' since we admit his existence, would—even if he were ever found, which is doubtful—be able to prove as good an alibi as young Greenhill."

"But I don't understand—"

"How the murder was committed?" he said eagerly. "Surely you can see it all for yourself, since you admit the 'nephew'—a scamp, perhaps—who sponges on the good-natured woman. He terrorizes and threatens her, so much so that she fancies her money is no longer safe even in the Birbeck Bank. Women of

that class are apt at times to mistrust the Bank of England.
Anyway, she withdraws her money. Who knows what she meant
to do with it in the immediate future?

"In any case, she wishes to give it after her death to a young
man whom she likes, and who has known how to win her good
graces. That afternoon the nephew begs for more money. They
have a row. The poor woman is in tears and is only temporarily
consoled by a pleasant visit at the theater.

"At two o'clock in the morning, young Greenhill parts from
her. Two minutes later the nephew knocks at the door. He
comes with a plausible tale of having missed his last train and
asks for 'a shake down' somewhere in the house. The good-
natured woman suggests a sofa in one of the studios and then
quietly prepares to go to bed. The rest is very simple and
elementary. The nephew sneaks into his aunt's room, finds her
standing in her nightgown; he demands money with threats of
violence. Terrified, she staggers, knocks her head against the gas
bracket, and falls on the floor stunned while the nephew seeks
for her keys and takes possession of the eight-hundred-odd
pounds. You will admit that the subsequent *mise en scène* is
worthy of a genius.

"No struggle, not the usual hideous accessories 'round a
crime. Only the open windows, the bitter northeasterly gale,
and the heavily falling snow—two silent accomplices, as silent
as the dead.

"After that the murderer, with perfect presence of mind,
busies himself in the house, doing the work which will insure
that Mrs. Owen shall not be missed—at any rate, for some time.
He dusts and tidies; some few hours later he even slips on his
aunt's skirt and bodice, wraps his head in a shawl, and boldly
allows those neighbors who are astir to see what they believe
to be Mrs. Owen. Then he goes back to her room, resumes his
normal appearance, and quietly leaves the house."

"He may have been seen."

"He undoubtedly *was* seen by two or three people, but no
one thought anything of seeing a man leave the house at that
hour. It was very cold, the snow was falling thickly, and as he
wore a muffler 'round the lower part of his face, those who saw
him would not undertake to know him again."

"That man was never seen nor heard of again?" Polly asked.

"He has disappeared off the face of the earth. The police are searching for him, and perhaps someday they will find him—then society will be rid of one of the most ingenious men of the age."

The old man had paused, absorbed in meditation. The young girl was silent. Some memory too vague as yet to take a definite form was persistently haunting her; one thought was hammering away in her brain, and playing havoc with her nerves. That thought was the inexplicable feeling within her that there was something in connection with that hideous crime which she ought to recollect, something which—if she could only remember what it was—would give her the clue to the tragic mystery and for once insure her triumph over this self-conceited and sarcastic scarecrow in the corner.

He was watching her through his great bone-rimmed spectacles, and she could see the knuckles of his bony hands, just above the top of the table, fidgeting, fidgeting, fidgeting, till she wondered if there existed another set of fingers in the world which would undo the knots his lean ones made in that tiresome piece of string.

Then suddenly—apropos of nothing, Polly *remembered*—the whole thing stood before her, short and clear like a vivid flash of lightning. Mrs. Owen lying dead in the snow beside her open window, one of them with a broken sash-line tied up most scientifically with a piece of string. She remembered the talk there had been at the time about this improvised sash-line.

That was after young Greenhill had been discharged and the question of suicide had been voted out.

Polly remembered that in the illustrated papers, photographs appeared of this wonderfully knotted piece of string, so contrived that the weight of the frame could but tighten the knots and thus keep the window open. She remembered that people deduced many things from that improvised sash-line, chief among these deductions being that the murderer was a sailor—so wonderful, so complicated, so numerous were the knots which secured that window-frame.

But Polly knew better. In her mind's eye she saw those fingers, rendered doubly nervous by the fearful cerebral excitement, grasping at first mechanically, even thoughtlessly, a bit of twine with which to secure the window; then the ruling habit strongest through all, the girl could see it—the lean and ingenious fingers fidgeting, fidgeting with that piece of string, tying knot after knot, more wonderful, more complicated than any she had yet witnessed.

"If I were you," she said, without daring to look into that corner where he sat, "I would break myself of the habit of perpetually making knots in a piece of string."

He did not reply, and at last Polly ventured to look up. The corner was empty, and through the glass door beyond the desk where he had just deposited his few coppers, she saw the tails of his tweed coat, his extraordinary hat, his meager, shriveled-up personality fast disappearing down the street.

Miss Polly Burton (of the *Evening Observer*) was married the other day to Mr. Richard Frobisher (of the *London Mail*). She has never set eyes on the old man in the corner from that day to this.

DAVID MORRELL

THE GOOD TIMES ALWAYS END

I knew she'd blame me, but I couldn't very well stand by and let the cops go in. Their uniforms, their badges and their guns—they would have scared her. This way, hearing it from me, she might go willingly, though with reluctance. She might realize she had no choice. She'd have a chance to leave with dignity.

The house had been her absolute domain for sixty years. She'd moved in at the age of twenty on the day she was married. She had given birth to each of us six children there. She'd raised us there. She'd seen my dad, her husband, die there.

Now she planned to die there, too. She'd always said that. The old homestead with its memories was all that really mattered to her. It embodied her whole life's achievement, everything she had ever worked for. She was proud that she had lived to eighty, proud that she could still maintain the property. Without that house, its every splinter intimate to her, without the farm, its every field and orchard one with her, she had no goal, no meaning.

Though I wasn't there the day she got the letter from the county, I heard how she phoned the planner who had signed the letter. He explained politely why the county had to build that road.

"We'll pay you market price," the planner said. "The farm. The house. You'll make a lot of money."

"I don't need the money. Go around me."

"Mrs. Wade, the square-foot cost of asphalt . . . If we curve the road, that's too expensive."

"I don't care. I'm *staying.*"

"Mrs. Wade, that isn't possible."

The planner must have had a premonition, must have sensed the trouble coming, when he heard the strength behind that brittle, feeble voice.

"The day I leave is when I die," Mom said. "You'll have to take me out feet first."

"The road—"

"Goes over my dead body."

I'll say this to give the planner credit. He went out there to the farm. He tried to do the decent thing by facing her instead of sending her another letter. He knocked bravely on the door, and when she opened it, he introduced himself.

I have to give my mother credit, too. She wasn't going to let some nice young man sweet-talk her. She slammed the door on him.

The planner later told me that he stood outside for half an hour, talking to the door. He knew she was listening from somewhere in the house while he explained about the law, about the county's right to buy up any property it needed in the name of progress. Sure, to move would inconvenience her, he said. He sympathized. But she'd be justly compensated, and the county's needs were more important than one person's inconvenience.

Still, he never got an answer, and he finally turned to other matters that required his attention. I'm not sure if he forgot about her, or if he naturally assumed she at last would see the sense of his position. When construction started, he was overwhelmed by final details, and I knew he never counted on Mom's lawyer showing up to threaten lawsuits, staying orders, and petitions to the county board.

"You mean she isn't gone?" the planner said, dismayed.

"My client totally refuses."

So of course the planner sent the sheriff out to scare her. An eviction notice through the mail was one thing, but delivered in person by a man in uniform, that clearly had more force.

My mother tore up the formal-looking document. She slammed the door. The sheriff gave her seven days.

The rest I'm sure you heard on radio or saw on television or at least read in the paper. Senior Citizen Takes On County. Aging Woman Claims Harassment. Widow Says Old Folks Described As Inconvenient. There were letters to the editor and arguments in county council, not to mention the indignant midnight phone calls waking up that planner. Sometimes pressure makes officials bend, and sometimes it makes them rigid. If there ever was a chance for compromise, it ended on the day the planner went to see her one last time and faced the double barrel of her shotgun.

All the while I kept in touch with her. My wife, two kids, and I have a house in town. I need two jobs, repairing cars from eight to five, then tending bar at night, to meet the payments on the house. But after all, I had one brother killed in Vietnam, another killed drunk-driving. My three sisters married and moved away. Mom had just me to watch over her, so I found time to phone her every day. I went there often, and I brought her into town to do her shopping or to go to church, so I kept up with all her news—how they were crazy if they thought she'd leave that house, how she would make them sorry if they tried to force her out.

I couldn't argue with her. Mom's word has always been the law. To tell the truth, the last year she'd been doing poorly, and this trouble seemed to liven her, to make her feisty once again. I liked the angry sparkle in her eyes.

I tried my best to help her, but it wasn't any use. The planner read me costs and schedules. I began to see that she was bound to lose. So since she hadn't made arrangements, without telling her I rented an apartment for her, close to where we lived. But every time I went to visit her, I saw dustclouds in the distance where the new road kept on stalking the house.

I knew that Wednesday was her deadline, so I took off work and drove out early, and the cops were there already with two squad cars and an ambulance. The biggest Caterpillar I had ever seen was pushing at the barn. The trucks and workmen waited. Earth removers rumbled, tearing through the cornfield, gouging deep rich topsoil.

Then the barn, its square nails screeching, toppled.

I turned, stunned, to where the planner stood grimly beside his car. I must have glared, because he quickly glanced the other way.

I walked up to the cops. And these weren't city cops. These were state cops, great big hulking brutes.

"Why the hell the ambulance?" I said.

"In case."

"In case of what?"

"Well, she might faint or something. Old the way she is, we want to make sure we take care of her. We want to show we're looking out for her."

I don't know how I missed the two reporters and the television news crew. Now I saw them, and I understood. With the publicity, the cops were trying to look good. And even so, I could imagine how this thing would look, these massive cops, my shrunken mother struggling in their arms (I knew for sure she wouldn't walk) as they evicted her.

The cops seemed nervous, glancing toward the news crew.

"Never mind. I'll bring her out," I said.

I saw relief spread over their faces.

"It's our job," one said, but it was obvious he wanted me to argue.

"She's my mother. Save your strength for writing traffic tickets."

Lord, their guns, their badges, they would scare her half to death.

So I just shook my head from side to side disgustedly and started toward the house.

It's funny. I'd been born and raised there, but since I had moved away, the house seemed foreign to me. Until now. I guess because this was the last time I would ever see it, I remembered all the good years I had spent out here. Its plain two stories and attic needed paint. Its simple porch could use a few new boards. But it was home. It was my youth. And as I turned the doorknob, I felt sadness—for my mother, for myself. The good times always end.

I stared back to that planner, to those cops, and I went in.

There was a narrow hallway first, where in the winter we had hung our coats and lined up all our boots. I saw the hooks on the bare wood wall. I saw the worn path on the wooden floor. For one brief instant, as my throat swelled shut, I thought I heard us laughing as we went in for our supper. Then I snapped back to the present with the sound of earth removers roaring, and I forced myself to go through with this awful business.

Out of habit I had shut the door behind me. I walked along the hall and reached the second door, the one that led to the front rooms of the house. But it was open slightly, which was not at all Mom's habit, and I frowned, not understanding. Then I pushed the door and stepped inside, and that was when the object struck me on the shoulder, hard and heavy, so surprising that I finched and groaned.

I rubbed my shoulder, peering down to where the thing had thudded loudly on the floor. I saw an iron, not a modern one, instead the old kind, black and solid, five pounds of metal. Mom preferred it. She would set it on the cook stove till it sizzled if she spat on it.

Sure, I thought. That's why the door was slightly open. Mom had balanced that big heavy iron up there so that someone coming in would have it fall on him. I was thankful I had closed the outside door. Those state policemen wouldn't have appreciated seeing the surprise that Mom had waiting for them.

But I wasn't injured badly. In a way, the iron was pathetic— Mom's last feeble effort to defend her home against invaders.

Now I shut the second door. The place was dark. The drapes were closed. I flicked the light switch, and I touched the water just before I felt the shock. The current jolted. Something flashed. I stumbled backward in the darkness, clutching at my hand, and snagged my foot against the wire Mom had stretched tautly across the floor.

I fell. My head cracked on a sharp-edge crate that Mom had placed strategically. I groaned again. The rumbling earth removers now seemed muffled by the ringing in my head.

I don't think I passed out, but I was dazed. I touched my head and felt the swelling and the sticky warmth of blood. In shock and anger I stood up slowly.

"Dammit, Mom, it's Charlie!"

Then I felt a nagging guilt. Mom never tolerated swearing. I tried hard to get control.

"Hey, Mom, it's me," I said, now calmly. "Tell me where you are."

She didn't answer. I was frightened. Not for me. For her. I don't know much about the law, but I suspected that these traps could be interpreted as criminal assault, as evidence she was not in her right mind. Despite her motives and her age, if anyone found out what she had done, she could be sent to jail or to a mental institution.

In the dark I couldn't find her, but I didn't trust the light switch, so I groped across the living room to reach the drapes. I barked my shins against a tea wagon, and I stumbled past a footstool.

Then I yanked the drapes and felt as if I'd grabbed a nest of hornets. Burning. Stinging. Fierce, hot, stabbing points of pain in both my hands. I screamed, fell, and struck my head again. I was now cursing in earnest. Never mind Mom's disapproval. This had gone too far.

But then I feared they had heard me outside. Favoring my tingling, bloody hands, I struggled to my feet and warily approached the drapes. I gently touched their edges.

Needles. She'd pushed needles through the edges, hundreds of them, all along both sides, their sharp points sticking out to harm any intruder. She'd anticipated every movement those policemen would have made. She was ahead of them, but Lord, how many other traps like this were set throughout the house?

I tugged the safest portion of the drapes. They fell and nearly smothered me. But this time I'd been clever. I had stepped back as I pulled. I saw the brilliant, welcome light. I blinked, trembled with relief. I saw the planner and the cops beside their cars outside the gate, and they did not appear alarmed, so I assumed they hadn't heard my scream.

But they were squinting toward me. They looked bored, preoccupied by the thought of other things they had to do. They wouldn't wait much longer. Soon they'd come in here to ask what made me take so long.

I waved to them and turned away. My heart was pounding.

"Mom, you've got to stop this! They can't find out what you planned for them!"

I waited, but she didn't answer. In the silent, muffled house I heard the roaring of the Caterpillar as it crunched across the parched boards of the fallen barn.

"We don't have time, Mom! Tell me where you are!"

I had to search for her. But if I didn't cut off all her exits, she might sneak from place to place until the cops came in to end this hide and seek. I had to do this systematically. The basement, then the kitchen, next to the living room, the sewing room, and finally upstairs. That way I knew for sure that she was not behind me.

As I heard the earth removers rumble, I hurried to the kitchen, past the pantry and the cupboards to the cellar door beside the stainless double sink that I'd installed for her when the original, old stone one finally had cracked apart. I vividly remembered how there'd used to be a bulky, squeaky hand-pump by the sink before the well went dry one blazing summer.

Then I heard three sharp blasts from a car's horn outside. No doubt the police and that planner were getting anxious. And my headache chased my reverie. I yanked the cellar door. It didn't open, and my wrist took all the pressure, jolting.

She had locked the cellar door.

I bit my lip. One needle-punctured hand spread blood on my throbbing wrist. I felt my face go pale.

"Unlock the door, Mom! Hey, it's me, Charlie! Look, I know you're down there!"

No reply. I heard three more horn blasts outside, and I knew I'd have to break the door down. Since the hinges faced the kitchen, all I needed was a hammer and a chisel.

In the top drawer of the cupboard by the stove. I yanked it open.

Tools fell through the unsupported bottom, slamming on my foot. I bumped against the kitchen table.

Once again she had outsmarted me, anticipating my next move. I fumbled for the hammer and the chisel. In two minutes I had knocked the final hinge-pin out. I pulled and heaved, and this time I was ready. As the door scraped free, I braced myself and stopped it from collapsing on me.

The cellar stairs led to a landing and a door that opened to the outside. The shadows thickened as I started down. I tried the door, and it was locked. The stairs turned left. I faced the pitch-black basement. Groping carefully along a shelf, I found the flashlight where it had always been kept. Had she forgotten it was on that shelf?

I aimed the flashlight toward the stairs, but they seemed normal. No sawed boards. No gaps along the railing. I crept down. I saw the furnace and the shelves of canning and the old-time wringer washer. I had told her I would buy a new washing machine for her. She'd insisted, though, that she preferred to do the wash the way she always had. I smelled the must, the dank moist mildew, like the bitter, fetid loam of old potatoes.

But I didn't see my mother. Was she crouched behind the furnace? Earlier I'd thought of hide and seek, and now I almost shouted, "Mom, I see you! Might as well come out!"

My footsteps scraped on the rough wood stairs. I thought I heard a scratch behind the washer, and I swung the flashlight, rushing down.

The stairs gave way. I screamed and dropped, my stomach rising in the darkness. As the flashlight fell and broke, my chin struck hard on a board. I hit the stone-cold floor. I couldn't breathe. I struggled as the pain raced through my body.

I had scanned the stairs, and they'd seemed normal. Now I rubbed my hand along a broken board and felt where she had sawed it. Not on top where I could have seen it. Underneath. She'd come down beneath the stairs and sawed them from below.

My fall could easily have snapped my neck or cracked my head and killed me. If those cops found out . . . This was worse than criminal assault. She'd been prepared to kill them. They could charge her with attempted murder.

Oh, my God, I've got to find her, get her out of here before . . . and that was probably my last clear thought. My pain-wracked body trembled uncontrollably. Shock had made me weak, delirious.

I left a trail of blood as, hobbling, moaning, I searched through the basement and then every upstairs room. I do recall more horn blasts from outside, a few shouts, but I was so confused by then that all I wanted was to win the game. I suddenly was six years old. I had to find my mother.

"I don't want to be alone," I wept and pulled the attic door. A bureau fell on me. But my pain had reached its zenith, soaring toward a nightmare state of senselessness, confusion. I crawled slowly from beneath the bureau and headed for the attic.

"Mom," I sobbed. "Don't hid on me. I'm frightened."

It seemed only yesterday when I had played up here among

the clothes trees and the dress forms and the moldy cardboard boxes filled with patterns, scraps, and outworn clothes. I used to try on my father's trousers up here, and I used to make believe that I was in a pirate's cave.

I crisscrossed aimlessly among the litter, tasting dust and wiping cobwebs from my face. I didn't find her.

There was only one last hiding spot. The crawlspace at the far end, underneath the eaves. I'd played there often. It was cramped and dark, a den where I had fought off Indians and stagecoach robbers, Dracula and Martians. I crept gratefully, approaching it. The low half-hidden door loomed closer, larger.

I clawed at the wooden latch.

I blinked, startled, at the double barrel of a shotgun pointed at my eyes. "No, don't Mom. Please. It's Charlie."

Click. I heard one hammer snicking back.

"No, please, Mom."

Click. The other hammer.

Swaying on my knees, I didn't have the energy to duck or run or try to hide. I just kept gaping toward the barrels.

I had hunted her, and having found her, I had lost.

The feeble, thin, frail voice came disembodied from the darkness of the crawlspace.

"Charlie?"

She was hesitant. Her voice was filled with disbelief. "Is that you, Charlie?"

"Mom, don't hurt me."

"You're supposed to be in school."

"I didn't go, Mom. I played hooky."

"When your father hears about this, he'll—you're hurt, son. What's the matter with you?"

"I was in an accident."

"Your face, your hands, your clothes! Dear Lord, I have to get some bandages! The blood!"

"I need a doctor. There's an ambulance outside."

She didn't even ask me why the ambulance was out there. She was in another time. I heard the hammers click down on the shotgun. She was groping out. I saw the rips on her own clothes and the blood on her, evidence of her own desperate effort to arrange her fierce surprises. She was hugging me,

wiping my tears. She raised her dress to swab the blood on my
face.

Then she was helping me to stand, but I was so disabled,
bleary, that I had to lean against her. In the end it wasn't me
who took her out. It was she who took me out.

We faced the blinding sunlight and the roar of heavy road
equipment. The policemen and the planner raced in through
the gate.

"My God, what happened to you?" one policeman asked,
alarmed.

But I was babbling, sinking to my knees.

"Why, any fool can see he's hurt," my mother told them with
indignant rage. "Don't stand there looking stupid. Help me get
him to the ambulance."

The two attendants had already grabbed a stretcher, rushing
toward me with their white coats flapping.

But I fainted, and the next thing I remember, I was on my
back inside the ambulance. Its siren wailed. The ambulance was
jolting down the dirt road to the back way into town.

I saw the bandages that the attendants were preparing and
the intravenous they had stuck into my arm. I saw my mother
crouched beside me, wiping my brow.

"That road equipment," Mom was saying, puzzled. "What's it
doing on our farm? Your father will be angry."

"Mom, it's a long story," I said weakly.

My last conscious thought was that the Caterpillar would by
now have pushed the house down, that the evidence of her
attempt to murder would have been destroyed. When I was
well, I knew I'd be able to control her, that in time she'd learn
to like the place I had rented for her. In the meanwhile, I had
done my duty. I had been my mother's loyal son. Through
swollen lips I tried to grin. Then I drifted and couldn't even
hear the siren's wail.

PETE HAMILL

THE MEN IN BLACK RAINCOATS

It was close to midnight on a Friday evening at Rattigan's Bar and Grill. There were no ball games on the television, old movies only made the clientele feel more ancient, and the jukebox was still broken from the afternoon of Red Cioffi's daughter's wedding. So it was time for Brendan Malachy Mc-Cone to take center stage. He motioned for a fresh beer, put his right foot on the brass rail, breathed in deeply, and started to sing.

> Oh, the Garden of Eden has vanished, they say,
> But I know the lie of it still,
> Just turn to the left at the bridge of Finaghy,
> And meet me halfway to Coote Hill . . .

The song was very Irish, sly and funny, the choruses full of the names of long-forgotten places, and the regulars loved Brendan for the quicky jaunty singing of it. They loved the roguish glitter in his eyes, his energy, his good-natured boasting. He was, after all, a man in his fifties now, and yet here he was, still singing the bold songs of his youth. And on this night, as on so many nights, they joined him in the verses.

> The boy is a man now,
> He's toil-worn, he's tough,
> He whispers, "Come over the sea,"
> Come back, Patty Reilly, to Bally James Duff,
> Ah, come back, Patty Reilly, to me . . .

Outside, rain had begun to fall, a cold Brooklyn rain, driven by the wind off the harbor, and it made the noises and the

179

singing and the laughter seem even better. Sardines and crack-
ers joined the glasses on the bar. George the bartender filled
the empties. And Brendan shifted from jauntiness to sorrow.

If you ever go across the sea to Ireland,
Then maybe at the closing of your day . . .

The mood of the regulars hushed now as Brendan gave them
the song as if it were a hymn. The bar was charged with the
feeling they all had for Brendan, knowing he had been an IRA
man long ago, that he had left Ireland a step ahead of the British
police who wanted him for the killing of a British soldier in the
Border Campaign. This was their Brendan: the Transit Authority
clerk who had once stood in the doorways of Belfast with the
cloth cap pulled tight on his brow, the pistol deep in the
pockets of the trenchcoat, ready to kill or to die for Ireland.

Oh, the strangers came and tried to teach us their ways,
And scorned us just for being what we are . . .

The voice was a healthy baritone, a wealth of passion over-
wheming a poverty of skill, and it touched all of them, making
the younger ones imagine the streets of Belfast today where
their cousins were still fighting, reminding the older ones of
peat fires, black creamy stout, buttermilk in the morning. The
song was about a vanished time, before rock and roll and
women's liberation, before they took Latin out of the Mass,
before the blacks and the Puerto Ricans had begun to move in
and the children of the Irish had begun to move out. The
neighborhood was changing, all right. But Brendan Malachy
McCone was still with them.

A little after midnight two strangers came in, dressed in black
raincoats. They were wet with the rain. They ordered whiskey.
Brendan kept singing. Nobody noticed that his voice faltered
on the last lines of *Galway Bay,* as he took the applause, glanced
at the strangers, and again shifted the mood.

Oh, Mister Patrick McGinty.
An Irishman of note,

He fell into a fortune—and
He bought himself a goat . . .

The strangers drank in silence.

At closing time the rain was still pelting down. Brendan stood in the open doorway of the bar with Charlie the Pole and Scotch Eddie, while George the bartender counted the receipts. Everyone else had gone home.

"We'll have to make a run for it," Charlie said.

"Dammit," Scotch Eddie said.

"Yiz might as well run, cause yiz'll drown anyway," George said. He was finished counting and looked small and tired.

"I'll see you gents," Charlie said, and rushed into the rain, running lumpily down the darkened slope of Eleventh Street to his home. Eddie followed, cutting sharply to his left. But Brendan didn't move. He had seen the strangers in the black raincoats, watched them in the mirror for a while as he moved through the songs, saw them leave an hour later. And now he was afraid.

He looked up and down the avenue. The streetlamp scalloped a halo of light on the corner. Beyond the light there was nothing but the luminous darkness and the rain.

"Well, I've got to lock it up, Brendan."

"Right, George. Good night."

"God bless."

Brendan hurried up the street, head down, lashed by the rain, eyes searching the interiors of parked cars. He saw nothing. The cars were locked. He looked up at the apartments and there were no lights anywhere and he knew the lights would be out at home, too, where Sarah and the kids would all be sleeping. Even the firehouse was dimly lit, its great red door closed, the firemen streched out on their bunks in the upstairs loft.

Despite the drink and the rain, Brendan's mouth was dry. Once he thought he saw something move in the darkness of an areaway and his stomach lifted and fell. But again it was nothing. Shadows. Imagination. Get hold of yourself, Brendan.

He crossed the avenue. A half block to go. Away off he saw the twin red taillights of a city bus, groaning slowly toward Flatbush Avenue. Hurry. Another half block and he could enter the yard, hurry up the stairs, unlock the door, close it behind him, undress quickly in the darkened kitchen, dry off the rain with a warm rough towel, brush the beer off his teeth, and fall into the great deep warmth of bed with Sarah. And he would be safe again for another night. Hurry. Get the key out. Don't get caught naked on the stairs.

He turned into his yard, stepped over a spreading puddle at the base of the stoop, and hurried up the eight worn sandstone steps. He had the key out in the vestibule and quickly opened the inside door.

They were waiting for him in the hall.

The one in the front seat on the right was clearly the boss. The driver was only a chauffeur and did his work in proper silence. The strangers in the raincoats sat on either side of Brendan in the back seat and said nothing as the car moved through the wet darkness, down off the slope, into the Puerto Rican neighborhood near Williamsburg. They all clearly deferred to the one in the front seat right. All wore gloves. Except the boss.

"I'm telling you, this has to be some kind of mistake, Brendan said.

"Shut up," said the boss, without turning. His skin was pink in the light of the streetlamps, and dark hair curled over th edge of his collar. The accent was not New York. Maybe Boston. Maybe somewhere else. Not New York.

"I don't owe anybody money," Brendan said, choking back the dry panic. "I'm not into the bloody loan sharks. I'm telling you, this is—"

The boss said, "Is your name Brendan Malachy McCone?"

"Well, uh, yes, but—"

"Then we've made no mistake."

Williamsburg was behind them now and they were following the route of the Brooklyn-Queens Expressway while avoiding its brightly lit ramp. Brendan sat back. From that angle he could see more of the man in the front seat right—the velvet collar of his coat, the high protruding cheekbones, the longish nose, the pinkie ring glittering on his left hand when he lit a cigarette with a thin gold lighter. He could not see the man's eyes but he was certain he had never seen the man before tonight.

"Where are you taking me?"

The boss said calmly, "I told you to shut up. Shut up."

Brendan took a deep breath, and then let it out slowly. He looked to the men on either side of him, smiling his most innocent smile, as if hoping they would think well of him, believe in his innocence, intervene with the boss, plead his case. He wanted to tell them about his kids, explain that he had done nothing bad. Not for thirty years.

The men looked away from him, their nostrils seeming to quiver, as if he had already begun to stink of death. Brendan tried to remember the words of the Act of Contrition.

The men beside him stared out past the little rivers of rain on the windows, as if he were not even in the car. They watched the city turn into country, Queens into Nassau County, all the sleeping suburbs transform into the darker, emptier reaches of Suffolk County, as the driver pushed on, driving farther away, out to Long Island, to the country of forests and frozen summer beaches. Far from Brooklyn. Far from the Friday nights at Rattigan's. Far from his children. Far from Sarah.

Until they pulled off the expressway at Southampton, moved down back roads for another fifteen minutes, and came to a marshy cove. A few summer houses were sealed for the winter. Rain spattered the still water of the cove. Patches of dirty snow clung to the shoreline, resisting the steady cold rain.

"This is fine," the boss said.

The driver pulled over, turned out the car lights, and turned off the engine. They all sat in the dark.

The boss said, "Did you ever hear of a man named Peter Devlin?"

Oh, my God, Brendan thought.

"Well?"

"Vaguely. The name sounds familiar."

"Just familiar?"

"Well, there was a Devlin where I came from. There were a lot of Devlins in the North. It's hard to remember. It was a long time ago."

"Yeah, it was. It was a long time ago."

"Aye."

"And you don't remember him more than just vaguely? Well, isn't that nice? I mean, you *were* best man at his wedding."

Brendan's lips moved, but no words came out.

"What else do you vaguely remember, McCone?"

There was a long pause. Then: "He died."

"No, not *died.* He was killed, wasn't he?"

"Aye."

"Who killed him, McCone?"

"He died for Ireland."

"Who *killed* him, McCone?"

"The Special Branch. The British Special Branch."

The boss took out his cigarettes and lit one with the gold lighter. He took a long drag. Brendan saw the muscles working tensely in his jaw. The rain drummed on the roof of the car.

"Tell me some more about him."

"They buried him with full military honors. They draped his coffin with the Tricolor and sang *The Soldier's Song* over his grave. The whole town wore the Easter Lily. The B-Specials made a lot of arrests."

"You saw all this?"

"I was told."

"But you weren't there?"

"No, but—"

"What happened to his wife?"

"Katey?"

"Some people called her Katey," the boss said.

"She died too, soon after—the flu, was it?"

"Well, there was another version. That she died of a broken heart."

The boss stared staright ahead, watching the rain trickle down the windshield. He tapped an ash into the ashtry, took another deep drag, and said, "What did they pay you to set him up, Brendan?"

He called me Brendan. He's softening. Even a gunman can understand it was all long ago.

"What do you mean?"

"Don't play games, Brendan. Everyone in the North knew you set him up. The British told them."

"It was a long time ago, Mister. There were a lot of lies told. You can't believe every—"

The boss wasn't really listening. He took out his pack of cigarettes, flipped one higher than the others, gripped its filter in his teeth, and lit it with the butt of the other. Then he tamped out the first cigarette in the ashtray. He looked out past the rain to the darkness of the cove."

"Shoot him," he said.

The man on Brendan's left opened the door a foot.

"Oh, sweet sufferin' Jesus, Mister," Brendan said. "I've got five kids. They're all at home. One of them is making her first Communion. Please. For the love of God. If Dublin Command has told you to get me, just tell them you couldn't find me. Tell them I'm dead. I can get you a piece of paper. From one of the polticians. Sayin' I'm dead. Yes. That's a way. And I'll just vanish. Just disappear. Please. I'm an old man now. I won't live much bloody longer. But the weans. The weans, Mister. And it was all thirty years ago. Christ knows I've paid for it. Please. Please."

The tears were blurring his vision now. He could hear the hard spatter of the rain through the open car door. He felt the man on his right move slightly and remove something from inside his coat.

The boss said, "You left out a few things, Brendan."

"I can send all my earnings to the lads. God knows they can use it in the North now. I've sent money already, I have, to the Provisionals. I never stopped being for them. For a United Ireland. Never stopped. I can have the weans work for the cause. I'll get a second job. My Sarah can go out and work, too. Jesus, Mister—"

"Katey Devlin didn't die of the flu," the boss said. "And she didn't die of a broken heart. Did she, Brendan?"

"I don't—"

"Katey Devlin killed herself. Didn't she?"

Brendan felt his stomach turn over.

The boss said, very quietly, "She loved Peter Devlin more than life itself. She didn't want him to die."

"But neither does Sarah want *me* to die. She's got the weans, the feedin' of them, and the clothin' of them, and the schoolin' of them to think of. Good God, man, have ye no mercy? I was a boy then. My own people were starvin'. We had no land, we were renters, we were city people, not farmers, and the war was on, and—They told me they would only arrest him. Intern him for the duration and let him out when the fightin' stopped. And they told me the IRA would take care of Kate while he was inside. Please, Mister, I've got five kids. Peter Devlin only had *two*."

"I know," said the man in the front seat right. "I was one of them."

For the first time he turned completely around. His eyes were a cold blue under the shock of curly dark hair. Kate's eyes in Peter's face. He stared at Brendan for a moment. He took another drag on the cigarette and let the smoke drift through his nose, creating lazy trails of grey in the crowded car.

"Shoot him," he said.

The man on his left touched Brendan's hand and opened the door wide.

MARJORIE CARLETON

MONDAY IS A QUIET PLACE

Emily went through the narrow outer closet dedicated to stationery, church bulletins, and the like, and, yanking open the inner door, propped it ajar with a shoulder. If it slammed shut, it stuck, and already the knob was loose from repeated tuggings. She hung her sweater at a decorous distance from Mr. Sanders' robes and then emerged hastily, for the janitor had been heavy-handed with the moth spray. Some of the reek followed her into the study, but the excellent ventilation would take care of it shortly.

She sat at her desk and looked around with her proprietary Monday eye. There were no windows but the cornices shed a concealed daylight, and unless you touched the walls you would think they were really paneled oak instead of patterned playwood. That, at least, was Emmy's innocent conviction. Mr. Sanders' desk was in order, with its single white carnation in a bud base; the lectern with its huge Bible brooded beneath a picture of the Sermon on the Mount. Everything was as it should be.

She was sharpening a pencil when the door opened sound-lessly and a choir boy stepped in. His robe was far too large, she noted with a practiced eye.

"You boys are not supposed to come in here—" she began and then saw that it was Vern Perrault. Her astonishment cut the rebuke short. No one had told her that Vern had been paroled from the county reformatory, and such a juicy bit of gossip should have flown rapidly around the town. Well, she had obviously missed it somehow, but it was quite incredible that even Mr. Sanders would have admitted him back into the choir.

As the great door started to swing back, the boy caught it and slipped the catch so that it locked behind him.

"Surprised, Miss Damon?"

"Surprised you're back in the choir," she said curtly. "And we don't lock the corridor door. Maybe we should."

He answered only her first comment. "Oh, I'm not in the choir—" he shrugged off the robe, let it drop to the floor "— just took it from the basement chest. How else do you think I got by Miss Lacey?"

He was wearing blue denims and a leather jacket buttoned to the throat, although it was a hot June day. He slid into the chair opposite Emmy, his pose alert by easy. She said nothing, waited. He would talk when he was good and ready, she knew, and after a while he did. "All fixed over in here, I see. But it's awfully quiet."

"Monday is a quiet place," Emmy nodded. She approved the slip of the tongue but corrected it. For all his intelligence, Vern was literal-minded. "Quiet day," she amended. "Sunday's over and most folks are too busy the first of the week to bother Mr. Sanders with their troubles. Come to think of it, they seldom die on Mondays, either."

"I didn't mean that. I mean you can't hear the choir practicing. Can't even hear the sawmill."

"When the study was made over, it was soundproofed," she said absently. And that was a slip she did regret, for his eyes narrowed triumphantly.

"Then I guess no one outside can hear anything *inside* here."

"Unless I push the buzzer," she agreed. "The bell rings in the parish room."

"I don't see any buzzer."

"There's one under each desk."

"Why would a minister hide a buzzer?"

She sighed with exaggerated patience. "He's a busy man, Vern. If some talkative old lady takes too much of his time, something has to be done about it; but naturally he doesn't want to hurt her feelings. So he presses the hidden buzzer and one of us comes in with something important for him to look at. Anything else you'd like explained?"

He warned, "Just don't touch the buzzer, that's all."

"Not unless you take too much of *my* time," she said meaningfully.

The first round was over and instinctively they settled back in their chairs. There was a little silence as they appraised each other for the first time in two years.

Vern was slim, blond, and a very undersized fifteen, with the innocent eyes and cherubic face that choir boys are supposed to possess and seldom do. He had actually be a choir boy for a brief six months. And that was a laugh, Emmy thought, without feeling in the least like laughing. Fourteen years his senior, she had had Vern in her seventh-grade class, and he had been one of the excellent reasons why she had given up teaching to become secretary to the Congregational minister.

Presently she said, "So they didn't parole you out of Dog-town—" (it was an accepted euphemism) "—you ran away. They'll catch up with you in a few hours, you know, so why not enjoy the great outdoors while you can?"

He glowered. "I'm waiting for Mr. Sanders."

"If you want help, why don't you go to the church where you were baptized?" Her eyes were grim. "The font water must have sizzled when it touched your little forehead."

He accepted the compliment with a curve of lips as delicately cut and tender as an angel's. But he remained practical. "Mr. Sanders is single and he'll have some dough he can spare. The Reverend Brown's got five children, so he wouldn't have none."

"My, how your grammar has deteriorated."

He bristled. "I was smarter than any of the other kids and you know it. Went clear through the Book of Knowledge before I was nine."

"Through it, is correct. None of it sank in. Anyway, you'd wait a long time for Mr. Sanders. He hardly ever takes his day off but he solemnly promised he wouldn't show up before afternoon. And I hope he's gone fishing. Besides, even if he wanted to help you run away—and he wouldn't—he hasn't a nickel to spare. Not one."

"Oh, yeah?"

"I mean it." She leaned forward earnestly. "The parish had to spend so much on church repairs that it will be two years before they can afford to carry the parsonage again. That's why they wanted a bachelor minister who'd be willing to live in a boarding house and take a lower salary for a while. Mr. Sanders is poor and the parish is poor."

Vern looked around sneeringly. "This room cost plenty of dough."

"A minister has to have at least one quiet place," she defended, "so the church voted to fix this up instead of buying the new Communion service."

The boy muttered an obscenity so familiar to Miss Damon's school-hardened ears that her frown was merely automatic. He went on savagely, "Thanks for the treasurer's report but I'm not interested. Mr. Sanders will find some way to help me. He'll hafta."

"You'll be seeing someone else first. Deacon Phipps comes in Mondays to sort the collection and take the cash to the bank." Emmy found that her eyes had wandered to the wall safe and she hurriedly glanced away.

Vern laughed. "Don't worry, I got no plans to rob the safe."

"And if you did, I don't have the combination any more than you do," she prevaricated. "But you'd better listen to what I'm saying. Deacon Phipps will be in any moment now and you won't win any argument with him, believe me."

"Won't have to argue. Just show him something." The knife was in Vern's hand then, the switchblade a sudden glitter beneath the cornice lighting.

Emmy stared at it without real surprise. Vern's swaggering order about the buzzer had already indicated that he was relying on something other than his own fragile physique to enforce his commands. And it was typical of his confused values that he should come armed to beg help from a clergyman. But she somehow hadn't expected a knife, not after what had happened two years ago. Well, no use taking a chance on the buzzer. She'd have to handle matters herself. The janitor was mowing, Mis Lacey would faint, the choirmaster was seventy-five and arthritic.

She said mildly, "Oh-oh. A knife like that is what brought you the heaviest sentence they could give a thirteen-year-old. Don't you ever learn anything, Vern? That sort of thing won't get you very far."

"Far enough. I'm waiting for Mr. Sanders, whatever Longnose Deacon Phipps tries to pull."

"Mr. Phipps is a big man."

"He makes trouble, this'll let a little air out of his paunch. He won't be so big them." He smiled.

A Victorian writer would have called that smile winsome. Miss Damon had her own adjective.

"And I'm a big girl," she reflected aloud. "Eight inches taller than you, forty pounds heavier. Brought up on a farm. I didn't develop these muscles cleaning blackboards, Vern. Think you can handle both of us at the same time?"

The knife blade did a bewildering ballet through the air. "Like that," he said complacently, "but thanks for the suggestion. Maybe I'd better settle you first, huh?"

Emmy's large and capable hands folded around the bronze paperweight. "I was good at baseball, too." Her eyes were bright as a mink's behind the heavy brows. "Of course, you might carve me up eventually. But I can guarantee to damage your handsome nose before you even reach this desk. Unfortunately, I can't guarantee it wouldn't split your skull, too. My goodness," she grumbled, "what makes you so ambitious this early on a Monday morning? Quite a change from your school days. Keep it up and you'll be Man of the Year—at least in the penitentiary."

He said sulkily, "Skip the wise chatter. Just push your chair back from the desk so's you can't reach the buzzer." She began to stir reluctantly. "And leave that paperweight on the desk."

Her expression altered. "Ha-ha and ho-ho, little wolf! That would be just a bit too easy, wouldn't it?" There was in her now the same mingled wariness and fierce good humor with which she had once gentled cattle and unruly classrooms. "I tell you what; you put the knife on the rug as far away as you can reach and I'll put this paperweight on the rug as far away as *I* can reach."

He said suspiciously, "Your arms are longer than mine."

"Then the knife will be nearer you than the paperweight is to me."

There was something wrong with this argument, but offhand Vern couldn't think what, so he muttered a grudging, "Okay."

Eyes alert, Emmy thrust the heavy chair back a foot, two feet, four feet. It was slow progress for the carpet was thick.

"Here we go," she said, "as far as you can reach and no cheating." Knife and paperweight were deposited on the rug simultaneously and then the two could relax.

Vern said admiringly, "You're not even sweating."

"Room's air-conditioned. But the day will be a broiler before it's through and you'll look mighty silly in that leather jacket. Stolen from a clothesline, I presume?"

"I presume," he mimicked. "What'd you expect me to do, wear a Dogtown jersey down Main Street?"

He sniffed at a sleeve, raised his head, frowned. "Something smells funny."

"The room," she said indifferently. "Para-dichloro-benzene."

"What the hell's that?"

"Moth crystals to you. Church closes for the summer after Children's Day next week. Why don't you come sing for us, Vern dear?"

"Go to hell."

"Two hells in a row. You used to be more original, Vern. That's what comes of being with bad companions. I mean, bad for your vocabulary and their morals."

He wasn't listening—his eyes were roaming. After a moment he demanded, "Where's the barrel?"

"What barrel?"

"One Mr. Sanders keeps his sermons in. I heard all ministers get their sermons from a barrel."

Miss Damon studied him thoughtfully. "You're incredible, Vern, quite incredible. You heard that storks brought babies, too, didn't you? But you never believed that. No, you knew."

Transparently fair as Vern's skin was, he was no longer capable of blushing. But for the first time he didn't meet her eye. "Aw, can it. All the guys—I mean, any guy—" His voice trailed, was cut off by a cough as firm as a period.

"Of course," Miss Damon agreed. "At certain ages, you're all horrible little beasts—and don't I know it. But all boys don't torture animals, they don't bully little children to death—oh, no, they're capable of love. Some of them are even afraid of God." She startled herself by that last comment. The deity's name belonged to certain well-defined rites or to the clergy; it was not to be bandied about in a duel of his nature. But if she were startled at this breach of etiquette, Vern was outraged.

"I said shut up!" he shouted fiercely, but as her eyes stormed at him he became a defensive fifteen—shrill, whining. "How'd I know there was rat poison on the floor? How'd I know she'd be silly enough to eat it?"

Emmy was dispassionate, musing now. "A three-year-old locked in a dark little harness closet for ten hours. No light, no water. No food except dry oats—and rat poison. Of course you wouldn't know it, Vern. All the Books of Knowledge in the world could never teach you nor reach you. Nothing ever reached you—nothing. And never will."

But the homily had been too long, she knew. And he had heard it too often. Before she had finished, his face was quite calm again, even faintly amused. "Babble, babble, o'er the pebbles—or however it goes. Anyway, save your breath. I been saying I'm sorry for two years now and I'm through, see? Fact is, it was her mother's fault. If kids are taught right, they don't go around eating things off a dirty floor. *I* didn't," he added virtuously. "Mom Perrault always said so."

"It wouldn't have hurt you," Emmy pointed out. "Most snakes are immune to their own poison."

He ignored that, his brief moment of weakness over. "Where do those other two doors go?" he demanded. "I don't remember 'em."

She was not to be betrayed into removing her eyes from the knife. "One's a closet. Other's a hall that leads outdoors. Private lavatory off one side. If you're feeling nervous, Vern," Miss Damon added generously, "I'm sure Mr. Sanders wouldn't mind you using the lavatory. You always did have weak kidneys when you were nervous."

"I'm not nervous and I'm not in seventh grade for you to be talking about my kidneys!" he flared. Inwardly, Emmy acknowledged her own flash of sadism. She had used the one weapon that could hurt him—and against the one failing for which he could not be blamed. She was not proud of herself.

"Sorry, but I can't waste any more time with you." She was suddenly brisk. "Monday's the one day I can work without being interrupted much. Listen, Vern, there's eighteen dollars and some change in my handbag. You can have it if you'll just leave here quietly and get yourself picked up somewhere else."

His eyes squinted with curiosity. "Why do you care where I might be picked up? Not that I will be." For a second Emmy wondered herself—but only for a second. Honesty lay deep in her, a granite ridge beneath the loose earthy soil of her everyday personality. She looked down at the broad hands folded in her lap, hands as freckled as her face.

"This place means a lot to Mr. Sanders. Mondays, too. Only room, only day he has to himself. He'll come back this afternoon with a sort of new look on his face, ready for the week ahead. I don't want the study and Monday spoiled for him. He needs them." For the first time she pleaded, "Listen, Vern, he came out of an orphanage the same as you did. He never had a private place or a private day before."

It was the wrong appeal. His voice was jerky, violent. "I never had 'em neither!"

"I know. But the way you're going, you'll have them sooner than you want, and they won't be the same kind as his."

"Gosh, I'm going to burst out crying any minute. But thanks for the loan of your dough and don't hold your breath till you get it back."

"Then you'll take it and go?"

"I'm not getting out till I see Mr. Sanders. Whatever you say, he'll hafta help me. He's my half brother."

"Dream on, little boy." But her tone was not unkind. How well she knew the fantasies of children who had been born or adopted into environments that didn't jibe with adolescent egotism. Even she herself on the good, dull farm . . . She knew a sudden joy that she had left that endless routine forever and without any wrench of ingratitude to mar her freedom. Her parents had died "in the fullness of their years," as Deacon Phipps had put it, and only then had the homestead been sold, with due and unhurried propriety. She would never have to go back to farm life. Never.

She smiled at Vern with the indulgence of memory. Perhaps he mistook the smile for a sneer.

"I mean it," he persisted. "He's my half brother."

Patience vanished. "Please, none of your dramatics, Vern. Of course you came from the same orphanage—there's only one in the state, so why not? But let me tell you something: everyone in Edgeville knows who Mr. Sanders' parents were—and that when his father died, his mother was too ill and hard up to take care of him and had to go back to her own family."

With pedagogic precision she was ticking off the points on her fingers now. "So Mr. Sanders became a state ward when he was twelve. When he was eighteen, he left and worked his way through college." She sat back triumphantly. "There's no mystery about him, none at all. You were a baby then, hadn't even been adopted yet."

He repeated stubbornly, "He's my half brother. One of the guys told me."

Emmy was really angry now. "Oh stop it! There's something else you're too stupid to know: when a child is adopted in this state, it's against the law to tell who his real parents were or are. The Perraults didn't know who you were when they adopted you, poor souls. They never knew."

"Now *you* listen." He was supercilious. "There's this guy come to Dogtown the other day. Seems he worked in the orphanage office his last year there. And someone left the files unlocked one day and he was looking through them for the names of fellas he knew. And he found me and Mr. Sanders in the same file. Same file, get it? His mother—my mother— married again. Only the second time, she got an A-one bum." The admission was made with quiet inverted pride. "And when she died he dumped me in the orphanage and claimed they wasn't married and I wasn't his kid."

Miss Damon felt a rising uneasiness but her voice was cool enough. "That's the corniest script yet. Mr. Sanders' mother wrote him regularly until she died of tuberculosis. He told me. And she didn't say anything about another marriage, let alone another child."

Vern said with one of his unnerving flashes of acuteness, "She wouldn't, natch. Look, she puts him in the orphanage because she's sick and her folks wouldn't take him, too. Well, maybe even a kid could understand that. But how'd he feel to hear she'd married again and started another family—leaving him

out in the cold?" Emmy's face was closed against him, disdain-
fully. His own hardened. "Anyway, he'll believe me and I'm
waiting for him, see? You think I'd be fool enough to skip
Dogtown if I wasn't sure he'd *hafta* help me?"

"Whether he believes you or not, he'll never help you break
the law."

There was a little silence, then Vern nodded slyly. "I thought
of that, too, but even if he makes me go back, I'll onlly be
twenty-three when I get out. Maybe less, if he pulls strings and
gets me paroled to him. He can do a lot for me then. Good
thing he isn't married. I'll need time and money to look around
till I'm really on my own." For an instant his face was incredibly
old and calculating, and Emmy had a vision of what it would be
like to have Vern "on his own" again—but this time an adult,
the cement of his wickedness hardened forever. It was a vision
from Hell.

"You think he's going to stay single eight years just to support
you when you get out?" Her voice cracked with outrage. "Just
on the off-chance that you're his half brother?"

"Off-chance, nuts. I can prove it."

"That's exactly what—" Emmy paused abruptly. She had
started to say, "what you can't do." But to complete the thought
aloud would merely be giving Vern another weapon, for could
his assertion ever be *dis*proved legally? The orphanage couldn't
officially open its files to Mr. Sanders, for the law had been
written to protect not only a child's anonymity, but that of his
natural parents, whether they were alive or dead.

Mr. Sanders could accept, deny—or wonder. He would never
know; he would live on the edge of an abyss. Of course a
sensibly selfish extrovert would shrug off the unprovable—with
a pang, perhaps, but with sturdy common sense. But not Mr.
Sanders, who too often let his Monday be nibbled away by far
more trivial exactions; not Mr. Sanders, who accepted a room
in a noisy boarding house and who was still filled with humble
awe at his possession of this study.

The fact was, he wasn't practical and no one would want him
to be. But Emmy was. Now it suddenly occured to her that the
orphanage was not the only source of information. One might
be able to find people who in later days had known Mr. Sanders'

mother and granparents—the grandparents who had accepted the care of an invalid daughter but who had refused responsibility for an active small boy. Well, they had been old, one couldn't exactly blame them.

Somehow it could be proved that Mrs. Sanders had never married again, had never had another child. And Vern's venomous little balloon would be punctured forever.

But all this would take time and money, for years had passed and the grandparents, like their daughter, were certainly dead or Mr. Sanders would have mentioned them, looked them up. There was no spite in him, no capacity for harboring resentments.

Emmy thought of her savings account, but almost immediately another thought, chilly and clairvoyant, perched like a bat on her shoulder. What is she spent time and money only to prove something she didn't want to know? What if she should look back someday to this very moment and say, "Dear God, why didn't I leave it alone?"

She closed her eyes an instant, calling Mr. Sanders' image to her inspection. Blond. Slimly built like Vern but, unlike Vern, ver tall. Vern had blue eyes—so had Mr. Sanders. But the boy's eyes were presented to the world on a plane almost flat with his cheeks, as though their bland transparency had nothing to hide. Mr. Sanders' eyes were caverned beneath projecting brows; kindly, shy. No, the two did *not* resemble each other.

She looked up, saw the boy lighting a cigarette. "Please don't smoke, Vern. There aren't any ashtrays and remember your asthma."

"My goodness," he grinned, "isn't our Miss Damon thoughtful today. Kidneys and asthma! Whyn't you just say 'drop dead.' You don't fool me any." He took a defiant puff, coughed. "It's not the cig, it's the stink in here. You must have a tough nose." But he pinched the lighted end of the cigarette, blew the ashes away, and pocketed the stub. "Not that I got any complaints about the asthma," he added complacently. "It took me outa farm work and into the liberry. They wouldn't believe me at first, they never do at Dogtown. But jeez, that first ten minutes in the hayfield I near strangled to death and turned blue in the face. Or so they say."

He threw a leg over the arm of the chair and went on, with an even broader grin. "I was clean out. Woke up in the infirmary and did I ever get service for a coupla weeks! Now I can pick and choose. For instance, makes me cough to dust books. So I just sit at the desk marked Information."

"And give it out, I'll bet," Emmy observed drily.

The buzzer rang. Vern leaped visibly. Perhaps he had not quite believed in the existence of that concealed bell. Emmy was almost as startled. She had been in the small purgatory, whose minutes were as endless as eternity. It was comforting to find that time actually existed—prosaic human time, measured in half and quarter hours.

"I'll have to signal back, Vern. It's probably Mr. Phipps."

He had snatched up the knife and was already on his feet. But he wasn't threatening her, for his eyes were swiveling, seeking a compass point in this windowless room.

Emmy had risen, too, swooping up the paperweight. Now she moved to the desk, opened a drawer, and took out her handbag.

"Don't lose your head, Vern. Just go out the hall door to the garden. That's the West Street side," she reminded him. "There's at least eighteen dollars here, maybe a little more. But if you have a scrap of sense left, you'll go back to Dogtown and do your week in solitary."

He shook his head. "Nix. And I don't want the money. Come to think of it, brother Sanders wouldn't think that was nice of me—" his eyes glinted at her "—and I want him to know I'm *real* reformed. I can see the front walk from the garden and when old Phipps leaves, I'm coming back to wait—even if it takes all day."

He was panting now, but she knew it was from excitement, not fear. Vern did not experience fear as other people did. In fact, he had few of the so-called normal reactions. That made him more difficult, of course, but in an odd way, more predictable.

Emmy could predict him now, as calmly as in the classroom. He would do the Vern-thing: at some point in figuring an equation, his very real intelligence would yaw wildly, would leap some unknown terrain—and come up with the wrong answer.

In a way, it was something like the death wish that psychologists talked about. Not that Vern's body wanted death. It was brilliantly alive, clutching, avid. It burned to survive; it would trample every obstacle to survive. But something in him always came up with the wrong answer.

Emmy stared at him curiously, almost with sympathy.

The buzzer rang again and added two little beeps like plaintive questions. Vern seized the choir robe from the floor, wadded it under his arm. "Which way to the garden? I'm coming back," he warned again.

"To tell Mr. Sanders he's your brother?" Emmy stood very still and her voice was still, too.

"Well, my half brother, at least. The good half." He grinned tauntingly. "And he's bound to think there's a good half to me too, or it'd make a monkey out of a parson, wouldn't it?"

Miss Damon let the handbag thud to the desk. She pulled open the closet door. "Here. Straight ahead to the garden through the next door."

Vern plunged in, and almost immediately started to back out. But Emmy was right behind him, bulking tall and solid.

"Jeez, I can't see nothing! Where's the other door?"

"Just put out your hand."

"Okay, go ring the ol' buzzer. But I'm coming back. You rat on me to Phipps, you'll be sorry. So will pie-face Sanders. He'll wish he was dead."

"Yes," Emmy agreed. She could see nothing in the inky darkness, but he must have the door to the inner closet open now, for the stench of the insecticide was a sudden blow to the lungs. Even Emmy coughed and the gasp from Vern was like a ripping blanket.

"Hey, what the hell! Hey, wait!"

Emmy didn't wait. She gave him a powerful thrust that must have thrown him against the robes, for there was a clatter of wooden hangers as he lost balance. The inner door shut. Let him have a taste of the harness room, a state of night and terror and death.

Emmy closed the outer door and sat at her desk, waiting for the sound of coughing, of fists pounding on wood. But the double closets must be as well insulated as the study itself, for there was nothing around her but the Monday quiet.

Even the buzzer was silent. Miss Lacey, however, puzzled, was keeping Mr. Phipps busy with gossip. And there would be gossip. By this time the whole town must know that Vern had run away from the reformatory.

She glanced up at the picture above the lectern. Blessed Are the Merciful. She looked away, but the other wall offered even less comfort, holding as it did the sampler worked in 1850 by old Mrs. Phipps's mother: Vengeance Is Mine, I Will Repay, Saith the Lord. The "I" stood out large and scarlet.

Emily stirred uneasily. There was no good half in Vern nor even a good ten percent. Of course, she conceded, there might be a good one percent. For all his swagger, was it possible that he was trying to bring a puny miserable little hope—to his brother?

She didn't believe it; only a fool would believe it. In that odd, suspended moment she thought: Maybe this time *I* was Vern's wrong answer. He was sure he knew me—and he didn't.

She sprang up, rushed through the outer closet, and yanked violently at the inner door. The knob came off in her hand.

She felt for the connecting bolt. At her mere touch it slid relentlessly through to the other side. The door was smooth now—a nightmare door.

She raced back into the study and toward the corridor to call the janitor, pausing only a moment to reset the catch that Vern had changed. And turned to see Mr. Phipps beaming down at her.

He was not allowed to linger. In fact, Miss Damon suggested firmly that his counting and accounting should be done in the parish room today. Anyone listening in would have *known* that she was trying to get rid of Mr. Phipps so that Vern and his asthma could be released from the closet. But he was a shrewd and stately old man. If she had been too rude, he might have grown suspicious and that wouldn't have helped Vern either, would it? Because he did know about the escape.

Her mind was suddenly full of contradictory choices, each canceling the other, holding her in an odd paralysis. Or was paralysis itself a choice?

It was particularly difficult because Mr. Phipps was in a rare and waggish moode for a Monday morning—full of sly, friendly little suggestions. For instance, church finances were doing much better than had been expected. The parsonage would be available again in another year and a fine young man like Mr. Sanders should be married. Makes parishioners selfish to have an unmarried pastor always on call. And then, in a clumsy attempt at a *non sequitur,* everyone liked and trusted Miss Damon. Everyone knew her background, her good solid practical folks. How long was she planning to remain a beautiful spinster? Wasting her sweetness on the desert air, so to speak— if an old man might say so without offense?

It didn't occur to Emmy to smile at his transparency. She was transparent herself, born of the same rural traditions, the same moralities, the same capacity for facing facts. She looked down at her wristwatch and faced a certain fact very quietly. By about eight minutes she had lost any right to be the future Mrs. Sanders.

After that recognition, she didn't find it hard to get rid of Deacon Phipps. She followed him down the corridor, her experienced eyes noting everything. Choir practice was over. Through the open east door she could see the janitor leaning on his power mower to chat with a passing workman. Sunlight glittered from the metal parts of the machine and there was the acrid, rebellious odor of young grass newly snipped. Miss Lacey's car was gone; she would be at the printer's, heckling him about the Children's Day programs. Emmy turned back, having seen Mr. Phipps safely established in the parish room. She could move swiftly now.

She found tools in the janitor's quarters and returned to the study, and then to the inner closet. No paralysis now—chisel and hammer were a duet of efficiency.

Propping the door open finally, she bent down. There was no pulse in the huddled body, but it was still warm and limp; it was a simple matter to shrug it into the oversized choir robe. And that big strong girl could carry Vern as easily as she had once carried calves or lambs dropped in desolate pastures.

She carried him to the chancel, up to the choir loft, and slid him into one of the choir benches. Once she had folded his arms along the bench in front of him, his head fell quite naturally on those arms. Just as naturally her hand smoothed back the soft blond hair. She lifted his chin an instant and saw that the blue was fading from his face.

She thought: Mr. Sanders will be sure the Prodigal Son came home to repent and die. Perhaps he did. I don't think so but how do I know? I'm just a farm girl who went to Teachers College two years.

She stood looking down from the chancel, tasting the quiet. The church was mid-Victorian gothic, far too large for its present parish. And in winter, a bit forbidding.

But now the June airs pulsing through it, it heaved and shone and breathed like some great and gentle ox whose strength had never fully been tried. She would miss it.

LORD DUNSANY

THE SHOP THAT EXCHANGED EVILS

I often think of the Bureau d'Echange de Maux and the wondrously evil old man that sat therein. It stood in a little street in Paris, its doorway made of three brown beams of wood, the top one overlapping the others like the Greek letter pi, all the rest painted green, a house far lower and narrower than its neighbors and infinitely stranger, a place to take one's fancy. And over the doorway on the old brown beam in faded yellow letters this legend ran: *Bureau Universel d'Echange de Maux.*

I entered at once and accosted the listless man who lolled on a stool by his counter. I demanded the wherefore of his wonderful shop, what evil wares he exchanged, and many other things I wished to know, for curiosity had led me: and indeed, had it not, I would have gone at once from the shop, for there was so evil a look in that fattened man, in the hang of his fallen cheeks and his sinful eye, that you would have said he had had dealings with Hell and won the advantage by sheer wickedness.

Such a man was the shopkeeper, but, above all, the evil of him lay in his eyes, which lay so still, so apathetic, that you would have sworn he was drugged or dead. Like lizards motionless on a wall they lay, then suddenly they darted, and all his cunning flamed up and revealed itself in what one moment before seemed no more than a sleepy and ordinary wicked old man. And this was the object and trade of that peculiar shop: you paid twenty francs, which the old man proceeded to take from me, for admission to the ship, and then had the right to exchange any evil or misfortune of your own for some evil or misfortune that anyone on the premises "could afford," as the old man put it.

There were four men in the dingy ends of that low-ceilinged

room, who gesticulated and muttered softly in twos as men who make a bargain, and now and then more came in, and the eyes of the flabby owner of the shop leaped up at them as then entered, seemed to know their errands at once and each one's peculiar need, and fell back again into somnolence, reeiving his twenty francs in an almost lifeless hand and biting the coin as though in pure absence of mind.

"Some of my clients," he told me. So amazing to me was the trade of this extraordinary shop that I engaged the old man in conversation, repulsive though he was, and from his garrulity I gathered these facts. He spoke in perfect English, though his utterance was somewhat thick and heavy. He had been in business a great many years—how many he would not say—and was far older than he looked. All kinds of people did business in his shop. What they exchanged with each other he did not care, except that it had to be evils; he was not empowered to carry on any other kind of business.

There was no evil, he told me, that was not negotiable there; no evil the old man knew had ever been taken away in despair from his ship. A man might have to wait and come back again the next day and the next and the day after, paying twenty francs each time, but the old man had the addresses of his clients and shrewdly knew their needs, and soon the right two met and eagerly changed their commodities. "Commodities" was the old man's terrible word, said with a gruesome smack of his heavy lips, for he took a pride in his business, and evils to him were goods.

I learned from him in ten minutes very much of human nature, more than I had ever learned from any other man. I learned from him that a man's own evil is to him the worst thing that there is or could be, and that an evil so unbalances all men's minds that they always seek for extremes in that small, grim shop. A woman who had no children had exchanged with an impoverished half-maddened creature with twelve. On one occasion, a man had exchanged wisdom for folly.

"Why on earth did he do that?" I said.

"None of my business," the old man answered in his heavy, indolent way. He merely took his twenty francs from each and ratified the agreement in the little room at the back of the ship where his clients conducted their business. Apparently the man who had parted with wisdom had left the shop on the tips of his toes with a happy though foolish expression all over his face, but the other went thoughtfully away wearing a troubled look. Almost always it seemed they did business in opposite evils.

But the thing that puzzled me most in all my talks with that unwieldy man, the thing that puzzles me still, is that none that had once done business in that shop ever returned again. A man might come day after day for many weeks, but once he did business he never returned. So much the old man told me, but when I asked him why he only muttered that he did not know.

It was to discover the wherefore of this strange thing, and for no other reason at all, that I determined myself to do business in the little room at the back of that mysterious shop. I determined to exchange some trivial evil for some evil equally slight, to seek for myself an advantage so very small as scarcely to give Fate, as it were, a grip, for I deeply distrusted these bargains, I knowing well that man has never yet benefited by the marvelous, and that the more miraculous his advantage appears to be the more securely and tightly do the gods or the witches catch him.

In a few days more, I was going back to England and I was beginning to fear that I should be seasick. This fear of seasickness—not the actual malady but only the fear of it—I decided to exchange for a suitably little evil. I did not know with whom I should be dealing, who in reality was the head of the firm (one never does when shopping), but I decided that not even the Devil could make very much on so small a bargain as that.

I told the old man of my project, and he scoffed at the smallness of my commodity, trying to urge me on to some darker bargain, but he could not move me from my purpose. And then he told me, with a somewhat boastful air, tales of the big business, the great bargains, that has passed through his hands. A man had once run in there to try and exchange death; he had swallowed poison by accident and had only a few hours to live. That sinister old man had been able to oblige him. A client was willing to barter even that commodity.

"But what did he give in exchange for death?" I said.

"Life," said that grim old man with a furtive chuckle.

"It must have been a horrible life," I said.

"That was not my affair," the proprietor said, lazily rattling a little pocketful of twenty-franc pieces.

Strange business I watched in that shop for the next few days, the exchange of odd commodities, and heard strange mutterings in corners among couples who presently rose and went to the back room, the old man following to ratify.

Twice a day for a week I paid my twenty francs, watching life with its great needs and its little needs spread out before me in all its wonderful variety.

And one day I met a comfortable man with only a little need—he seemed to have the very evil I wanted. He always feared the elevator was going to break down. I knew too much of hydraulics to fear things as silly as that, but it was not my business to cure his ridiculous fear. Few words were needed to convince him that mine was the very evil for him—he never crossed the sea, and I, on the other hand, could always walk upstairs—and I also felt at the time, as many must feel in that shop, that so absurd a fear could never trouble me.

When we both had signed the parchment in the spidery back room and the old man had ratified (for which we had to pay him fifty francs each), I went back to my hotel, and there I saw the deadly thing in the basement. They asked me if I would go upstairs in the elevator. From force of habit I risked it, and held my breath all the way up and clenched my hands.

Nothing will induce me to try such a journey again. I would sooner go up to my room in a balloon. And why? Because if a balloon goes wrong you have a chance—it may spread out into a parachute after it has burst, it may catch in a tree, or a hundred and one things may happen—but if the elevator falls down its shaft, you are done. As for seasickness, I shall never be seasick again—I cannot tell you why except that I know that it is so.

And the shop in which I made this remarkable bargain, the shop to which none return when their business is done: I set out for it next day. Blindfold, I could have found my way to the unfashionable quarter in which the mean street runs, where you take the alley at the end, whence runs the cul-de-sac where the queer shop stood. A shop with pillars, fluted and painted red, stands on one side; its neighbor is a low-class jeweler's with little silver brooches in the window. In such incongruous company stood the shop with the three brown beams of wood and all the rest of it painted green.

In half an hour I stood in the cul-de-sac to which I had gone twice a day for the last week. I found the shop with the ugly painted pillars and the jeweler who sold brooches, but the green house with the three brown beams was gone.

Pulled down, you will say—although in a single night? That can never be the answer to the mystery, for the shop of the fluted pillars painted red, and the low-class jeweler's shop with its silver brooches (all of which I could identify one by one), were standing side by side.

BROOKE WELD

THE BAG MAN

There was a piece in the paper once about this woman in California who burned down her house. There wasn't much insurance on it, but still they found out it was she who did it; so she admitted it—yes, she said, she just hadn't felt like cleaning it up. What a gorgeously simple solution—though it does make one wonder, doesn't it?

I was sitting on the landing by a pile of laundry, just smoking and thinking about this woman who burned down her house, almost enviously, when the front doorbell rang.

The front door had been stuck so that you can't open it for quite a while, so my friends who drop in for coffee—and even the tradesmen—have finally learned to come to the back door. No one in his right mind would try to sell encyclopedias or collect for charity at ten o'clock on a Monday morning, so I couldn't think who could possibly be at the front door. Well, at least I was dressed, so after I let it ring a few more times I went to see who it was. I admire the sport of people who can ignore bells and burn down houses—but I do know my own limitations.

Shouting through the window to please come to the rear, I went back to the kitchen and opened that door and began to explain about the front one when I stopped suddenly. I couldn't place the man standing there at all.

To begin with, he was terribly tall—maybe only six-four, but he looked even taller because he was thin and stooped, the way people are who have been told stand-straight, shoulders-back too often and have bumped their heads. Though his soft brown hair was longish and combed to hide a thin patch, I didn't judge him to be much older than I am, but I didn't like his looks one bit.

His eyes were too far apart and his features had a soft crumply look and he was much too pale—an unhealthy pallor that

reminded me of those horrid maggots the boys will put in their
pockets for fishing and then forget. He had a thin moustache
drooping over but you could still see his mouth was weak and
he had a receding chin a beard might have helped, except he'd
evidently decided not to go the whole hog. A well cut tweed
jacket only added to his generally cadaverous air—it looked left
over from some time when he'd weighed more.

He'd insinuated himself into the kitchen by the time I finished
apologizing for the front door, and then he began to apologize
for disturbing me. He didn't have the manner of a salesman and
his voice was soft and so low that it was difficult for me to hear
him. But he didn't say what he'd come about. I decided not to
apologize for the kitchen being in rather a mess. I had a sudden
impulse to push him clear out of it, but I didn't.

It wasn't that I was afraid—my neighbors are in hollering
distance, and I could hear Millie Clark over the fence yelling at
Bobby to stop splashing mud like that—but this man looked as
if he ought to be squashed. And why should I have him in my
kitchen at ten o'clock on a Monday morning, and him staring at
his muddy shoes in awkward silence and not explaining who
he was and why he was there? I made up my mind right then to
get that front door fixed so I could begin with a cold yes-what-
is-it and keep people out.

He stood there another full minute looking at his shoes
instead of my pleasant inquiring smile, which was getting pretty
stiff, and twisting the brim of his soft black hat. His whole
appearance was so strange, so unnerving somehow, that it was
only then that I noticed the enormous burlap sack in his other
hand. You'd think that would have been the first thing I'd have
seen, but I hadn't—or maybe I had and just hadn't taken it it,
the way you don't notice something that's wrong, like a mack-
erel in a magnolia tree.

"I lived here once." He flushed as his voice cut the resounding
silence, and it made him look a lot more human. The pale-
brown eyes seemed to plead for help the instant before they
slid away again to study his shoes, and suddenly I felt in
command of the situation and rather sorry for him.

We'd been in the house less than a year, and it was the sort
of old house a lot of people might have lived in. He might even

have lived in it as a child—the only circumstance in which I could imagine anyone becoming actually attached to it. I'd wondered how long the Florida coastline crack had been in our bedroom ceiling and who all the people were who had lain staring at it before me. If he thought he was going to make a sentimental journey through the house at this hour—and on a Monday—he was mistaken, but I still didn't think it would do any harm to be civil.

"Oh, really? That's interesting," I said. "I was just going to put the coffee on—would you like a cup?"

He shook his head, and mumbled, "Thank you very much, but I can't stop—I've only come for my things, if you don't mind."

What things? I wondered, taken aback. There was some junk in the attic and in the basement—some ours, some left by a previous owner. I hadn't got around to a really good clear-out, but nothing had looked the least bit valuable.

"What things? Where are they? I'm afraid I really don't know what you're talking about."

If I sounded irritated, I was, but he only passed his long bony white hand over his face as if, strangely, he didn't know himself what he was talking about.

"That's the trouble. I can't quite remember. But if I could look around, if you would just let me look, I might find it." He gave his big bag a nervous twitch. "I would take away anything that you wanted to get rid of—anything spoiled or stained, anything ragged or broken or torn, anything I could take away in my bag—" He paused. "Anything that has failed or been left unfinished or forgotten."

He looked at me suddenly, meeting my eyes for an instant with the same pleading look, but I simply stood there, frozen. It was like my whole life was spinning around—knowing that I had failed French, failed to write a hundred and eleven thank-you notes, failed my friends, left the P.T.A. project unfinished, and the curtains, and the crèche; forgotten to take Jim's suit to the cleaners, forgotten the kettle boiling until there was this terrible smell. Everything seemed to drain away to make a hollow for this misery of self-loathing.

You probably haven't ever had that sort of feeling, but I get it quite often, even though I know I'm very nice in some ways. I think about the things I haven't done, and how things might be different, if only I had. Well, anyway, I just stood there like a gawk, wishing I were dead, until suddenly I came to my senses and realized this was all perfect nonsense.

"I'm afraid I really don't have anything for you, and I am very busy this morning." I had to cross in front of him to open the door, but I did it, and felt a lot better.

"If I could just look in the cellar or the attic. Please, I wouldn't ask, but it matters such a lot—"

"What *is* it then? I'll have a look for you when I get time. If you'll only give me some idea of what to look for."

He shook his head sadly, still staring at his muddy brown shoes. "I can't remember it, you see—it's something forgotten, unfinished, undone—But everything would be all right if I could just remember and find it and do it—everything would come out right then."

Obviously the poor man was some sort of lunatic, but all I wanted to do was to get him out of that door.

"I'm sorry, but you really can't look now. Not this morning. I'll look later on. Later, when I have time, I'll look for whatever it is."

"Thank you—thank you for being so kind, so understanding. I believe you will find it for me. I'll leave my bag for you to put it in and come back next week if I may—if it won't disturb you."

"Yes, yes—next week will be fine. I'll try to put everything that was left here in your bag, or let you look for it then. Not now. Next week."

He seized my hand and gave it a grateful wring. Then, with a little bow, he left.

I shut the door after him and locked it. Half the time I forget to lock it, even at night, but I locked it then. Everything seemed to be jumping uncontrollably in my head, widening and narrowing like the reflections in a crazy mirror. That is supposed to be just your pulse beating.

I lit a cigarette, and then made the coffee and had another cigarette. I'd have thought I was going crazy myself—except there was the burlap bag, lying where he'd left it by the door.

The natural thing would have been to run over to Millie Clark's and tell her about this weird experience, but I couldn't. I couldn't tell anyone. And I couldn't forget about it, either. You can judge the effect it had on me when I tell you I started cleaning that house and I didn't stop all week. I had the front door fixed too, along with the bedroom window that was also stuck, and the dripping faucet, and a lot of little things like that.

Of course, Jim was still away in Cleveland, trying to swing that big deal, and with the children spening the summer at their grandmother's in Crescent Beach, it wasn't as if I had all the normal grind. But the only thing I didn't do was go near the attic or the cellar—I simply couldn't, though I thought about it all the time.

I had it in my mind that the bag man—that's the way I thought of him—would be back the next Monday, the same time as before, so I got up and dressed very nicely that morning, in a skirt instead of jeans, and then I went around the house putting finishing touches here and there until ten o'clock. After that I kept trying to see out of the upstairs window, and smoking and drinking coffee, feeling as if I were waiting to take an exam or was coming down with flu or something.

About three o'clock I decided he definitely wasn't coming, but I locked both doors to make sure he couldn't just walk in and then I went down to the cellar.

That enormous burlap bag was lying halfway down the cellar stairs where I'd pitched it after he'd left a week ago. I kicked it aside and kept on down. The cellar wasn't really too bad—there was only the boiler down there and a huge old icebox someone had abandoned, and some of our empty packing crates.

I had pushed along one wall all the things previous tenants hadn't bothered to pay the trash man to take away. There were untidy stacks of old *Saturday Evening Posts* with a few *National Geographics* mixed in, a broken ladder and a roll of chicken wire, an enormous rusty ax and a pitchfork with a missing tine, a simply filthy army blanket, an old photograph album without any snapshots in it, and a cheap edition of *Pollyanna.*

That was the lot. I even opened the icebox, but it was quite empty—no golden doubloons or fading love letters or forgotten bodies there. That left the attic.

It is a low-beamed spooky place—one large shadowy room stretching under the roof, with slat walls parallel to the eaves. By the light from the one small window I could see the looming shapes of our own trunks. I turned my attention to the other wall, where I'd left the discards of former owners, but I knew what was there: the unframed oil painting of amateur execution—dispirited cows beneath a noble oak, a broken high chair, a rather pretty oval mirror, badly cracked, several cartons of empty glass jam jars, a dressmaker's dummy of prim but ample contour, a stack of old Richmond *News Leaders,* and a thick layer of dust over everything. Nothing undone, nothing unfinished.

And yet looking at that line of discards, all at once I felt an unreasonable terror. I got out of there fast and ran over to Millie's.

We had coffee and everything seemed blessedly normal in her cheerful kitchen as she griped about her husband's latest craze, photography, going on about how messy and expensive it was. The afternoon mail came while we were chatting, so I ran back to my house to see if there was anything interesting. There was just a letter from Jim, but I felt terribly let down to learn he wouldn't be home for another week. I mean, the house was really sparkling and he'd think I'd made the extra effort for him and be pleased, and I could easily think of some reason for him to have a good look around the attic.

The thing I'd noticed about the attic was that the discards I had lined against the wall were too close to the stairs. The stairs went right up the middle, with the window centered above them in the front; but that side didn't go back as far as the other side, and that slat wall was taller.

I was perfectly sure the slat wall had a door—the door to a narrow room that someone, sometime, for some reason had partitioned off. And I knew *I* wasn't going in it—not for all the rubies in Rajput, and not to see if someone had left forgotten there a few bits of Meissen or an Early American spinning wheel—or perhaps some contemporary bones.

The week went by somehow, and when if finally ended without the bag man showing up again, it seemed unlikely that he ever would—I hoped not, anyway. But I decided to go over to Millie's before ten on Monday, just in case.

When the front doorbell rang at nine-thirty I knew I was too late. I didn't want to answer it, but the back door was unlocked and I was even more afraid of his walking in and finding me—somehow that would be even worse than confronting him. Sometimes you have to get things over with.

"Good morning." He tried a smile, a baring of tobacco-stained teeth that made him look even worse than I had remembered. "I don't know if you remember, but I came here two weeks ago. You remember?"

"Yes." I did remember.

"I left my bag."

"But you were supposed to come for it last week."

"I know, and I'm sorry about that. I wasn't free, though I wanted to come very much. I felt sure, last Monday, that you'd found what I'm looking for."

"No. There isn't anything but a lot of junk. I looked."

His face fell, and for a panicky moment I thought he might cry.

"You didn't find it? It must be here—if only you'd let me look I'm sure I'd find it. Please let me come in and look for it."

He appeared so miserable that my terror fell away, leaving me strangely calm. After all, I wasn't alone in the middle of the country on a dark night or anything like that. I'd let my imagination run away with me because I didn't like his looks, and that wasn't his fault. But I'd think of some way to avoid the attic—no, not the attic.

"Your bag is in the cellar. There are a few things there—"

I led the way to the cellar steps, but I made him go down ahead of me. His face fell as he saw the useless little collection. With a new spasm of terror I realized that the rusty ax and the broken pitchfork would make effective if horrid weapons. Yet he barely glanced at them. He picked up the photograph album, but lost interest when he found its pages empty, and then his attention turned to the icebox.

"It's quite empty—I opened it and looked." My voice was

thin and strained, as if I were lying, but he paid no attention and opened it.

"How big it is! They're big enough to hold an ox, this old-fashioned kind."

Or a man, I thought. I don't know what made me think that, but the same idea must have come into his head.

"Even a person could fit into it—" He looked at me inquiringly, as if to ask what I thought of this notion, and I took an involuntary step backward. I'm only five feet two and small-boned. I could easily fit into that icebox—or into his bag.

"A tall person, like yourself?"

He looked at it gravely, considering. "I think so—and if I could anyone could, I guess." He gave a low chuckle and bared the yellow teeth again.

"Oh, yes, anyone could if you could—but I shouldn't think it would be very comfortable." I giggled, pointlessly. What a delightful, witty conversation we were having.

But he was actually climbing into the thing—he had to hunch way over, but in the natal position, with his head resting on his drawn-up knees, he managed quite nicely. A few steps forward brought me to the center of the cellar where I watched, fascinated, the little wriggles he was making to get himself comfortable. There's no use at all in trying to describe it—you'd have to see him yourself at that moment to realize how much a man can look like a maggot.

It took me only three more steps to reach the icebox door and slam it shut.

In another instant I was out of the house, outside breathing the soft air, hearing the voices of children quarreling and the Robinsons' basset giving tongue over a cat. The Number 23 bus stops just across the street, and as one was just pulling in I jumped on. I almost jumped off at the next stop, though, because I had started thinking about the thing I had done.

How long would it take for someone to die shut up like that? If I went right back he might be all right. What could you say to a perfect stranger you had shut up in an icebox? It wasn't just the social awkwardness of the situation that stopped me, it was that I was too scared. I simply couldn't.

Suppose he was already dead.

Or suppose he wasn't.

It's a forty-minute ride to the end of the bus line, but I didn't notice it and the driver had to tell me to get off when we reached the terminus. Maybe it hadn't taken the bag man long, just a moment perhaps of terror and panic and disbelief and trying to get his breath and choking. I hoped it hadn't taken long.

If only I'd had the front door fixed sooner he might never have got into my kitchen; if only I'd cleared everything out when we'd first moved in; if only I'd got to Millie's earlier today; if only Jim had come home; if only I'd asked the Clarks or the police or someone to look in the attic; if only I'd just stayed upstairs and told him to look in the cellar for himself. I guess a hundred little things could have prevented it. I wondered what kind of man he'd been, and what his life had been, and what it was that he had wanted so much to find—something unfinished, but finished now.

On the ride back I started to think about what I must do. That is the sort of courage I do have, the kind a lot of women have— more than men, I think—about getting through anything you absolutely have to get through. Fortunately, I'd committed the sort of crime that is difficult to solve—I'd murdered someone I didn't know, and without reason. There was no possible way to connect his life with mine. There would be no sign of struggle, no blood, no weapon, no clue. Except his body.

I would have to take him out, this evening, and if I could get him even halfway into that big burlap bag I could drag him up the cellar steps and through the inside door to the garage without anyone seeing. But Jim had the car. I would pretend I needed another load of leafmold for the azaleas and borrow the Clarks' car.

Then when I was sure no one was around I would dump him in some underbrush, and drive to another part of the wood for the leafmold. Even if he was found right away, it would be just one of those odd cases that are never solved. The worst part would be to go down to the cellar and open that icebox door.

Thinking about that, I was almost glad to see the police already there. They'd had to wait quite a while, and I certainly wouldn't have minded if they'd helped themselves to some coffee—but they had just waited.

The bag man really was a lunatic, you see, but they were beginning to give him a little freedom at the sanitarium because he seemed so much better and was so very gentle. That Monday—the first time he came to my house—was his first excursion by himself. They hadn't let him leave the following Monday, though, because he seemed overexcited, and the next Monday—today—they had sent someone along to follow him, just to make sure that nothing went wrong.

The guard from the sanitarium had been watching from the bus stop across the street, and when he saw me tear out of the house and onto that bus like a loony, he'd waited a minute or two, and then gone in the front door I'd thoughtlessly left wide open. I'd left the cellar light on too, so that guided him down there, and he was just in time.

I'm thankful for that. Otherwise there would have been a trial—but mainly I am thankful for his sake, the bag man's. The chief of police was really on my side—said they shouldn't go around turning lunatics loose on helpless housewives like that.

I told them about the attic. Behind the partition they found the butterfly collection that he was looking for, and all the paraphernalia of the hunter, with empty cases for mounting, and one half-done. That must have been "the unfinished thing." He'd begun collecting butterflies when he was just a little boy, but by the time he was sixteen it had become a mania, and his mother couldn't get him to pay attention to anything else. They had a lot of rows about it, naturally, and finally she hid all the butterfly equipment in the attic and told him she had given it away to the trash man.

He was the sort of adolescent they now call disturbed, because he took after his mother with an ice pick. Funny, isn't it—an ice pick and an icebox. He wasn't successful with his murder, either—his mother is still living with her daughter in Fort Lauderdale—but he gave her a couple of nasty punctures, and remorse or something sent him clean over the edge and he's been in the sanitarium ever since. I can understand why his mother just left the butterflies there behind the partition where she'd hidden them. It's a pitiful sort of story if you think about it, and I'm terribly glad I didn't really kill him and that he has his butterfly collection back.

Well, if you've been following all this in the *Times Dispatch* or the *News Leader,* you know they decided it was temporary insanity due to fright, but the papers don't give any idea of how it really happened, and you may have wondered—the way I did about that woman who burned her house down. It is a little hard to understand, when you realize that *any* little thing could have prevented it, but Jim says they'll say that about the atom bomb someday.

It's silly—nothing can possibly happen—but there's one thing that frightens me. After I get out of this hospital where they've been observing me, I'll have to go to the sanitarium, or it wouldn't look right.

But suppose I run into the bag man there? That's what I can't stop thinking about.

JOHN GALSWORTHY

THE NEIGHBORS

In the remote country, nature, at first sight so serene, so simple, will soon intrude on her observer a strange discomfort; a feeling that some familiar spirit haunts the old lanes, rocks, wasteland, and trees and has the power to twist all living things around into some special shape befitting its genius.

When moonlight floods the patch of moorland about the center of the triangle between the little towns of Hartland, Torrington, and Holsworthy, a pagan spirit steals forth through the wan gorse, gliding round the stems of the lonely, gibbetlike fir trees, peeping out among the reeds of the white marsh. That spirit has the eyes of a borderer, who perceives in every man a possible foe. And, in fact, this high corner of the land has remained border to this day, where the masterful, acquisitive invader from the North dwells side by side with the unstable, proud, quick-blooded Celt-Iberian.

In two cottages crowning some fallow land, two families used to live side by side. The long white dwelling seemed all one, till the eye, peering through the sweetbrier which smothered the right-hand half, perceived the rude, weatherbeaten present-ment of a running horse, denoting the presence of intoxicating liquors; and in a window of the left-hand half, that strange conglomeration of edibles and shoe-leather which proclaims the one shop of a primitive hamlet.

Those married couples were by name Sandford at the eastern, and Leman at the western end; and he who saw them for the first time thought: What splendid-looking people!

They were all four above the average height, and all four as straight as darts. The innkeeper, Sandford, was a massive man, stolid, grave, light-eyed, with big fair moustaches, who might have stepped straight out of some Norseman's galley. Leman was lean and lathy, a regular Celt, with an amiable, shadowy, humorous face. The two women were as different as the men.

Mrs. Sandford's fair, almost transparent cheeks colored easily, her eyes were grey, her hair pale-brown. Mrs. Leman's hair was of a lusterless jet-black, her eyes the color of a peaty stream, and her cheeks had the close creamy texture of old ivory.

Those accustomed to their appearance soon noted the qualifications of their splendor. In Sandford, whom neither sun nor wind ever tanned, there was a look as if nothing would ever turn him from acquisition of what he had set his heart on; his eyes had the idealism of the worshipper of property, ever marching towards a heaven of great possessions. Followed by his cowering spaniel, he walked to his fields (for he farmed as well as kept the inn) with a tread that seemed to shake the lanes, disengaging an air of such heavy and complete insulation that even the birds were still. He rarely spoke. He was not popular. He was feared, no one quite knew why.

On Mrs. Sandford, for all her pink and white, sometimes girlish look, he had set the mark of his slow, heavy domination. Her voice was seldom heard. Once in a while, however, her reserve would yield to garrulity, as of water flowing through a broken dam. In these outbursts she usually spoke of her neighbors, the Lemans, deploring the state of their marital relations.

"A woman," she would say, "must give way to a man sometimes; I've had to give way to Sandford myself, I have." Her lips, from long compression, had become thin as the edge of a teacup; all her character seemed to have been driven down below the surface of her long, china-white face. She had not broken, but she had chipped; her edges had become jagged, sharp. The consciousness that she herself had been beaten to the earth seemed to inspire in her that waspish feeling towards Mrs. Leman—"a woman with a proud temper," as she would say in her almost ladylike voice, "a woman who's never bowed down to a man—that's what she'll tell you herself. 'Tisn't the drink that makes Leman behave so mad, 'tis because she won't give way to him. We're glad to sell drink to anyone we can, of course, but 'tisn't that what's makin' Leman so queer. 'Tis her."

Leman, whose long figure was often to be seen seated on the wooden bench of his neighbor's stone-flagged little inn, had, indeed, begun to have the soaked look and scent of a man never quite drunk, and hardly ever sober. He spoke slowly, his tongue seemed thickening; he no longer worked; his humorous, amiable face had grown hangdog and clouded. All the village knew of his passionate outbreaks and bursts of desperate weeping; and of two occasions when Sandford had been compelled to wrest a razor from him. People took a morbid interest in this rapid deterioration, speaking of it with misgiving and relish, unanimous in their opinion that "summat'ed 'appen about that; the drink were duin' for George Leman, *that* it were, praaperly!"

But Sandford—that blond, ashy-looking Teuton—was not easy of approach, and no one cared to remonstrate with him; his taciturnity was too impressive, too impenetrable. Mrs. Leman, too, never complained. To see this black-haired woman, with her stoical, alluring face, come out for a breath of air and stand in the sunlight, her baby in her arms, was to have looked on a very woman of the Britons. In conquering races, the men, they say, are superior to the women; in conquered races, the women to the men. She was certainly superior to Leman. That woman might be bent and mangled, she could not be broken; her pride was too simple, too much a physical part of her.

No one ever saw a word pass between her and Sandford. It was almost as if the old racial feelings of this borderland were pursuing in these two their unending conflict. For there they lived, side by side under the long, thatched roof, this great primitive, invading male, and that black-haired, lithe-limbed woman of an older race, avoiding each other, never speaking— as much too much for their own mates as they were, perhaps, worthy of each other.

In this lonely parish, houses stood far apart, yet news traveled down the May-scented lanes and over the whin-covered moor with a strange speed, blown perhaps by the west wind, whispered by the pagan genius of the place in his wanderings, or conveyed by small boys on large farm horses.

On whit-Monday it was known that Leman had been drinking all Sunday, for he had been heard on Sunday night shouting out that his wife had robbed him and that her children were not his. All next day he was seen sitting in the bar of the inn soaking steadily. Yet on Tuesday morning Mrs. Leman was serving in her shop as usual—a really noble figure, with that lusterless black hair of hers—very silent, and ever sweetening her eyes to her customers. Mrs. Sandford, in one of her bursts of garrulity, complained bitterly of the way her neighbors had "gone on" the night before. But unmoved, ashy, stolid as ever, Sandford worked in the most stony of his fields.

That hot, magnificent day wore to its end; a night of extraordinary beauty fell. In the gold moonlight, the shadows of the lime-tree leaves lay, blacker than any velvet, piled one on the other at the foot of the little green. It was very warm. A cuckoo called on till nearly midnight. A great number of little moths were out and the two broad meadows which fell away from the hamlet down to the stream were clothed in a glamorous haze of their own moonlit buttercups. Where that marvelous moonlight spread out across the moor it was all pale witchery; only the three pine trees had strength to resist the wan gold of their fair visitor, and brooded over the scene like the ghosts of three great gallows. The long white dwelling of "the neighbors," bathed in that vibrating glow, seemed to be exuding a refulgence of its own. Beyond the stream a nightjar hunted, whose fluttering harsh call tore the garment of the scent-laden still air. It was long before sleep folded her wings.

A little past twelve o'clock there was the sound of a double shot. By five o'clock the next morning the news had already traveled far; and before seven quite a concourse had gathered to watch two mounted constables take Leman on Sandford's pony to Bideford jail. The dead bodies of Sandford and Mrs. Leman lay—so report ran—in the locked bedroom at Leman's end of the neighbor's house. Mrs. Sandford, in a state of collapse, was being nursed at a neighboring cottage. The Leman children had been taken to the Rectory. Alone of the dwellers in those two cottages, Sandford's spaniel sat in a gleam of early sunlight under the eastern porch, with her nose fixed to the crack beneath the door.

It was vaguely known that Leman had "done for 'em"; of the how, the why, the when, all was conjecture. Nor was it till the assizes that the story of that night was made plain, from Leman's own evidence, read from a dirty piece of paper:

"I, George Leman, make this confession—so help me God! When I came up to bed that evening, I was far gone in liquor and so had been for two days off and on, which Sandford knows. My wife was in bed. I went up and I said to her: 'Get up!' I said, 'Do what I tell you for once!' 'I will not!' she said. So I pulled the bedclothes off her. When I saw her all white like that, with her black hair, it turned me queer, and I ran downstairs and got my gun, and loaded it. When I came upstairs again, she was against the door. I pushed, and she pushed back. She didn't call out, or say one word—but pushed, and she was never one to be afraid. I was the stronger, and I pushed in the door. She stood up against the bed, defying me with her mouth tight shut, the way she had; and I put up my gun to shoot her. It was then that Sandford came running up the stairs and knocked the gun out of my hand with his stick. He hit me a blow over the heart with his fist, and I fell down against the wall and couldn't move. And he said: 'Keep quiet!' he said, 'you dog!' Then he looked at her. 'And as for, you,' he said, 'you bring it on yourself! You can't bow down, can't you? *I'll* bow you down for once!' And he took and raised his stick. But he didn't strike her, he just looked at her in her nightdress, which was torn at the shoulders, and her black hair ragged. She never said a word, but smiled at him. Then he caught hold of her by the arms, and they stood there. I saw her eyes; they were as black as two sloes. He seemed to go all weak of a sudden, and white as the wall. It was like they were struggling which was the better of them, meaning to come to one another at the end. I saw what was in them as clear as I see this paper. I got up and crept round, and I took the gun and pointed it, and pulled the triggers one after the other, and they fell dead, first him, then her. They fell quietly, neither of them made a noise. I went out and lay down on the grass. They found me there when they came to take me. This is all I have to write, but it is true that I was far gone in liquor, which I had of him . . ."

DAVID ELY

A QUESTION OF NEIGHBORLINESS

A chill spring storm burst across the meadow and shook the heavy-headed trees beyond. It blew in with the dusk, and the first raindrops seemed black, like bits of night torn out of the sky.

The young man limped toward the Hall. Its upper story was tightly shuttered, but some of the ground-floor rooms were lighted, and one window was touched with the soft irregular coloration that suggested a warm fire within. There was a cascade of thunder. The sky split, wild and bright. In the flash, the young man noticed a figure standing behind one of the unlighted windows, but it vanished as the lightning died.

Anxious to accomplish his mission, the young man hurried ahead, reached the massive door, and knocked. Almost at once, the inside bolt was drawn and the door swung open.

"Come in, Mr. Smythe." The Colonel's voice was hearty and the handshake that accompanied it was firm. "Nasty turn of weather, eh? Ah, you've caught a bit of rain, I see. Come, I've got a fire. You'll soon warm up. And we'll put that coat of yours on a chair nearby to dry."

The young man readily removed his coat and stood before the fire. The paneled room, he judged, had once accurately reflected the solid prosperity of a successful landowner, but that must have been many years ago, long before the Colonel's time, for the rugs were frayed, the upholstery well worn, and the tables dull from lack of polish.

"You'll have a drink, Mr. Smythe? Of course!" the Colonel declared. He kept his bottles handy on a table near the hearth, and as he poked among them for the particular one he sought the fire made the shadows of his fingers do a clumsy dance on the opposite wall.

227

"Here we are!" He grunted with satisfaction as he plucked the bottle up. "Well, sir, if you'll accept that chair, we'll draw up snug-like, see, and get to business." He puffed as he eased himself into his own chair and then cleared his throat noisily. "But first," he said with a wink, "we'll have a toast. To neighborliness, eh?"

"Gladly," said Smythe.

"Capital!" the Colonel responded. He tilted his upraised glass and drank with gusto. "Um!" He smacked his lips, then gave his visitor a thoughtful look. "Sounds as though you had a bit of a cold, sir. Your voice is thick, I mean."

"I'm afraid so."

"Ah, well. This is the medicine for it, eh? You can't go wrong with a couple of doses of this prescription!" The Colonel chuckled and drank again. He was elderly, but as sturdy as a draft-horse, and his fleshy face was stained by years of weathering. He was an avid hunter, it seemed, for guns and rifles were hung on the walls or leaned in corners, each weapon glistening with fresh oil.

"Now," the Colonel barked cheerfully, as if he were convening a regimental officers' meeting. "You phoned me, sir, about my cows?"

"Yes. I'm afraid they found a gap in your fence and wandered into my meadow—"

"Ah, so you informed me, Mr. Smythe. Well, the problem seems a simple one, eh? Come morning, I'll trot down to have a look at that fence and then get it patched up, that's all."

"I'd be much obliged, sir."

"No problem at all, Mr. Smythe. Never a problem between neighbors if there's fair dealing and honesty, is my opinion." The Colonel nodded in self-agreement and the firelight winked on his bald dome. "It's an honest county, this," he added, "though I've known it but a few short years. And yet I'm not such a newcomer as yourself, sir, since this is your first season, eh? Strange about those cows, though," the Colonel rambled on. "Old Towsley, he's my dairyman—my whole staff, to tell the truth—he mumbled something about the beasts, come to think of it. Said of the eight he counted but seven. In short, one missing."

"Oh, I say, really?" Mr. Smythe seemed taken aback. "I was almost positive I'd sent the lot back through—"

"Undoubtedly you did, sir, undoubtedly you did! Old Towsley's half blind and can't handle numbers besides. You could have driven a dozen of your own to my barn and the old chap wouldn't have noticed!"

"But seriously, sir, I shall certainly have a talk with my men first thing tomorrow—"

"Think no more about it, Mr. Smythe!" The Colonel chuckled heartily. "I mentioned it simply to illustrate old Towsley's muddled ways. No indeed, sir, it isn't a question of one cow more or less, but of neighborliness, as I have said." He paused— then, with an embarrassed glance at Smythe, he added, "Excuse my thoughtlessness for referring to Towsley's eyes troubles. I meant no personal allusion to yourself."

"Not at all, Colonel," Smythe said hastily. He removed his dark glasses, gave them a quick polish on his sleeve, and replaced them. "I've had a sensitivity to light ever since childhood."

The Colonel made a clucking sound. "Pity!" He rose to replenish their drinks. "Neighborliness, Mr. Smythe, that's the drill in these parts, and I can honestly say I'm delighted to have such a considerate young man as yourself next door to me. Your glass, sir. Ah!" He sat down again. "I treasure such a relationship all the more, you see, because I had an unusually nasty experience in the opposite way five years back when I was living up north. A rotten show it was, all the way through!" He leaned toward Smythe confidentially. "Had a chap adjoining me who was one of those odd quirky types—paranoia."

"Really!" remarked Smythe.

"Worst of it was," the Colonel went on, scowling at the recollection, "that nobody in the village had the decency to warn me. No, not them. They'd let the trusting old fool march in and buy his bit of land to settle down to a modest country existence—and not a word from them, not one! I had to find out for myself. 'Twas like living on a powder keg!"

"Good heavens," said Smythe. "What happened, sir?"

The Colonel took a healthy swallow from his glass. "Ah, it began quietly enough. That's the way with those chaps. To look at 'em, you'd never suspect a thing. Fellow rapped at my door one day, polite as pie. He told me in a roundabout way that one of my dogs had slipped over and killed a fowl of his. Oh, he was full of apologies. Could hardly bear to disturb me about it—that kind of thing. But I caught a glint in his eye, and I said to myself, Oho! Something's up here! But naturally, I returned his politeness with my own."

"Of course," said Smythe.

"For the sake of appearances," the Colonel continued, "I went over with him to investigate, but I knew straightaway there was something odd, because neither of my pups had a taste for fowl. Good dogs both, they were. I suggested the presence of a fox, but the fellow claimed that one of his men had seen the culprit fleeing and could swear it was a dog, and a collared dog at that. So what could I do but defend my own, eh? I denied it was possible. A dog, perhaps, but mine? Nonsense!"

"Did your neighbor become—er—violent?"

"Ah, not him!" the Colonel declared grimly. "That's not their way, you see, sir. They're clever, these creatures. Oh, he had a disarming way about him. A young chap, several years your junior, I would judge, Mr. Smythe—a bit slenderer, too, and with a rather high-pitched voice. When I spoke my little piece, he simply bowed his head a bit, as if he were accepting a challenge almost, and again I was struck by the look in his eye." The Colonel shrugged and shook his head. "I've been through some sticky places in my lifetime, I can tell you, but I'd never before seen a slyer, more ingratiating devil than that chap up north!"

"What did he do, Colonel?"

"Mr. Smythe, that was the very question that troubled me. Rather, I wondered what *would* he do? Not that I thought he was a loony then, but I can assure you I was a bit uneasy." The Colonel pursed his lips reflectively. "First, I decided to find out more about the man. I went to the village and made inquiries. I spoke to the banker and to some of the tradespeople. Right off, I could tell that this neighbor of mine had them scared speechless, for they claimed to have heard nothing bad about him, and on the contrary vowed that he was an altogether pleasant person. Not only that, sir, but I got the distinct impression that these poor folk would side with him in any dispute—out of sheer terror, you see. Why, in a week's time they turned positively hostile toward me!"

Smythe nodded in response, and thoughtfully stroked his close-cut brown beard. "And then, Colonel?"

"Then the game broke out into the open," said the Colonel. "A day or two later, the fellow appeared again at my door, still pretending civility, you understand. He told me he'd lost a second bird the night before. I looked him in the eye. 'What's that to me, if I may ask?' I said, as any honest man would, and he dropped his gaze then—couldn't brazen it out, you see—and mumbled some kind of apology and off he went. But it gave me the shivers to see the way he slunk along, casting his eye left or right, for it put me in mind of the way a hunter will study the terrain where he intends to ambush his prey.

The Colonel paused to blow his nose. His listener remained silent, staring down into his glass.

" 'Twas then," the Colonel went on, "that I smelled danger. I thought at first the rascal might try to poison my beasts—and then it occurred to me that he would hardly be satisfied with that. No, once these chaps get a grudge started, there's no easy ending, that I knew. Well, sir, I made a second foray into town, and I was a determined man by then. I cornered the banker and this time I held on. I wouldn't be shaken off, sir! For hours I worried at him, presenting the plain unvarnished facts, you see, and finally he had to admit sir, that I was right. He seemed shocked and amazed, Mr. Smythe, and not a little frightened.

"You convinced him you were dealing with a madman?"

"Ah, not convinced, Mr. Smythe. He had known it all along, of course. No, I merely forced him to concede the truth, although he still pretended that this was the first hint of trouble that had come to him. Bankers are craft that way, sir!" The Colonel set down his glass and fumbled in his pocket for a pipe.

"He told me something about my neighbor's background. It seems that the young fellow was an orphan, of indifferent stock, who had got some kind of education and scraped up enough money to come to that county and buy his piece of land. Ah, in another type such a story would be admirable, Mr. Smythe, but with this fellow his struggle to succeed had merely puffed up his wild suspicions of the world until he had gone clear over the edge! The banker confided in me further. The young man, he said, had overextended himself somewhat and was even then applying for a loan to see him through. Without it, he might be in deep trouble with his creditors.

"The opening was too obvious not to be seized. I said to him, 'Surely, you're not going to approve the loan?' And he replied, 'On the contrary, Colonel, I believe we will approve it.' The blindness of some folk! I argued with him, as you may imagine, saying that here was a heaven-sent opportunity to get rid of this creature. 'Deny the loan, sir, and you'll topple him.' I cried. He was uncertain at first—and I could hardly blame him, for a banker is by nature a timid animal—but after I had been at him for another hour or two, he agreed that the time had come for firmness. Yes, Mr. Smythe I managed to stiffen his backbone. He promised he would turn down the application."

"Admirable," muttered Smythe.

"But there was much else to do," the Colonel continued, stuffing his pipe with tobacco. He brought it to his lips and struck a match, glancing sharply over the flame at the face of his guest. "I had to make certain of it. So in the next few days I visited each of the important tradesmen in turn, those who had extended credit to my neighbor. I didn't waste time in trying to overcome their terror of the lunatic. No, with them I pursued a subtler course. After gaining their confidence, sir, I let it slip, as if by accident, that the chap's attempt to get a loan from the bank was being turned down."

"A clever strategem," said Smythe.

The Colonel inclined his head in acknowledgement. "The effect was like one of these chain reactions, sir. First one creditor called for payment of his bill, then another, then a third and fourth, and, sure enough, within a few days that young devil was beating a path to the bank, hoping to speed up his loan. I happened to be in town that day myself. As a matter of fact, I had just visited the banker, for I anticipated what would happen. I wanted to put some more iron in his nerve, you see, so he wouldn't back down at the last minute. I drew myself up, sir, to full height, and I told that banker in no uncertain terms, sir, that if he turned tail and approved the loan, I could not be held responsible for the consequences."

"And he followed your—ah—advice?"

"He did indeed, Mr. Smythe! I was standing near the bank when the young chap came out. Oh, you could tell he had suffered a blow. He thought he had the village under his thumb, like some feudal tyrant, you see, and then all of a sudden—" The Colonel brought his hands sharply together and laughed shortly. "He was ruined, sir! He staggered toward me, pale and trembling. He gave me one glance—ah, the hatred in it, Mr. Smythe!—'twas like the mask of a demon, sir! But like a coward, he said nothing, and passed on by. The next day his land went on the market!"

"You had finished him, then," remarked Smythe.

"Not quite! Ah, but there was another factor I almost forgot. It seems that my intervention had prevented a great tragedy, sir. The young schemer was engaged to marry the daughter of one of the other landowners, a lovely girl she was, and naturally, when his bankruptcy came to public notice, the engagement was canceled—"

"Naturally."

"And the girl herself, saved from a life of horrors, was dispatched by her family to France to avoid the villain's revenge. These chaps will stop at nothing, Mr. Smythe! But I should tell you of that look he gave me there in the street outside the bank. As plain as day, sir, that look spoke in unutterable passion for vengeance, as if that young devil had screamed aloud his intention of murdering me, of hunting me down, sir, no matter what the cost, no matter how long it might take."

"Ah," remarked Smythe, "but he appears to have been unsuccessful thus far."

The Colonel chuckled. "True enough, sir, true enough! I was too quick for him, I think."

"You sold your own property and moved down here, I would gather."

"Correct, sir."

"To remove yourself from the possibility of being shot down by this—this madman," said Smythe. He reached over to feel his coat. It was quite dry now, except, it seemed, for the area around the shoulders.

The Colonel watched his movements. "Well, sir, not precisely for that reason," he said slowly.

"Don't mistake my meaning, Colonel," said Smythe quickly. "I don't imply that you had any personal fear—"

"Understood, sir!" boomed the Colonel. "No, let me tell you. It was a rather unpleasant incident, and at its conclusion I chose to move away, for there was some hard feeling among ignorant persons up there.

"Well, sir, the morning after the scene at the bank, I was out walking along the edge of my property when I thought I heard a noise nearby. It seemed to come from the direction of the lunatic's fields, so I slipped across the fence to investigate.

"Over a rise I saw him. He was on his knees in the meadow, sobbing. A fit had taken him, Mr. Smythe. I could tell that he was nerving himself to some desperate deed, and I saw with alarm a bulge in his coat pocket which I took to be a pistol, but which actually was a knife. One of these little fold-up affairs, sir, but capable of carving a man to ribbons!"

Smythe reached again toward his coat. "How frightful, Colonel. And did he attack you?"

"He would have, sir, he most certainly would have!" The Colonel puffed heavily on his pipe, and the smoke obscured his face. "But again, I was too quick for the chap. I pulled out my revolver—and fired!"

"You disabled him, sir?"

The Colonel coughed from the smoke and turned his head aside. "Not exactly, Mr. Smythe." He paused and coughed again. "No, I killed him, sir. Killed him on the spot. There was some nastiness about it later, but the jury at length agreed it was clearly self-defense on my part. It was after that, Mr. Smythe, that I moved here."

The Colonel's voice faded and the echoes of his last words whispered along the walls. The dying fire glowed fitfully with little resentful spikes of reddish flame. The room hardened in silence.

The Colonel turned his head toward Smythe. His features seemed fleshier than before and his eyes were drawn into a squint.

When he spoke, his voice was thick, and it had a querulous

tone. "But about our business, sir. About that so-called gap in my fence. Strange, most strange. I had not noticed it before you moved in, sir. Nor had my man Towsley, sir, and he's got a keen pair of eyes, Towsley has. What—leaving so soon, Mr. Smythe? Come now, sir, is that quite neighborly? And before your coat is dry?"

JOHN D. MACDONALD

WHO'S THE BLONDE?

It was well after seven when he asked them again if he could call Helen. It had become an almost automatic question on Tom Weldon's part, and each time he had asked there had been neither permission nor denial—just an infuriating obtuseness, as though he had spoken in Arabic or had been a silly child asking for the moon.

His throat felt dry as he said again, "Please, could I call my wife? She'll be worried."

At the moment there were three of them in the bank president's office, three of them looking at him with those coldly amused eyes. There was Durand, from the police; Elvinard, one of the bank examiners; and Vic Reisher, the chief teller.

This time Reisher looked at Durand. Durant nodded and gestured toward the telephone with a thick thumb. "On a night plug, isn't it? Go ahead, Weldon."

Tom reached over and pulled the telephone toward him. He heard the dial tone and dialed his home number. It rang twice before a man answered. "Who is this?" Tom said. "Who's talking?"

"Who are you, friend?"

"This is Weldon. Is this my home? I'm positive I dialed the right number."

The voice sounded amused. "Hold it, friend. I'll put your wife on."

He could tell from Helen's voice that she had been crying. "Tom? Oh, Tom, what's happened?"

"Who is that man? What's he doing there?"

"He's a policeman. A detective. There are two of them. They wouldn't let me try to phone you. Oh, Tom, I've been frantic. What's it all about?"

"It's a mistake, dear. Some kind of—terrible mistake."

There were often mistakes when it came time to balance up

at three o'clock. Sometimes there had been a stupid transposition of figures. There were formulas to apply which would pinpoint the error. Today had been different, very different. The guards had locked the door at three o'clock, standing nearby to let the last few customers out. It hadn't been a particularly tough day. There had been time, off and on, for Tom—teller number three—to kid around with Jud Fergol in the second cage at his right and Arthur Maldrick in cage four at his left.

On tough days there was the knowledge of being a working team, a fast team operating under the guidance of wry Vic Reischer. Jud Fergol was a thin-faced, quiet man about Tom's age, who handled money with an almost dazzling manual dexterity. Arthur Maldrick, on the other side of Tom, was younger, but he was one of those big, plodding, ponderous young men who seem to have been born middle-aged. Arthur's extracurricular passion was tree peonies, and his rather heavy-handed sense of humor did not extend to that topic.

This was one of those days when you knew the balancing up would be routine and you'd be home earlier than usual. Tom had worked quickly, hoping that neither Jud Fergol nor Arthur Maldrick had made mistakes. Vic Reisher clung to the old tradition of keeping all tellers on hand until the balancing was complete and perfect.

Tom could hear the quick whip-slap of currency in Jud's agile fingers and the tone-deaf humming of Arthur. His own error was so large that he grinned at it, suspecting a simple arithmetic error. He quickly ran another tape—and another. He began to sweat. Arthur had finished and gone with Vic to the vault to lock up his drawer. Jud had finished and was waiting for Vic.

"Trouble, Tom? Find it fast. I've got a lawn to mow."

Tom nodded, and kept struggling with the figures. Vic and Jud went into the vault to lock up Jud's drawer. They came back and stood behind the wire door of Tom's cage, chatting and smoking.

"Can you hurry it up, Tom?" Vic asked.

"You better help me, Vic."

Vic raised one eyebrow and came through the wire door as Tom unlatched it on the inside. "How big is your error?"

"Uh—four thousand, Vic."

In the silence of the bank the words carried clearly. Tom heard Jud's gasp, glanced quickly at Arthur's puzzled face. He felt the tension as he stood aside and watched Vic go through the procedure with the ease of years of practice. Vic ran his tapes, then straightened up slowly. His eyes were cool. "Your cash is short an even four thousand, Tom."

He had been a part of the team and now he was standing on the outside and they were all looking at him.

"What have you done, Tom?" Jud asked softly. "Why did you do it?"

"But I—I haven't—"

"I can't sit on this, Tom," Vic said, his voice as emotionless as a comptometer. "There's a crew of examiners in town. They've been checking Federal. I'll get in touch with them. I'm sorry, Jud, Arthur. You'll have to stay around. Better phone your homes."

"Vic, could I phone?"

"I'd rather you stand right where you are, please."

And that had been the beginning of a nightmare—to find yourself unaccountably on the wrong side of the fence from the rest of the team. Deny it until your mouth was dry and there was a rasp in your throat, but they still kept looking at you in that certain, unmistakable way . . .

His hand was damp on the telephone. "Don't worry about it, Helen. Everything will be all right."

"They—they say you took money."

"Do you believe that?"

"Of *course* not!" she said hotly. And she added, in a more uncertain tone, "They have a warrant or something and I had to let them go through all your things."

"Just don't worry about it, please, honey. Kids okay?"

"I fed them early and put them to bed. But you know how they are. They sort of sense it when anything is wrong. And these men keep asking me all sorts of questions."

"Answer everything they ask. I don't have to tell you that. They're off on the wrong tangent. I'll explain when I see you. Don't worry if they don't let me come home."

"I'm—I'm so glad you called."

"I tried to call before. They wouldn't let me."

"I'll be waiting for you, darling. They'll have to let you come home."

Tom hung up and leaned back in the straight chair. "There are men at the house, and they've upset my wife. I resent that." He tried to summon up righteous anger, but the hours of anger and indignation had drained him.

Durand was a stocky, nervous, bright-eyed man with thick white hands that were in constant motion, plucking at his suit, ruffling his hair, pulling at his ear lobes.

"Those men," said Durand, "Harkness and Lutz. They're okay. Nothing rough about them. You want to get your wife off the hook, you tell us about the girl friend."

Tom looked dully down at his hands and said, as he had said so many times before, "I never saw the girl before in my life. Never."

"Okay," said Durand. "We take it again. Today's Wednesday— a slow day. It's a quarter after two and the bank closes at three. There you are. Window three. There's another window vacant and you got one customer. But she comes right to your window and waits. A dish like that, people notice her. A real blondie. One of those tight-skirt, go-to-hell blondies. Fergol at window two hears her call you Tom and then she talks so quiet he can't hear her. But he sees you lean forward to listen."

"I never saw her before in my life. I've told you that. I can't help what she called me. My name is on the window, you know. Thomas D. Weldon. She called me Tom and it startled me. Then she talked so low I had to lean forward to hear her."

"Why don't you tell us what she actually said to you?"

"She said, 'Tom, if I gave you a fifty, could I get fifty nice crisp new ones?' She looked and acted funny. I had my foot on the button, ready to let the alarm go. She slid the fifty under the grille. I took a good look at it, just in case. It was okay. I gave her the fifty ones, and she jammed them into her purse and turned and went out fast."

"She went out fast because you gave her four thousand bucks, Weldon. And she was in a big hurry to get away. What does she have on you, boy?"

"I never saw her before in my life. It's the truth. I swear it."

Vic Reisher said, "Tom, damn it, this isn't going to do any good."

Tom stared at his friend. "You believe I gave her that money, don't you?"

Vic was a gaunt man with shaggy hair, deep-set eyes, and a wry smile. He shrugged, "What else can—"

"Let me try again, Mr. Reisher," Elvinard, the examiner, said. He had a face like a small, neat grave marker. His voice was metallic. "Now look, Weldon. Listen carefully. You got your drawer out of the vault this morning and you were checked out by Mr. Reisher, everything in order. You worked from ten until twelve-thirty and then took an hour for lunch. When you went to lunch, you and Mr. Reisher locked your drawer with the two keys necessary. When you came back, you both unlocked it. No one had a chance to tamper with your cash on hand. At all times when the cash was—shall we say—available, you were there in your cage. Yet, when the doors closed at three o'clock you seemed to be having trouble balancing out. Mr. Reisher came over to you and helped you check. And you were four thousand dollars short.

"Now, let us suppose for a moment that you are telling the truth about that young lady who spoke to you by name. We will assume that she *was* a stranger and that you gave her fifty ones. All right, then. If she didn't get the money, Mr. Weldon, exactly how did it disappear and where did it go?"

Tom braced his elbows on his knees, the heels of his hands hard against his eyes. "I don't know," he said hopelessly.

Durand said, "We're going to find out. The more work it makes for us, the more trouble it means for you. Open up, and we'll try to give you every break in the book. Maybe we can get a recovery on the funds. Maybe you can draw a suspended sentence. Who knows? But the starting place is for you to come clean, boy." His voice turned wheedling, confidential. "A lot of nice guys get taken over the jumps by a blondie. Come on, boy. What's she got on you? Hell, we *know* you've been playing around."

Tom felt the return of dull anger. He straightened up. "I explained all that to you. I was being frank with you. I told you that I've been sort of restless lately—the last six months, I guess.

Vic told you about me telling him that Helen and I were scrapping. I guess every married couple goes through times like that. It's—hard to live on the pay. It makes a strain. You know what I mean. So it gets on your nerves, with prices going up all the time and a couple of kids. I walked out a couple of times and went to a neighborhood beer joint. Tige's Grill. Just a few beers. Ask Al, the bartender. No women. No blondes. Just a few beers to take the strain off."

Durand had been out of the room several times in the past three hours. He grinned in an unpleasant way and took a notebook out of his pocket. "The bartender is Albert Kelling, and he knows you by name. He states that to the best of his recollection you were in there on a Friday night three weeks ago and that you went over to one of the booths and engaged in conversation with a woman about thirty years of age, dark hair, and a younger woman who was a blonde. Albert Kelling stated that he had never seen either of the women before and they have not been in since. He is willing to make a formal statement to that effect, and to the effect that you left said Tige's Grill accompanied by the two women."

Tom tried to smile in a confident way. He was aware of the trembling of his hands. "That's plain silly! I knew that dark-haired girl in high school. She remembered my name, but I couldn't remember hers. Sure, I spoke to them. Who wouldn't? Her friend was younger and blonde, but she didn't look anything like the girl who came into the bank. And I walked out the door with them, yes. We talked for a couple of minutes on the sidewalk, then they went one way and I went the other."

"What was this woman's name?"

"I tell you I can't remember. I'm no good about names. I never have been."

"Where does she live?"

"She didn't say."

"And she didn't refresh your memory and give you her name?"

"You know how it is when you can't remember a name. You try to cover up. She introduced her friend. I think it was Mary something. Or Marie, maybe."

"Can you describe the blonde friend? This Marie?"

"Well, about twenty-five. Medium height. Sort of thin, I think."

"So you picked up a blonde in a bar and got more than you bargained for."

"I—I know how it sounds to you. When I tell you, everything sounds so weak. But believe me, I've never stolen anything in my life. I've got a good record. Ask Vic."

Durand said heavily, "You *had* a good record, young man." He looked at his watch. "Go on home, Weldon. I advise you to talk it over with your wife. Harkness told me over the phone she seems like a good, sound person. Come clean with her, Weldon. I advise it. Tell her everything and I'm sure she'll tell you to do the right thing."

Tom was startled. "I can go home?"

"Go ahead. Will you let him out, please, Mr. Reisher? Don't try to leave town, Weldon. We'll pick you up when we've got everything we need."

They went down the dark staircase to the side entrance. Vic started to unlock the door and then turned. "How could you do it, Tom? You knew that if you were in a jam, all you had to do was come to me and tell me the story."

"If you don't believe me, who else is going to? Just unlock the damn door."

Vic stood still for a few moments, then unlocked the door. He didn't speak. Tom heard it close crisply behind him. He went back to the parking lot behind the bank and started the six-year-old sedan and drove slowly home. Twice he stopped for red lights and then didn't start up again until the cars behind him honked indignantly.

He lived in the top half of a two-family house. As he turned into the narrow driveway between the house and the one next door, his headlights swept across the police cruiser parked at the curb. Oh, fine! Nice questions for the kids. "Tommy, what were the police at your house for? What's your daddy done?"

It gave him a feeling of acute helplessness. You went along thinking that if somebody ever tried to persecute you, mess up your life, kick you around, you were a citizen and you could call the cops. Get a lawyer. Get an injunction or something. But who did you yell to when it was the forces of law and order

sitting on your chest, making your wife cry, ruining your hopes
and your chances and your future?

None of it made sense. He had the crazy feeling that maybe
he had been hypnotized somehow into thinking four thousand
dollars were fifty ones. He could see the blonde, teetering
hastily away from his teller's cage, hurrying out of the bank,
holding that shiny blue pocketbook. She was the kind men
looked at, the kind they would remember. So all you remembered was the ripe figure and the wide, damp mouth and
nothing else.

He went slowly up the stairs. The door opened off the living
room and a tough-faced young man in a pale suit looked at him
and said, "Weldon. Know you from your picture on the bureau.
Welcome home."

Tom ignored him and went on down the hall. Helen had
heard the man and she came, half running. He held her close
and felt the trembling of her body. Her eyes were red and
puffed, but she wasn't crying.

He kissed her. "It's okay. It's a mistake."

Over her shoulder, he saw a paunchy young man come out
of the kitchen with a glass of milk in his hand. His look of
relaxation, of being at home, infuriated Tom. He said, "Why
don't you two get the hell out of here?"

The paunchy young man drained the glass and set it on the
bookcase. He wiped his mouth with the back of his hand. "On
our way, Weldon. This very minute." He came over and held his
hand out to Helen. She took it shyly. He said, "Sorry we had to
bother you this way, Mrs. Weldon, but you know how those
things are." He gave Tom a bleak look. "You got you a good lady
here, friend. Come on, Willy."

They clumped heavily down the stairs. Tom heard one of
them chuckle at something the other one said as they went out
the front door. He walked to the front windows and watched
the car move slowly down the street.

"They've got no right," Tom said in a thick voice.

"It's something they had to do. They explained that. Darling,
have you had anything at all to eat?"

"No, but I couldn't eat anything."

"You must. You look so dreadful, so tired. Scrambled eggs, maybe. Bacon?"

"I—guess so."

"Come out to the kitchen and tell me about all this while I fix it, honey. What makes them think you could do anything— crooked?"

"My furtive expression, I guess." He sat at the kitchen table and lighted a cigarette. He said, "I'll tell you the facts. It's what they're going by. In a crazy way, I don't blame them."

It didn't take long to tell her. The eggs were done and she was putting them on the plate when he finished. Frowning, she walked to the table and sat down.

"And Vic doesn't believe you?"

"No."

She said fiercely, "When they find out you didn't do it, Tom, neither one of us will ever speak to him again."

He felt the sting in his eyes. "I have expected you to wonder whether I—"

"Tom!"

"Well, I *have* been kind of mean lately—yammering at you, going off in my little private huff."

"But I *know* you. I *know* you couldn't steal."

"And I know I *didn't.* So where did the money go? Evaporation? Hundreds and fifties. Wrapped. A little pack. Easy to hide. They had me strip, you know. And went through my locker." His voice had gone shrill, harsh.

"Please, Tom. Please. Don't do that to yourself. You have to think, you know. You didn't take the money. You didn't give it to that girl. Somebody took it. It didn't walk away."

"We went over that during my—interview. There are a lot of slick tricks. Every teller knows that. Bent pins and adhesive tape and chewing gum on the end of a cane. It gets to be second nature to be conscious of the money, to make sure it's well back from the cage opening."

"Can you remember any other strangers who came to your window?"

"We had the usual last-minute rush from quarter of three until closing. There were several strangers. Nothing special about them. One with a traveler's check. One at the wrong

window. Others, probably—I can't remember. You see, I didn't
know then that it was going to be important to remember."

"And you didn't notice that the stack of bills was gone until
you started to balance out for the day?"

"No, I didn't."

"When was the last time you did any housekeeping behind
your window?"

"Around two-thirty, I think. If the money had been gone then,
I think I would have noticed it. Just noticed the physical lack of
it."

"Was the whole stack gone?"

"One whole stack."

Helen and Tom sat up and went over it again and again. He
was sick with emotional fatigue. Finally Helen said, "We're not
making sense any more. We've got to sleep, darling."

He thought he would be unable to sleep. But sleep come
over him like a black tide in flood. When he woke up it was
morning and Helen was up. He heard the kids chattering in the
kitchen. He knew he should go out and speak to them, go out
with a morning smile and a confident manner. But somehow he
couldn't quite manage it. He waited until he heard Helen at the
door with them, giving Tommy the usual morning admonition
not to let his sister cross the streets without holding her hand.
He heard the staccato sound of their feet on the wooden stairs,
heard the front door slam lustily.

When he went out to breakfast, his high-school yearbook was
beside his glass of orange juice. He frowned at it and then
suddenly grinned at Helen. "You're a smart kid."

"I thought if you could find her you could tell them her
name, and then they could find out you didn't lie."

He sat there at the breakfast table and went through all the
pictures. He could not find her among the graduates. Conceal-
ing his sense of dismay, acting confident for Helen's sake, he
turned to the group pictures in the back, pictures that had been
taken during the school year.

"Come here," he said. "This one. Right here."

"Are you absolutely certain, dear?"

"Let me see. The names are down here. Second row. Third
from the left. One, two, here it is—Martha Dolvac."

He phoned police headquarters and asked for Lieutenant Durand. There was a long wait after he gave his name. "Lieutenant? This is Tom Weldon."

"Did your wife give you the right steer? Ready to talk?"

"I haven't got any confession, if that's what you mean. I want to give you a name. The dark-haired woman in the bar. Martha Dolvac. Maybe you could trace her from the Briggs High School records."

"If you didn't make up the name."

"I've got a picture of her here. Out of my yearbook. I think I remember that she was a junior when I was a senior. Will you check it?"

"Sure. And suppose it nails it a little tigher, Weldon?"

"It won't," Tom said, trying to make his voice sound confident. He hoped that it did. "Will you let me know?"

"You want to come in this morning and give us the straight story?"

"You've had the straight story, Lieutenant."

Tom hung up quickly, the palms of his hands sweaty. Even if he straightened out the distorted version of that conversation at Tige's Grill, it didn't solve the problem of how the money disappeared.

He took a sheet of white paper and a ruler and made a scale drawing of his cage, looking down at it from above. After the years he had spent in the cage, he could remember every detail of it. It was roughly six feet by five feet. On the window side, where he faced the public, it was five feet across. The wall was eight feet high, with the bronze grille set into it. There was a three-and-a-half-inch gap between the bottom of the window and the counter, but the grille could be unlatched from the inside and swung outward to permit the passage of bulky items. Inside his cubicle there was a counter on each side of him, with his cash drawer under the counter on his right. He usually stacked the bills on the counter above the cash drawer. The change machine was between the stacked currency and the barred window. The sides of his cubicle, of wire mesh in a three-quarter-inch diamond pattern, were about six feet high.

At the rear of his cage was a wire door which could only be opened from the inside. He remembered the days when the front wall, between the windows, had been of wood. It had given the tellers too much of a closed-in feeling, so it had been changed to heavy, shatterproof plate glass.

On his detailed sketch he marked the location of the stack of bills which had disappeared. It had been, he remembered, a stack of wrapped packets, with a rubber band encircling the stack.

Helen stood beside him and examined the drawing. "We'll say the money was there at 2:30."

"I can't be sure of that. I just think it was. It could have been gone."

"Could it have been gone before the girl came in?"

"I don't think so."

"Was anybody in your cage between the time she was in and when the bank closed."

"No, Helen. I'm positive of that."

"Jud Fergol is here, at window two. And Arthur Maldrick on the other side of you. They didn't see anything?"

"Nothing. Jud heard the girl call me Tom, but then she talked too low for him to hear what she said."

"Did she seem nervous?"

"Just kind of—odd. I thought she was maybe a little crazy."

"I—I just can't understand it, Tom."

"Neither can anyone else."

"They can't send you to prison, can they?"

"I don't know. Maybe. I think they let me go so they could follow me and see if I got in touch with that blonde, or she with me. I *know* that money didn't go through the window. I *know* that."

"And your door was not opened. There's only one other place. Over the walls. They say women aren't logical. That's the only other place it *could* go!"

"That isn't being logical. That's being simpleminded. Somebody twelve feet tall reached over and picked it up." He flushed. "Damn it, Helen, you know better than to try to tell me that."

The doorbell rang. It was Harkness and Lutz. It was two in the afternoon. They took him to Durand's office. Elvinard was there.

"I'll give you this," Durand said. "It checked out. She got

married, and she lives on West Pershing. Her name is Mrs. Henry Votronic. She remembers the evening very well. She backs you up. Her friend is named Marie Gold. We questioned Marie separately. She told the same story. The guards took a look at Marie. Too thin, they say, to be our friend. Or should I say *your* friend?"

"If I wasn't lying about that—"

"It doesn't mean you couldn't have been lying about everything else. Who's the blonde?"

"I didn't give her the money. I didn't take it myself."

Durand gave him a look of disgust. He leaned back in the chair and cracked his knuckles. "You got any theories?"

Tom flushed. "My wife says if it didn't go through the window or through the door, it had to go over the wall."

"Nonsense!" Elvinard said in his sharp, metallic voice. "I've seen a lot of slickers in action. They haven't developed any methods of hoisting money over an eight-foot wall between your cage and the bank floor. You're wasting our time, Weldon."

"Maybe," said Durand slowly, "if everybody's attention was attracted some other place—I read upon one deal where an accomplice sets a sort of accidental fire in one of the wastebaskets out on the floor and then his buddy, with one of those collapsible fishing gaffs, lifts a package out of a teller's window while the guy is watching the fire."

"We've been over that," Elvinard explained impatiently. "There was no incident of that sort. The only odd thing noticed in the bank yesterday afternoon was the blonde young lady. There was no—ah—diversionary attempt." He coughed in a dry way. "Weldon, this isn't a big theft. We're more interested in the money than in a successful prosecution. Produce the four thousand, or tell us where we can get it, and I can almost guarantee you a suspended sentence."

"And if I can't?"

Elvinard leaned forward. "I'll see that you get a prison sentence. And once you get out, we'll still be looking for that money, and for the blonde."

Something was nibbling at the back of Tom's mind. Some memory. Something ludicrous. He didn't answer.

"Well?" said Elvinard.

"Please shut up a minute," Tom said patiently. No diversionary attempt. Over the all. What constituted a diversionary attempt? Something that would focus all eyes on one specific object. There had been laughter as the girl reached the door. Something had happened to make both the tellers and the customers laugh. He remembered seeing the irate face of a vice-president who glared at the unseemly sound. And Helen had said the money had to go over the wall.

He said to Elvinard, "Go away for a while. I want to talk to the Lieutenant."

"I certainly will not go—"

"Humor the guy, humor the guy," Durand said. Elvinard stalked out and shut the door. "What's on your mind?" Durand asked Tom.

"Lieutenant, that girl had high heels and a tight skirt, and she set those heels down hard. They made a lot of racket. She was hurrying. And when she was ten feet away from my window, somebody whistled. You know, one of those wolf whistles."

"So?"

Tom stood up, too nervous to stay sitting down. "It made me think. When that whistle came, everybody looked at her. I guess she was the only woman on the bank floor anyway. And they laughed when she got to the door."

"Make sense, will you?"

"Don't you see it? That whistle did it. It made everybody look at her. Just like they'd look at a fire in a wastebasket. I don't like to say this—but I know who whistled. It came from my right. It was Jud Fergol, and I remember now thinking that it wasn't like him at all. It was a funny thing for him to do."

Durand laced his fingers at the back of his neck. "Weldon, any bank job puts the heat on the local cops, and it brings in a lot of help. The F.B.I. has been on this, you know. You've got an appointment with them a little later on. Judson Fergol, Arthur Maldrick, Victor Reisher—fine-tooth combs on all of them. Okay, so Fergol whistled. Sometimes a blonde will make a sedate-type guy forget where he is. Judson Fergol is a very sober citizen. To bed at ten. No booze. No gambling. No ladies. Does it match?"

"Not exactly. Vic told me three months ago he was worried

about Jud. He said Jud always chewed mints after lunch. One day he forgot them. Vic sent him home. He was afraid one of the vice-presidents might smell Jud's breath."

Durand closed his eyes for long seconds. He was immobile. For once, the restless white hands didn't move. He opened his eyes. "You interest me strangely. Your wife said the dough had to go over the wall?"

"Yes, but I don't see—"

"Maybe she's a smart girl."

"What are you going to do?"

Durand smiled in an exceedingly unpleasant way. "Take Mr. Fergol's life apart, just for the kicks. Like we did yours. Know we vacuumed your car? Checked the ashtray? Went over your clothes? The face powder we got matched your wife's. The lipstick we got off a dirty shirt was your wife's brand. Same with lipstick on the butts in the car ashtray. A guy thinks he's smart, you know, destroying match covers, parking-lot stubs, love notes. He forgets you can identify one blonde hair, vacuum face powder, run a spectroscopic analysis of lipstick. Get the cops looking for the 'other woman,' and they're worse than any wife could ever think of being. That was the only thing about you that bothered me. Couldn't find evidence of any outside fun. Go on home. I'm going to cancel your F.B.I. appointment for now."

Sunday afternoon in the bank: shades drawn on the doors, autumn sun slanting in the high windows. Durand said, "Okay, Mr. Weldon. Go on into your cage and shut the door behind you. You watching this, Mr. Fergol?"

"I'm watching," Jud said, his face white, "but I'm afraid it doesn't mean very much to me, Lieutenant." Harkness and Lutz were there, and Vic Reisher, and several almost dapper young F.B.I. men, and some others Tom wasn't able to identify.

Durand went into the adjoining cage—Jud Fergol's cage, teller number two. The men moved to where they could see him. Durand said, "Okay, Weldon, put that package of ones where the big bills were. Fine. Right there. Now make like you're working. Fine. Now turn back and look at the bills. Look okay?"

Tom looked at the money. "Yes, I can't see—"

"Fine. Now, Lutz, you be the blonde." Lutz put his hand on his hip and swayed up to the window. "Don't clown it!" Durand said sharply. "Weldon, act as though you're making change. Okay. Now, Lutz, turn around and walk fast toward the main doors. Set your heels down hard. Keep watching him, Tom."

Tom watched. There was a prolonged shrill whistle.

"Now," said Durand, "turn around slow and take another look at the money."

Tom turned around and gasped. *The money had completely disappeared!* It was gone. He looked at Jud Fergol. He saw the sweat beaded on the man's upper lip. Funny how you could work beside a man and never . . . "How did you do that?" Tom demanded.

Durand smiled. "Like your smart little wife said, Weldon. Over the wall. A while ago I stretched, casual-like, and when my hand was over the edge of the wire fence—and it's only six feet high in here, you know—I let some nylon monofilament fishing line fall down on your side, right where that money is. It's leader material, two-pound test, and it's camouflaged. Hell, you can hardly see it even when you know it's there. On your end was a trout hook. Nothing on my end. I just let it hang down in here.

"When Lutz was standing at your window, I stuck two fingers through the wire grille and hooked the trout hook onto the rubber band. Right after I whistled, I hoisted away. The money dropped on my side. Every man, on that day the blonde was here, was watching that tight skirt and that walk. I shoved the money out of sight, just like Fergol did."

"It's crazy!" Jud said much too loudly. "I never did that."

"The guy where you bought the leader material identified you from a picture. Your wife showed us where you keep your fishhooks. In fact, this is one of yours. When we told her about powder and lipstick that wasn't hers, she stopped kidding us and told us about you sneaking out in the middle of the night too often. So where is she, Fergol, and what's her name?"

Fergol seemed to dwindle as Tom watched him. He looked through them all, looked beyond them to some far, cold, hopeless pace. "Her name is Connie Moran. Westlake Hotel

Apartments. Brown hair. She used that dye that washes out. She had to have the money. She took it all—all but five hundred."

Durand gave him a wise, complacent smile. "You were followed there Friday night. She's in custody, chum. But she's a tougher apple than you are. She never would have talked."

One of the unidentified men said, "Okay to phone in it, Lieutenant?"

"Hold it, Marty. Tell your rewrite boys to give this Weldon a break. Give us the put-out, but give this Weldon an assist on the play. His wife ought to have it, but he needs it more. His kids have to think the old man was working with the cops, Okay?"

"Okay, Lieutenant."

Vic Reisher walked over to Tom, looking miserable. He put his hand out. Tom looked at the man he had considered his friend as well as his boss. He looked at the outstretched hand and knew, suddenly, that to refuse to take it would be a childish gesture.

"Tom—maybe I've been here too long. Maybe I've run too many columns of figures through the machines, totaled too many tapes. My thinking has gotten too black and white. I forgot that I ought to trust my instincts. Your cash account was short; so I had you accused, convicted, and sentences, all in my mind. It adds up to a man who isn't—anyone I'd want to work for. I'm deeply ashamed, Tom."

"Vic, I really don't know whether I'm going to stay or not."

Vic's wry smile was oddly shy. "Wish you would. I guess it won't be exactly the same, but I wish you would."

"I'll talk it over with Helen," Tom said. He suspected that, when his outrage and anger had faded, when his bitterness was gone, he would probably decide to stay. It was work he liked, work he could do well. There would be a new man in Jud's cage. Maybe, with care, the four of them—Vic Arthur, Tom, the unknown newcomer—could once again achieve that sense of unity, of being a quick, clever, functioning unit.

Helen was waiting. He lifted her off the floor when he kissed her. In the mysterious way children have, the kids knew that this was a holiday, this was special. They clung to his legs and yelped.

He said, "Look, among other things, honey, I want to tell you there won't be any more of that storming out of here—"

She stopped his lips with her fingertips. "Hush up. Just take me along next time."

Which, he decided later, was another proof that she was probably just as smart as Durand had said she was.

ROBERT L. FISH

IN A COUNTRY CHURCHYARD

It was on the return trip from the churchyard cemetery that Martin Blackburn felt the first indication of nervousness. As husband of the deceased he rode in the carriage immediately behind the now-empty hearse, and as he sat rigidly on the edge of the seat and stared out of the streaked window at the bleak Northumberland sky, a tremor swept through his body.

He was a tall, gaunt man in his early forties. The taut skin that stretched over the sharp-boned face gave him a skeletal appearance, and the long, thin fingers of his large hands enhanced this imagery. His forehead was high and slightly bulging, and his small ears lay flat against his head, completing the picture of a drawn skull. Only his eyes, sharp and piercing, gave a touch of animation to his face. The black of his costume was quite usual for him, and the occasion had required no change in his normal Sunday attire beyond a funeral band sewn about the sleeve of his greatcoat. All the neighbors and the new families working on his farm had always stood in awe of his aloof figure, for by nature he was neither friendly nor communicative. Now, alone in the dim, heaving carriage he braced himself against the hard seat and relived the past month . . .

It had actually been surprisingly easy. Loretta's illness had been quite natural in its inception; in fact, it was not until she had been forced to remain in bed for a second week that the possibility of actively arranging her death had even occurred to him. Of course, the idea of her dying and the idea of his subsequently inheriting the large farm and her larger personal income had, on occasion, presented itself to him, for his unattractive and shrewish wife had never relinquished her control over the dowry she had brought to their barren marriage.

But the thought of murder to accomplish these desired ends

had only suggested itself since the second week. Then all the details had sprung to mind with such remarkable clarity that he could almost convince himself he was simply an instrument, an agent, directed by forces beyond himself, for Loretta's deserved removal from this vale of life.

He had never been affectionate, either during courting days or after marriage, and he did not make the mistake of changing his ways once his plans were completed. The doctor, for one thing, was far from a fool; nor was Mrs. Crimmins, their house-keeper. He continued to visit his wife's room with the same regularity—as well as the same air of distaste—and to ask the same questions of her, the housekeeper, and the doctor.

His routine for handling the farm was rigorously maintained, and by every carefully calculated action he appeared to be the same man, irritated as he would naturally be by the inconven-ience of illness in the house, but expecting that sooner or later his wife would get up from the sickbed and resume responsibil-ities.

But behind this facade of normality the details of the murder were being carefully decided upon. Loretta Blackburn had never been too strong; her heart, while not sufficiently weak to cause either herself or her doctor any immediate anxiety, had still required constant medication. Her illness had begun as a simple catarrh and had been aggravated by the damp weather and the poor location of the fireplaces their farmhouse afforded. Her doctor had warned Blackburn of the danger of lung fever and the attendant possibility of a further weakening of her heart; but Blackburn had no intention of depending upon a kindly Fate to resolve his problem.

A small kettle lit by an alcohol-spirit lamp stood by the patient's bedside, and each evening Loretta propped herself up complainingly upon the pillows of the great four-poster and inhaled the fumes of a benzoin preparation to clear her head. The murder plan reduced itself to the utmost simplicity: to add to the benzoin solution a small quantity of sulphuric acid and the tiniest of cyanide pellets, and to allow the fumes of this potent concoction to kill his wife.

The mechanics of administration were given particular con-sideration, for Martin Blackburn had no wish inadvertently to join his wife in death. The odor would, he was sure, be disguised by the sharp aroma of the benzoin itself in a strengthened solution, and a thorough airing of the room would strengthen the appearance of innocent surroundings.

And it had all worked perfectly. He began by taking over the housekeeper's daily task of preparing the benzoin solution. It was done subtly, grudgingly, on the basis that Mrs. Crimmins was using the task as an excuse for shirking her other duties, and the housekeeper was pleased to be relieved of any duty, since the illness of Mrs. Blackburn had thrown the entire burden of the household upon her.

On the evening of the fourth day after Blackburn had assumed the extra sick-room responsibility, he deemed the time ripe, for the crisis had passed and his wife was showing signs of improvement, and the regular visit of the doctor fell on the following day. To the usual preparation he added the acid, and at the last moment slipped in the tiny pellet. Holding his breath tightly, he pressed the cone to his wife's thin and unattractive face. The response to the gas was almost immediate; still holding his breath, he swiftly flung the contents of the flask into the darkness beyond the open window, leaning out into the brisk breeze that swept past.

When his aching lungs could no longer stand the pain of their confinement, he cautiously allowed a breath of night air to filter into his lungs, and then stood inhaling for several minutes. He then softly closed the window, added a scuttle of coals to the fire to remove the unusual chill, returned to the bedside, and rapidly prepared a harmless solution.

His fear of detection was slight; the odor was almost indistinguishable, and throughout he had heard the constant rattling of dishes as Mrs. Crimmins finished her work in the kitchen below. Steadying himself against one of the bed-posts, he called to the housekeeper, his voice tinged with an edge of panic that was far from pretense.

And that had been all. The hastily summoned doctor may have been a bit puzzled by the suddenness of death, but if so, his wonder did not extend to any suspicious questions. The death certificate had been duly signed, with heart-seizure given as the immediate cause. Blackburn had been careful to avoid the error of being too obviously overcome with grief; the relationship between his wife and himself had never been anything but poorly disguised enmity, and that fact was known to everyone in the village. Sad, sober in his mourning, he had made the necessary arrangements for burial in the country churchyard and carried them through.

His crowning stroke was to hide both the bottle of acid and the box of cyanide pellets beneath the cerements in those moments he had requested to be alone with his wife before the coffin-lid was screwed down . . .

Yes, it had been so easy! He felt the tremor return and gripped his knee with his free hand, fighting down a momentary panic that he knew was truly unfounded. There could be no questions; there had been no slips. A laugh of successful attainment welled within him, replacing the panic; a wide grin, part relief and part hysteria, twisted his lips. And at that moment the wrinkled face of one of the walking mourners bobbed up beside the carriage window, peering curiously in at him.

The horrible smile froze on his lips. Idiot! he cried to himself, recoiling into the deeper shadows of the rocking vehicle. Fool, fool! Control yourself! To be observed laughing at a time like this!

A lurch of the carriage and the hobbling figure had disappeared into the gloom behind. The dark moor swayed past as he slowly regained control, but he was certain there must already be whispering groups in the rutted road behind, marking and discussing his idiotic grin.

In the days that followed, Martin Blackburn watched anxiously for any sign that his suspicious demeanor on the day of the funeral had become public knowledge, but to all appearances it had passed unnoticed. At least, those with whom he came into contact never seemed to reveal by word or deed that they had heard of the incident, or, having heard of it, had put any suspicious interpretation upon it. He gave himself over to the running of the farm, his inner turmoil assuaged.

The question of getting in touch with the solicitors who handled his wife's estate was one to which he gave careful thought. There was a certain correct timing necessary, for he felt that to be either too precipitous or too hesitant might be equally damaging. He had finally decided that an inspection of his wife's papers would be of aid in properly assessing the matter, when he received his second shock.

He had gone to her bedroom for the papers he knew his wife had kept in an old wooden trunk-case bound with leather straps. After closing the door of the room, he pulled the trunk from the closet and, kneeling beside it, threw back the lid. Atop the pile of papers lay some old daguerreotypes of his wife and members of her family, shiny, stiff relics now turned purplish-brown with age.

He was removing these to rummage underneath when he heard the door open and felt, rather than saw, the cold eye of the housekeeper upon him. The dread panic he had suppressed rose within him again. Too early, you fool! he thought, almost snarling in his self-disgust. You appear too anxious!

He turned his head, afraid to meet the suspicion in her eyes, and spoke dully. "Yes, Mrs. Crimmins? You wanted something?"

Even the slight hesitation in her reply was accusative.

"The roses," she finally said, and he could hear the sarcasm behind the innocent words, "the ones outside her window—this window. They're all brown and burned, like. I thought you might want to—" She stopped.

The roses! Of course—the acid he had thrown out the window! He fought down the gush of fear, his anger at himself suddenly shifted to this implacable nemesis above him, watching him coldly, silently taunting him. His voice lost control.

"Get out! At once, do you hear? Leave the house! Go to the village; anything, anywhere, but get out!" And then he added with quiet hatred: "You will never disturb me when I am in this room!"

He slumped there with head bent, like a gyved body awaiting the executioner's axe, and heard the door close and, a few moments later, the creak of the outside gate. For one wonderful moment he felt a sudden peace at the silence, at being alone, at the feeling of motionlessness that possessed him.

But his flare of temper had been foolhardy, and he knew it. He had come to consider himself two people: the careful, clever, watchful man who had carried out the audacious plan of murder with no oversights; and a blind, raving fool seemingly intent upon destroying everything with the ill-advised and reckless actions of a maniac. Now, still kneeling in the quiet room beside the empty four-poster, he clenched and unclenched his trembling fingers and in a steady, maddening monotone cursed all his enemies, but particularly the most dangerous of all, that second Martin Blackburn inside him.

To lose his control with Mrs. Crimmins, of all people! With her steel-trap mouth, her rigid bewhiskered lips, her icy eyes! He could hear her now, bending over the cluster of attentive heads in the village, whispering her suspicions, telling of the discord between Loretta and himself, the evidence of his guilty conscience, remarking on the suddenness of her death when she obviously had been recovering . . .

He could hear it all, see the lifted eyebrows, the slowly nodding heads. With a sudden resurgence of fury he slammed the lid shut on the battered chest and, arising, kicked it violently against the wall. He stumbled down the stairs and sought to calm his nerves with huge gulps of brandy.

His third shock came the following day, although it was postponed until the evening. He was sitting, staring somberly into a glowing fire, when Mrs. Crimmins came in and announced with obvious satisfaction that the constable had come to see him. Behind her as she spoke there appeared the gross figure of the village's only police officer, but before Blackburn could leap from his chair, the constable came forward, eyeing him steadily.

"Me wife was after sayin'," mumbled the constable with an implied *non sequitur* that held Blackburn bound to his chair with terror, "that a game of draughts might be what 'e gentleman was needin'." He shook his head lugubriously. "Not that I 'ave any 'opes of winnin'—at draughts, that is—but . . ." He allowed the words to trail off in silence.

Blackburn choked down the hysterical laugh that was inadvertently rising in his throat; it had been just such a nervous laugh that had been the first link in his chain of adversity. So it was to be cat-and-mouse, eh? The full import of the danger seemed to wipe away all fear and substitute a new watchfulness.

And with it a new decision: tonight *he* would take charge,

and not his stupid, reckless alter ego. His mind seemed clear and sharp for the first time since the funeral, his fear and panic for the first time under confident control.

To an impartial observer, the game of draughts might have served as a pleasant example of an ordinary evening's entertainment in that solid, dependable Victorian year, with the portly housekeeper stepping from the kitchen on occasion to see that the ale mugs were well filled and the tin of biscuits ready at hand. Although it was late spring and a full moon glanced in at the narrow recessed windows, the fire was kept burning brightly and, together with several tapers, provided the light by which the two men played.

To a less impartial observer, the scene would have blended the dramatic with the grotesque. In the flickering shadows cast by the flames, the two men presented a sharp contrast: Blackburn, thin and tense, making contemptuously swift moves and then falling back in his chair to search the face of his opponent for some key to his thoughts; the constable, bulky and stolid, his heavy fingers curled in hesitation over this checker or that, puffing on his stubby pipe with the rhythm of breathing, his eyes fixed steadily on the board before him.

Blackburn, in a sudden, crystal clarity of perception, almost smiled. His enemies also made mistakes. The patent hollowness of the constable's excuse to visit the farm; the regularity of Mrs. Crimmins' inspection from the doorway—all a bit too obvious. They were trying to wear him down, wait him out, force his nerve to fail. The careful plotter within him studied the scene impassionately, answering each move of his opponent rapidly, paying small attention to that game; but watching, watching, in the larger game.

When at last Blackburn had been defeated and the pieces laid back in their box, he felt a surge of relief, a feeling that he had withstood the preliminary assault on his nerves, and was prepared for the next attack. But the constable, muttering something about an early rising, swallowed the remainder of his ale and left soon after.

Blackburn returned to his chair in suspicious doubt. Was it possible their plan was a different one? Quite obviously it was. His fears began swiftly to gather once again.

It was quite apparent that any hopes of safety that he might have cherished regarding his idiotic laugh on returning from the funeral were pure self-deception. Of course the grin had been noted; how could it have been otherwise? It was equally evident that Mrs. Crimmins had spread her tale in all directions. The visit of the constable had not been very subtle, but in truth what need did they have for subtlety?

There was, of course, one saving grace: there could be no evidence, no proof. The suspicions which his stupid actions had aroused might have convinced the police that he had murdered his wife, but if he kept his wits—and if that damned idiotic beast within him made no future slips—they could never prove anything against him. There were no traces of cyanide gas, certainly not after this length of time. And an autopsy would not—

An autopsy! Suddenly he sat upright. The bottle of acid, the box of pellets! A paralyzing cold hand gripped his stomach. You fool! he cried to himself. You utter, complete, unmitigated fool! The dozens of places you might have hidden them, the hundreds of ways you might have destroyed them! To leave them where their mute testimony was bound to be fatal! All other thoughts were swept from his mind. He had to get the bottle and box from the coffin!

He arose from his chair, shaking, and called out to Mrs. Crimmins. She hurried in from the kitchen, drying her hands, eyeing him slyly. He forced himself to disregard the cynicism he saw in her eyes and to keep his voice down.

"Mrs. Crimmins," he said, steadying himself against the fireplace, "there is no need for you to remain any longer tonight. You may leave things as they are. I—I have some accounts to go over and I—I would rather not be disturbed."

He seemed to hear his own voice as from a far distance. There was something dreamlike in the housekeeper's getting her wraparound and kerchief, something unreal in watching her move to the door. The sound of her footfalls hurrying down the path seemed to come to him through a misty curtain, like distant, imagined echoes. He placed his shaking hands over his eyes, forcing his tired brain to plan.

Several brandies seemed partially to dissipate the fog in his head, and then he set to work. Wrapping a scarf about his neck, he went quickly to the stables, saddled a horse, and led the animal to the shed where the tools were kept.

Somewhere from within his hot, pounding head a cold voice seemed to direct his movements; he acted on this inner compulsion. His own emotions flickered in and out of focus, now filling him with dread, and alternately disappearing into a warm, soft lassitude.

He found himself riding furiously along the hard road to the cemetery, one hand gripping the reins, the other holding a shovel tightly across the pommel. The damp night air seemed to clear his brain, and he saw again the terrible position he was in. Terror came with awareness as he spurred his horse even more fiercely over the rolling moor.

The churchyard cemetery appeared above a rise in the road, the ancient fence and drooping trees momentarily silhouetted against the white disk of the full moon. Blackburn threw himself from the saddle, dropping the reins to the ground, hurrying through the scattered monuments to the relatively fresh mound covering his wife's grave. Without a pause he began to dig, his heart pounding, his breath harsh in the night silence.

A sudden sound brought him to a startled standstill and he stopped, panting, to search the gloom. It was only his horse, untethered, moving away in the darkness. For an instant he contemplated going after it, but the urgency of his mission forced him to abandon the idea. With a choked curse he threw himself back into his labors, tearing at the stubborn earth, flinging the dirt from the grave with frenzied, jerking motions. The bright moon threw wavering shadows over the scene, and the rising wind whispered through the overhanging branches bent in solemn contemplation of the weird view below.

Suddenly metal grated on wood. With a savage grunt of satisfaction he redoubled his efforts, scraping the clinging clods from the coffin lid with the edge of the shovel. The moon peered over the rim of the black pit, throwing into relief the struggling, disheveled figure, the partially uncovered coffin.

Blackburn slipped the edge of the shovel under one corner of the lid, pressing the shovel down with a strength born of desperation; with a sharp tearing sound the screws ripped free and a board came away. Bits of dried earth fell into the opening, covering the half exposed, sunken face within.

With frantic haste Blackburn dropped to his knees, slipping his fingers beneath the cerements, searching for the containers. One came to hand readily; he slid it into his pocket and continued his search.

Where could the other have gotten to? He reached further, feeling the weight of the lifeless body pressing against his fingers, the rough wood of the coffin scraping his skin.

And then he had it! And at the same moment he became aware of the commotion above him.

There was a flickering of a bull's-eye lantern thrust over the edge of the grave. He heard his name being called.

"Hold on! Mr. Blackburn! None of that, now!"

No sound could make itself issue from his paralyzed throat. He made one move towards the far wall of the shallow pit, stumbling over the coffin, spurning the huge arm extended in his direction. His eyes bulged in terror, searching for escape. There was none. With his mouth open in a vain attempt to scream his rage, his frustration, he tore the cover from the box in his hand and dropped a pellet down his throat . . .

The old crone had few opportunities to bask in public attention, and she didn't mean to let this one pass by. Her hand gripped the polished rail of the witness box of the coroner's inquest like a vulture's talon.

"So bin to 'is 'elf, 'e was," she said. "I seed 'im through the carriage winder arter the funeral. Ah, it were darkish an' me eyes mayn't be what they was, but I seed 'im clear enough. Her dyin' 'it 'im 'arder not he let on. It allus does," she added, picturing with dark satisfaction the future reaction of her own undemonstrative husband at her demise.

"There he was," Mrs. Crimmins told the solemn courtroom. "Poor man! Going over her old tintypes, one by one. And me, like the fool I be, disturbing the poor man in his sorrow. Oh, he felt it deep, never you mind!"

"I knowed it was still botherin' the poor man," the constable said with a sad shake of his head, " 'im losin' a game o' draughts to the likes o' me! Then when Mrs. Crimmins comed over t'house sayin' she was sure 'e meant to 'arm 'isself, well, I 'ad to get young Griggs an' the others, didn't I? And o' course we wasted time lookin' about 'is 'ouse and the barns afore we often thought of 'e cemetery." He shook his head in the ensuing silence.

"Anyway," he resumed, "if 'e 'adn't done it with one o' them pills, 'e'd of jumped off a bridge, or 'ung 'isself. When they're grievin' deep like that, there ain't never no stoppin' them."

MARY BARRETT
DÉJÀ VU

Mrs. Oliver was puzzled. She always liked to pay cash, now that she could, and she no longer kept in touch with anyone out of town. Therefore she received almost no mail. The package which the mailman handed her was a surprise, and, like many surprises, unwelcome.

"There must be a mistake," Mrs. Oliver said uncertainly.

"No mistake, lady." And the mailman walked away.

Mrs. Oliver inspected the parcel. It was wrapped in brown paper and sealed with tape. Her name and address were clearly spelled out in neat block letters. The stamps were canceled with the local postmark.

She put the parcel down on the dining table. For some reason she was reluctant to open it. At the edge of awareness, the sensation gnawed at her that she had experienced this same event before. *Déjà vu.*

Don't be a fool, Mrs. Oliver said sternly to herself. She hoped that she wasn't getting eccentric, living alone as she had been since John died. Surely a package in the mail was nothing to be so upset about.

She pulled at the sealing tape. Under the paper was a plain white box bearing no identification. Its very impersonality somehow increased Mrs. Oliver's uneasiness.

The box was lined with white tissue paper. Lying in the center, like a cherished treasure, was a little music box with a dainty lady dancer on top.

Mrs. Oliver gasped. She picked up the box. She wound the little key. The lady dancer turned slowly, gracefully, and the music box tinkled "The Blue Danube Waltz."

It was impossible!

Mrs. Oliver sat down. Her hands were suddenly cold and her heart was beating fast.

It was the very first gift that John had sent to her. It came before they were married, when John was still courting her. The little Bavarian music box had arrived, then as now, in a parcel in the mail. Then, as now, it had been carefully wrapped and sealed. John was always a careful man.

She looked again at the address on the wrapping paper. It told her nothing. The printed words were impersonal, unrevealing.

Panic hit Mrs. Oliver like a sonic boom. She knew very well where she had last seen the music box—in Mr. Stover's store, where she had taken it to be sold.

She stood up shakily and forced herself into action.

"Mr. Stover, I would like to see the Bavarian music box which I sold to you."

Mr. Stover had been afraid of this. How much of the truth could he tell her? He looked at her closely. No, he decided, she was too agitated; even part of the truth would be too great a shock.

"I remember it," he said. "Had a little dancing girl, didn't it? That was sold some time ago."

Mrs. Oliver was uncertain whether to feel relief or apprehension.

"Do you remember who bought it?"

"No. I didn't know the man. He was a stranger who happened in. A young fellow. Didn't quibble about the price."

Mrs. Oliver felt dizzy. That would have been John's style.

"A young man, you said?"

"That's right. In his early thirties, I'd say."

Mrs. Oliver slept restlessly that night. She had distressing dreams from which she woke perspiring, her heart pounding, the thought of her dead husband vivid in her mind.

John. *He* was in his early thirties when they first met. He was handsome and ambitious, already a successful lawyer. It was inevitable that he would become an important man in state politics.

He was a good catch for any woman. And how persuasively he had courted her, showering her with attention and presents!

He had this house built for her, and had it furnished with the finest things. She appreciated all this. There was no passion on her part, but she couldn't, finally, resist him. Her family was an old one, far more distinguished than his, but their money had long ago trickled away. She could not afford not to marry for money. So it might as well be John.

If he was ever disappointed he was too gentlemanly to let it show.

She hid the music box in a drawer under the linen tablecloths and tried to forget it. It was not that simple. Whoever was manipulating Mrs. Oliver's state of mind was not only very clever but astonishingly well informed.

Only a week after the arrival of the music box another parcel was delivered. It, too, was carefully wrapped and sealed. The box was, again, disquieting in its impersonality.

Mrs. Oliver opened it and felt her knees go weak. Deep in tissue paper the box held the exquisite emerald brooch which John had given her on the day they were married. It was a lovely thing, of superb craftsmanship. Mr. Stover had given her a very good price for it. Now it lay in her hand, as sparkling as it was the day John had pinned it so tenderly on her bridal dress.

Mrs. Oliver tried to slow the beating of her heart. It wasn't good for her to be so upset. The doctor would be cross with her.

If this eerie procedure continued, she would receive many packages. John had been very generous with gifts. His practice brought in a great deal of money. To outside observers she seemed a very lucky woman. She had only to drop the smallest hint and John would buy her whatever she wanted.

Still, as time went by, she had felt more and more like a kept slave. She yearned for a little cash of her own. Not much. Just enough so that she could be free to buy some small things for herself. He never let her have a personal checking or bank account, and he gave her a minimum of pocket money.

"I would rather take care of you myself, dear," he said.

John overlooked nothing. He established charge accounts with the grocery store, the milkman, the dry cleaners. He bought all her clothes himself. In all the days of her marriage she never had more than a five-dollar bill of her own. Of course, John paid all the bills himself.

The packages continued to come. Mrs. Oliver lived in a state of constant agitation. The parcels arrived with no regularity, and she never knew on which day one would be delivered. There was, however, one thing she could be certain of ahead of time—the contents of each box. For the presents were coming back to her in the exact order John had given them to her.

Her birthday present, the diamond bracelet, was followed by the matching earrings John had given her for Christmas.

At first, when she was a new bride, she had been charmed by John's generosity. She had never owned beautiful things before, and the shower of extravagant gifts was like a dream come true. It was only in time that the longing for the illusion of financial independence came to sit on her soul like a lead weight; and in time the longing became an obsession.

John refused even to consider the possibility of her looking for a job.

"We're rich, dear," he said. "It would be ridiculous for you to work. You know that I'll get you anything you want."

As time passed, John's gifts brought her no joy. They seemed merely symbols of her bondage. She even had trouble pretending to be pleased.

Now, receiving them a second time, she felt even less pleasure. She felt only horror and repugnance. As each gift arrived she quickly hid it away.

His anniversary present of silver demitasse spoons came only shortly before the hand-blown crystal vase which John had brought back from a short trip out of town.

Mrs. Oliver's panic was now beginning to overwhelm her. There was only one gift left—the last one John had given her. She knew what it would mean if that one came back. And she knew with dreadful certainty that though it had been, in life, John's last gift, it would not now be. She knew that the final gift would come to her from the grave.

Mrs. Oliver, never a hardy woman, was not well. She hardly ever slept. When, finally, she did drop off, her dreams were terrifying, and she often woke up screaming.

She no longer had any appetite. She had lost so much weight that her dresses hung like bags. She hardly recognized herself in the mirror. Her eyes stared back at her from sunken sockets like glass globes in a skull.

The package came.

John's last gift.

She knew very well what the package contained even before she opened it. He had brought this gift on no special occasion—it had been a sudden whim. He had seen it in a store window and, on impulse, had gone in and bought it for her.

Her hands shook. She could hardly tear off the paper. Inside the white box lay the gift. It was a beautiful little emerald pillbox, made by an expert craftsman. It was truly a work of art. Mrs. Oliver put it out of sight as quickly as she could.

She tried to brace herself for what she knew was bound to come next. But what could she do? There was no way to anticipate how it would come, or in what form. There was no way to protect herself.

That night she went to bed early and lay there, wide-awake. Her eyes were open, staring unseeingly at the ceiling.

There was a knock at the door. It was not imperative—simply firm and sure.

Mrs. Oliver stepped into her bedroom slippers and put on her robe. She went silently down the stairs. She could no more have ignored that self-assured knock than she could have left the packages unopened. She was moved by an irresistible compulsion.

The knock sounded again—no louder than before, but still firm and self-confident.

Mrs. Oliver went to the door. She stood there, dizzy. Her hand was on the doorknob.

She was faint with panic and fatigue. Her body shock, out of control. She sank to the floor and her face pressed against the hard wood of the door.

Again the knock sounded.

There was a pounding in her ears. The hall seemed to tilt, first one way, then another.

"John," she whispered, "how did you know?"

It *was* John on the other side of the door. She was certain of that. And somehow he had learned the truth.

She had taken the poison out of the little enamel pillbox. She had put it in his demitasse. She was sure he hadn't seen her do it. She had sat there calmly and watched him drink the coffee, and die. And, finally, she had money of her own.

She should have known better, she thought fuzzily. She should have known she couldn't outwit John, that he would never stop giving her things.

She lay, a crumpled disorderly heap, on the floor of the hall. She was shrunken and unadorned. She looked old. She sighed, a long sigh, and then she died.

There was a final knock on the door, and then the sound of footsteps going away.

Mr. Stover was disappointed. He had waited until he had sent back all her lovely things, in the same order she had sold them, to tell her he loved her. Well, he would call again tomorrow.

STEPHEN WASYLYK
FISHING CAN BE FATAL

The man who came into the sheriff's office in Fox River was a little over six feet tall, with a hewn-from-granite face above a short neck, wide shoulders, and a big chest that strained the buttons of his short-sleeved plaid shirt.

He stopped just inside the door, spread his arms wide, and grinned. "How is this Mickey Mouse police force doing?"

With the feeling that his jocularity was a little forced, I motioned to Julio. "You're the chief deputy, Julio. Arrest Mr. Masterman for disturbing the peace."

Julio's teeth showed white below his black moustache. "You're the sheriff. You arrest him."

"Hold it," said Masterman. "You are dealing with a handsome, intelligent, law-abiding New York City detective with a legitimate complaint." The good humor gave way to a puzzlement edged with anger. "I was out this morning fishing in the Little Stoney when someone took a shot at me. Three shots, as a matter of fact."

Julio knew Masterman as well as I did. "This isn't one of your jokes, is it?"

"Shooting is one thing I never joke about."

I motioned toward a chair. "Let's have it, Milo."

He grinned wryly. "Getting shot at while I'm on duty in New York is something I can expect, but up here, on vacation, I put away my gun and forget all that. I've always been a little envious of you, Gates. I've seriously considered giving up and moving to a place like this many times." He shook his head. "But I guess it's the same all over.

"At seven this morning I was ten or fifteen yards out in that pool below the rapids about a mile south of Cooper's place, casting upstream and minding my own business, when *bam,* the first shot hit about a foot in front of me. I didn't spend any time wondering what it was all about. I hauled for the bank as fast as I could, which wasn't very fast because I was wearing waders. The second one cut water alongside me, then the third.

"I dove for cover below the lip of the bank, crawled to where the trees grew close to the creek, and came up running, heading uphill toward where I thought the shots had come from. If I could have put my hands on the guy, I would have killed him, but he was gone when I got there. Found the place he fired from, though. Weeds matted down behind a fallen oak, three empty rifle shells on the ground."

Julio and I glanced at each other. The summer had been quiet so far, a situation we appreciated because we'd been working one man short since winter. Our annual influx of visitors had been exceptionally well behaved, and the year-round residents had been too busy taking care of them and counting money to get into trouble. Someone shooting at Masterman was the first violence we'd had since spring, when Fergo Pyrum had chased his young wife and her lover through town, intent on carving them up with the machete he had brought back from the South Pacific during World War II.

Now the thought of an unknown sniper on the loose among all the vacationers chilled me. If the news got out, a great many of them would pack up and go home, but that didn't concern me as much as the vision of innocent people dying.

"Did you bring the shells in?" I asked.

"I touched nothing. I'm a city boy. I figured you were the Daniel Boone type who could study the scene, pick up a bent twig, and give me the name and address of the guy so I could go punch his face in."

"Don't joke, Milo," I said. "This is damned serious."

"I'm not joking," he said quietly. "If the guy wasn't a bad shot, I'd be floating down that creek face down, and I wouldn't have even known why I was suddenly dead."

"No one from around here would have reason to shoot at you," I said slowly. "How about your New York acquaintances? Could one of them have followed you up here?"

"The people I know prefer handguns and dark alleys. It has to be some sort of local flake."

"It might be, but if someone has come unglued, you were his first target and we'd better put a stop to it right now before his aim improves. Let's go. Show me where it happened so I can pick up those shells."

I spun the four-wheel drive toward the street on screaming tires.

"Let's get a cup of coffee first," said Masterman. "I was up at six and haven't had breakfast yet and I could use something to settle me down."

I hoped the half-hour delay wouldn't matter and swung into the parking lot behind the old hotel, which aside from the diner was the most popular eating place in town, in spite of the nineteenth-century decor and the elderly waiters. Beyond those two you hit the highways for the better restaurants and the fast-food places.

We found a table and I impatiently watched Masterman go to work on a double order of ham and eggs he couldn't resist once he sat down.

This was his third summer visit to Fox River. I had first met him at Cooper's Lodge, which was located about ten miles out of town along the Little Stoney Creek. Cooper catered to fishermen, many of whom came not so much to fish as to sit in his recreation room in the evening and play poker while they argued over the merits of assorted gear and told lies about the fish they had caught.

While I knew Masterman was a detective, I knew little else about him because, like everyone else, he considered a vacation his annual opportunity to leave his daily life behind.

He finished his breakfast and we stepped out of the door of the dining room just as three men approached across the lobby.

I knew the one in the lead. He was slender and middle-aged with thinning, stringy hair and a hawknose. His name was Schuyler and he had made quite a name and a great deal of money as a criminal attorney, some of which he had spent for a luxurious private lodge about two miles below Cooper's on Little Stoney Creek.

One of the men with him was heavyset, his body leaning toward fat rather than muscle, his features coarse like an unfinished sculpture. The other was short and thin, with a face so pale it looked as though it had not only never been exposed to sunlight but had been hidden from light itself.

The heavy man stopped and grinned at Masterman.

"You, detective," he said. "Why aren't you in New York beating up innocent people?"

Masterman pushed by without a word.

As I pulled out of the parking lot, Masterman sat beside me, his arms folded, his jaw clamped shut, staring ahead.

I drove for a few miles before I said, "What was that all about?"

"I guess I should have told you up front," he said slowly. "I'm not here on vacation. I'm here because I drew a ten-day suspension for slugging that guy back there."

"Who is he?"

"His name is Pomp. He's one of those bad guys we like to think we'll put away some day but never do because no connection ever leads directly back to him. I guess he has a piece of everything rotten in my precinct but we can't touch him. The white-faced creep with him is Lonnie, his bodyguard."

"Did you slug him on general principles or for a specific reason?"

"A little of both. A year ago he took a fancy to one of the young waitresses in a bar he owns and set her up in an apartment. She was a nice kid and she should have known better because when guys like Pomp get tired of them, they send these women down the ladder and in a few years the women are either hustling or dead. I guess she wouldn't go, or else she saw or heard something she shouldn't have, because about a month ago she turned up in the gutter beaten to death.

"The street talk was that Pomp was responsible, so we brought him in for questioning. It was a waste of time, of course, but as he was walking out, Pomp and I had a few words. He laughed at me and I hit him. They pulled me off the case and a couple of weeks later the suspension came down."

"You said no one had any reason to shoot at you."

"You mean Pomp? If that was what he wanted, he would have had it done weeks ago. Besides, he would have given the job to a professional and no pro would miss three times. He'd rather have it this way, so he can needle me. It also helps his image because he can claim he got me suspended. What he's doing here, I don't know."

"He's probably staying at Schuyler's lodge. Schuyler has brought clients here before to do some fishing, but it's the first time for Pomp."

"The bum does like to fish. I've heard him talk about it."

"Still, could he have known you were coming here?"

"The whole precinct knew. The lieutenant even suggested it."

"Fishing could be a cover for his real reason, namely, to have you knocked off."

"Forget it. No one, including Pomp, has any big reason to see me dead. I can't say the same for him. Plenty of people would like to blow him away."

I thought for a moment. "Maybe that's the answer. The two of you are built along the same lines. Schuyler's lodge is downstream of Cooper's place. If someone was expecting to see Pomp in that creek this morning, he could have mistaken you for him."

I could feel Masterman staring at me.

"You just might have something." He grinned a little. "Maybe you better not look too hard for the man who fired those shots. Give him a chance to try again. He could be luckier next time."

"Not in my county," I said as I turned into the road leading to Cooper's Lodge. I used Cooper's phone to call Schuyler at the hotel dining room.

"Would you mind telling me if your guest was out fishing this morning?" I asked.

"I see no reason—"

"You might. Was he?"

"Yes. The both of us went out early."

"Above seven?"

"About that time."

"Did you hear any rifle fire?"

"We heard three shots. What is this all about?"

"Those shots could have been intended for him."

"I don't understand."

"Neither do I, but just in case they were, and the man intends

to try again, keep Pomp inside until I get back to you." I
dropped the phone on his response.

I followed Masterman to a spot where the creek swirled slowly
in wide pools below a rough stretch of water. Behind us a
natural meadow sloped upward. Masterman pointed. "I was out
there. Like I told you, the first shot was in front of me, the other
on either side." He turned. "He fired from that fallen tree up
there."

Halfway up the slope the trees began again, widely spaced
and scattered. Masterman stopped beside one that had lost its
battle with a storm. "Here," he said.

I knelt and studied the ground. Some of the grass that had
been trampled had started to spring up again, but enough had
been permanently bruised and damaged to indicate a body had
pressed it down. Lying almost side by side were three empty
brass shells. I pulled a ballpoint pen from my pocket, slipped it
into one of them, and held it up so I could read the numbers
stamped into the base.

.243

The caliber of the rifle worried me. A .243 was fine for small
game and with a 100-grain bullet could be used for a deer; but
even with the heavier load it couldn't be considered an ideal
hitman's weapon. A professional out to eliminate Pomp or
Masterman would want something with more knockdown
power and, as Masterman had said, would not miss three times.
If anything, the shells indicated that the shooter was a local
man.

I measured the distance to the creek with my eyes. About
two hundred yards. Almost any rifleman should have been able
to hit Masterman at least once, especially with the fallen tree
serving as a rest.

I placed the shells in an envelope and stood up. "What I'd
like to know is, was he shooting at you specifically, or imagining
he was shooting at Pomp, or was he just shooting at any
fisherman he saw?"

"If you think I have the answer, you're nuts," said Masterman.

"This bodyguard of Pomp's, Lonnie—"

"Forget him. He's the type to wait in the bushes, then shoot me in the back after I walked by."

I looked out over the small valley. Talk of murder sounded out of place in these peaceful surroundings and the crisp clean air somehow seemed dirtier now.

"Have you told anyone about this?" I asked Masterman.

"I saw no reason to."

I thought for a moment. It had been necessary to mention the shooting to Schuyler to protect Pomp. Should I tell Cooper to keep the fishermen out of the creek for the rest of the day—and why? That would panic some, anger others, and be ignored by most. I decided to gamble that the rifleman was through for the day. If someone was shot, I would have to live with my conscience, but I had the feeling that he wasn't running around sniping at people just for the hell of it.

"You'd better stay inside," I told Masterman. "You could be the target again."

"Nuts to that. If someone is out to get me, I'd just as soon be killed doing something I like rather than sitting around waiting for it to happen. I'll be out again this evening. You know what's a good time for smallmouth bass."

"You'll stay inside," I said coldly. "Drink beer. Watch television. Play poker with Cooper. I don't care which, but keep out of sight. Now, let's go."

I sped into town, dropped Masterman off at his car, and double-parked in front of Avery's Sporting Goods. Avery himself was behind the counter. He was a small, thin, wiry man with half spectacles hanging on the tip of his nose, an expert on everything he sold, and noted for the excellent free advice that went with each sale, whether the purchaser wanted it or not. He peered at me above his spectacles.

"How many people do you know who own a .243 rifle?" I asked.

He frowned. "Maybe a half dozen. Why?"

I didn't answer. "Check your sales of .243 ammunition for the past twelve months and see how many names you can find."

"That's a big job."

"Not so big. I'll wait."

"If I knew why—"

"Avery," I said, "I'm in a hurry. Look up the names and do it now."

Twenty minutes later he handed me a slip with eight names.

"These are all local people?" I asked.

"Every one."

I drove to the office and handed the names to Julio. "They own .243 rifles," I said. "Find out where those rifles were at seven this morning. Do it fast."

"This is the Masterman thing?"

"Yeah, and don't tell anyone why you're asking."

After Julio had gone, I shook the three brass shells out on my desk and carefully brushed them for fingerprints. I found nothing but smudges. I propped one up and examined it through a magnifying glass.

The distinctive scratches every rifle leaves on a casing were sharp and clear, especially the ejector marks, which indicated a new rifle or one that had been little used. I put the shells away in my desk drawer. If Julio found one of those rifles had been out this morning, I'd be able to run a shell through it and see if it matched. In the meantime all I could do was hope the sniper didn't try again.

Time stretched into early evening and the streets of the town filled with summer vacationers who, for something to do, came in from the cabins and the motels to poke around in the shops.

Julio had checked in twice by radio, the last time to tell me five of the rifles had been hanging on walls or standing in closets at seven that morning.

The phone rang. I picked it up. Schuyler's voice was flat and emotionless, as if he were reporting something routine.

"In view of your earlier warning," he said, "you will be interested to learn Pomp has been shot and killed."

I felt my throat grow tight.

"You damned fool. I told you to keep him inside. Didn't you believe me?"

"I did, he didn't. To quote him, he said, 'What does a hick sheriff know?' He wanted to fish, so he went. He took his bodyguard with him this time. Lonnie stayed on the bank. Pomp was a few yards into the stream just north of the house. There was one shot. Lonnie brought the body back."

"Leave everything the way it is," I snapped. "I'll be right out."

I arranged for an ambulance to meet me at Schuyler's lodge, called Julio on the radio while en route, and skidded to a halt in Schuyler's driveway twenty siren-screaming minutes later.

From the patio at the rear of the house a smooth lawn sloped to the creek. At the foot of the slope Schuyler and Lonnie were standing near a crumpled figure. I went down the slope and knelt by the body. The clothes were soaked, the hair matted. The bullet had hit Pomp in the right side of the chest and a slight trickle of blood from his mouth showed it had torn him up inside.

"All right," I said. "How did it happen?"

Lonnie stared at me without expression. Like Pomp, his clothes were dripping wet.

"Tell him," said Schuyler.

"The boss wanted to go out," he said slowly. "Schuyler told him not to go. He laughed. 'Lonnie will take care of me,' he said. He put on his boots and we walked along the creek that way." He pointed north. "He found a spot he liked and walked out into the creek. I stayed on the bank. We were out for maybe half an hour when the shot came from the trees behind me.

"The boss went down into the water. In those shadows under the trees I couldn't see a damned thing to shoot at, but I threw a couple of shots in there anyway. I couldn't go looking because I had to get Mr. Pomp out of the water. For all I knew he was still alive and could drown out there, but when I reached him he was dead. He was too heavy for me to carry, so I sort of floated him down the creek to here and called Schuyler."

"Did you hear the shot?" I asked Schuyler.

"No. I was in the house. The first I knew of it was when I heard Lonnie yelling for me. I think it's obvious who killed him."

"Masterman," Lonnie spat the name out. "It had to be that pig cop. He said he would get the boss."

"I can testify to that," said Schuyler. "I heard him threaten Pomp."

"Someone shot at Masterman this morning," I said.

"Do you have only his word?" asked Schuyler.

"There were no witnesses."

"He probably lied to throw suspicion off himself," said Schuyler.

Two men in tan uniforms came down the slope, carrying a stretcher.

"Anything to be done?" asked one.

I shook my head. "Ask Dr. Blenheim to recover the slug immediately and call me when he has it. The full autopsy can come later."

On the way up the slope they passed Julio jogging toward me.

"All those rifles on the list are out of it," he said. "What's the story here?"

"It looks like the guy who fired at Masterman didn't miss this time."

"Damn. Anything I can do?"

"Call the county attorney when you get back to the office. I'll need him tomorrow at nine."

I went back to Lonnie and Schuyler.

"You going to pick up Masterman?" asked Lonnie.

"I'll see him," I said.

He shrugged. "Don't matter. I know how you cops stick together. I'll take care of him myself."

I held out my hand. "Let's have it."

"He has a permit," said Schuyler.

"I'm sure," I said. "I still want it."

Lonnie's eyes locked with mine, then he lifted his loose shirt. Tucked inside his belt was a small holster. He pulled the weapon loose and handed me a .38 special. I checked the cylinder.

"I told you I fired into the trees," he said.

"You told me." I slid the revolver under my belt.

"Hey, wait a minute," he said. "You can't—"

"Sure, I can," I said. "Besides, you don't need it. You no longer have anyone to guard. I'll expect you both in the office at nine tomorrow morning. If either of you doesn't show up, I'll have a warrant issued, find you, and drag you back by the heels."

"Is that a threat?" asked Schuyler coldly.

"It certainly is," I said.

"I tell you Masterman did it!" screamed Lonnie.

"Then there is no reason for you not to show up tomorrow morning," I said.

I drove slowly to Cooper's. Whatever daylight remained was high in the sky and would soon fade; the creases of the valleys were already purple. By the time I reached Cooper's driveway, night had caught up to me.

Cooper was a wide-shouldered man with a flat stomach, tanned weatherbeaten skin, and a full head of snowy hair.

"Where's Masterman?" I asked.

He pointed. "Head of the hall upstairs. He came in fifteen minutes ago."

I tapped at Masterman's door.

He opened it, a can of beer in his hand. He held it up. "Want one?"

I shook my head. "I told you to stay inside. Where were you?"

"Out in the creek, fishing. I told you I would go."

"North or south?"

"South."

"Toward Schuyler's place?"

"If that's south."

"Anyone see you?"

"No. Why?"

"Someone shot and killed Pomp."

He rubbed the top of the can thoughtfully. "I thought I heard a shot, but I wasn't sure. It looks like you were right about this morning. Someone thought I was Pomp, missed, and tried again."

"Maybe," I said. "But you're the only one in the area I know who would want Pomp dead and you were in the vicinity."

He pointed to the fishing rod standing in the corner. "I could hardly shoot him with that."

"Come off it, Milo," I said. "If you killed Pomp, I wouldn't expect you to be walking around the rifle in your hand."

He studied me for a moment. "You really think I could have done it, don't you?"

"Sure," I said. "You *could* have done it."

"You want to question me, go ahead."

"What for? If you did it, you'll have the answers. I stopped by to tell you to be in my office at nine tomorrow morning."

"The answers will be the same then."

"The questions may be different. Nine tomorrow."

I left him staring after me.

Through the office window I watched Julio drive away toward home and dinner, to be back the following morning at six. The shopping crowds had thinned out and the stores would be closing shortly.

The phone rang. It was Bleinheim at the hospital.

"Now that I have your slug, what do I do with it?"

"Weigh it," I said.

"I already have. Call it about a hundred and fifty grains."

I sat upright. "Are you sure?"

"My scale doesn't lie."

"What about the angle of penetration?"

"Level."

"Not as if the man was standing in a creek and the shooter was on the bank?"

"I can tell you it didn't happen that way, even though the man's clothes were soaked. Death was quick but not instantaneous. If the man had been standing in water when he was shot, he would certainly have taken water into the lungs. There was none. He was dead when he entered the water."

"Listen," I said. "If your secretary's typewriter has a red ribbon, I want that part in caps, underlined, and in red."

"It's that important?"

"It gives me the killer."

I hung up, strapped on the gunbelt I wore only when necessary, and called Julio to tell him I would need him for an hour.

There was no jocularity in Masterman when he came into the office at nine the following morning. His face was impassive, almost cold.

"I'm here," he said. "Where are the others?"

"What others?" I asked innocently.

"Schuyler and Lonnie."

"I guess Schuyler is on his way to New York." I jerked my

thumb over my shoulder. "Lonnie is in a cell back there. He'll have a preliminary hearing later this morning, but he's not going anywhere after that."

"He killed Pomp?"

I poured two cups of coffee and handed one to him. "Sit down."

I placed the coffee on my desk to cool a little. "Lonnie is like a great many people who are born and grow up in big cities. They seem to have the idea that intelligence and common sense disappear once you cross the city limits. I told Schuyler that there was a possibility that an unknown rifleman might take a shot at Pomp, so Lonnie decided to take advantage of the situation and try to hang it on you. I don't know why he killed him. He won't say. But kill him he did.

"He thought all he had to do was shoot him, dunk the body in the creek, and come up with a story that an unseen rifleman had done it. What he didn't know was that I had the empty shells that came out of the .243-caliber rifle that fired at you and the slug had to be either eighty- or one-hundred grain. Pomp was killed with one that weighs a hundred and fifty grains. Lonnie was carrying a .38 special which normally takes a slug of that weight, so the rifle that fired at you couldn't have killed Pomp, but Lonnie's gun could have. The state police ballistics lab will probably prove that it did. And then, of course, he had no way of knowing Dr. Blenheim, who performs the autopsies for the coroner, could very easily prove that he lied about how it happened."

I sipped the coffee. "So you can go enjoy your fishing and not worry about a thing."

"Like hell," said Masterman. "You still haven't found the man who shot at me."

I took the time to finish the coffee. "I really worried about that after I put Lonnie away, but now I think I have the answer. Come with me. We'll talk with an expert."

We walked down the street to Avery's sporting-goods store and found Avery behind the gun counter at the rear. He looked up over his glasses and blinked.

"You looking for more names?" he asked.

"One more," I said. I nodded at Masterman. "This is Milo

Masterman. He was out in Little Stoney Creek yesterday morning when someone shot at him with a .243 rifle. Luckily the man missed."

"Probably the same man who killed that fellow Pomp last night," said Avery.

"Well, no, it wasn't," I said. "Although there is a connection. Masterman is a New York City detective. He's here because he was suspended for slugging Pomp. He slugged him because he felt Pomp was responsible for the death of a young woman a month ago."

Avery's eyes flicked to Masterman and back to me. "Should have given him a medal," he grunted. "But I can't see how I can do more for you than I already have."

"Sure you can," I said. "The caliber of that rifle bothered me from the beginning. It just had to be a local gun, even though the names you gave me were no help. Then I remembered there is one man who could use all the ammunition he wanted and his name would never appear on the records."

He drew himself up. "I comply with the law. When someone buys ammunition the purchase goes into the book."

"I said *use*, not *buy*, Avery. You own the store. Who would know if you took a few shells?"

He blinked at me coldly. "What reason would I have to shoot at this man? I don't even know him."

"That was the part I couldn't understand until I made a few phone calls last night. One was to Masterman's precinct. The sergeant there told me that when the young woman was killed, an ex-husband in Chicago was notified as next of kin. He never showed up, but he must have called the woman's parents. They claimed the body. Masterman didn't know because he was off the case."

Avery stared at me, his eyes expressionless and dark.

"How is *your* daughter, Avery?" I asked softly. "The one who married three years ago and moved to Chicago?"

His eyes suddenly became misty, his voices soft. "Damn you, Gates. Can't anyone in this town keep a secret from you?"

"As long as no one is hurt and no law is broken, you can have all the secrets you want," I said.

He placed his elbows on the glass-topped case and lowered his face into his hands.

"But you learned about Pomp in New York when you claimed your daughter's body," I continued, "and you recognized Pomp when he walked in the other day with Schuyler to pick up a new rod. Schuyler told me you gave Pomp some of your free advice. Get out on the creek early in that pool below Cooper's place. He said he would. That was when you made it my business, because the next morning you look a .243 off the rack and went out there and thought you saw him, but your eyes aren't what they used to be and you missed, which was a damned good thing because you would have killed the wrong man. I just couldn't figure out why you used something as light as a .243." I waved at his gun rack. "You have rifles here that will blow a man apart."

He lifted his head. "Following my own advice," he said dully. "I always tell people, use the rifle you feel most comfortable with." His eyes held an appeal. "What will happen to me, Gates?"

"Tell me, Avery," I said. "After you missed yesterday morning, would you have tried again?"

He shook his head. "It was the one insane moment of my life. When I heard someone else had killed him I wasn't sorry, but I was happy it hadn't been me."

I turned to Masterman. "It's up to you."

He rubbed his jaw thoughtfully. "You know, Avery, I've been out in that pool below Cooper's twice now with zero results, yet everyone says it's a great place."

Avery straightened, his eyes bright above the half spectacles. "Well, a great deal depends on the rig you're using." He came around the counter and took Masterman's arm. "Come down here and I'll show you what you should have."

They walked away from me, Avery talking about water temperature and deep holes and rocks.

I went back to the office.

CORNELL WOOLRICH

REAR WINDOW

I didn't know their names. I'd never heard their voices. I didn't even know them by sight, strictly speaking, for their faces were too small to fill in with identifiable features at that distance. Yet I could have constructed a timetable of their comings and goings, their daily activities. They were the rear-window dwellers around me.

Sure, I suppose it *was* a little bit like prying, could even have been mistaken for the fevered concentration of a Peeping Tom. That wasn't my fault, that wasn't my idea. The idea was, my movements were strictly limited just around this time. I could get from the window to the bed, from the bed to the window, and that was all.

The bay window was about the best feature my rear bedroom had in the warm weather. It was unscreened, so I had to sit with the light out or I would have had every insect in the vicinity in on me. I couldn't sleep, because I was used to getting plenty of exercise. I'd never acquired the habit of reading books to ward off boredom, so I hadn't that to turn to. Well, what should I do, sit there with my eyes tightly shuttered?

Just to pick a few at random: straight over, and the windows square, there was a young couple, kids in their teens, only just married. It would have killed them to stay home one night. They were always in such a hurry to go, whenever it was they went, they never remembered to turn out the lights. I don't think it missed once in all the time I was watching. But they never forgot altogether, either. I was to learn to call this delayed action, as you will see. He'd always some skittering madly back in about five minutes, probably from all the way down in the street, and rush around killing the switches. Then fall over something in the dark on his way out. They gave me an inward chuckle, those two.

The next house down, the windows already narrowed a little

with perspective. There was a certain light in that one that always went out each night, too. Something about it, it used to make me a little sad. There was a woman living there with her child, a young widow, I suppose. I'd see her put the child to bed and then bend over and kiss her in a wistful sort of way.

Then she'd shade the light off her and sit there painting her eyes and mouth. Then she'd go out. She'd never come back till the night was nearly spent. Once I was still up and I looked and she was sitting there motionless with her head buried in her arms. Something about it used to make me a little sad.

The third one down no longer offered any insight—the windows were just slits like in a medieval battlement, due to foreshortening. That brings us around to the one on the end. In that one, frontal vision came back full-depth again, since it stood at right angles to the rest, my own included, sealing up the inner hollow all these houses backed on. I could see into it, from the rounded projection of my bay window, as freely as into a doll house with its rear wall sliced away. And scaled down to about the same size.

It was a flat building. Unlike all the rest, it had been constructed originally as such, not just cut up into furnished rooms. It topped them by two stories, and had rear fire escapes to show for this distinction. But it was old and evidently hadn't shown a profit. It was in the process of being modernized. Instead of clearing the entire building while the work was going on, they were doing it an apartment at a time, in order to lose as little rental income as possible. Of the six rearward apartments it offered to view, the topmost one had already been completed but not yet rented. They were working on the fifth-floor one now, disturbing the peace of everyone all up and down the inside of the block with their hammering and sawing.

I felt sorry for the couple in the apartment below. I used to wonder how they stood it with that bedlam going on above their heads. To make it worse, the wife was in chronic poor health; I could tell that even at a distance by the listless way she moved about over there and remained in her bathrobe without dressing. Sometimes I'd see her sitting by the window, holding her head. I used to wonder why he didn't have a doctor in to in to look her over, but maybe they couldn't afford it. He seemed to be out of work.

Often their bedroom light was on late at night behind the drawn shade, as though she were unwell and he was sitting up with her. And one night in particular he must have had to sit up with her all night. It remained on until nearly daybreak. Not that I sat watching all that time, but the light was still burning at three in the morning when I finally transferred from chair to bed to see if I could get a little sleep myself. And when I failed to, and hopscotched back again around dawn, it was still peering wanly out behind the tan shade.

Moments later, with the first brightening of day, it suddenly dimmed around the edges of the shade, and then shortly afterward, not that one, but a shade in one of the other rooms—for all of them alike had been down—went up, and I saw him standing there looking out.

He was holding a cigarette in his hand. I couldn't see it, but I could tell it was that by the quick, nervous little jerks with which he kept putting his hand to his mouth and the haze I saw rising around his head. Worried about her, I guess. I didn't blame him for that. Any husband would have been. She must have only just dropped off to sleep after nightlong suffering. And in another hour or so at the most, that sawing of wood and clattering of buckets was going to start in over them again. Well, it wasn't any of my business, I said to myself, but he really ought to get her out of there. If I had an ill wife on my hands—

He was leaning slightly out, maybe an inch past the window frame, carefully scanning the back faces of all the houses abutting on the hollow square that lay before him. You can tell, even at a distance, when a person is looking fixedly. There's something about the way the head is held. And yet his scrutiny wasn't held fixedly to any one point, it was a slow, sweeping one, moving along the houses on the opposite side from me first. When it got to the end of them, I knew it would cross over to my side and come back along there. Before it did, I withdrew several yards inside my room to let it go safely by. I didn't want him to think I was sitting there prying into his affairs. There was still enough blue night-shade in my room to keep my slight withdrawal from catching his eyes.

When I returned to my original position a moment or two
later, he was gone. He had raised two more of the shades. The
bedroom one was still down. I wondered vaguely why he had
given that peculiar, comprehensive, semicircular stare at all the
rear windows around him. There wasn't anyone at any of them
at such an hour.

It wasn't important, of course. It was just a little oddity, but
it failed to blend it with his being worried or disturbed about
his wife. When you're worried or disturbed, that's an internal
preoccupation; you stare vacantly at nothing at all. When you
stare around you in a great sweeping arc at windows, that
betrays external preoccupation, outward interest. One doesn't
quite jibe with the other. To call such a discrepancy trifling is
to add to its importance. Only someone like, me stewing in a
vacuum of total idleness, would have noticed it at all.

The apartment remained lifeless after that, as far as could be
judged by its windows. He must have either gone out or gone
to bed himself. Three of the shades remained at normal height
and the one masking the bedroom remained down. Sam, my
day houseman, came in not long after with my eggs and
morning paper, and I had that to kill time with for a while. I
stopped thinking about other people's windows and staring at
them.

The sun slanted down on one side of the hollow oblong all
morning long, then it shifted over to the other side for the
afternoon. Then it started to slip off both alike and it was
evening again—another day gone.

The lights started to come on around the quadrangle. Here and
there a wall played back, like a sounding board, a snatch of
radio or TV program that was coming in too loud. If you
listened carefully, you could hear an occasional clink of dishes
mixed in, faint, far off. The chain of little habits that were their
lives unreeled themselves. They were all bound in them tighter
than the tightest straitjacket any jailer ever devised, though they
all thought themselves free.

The gadabout couple made their nightly dash for the great
open spaces, forgot their lights, he came careening back,

thumbed them out, and their place was dark until the early-morning hours.

The woman put her child to bed, leaned mournfully over its cot, then sat down with heavy despair to redden her mouth.

In the fourth-floor apartment at right angles to the long interior "street," the three shades had remained up, and the fourth shade had remained at full length, all day long. I hadn't been conscious of that because I hadn't particularly been looking at it or thinking of it until now. My eyes may have rested on those windows at times during the day, but my thoughts had been elsewhere. It was only when a light suddenly went on in the end room behind one of the raised shades, which was their kitchen, and I realized the shades had been untouched like that all day.

That also brought something else to my mind that hadn't been in it until now: I hadn't seen the woman all day. I hadn't seen any sign of life within those windows until now.

He'd come in from outside. The entrance was at the opposite side of their kitchen, away from the window. He'd left his hat on, so I knew he'd just come in from outside.

He didn't remove his hat. As though there was no one there to remove it for any more. Instead, he pushed it to the back of his head by pronging a hand to the roots of his hair. That gesture didn't denote removal of perspiration, I knew. To do that, a person makes a sidewise sweep. This was up over his forehead. It indicated some sort of harassment or uncertainty. Besides, if he'd been suffering from excess warmth, the first thing he would have done would be to take off his hat altogether.

She didn't come out to greet him. The first link of the so-strong chain of habit, of custom, that binds us all had snapped wide-open.

She must be so ill that she had remained in bed in the room behind the lowered shade all day. I watched. He remained where he was, two rooms away from there. Expectancy became surprise, surprise incomprehension. Funny, I thought, that he doesn't go in to her. Or at least as far as the doorway and look in to see how she is.

Maybe she was asleep and he didn't want to disturb her. Then immediately: But how can he know for sure that she's asleep without at least looking in at her?

He walked forward and stood there by the window, as he had at dawn. Sam had carried out my tray quite some time before and my lights were out. I held my ground; I knew he couldn't see me within the darkness of the bay window. He stood there motionless for several minutes. And now his attitude was the proper one for inner preoccupation. He stood there looking downward at nothing, lost in thought.

He's worried about her, I said to myself, as any man would be. It's the most natural thing in the world. Funny, though, he should leave her in the dark like that, without going near her. If he's worried, then why didn't he at least look in on her on returning? Here was another of those trivial discrepancies between inward motivation and outward indication.

And just as I was thinking that, the original one that I had noted at daybreak repeated itself. His head went up with renewed alertness and I could see it start to give that slow circular sweep of interrogation around the panorama of rearward windows again.

True, the light was behind him this time, but there was enough of it falling on him to show me the microscopic but continuous shift of direction his head made in the process. I remained carefully immobile until the distant glance had passed me safely by. Motion attracts.

Why is he so interested in other people's windows, I wondered detachedly. And of course an effective brake to dwelling on that thought too lingeringly clamped down almost at once: Look who's talking. What about you yourself?

An important difference escaped me. I wasn't worried about anything. He, presumably, was.

Down came the shades again. The lights stayed on behind their beige opaqueness. But behind the one that had remained down all along the room remained dark.

Time went by. Hard to say how much—a quarter of an hour, twenty minutes. A cricket chirped in one of the back yards. Sam came in to see if I wanted anything before he went home for the night. I told him no, I didn't—it was all right, run along. He

stood there for a minute, head down. Then I saw him shake it
slightly, as if at something he didn't like.

"What's the matter?" I asked.

"You know what that means? My old mammy told it to me,
and she never told a lie in her life. I never once seen it to miss,
either."

"What, the cricket?"

"Any time you hear one of them things, that's a sign of death
someplace close around."

I swept the back of my hand at him. "Well, it isn't in here, so
don't let it worry you."

He went out, muttering stubbornly. "It's somewhere close
by, though. Somewhere not very far off. Got to be."

The door closed after him and I stayed there alone in the
dark.

It was a stifling night, much closer than the preceding one. I
could hardly get a breath of air even by the open window at
which I sat. I wondered how he—that unknown over there—
could stand it behind those drawn shades.

Then suddenly, just as idle speculation about this whole
matter was about to alight on some fixed point in my mind,
crystalize into something like suspicion, up came the shades
again and off it flitted, as formless as ever and without having
had a chance to come to rest on anything.

He was in the middle windows, the living room. He'd taken
off his coat and shirt, was bare-armed in his undershirt. He
hadn't been able to stand it himself, I guess—the sultriness.

I couldn't make out what he was doing at first. He seemed to
be busy in a perpendicular, up-and-down way rather than
lengthwise. He remained in one place, but he kept dipping
down out of sight and then straightening up into view again at
irregular intervals. It was almost like some sort of calisthenic
exercise, except that the dips and rises weren't evenly timed
enough for that. Sometimes he'd stay down a long time, sometimes he'd bob right up again, sometimes he'd go down two or
three times in rapid succession.

There was some sort of widespread black V railing him off
from the window. Whatever it was, there was just a sliver of it

showing above the upward inclination to which the windows sill deflected my line of vision. All it did was strike off the bottom of his undershirt, to the extent of an inch maybe. But I hadn't seen it there at other times and I couldn't tell what it was.

Suddenly he left it for the first time since the shades had gone up, came out around it to the outside, stooped down into another part of the room, and straightened again with an armful of what looked like varicolored pennants at the distance at which I was. He went back behind the V and allowed them to fall across the top of it for a moment, and stay that way. He made one of his dips down out of sight and stayed that way a good while.

The "pennants" slung across the V kept changing color in front of my eyes. I have very good sight. One moment they were white, the next red, the next blue.

Then I got it. They were a woman's dresses, and he was pulling them down to him one by one, taking the topmost one each time. Suddenly they were all gone, the V was black and bare again, and his torso had reappeared.

I knew what it was now, and what he was doing. The dresses had told me. He confirmed it for me. He spread his arms to the ends of the V and I could see him leave and hitch, as if exerting pressure, and suddenly the V had folded up, become a cubed wedge. Then he made rolling motions with his upper body and the wedge disappeared off to one side.

He's been packing a trunk, packing his wife's things into a large upright trunk.

He reappeared at the kitchen window presently and stood still for a moment. I saw him draw his arm across his forehead, not once but several times, and then whip the end of it off into space. Sure, it was hot work for such a night. Then he reached up along the wall and took something down. Since it was the kitchen he was in, my imagination had to supply a cabinet and a bottle.

I could see the two or three quick passes his hand made to his mouth after that. I said to myself tolerantly: That's what nine men out of ten would do after packing a trunk—take a good stiff drink. And if the tenth didn't, it would only be because he didn't have any liquor at hand.

Then he came closer to the window again and, standing edgewise to the side of it so that only a thin paring of his head and shoulder showed, peered watchfully out into the dark quadrilateral, along the line of windows, most of them unlighted by now once more. He always started on the left-hand side, the side opposite mine, and made his circuit of inspection from there on around.

That was the second time in one evening I'd seen him do that. And once at daybreak made three times altogether. You'd almost think he felt guilty about something. It was probably nothing, just an odd little habit, a quirk, that he didn't know he had himself. I had them myself—everyone does.

He withdrew into the room again, and it blacked out. His figure passed into the one that was still lighted next to it, the living room. That blacked out next. It didn't surprise me that the third room, the bedroom with the drawn shade, didn't light up on his entering there. He wouldn't want to disturb her, of course—particularly if she was going away tomorrow for her health, as his packing of her trunk showed. She needed all the rest she could get before making the trip. Simple enough for him to slip into bed in the dark.

It did surprise me, though, when a match flare winked sometime later, to have it still come from the darkened living room. He must be lying down in there, trying to sleep on a sofa or something for the night. He hadn't gone near the bedroom at all, was staying out of it altogether. That puzzled me, frankly. That was carrying solicitude almost too far.

Ten minutes or so later, there was another match wink, still from that same living-room window. He couldn't sleep.

The night brooded down on both of us like, the curiosity-monger in the bay window, the chain smoker in the fourth-floor apartment, without giving any answer. The only sound was that interminable cricket.

I was back at the window again with the first sun of morning. Not because of him. My mattress was like a bed of hot coals.

Sam found me there when he came in to get things ready for me. "You're going to be a wreck, Mr. Jeff," was all he said.

First, for a while, there was no sign of life over there. The suddenly I saw his head bob up from somewhere down out of sight in the living room, so I knew I'd been right; he'd spent the night on a sofa or easy chair in there. Now, of course, he'd look in at her, to see how she was, find out if she felt any better. That was only common ordinary humanity. He hadn't been near her, so far as I could make out, since two nights before.

He didn't. He dressed and went in the opposite direction, into the kitchen, and wolfed something in there, standing and using both hands. Then he suddenly turned and moved offside, in the direction in which I knew the entrance to be, as if he had just heard some summons, like the doorbell.

Sure enough, in a moment he came back and there were two men with him in leather aprons. Expressmen. I saw him standing by while they laboriously maneuvered that cubed black wedge out between them in the direction they'd just come from. He did more than just stand by. He practically hovered over them, kept shifting from side to side, he was so anxious to see that it was done right.

Then he came back alone, and I saw him swipe his arm across his head as though it was he, not they, who was all heated up from the effort.

So he was forwarding her trunk to wherever it was she was going. That was all.

He reached up along the wall again and took something down. He was taking another drink. Two. Three. I said to myself, a little at a loss: Yes, but he hasn't just packed a trunk this time. That trunk has been standing packed and ready since last night. Where does the hard work come in, the sweat and the need for a bracer?

Now, at last, after all those hours, he finally did go in to her. I saw his form pass through the living room and go beyond, into the bedroom. Up went the shade that had been down all this time. Then he turned his head and looked around behind him. In a certain way, a way that was unmistakable even from where I was. Not in one certain direction, as one looks at a person, but from side to side and up and down and all around, as one looks at—*an empty room.*

He stepped back, bent a little, gave a fling of his arms, and an unoccupied mattress and bedding upended over the foot of a bed, staying that way, emptily curved. A second one followed a moment later.

She wasn't in there.

They use the expression "delayed reaction." I found out then what it meant. For two days, a sort of formless uneasiness, disembodied suspicion, I don't know what to call it, had been flitting and volplaning around in my mind like an insect looking for a landing place. More than once, just as it had been ready to settle, some slight reassuring thing, such as the raising of the shades after they had been down unnaturally long, had been enough to keep it winging aimlessly, to prevent it from staying still long enough for me to recognize it.

The point of contact had been there all along, waiting to receive it. Now, for some reason, within a split second after he tossed over the empty mattresses, it landed—*zoom!* And the point of contact expanded, or exploded, into a certainty of—*murder.*

In other words, the rational part of my mind was far behind the instinctive, subconscious part. Delayed reaction. Now the one had caught up to the other. The thought message that sparked from the synchronization was: He's done something to her.

I looked down and my hand was bunching the fabric over my kneecap. I forced it to open. I said to myself, steadyingly: Now wait a minute, be careful, go slow. You've seen nothing. You know nothing. You only have the negative proof that you don't see her any more.

Sam was standing there looking over at me from the pantry-way. He said accusingly, "You ain't touched a thing. And your face looks like a sheet."

It felt like one. It had that needling feeling, when the blood has left it involuntarily. It was more to get him out of the way and give myself some elbow room for undisturbed thinking than anything else that I said, "Sam, what's the street address of that building down there? Don't stick your head too far out and gape at it."

"Somethin' or other Benedict Avenue." He scratched his neck helpfully.

"I know that. Chase around the corner a minute and get me the exact number on it, will you?"

"Why do you want to know that for?" he asked as he turned to go.

"None of your business," I said with the good-natured firmness that was all that was necessary to take care of that once and for all. I called after him just as he was closing the door, "And while you're about it, step into the entrance and see if you can tell from the mailboxes who has the fourth-floor rear. Don't get me the wrong one now. And try not to let anyone catch you at it."

He went out mumbling something that sounded like, "When a man ain't got nothing to do but just sit all day, he sure can think up the blamest things—"

The door closed and I settled down to some good constructive thinking.

I said to myself: What are you really building up this monstrous supposition on? Let's see what you've got. Only that there were several little things wrong with the mechanism, the chain belt, of their recurrent daily habits over there.

1. The lights were on all night the first night.

2. He came in later than usual the second night.

3. He left his hat on.

4. She didn't come out to greet him—she hasn't appeared since the evening before the lights were on all night.

5. He took a drink after he finished packing her trunk. But he took three stiff drinks this morning, immediately after her trunk went out.

6. He was inwardly disturbed and worried, yet superimposed on this was an unnatural external concern about the surrounding rear windows that was off-key.

7. He slept in the living room, didn't go near the bedroom, during the night before the departure of the trunk.

Very well. If she had been ill that first night, and he had sent her away for her health, that automatically canceled out points

1, 2, 3, and 4. It left points 5 and 6 totally unimportant and unincriminating. But when it came up against 7, it hit a stumbling block.

If she went away immediately after being ill that first night, why didn't he want to sleep in their bedroom last night? Sentiment? Hardly. Two perfectly good beds in one room, only a sofa or uncomfortable easy chair in the other. Why should he stay out of there if she was already gone? Just because he missed her, was lonely? A grown man doesn't act that way. All right, then she was still in there.

Sam came back at this point and said, "That house is Number 525 Benedict Avenue. The fourth-floor rear has the name of Mr. and Mrs. Lars Thorwald up."

"Shh," I silenced, and motioned him backhand out of my sight.

"First he want it, then he don't," he grumbled philosophically, and retired to his duties.

I went ahead digging at it. But if she was still in there in that bedroom last night, then she couldn't have gone away to the country, because I never saw her leave today. She could have left without my seeing her in the early hours of yesterday morning. I'd missed a few hours, been asleep. But this morning I had been up before he was himself and I only saw his head rear up from that sofa after I'd been at the window for some time.

To go at all, she would have had to go yesterday morning. Then why had he left the bedroom shade down, left the mattresses undisturbed, until today? Above all, why had he stayed out of that room last night? That was evidence that she hadn't gone, was still in there.

Then today, immediately after the trunk had been dispatched, he went in, pulled up the shade, tossed over the mattresses, and showed that she hadn't been in there. The thing was like a crazy spiral.

No, it wasn't either. *Immediately after the trunk had been dispatched—*

The trunk!

That did it.

I looked around to make sure the door was safely closed

between Sam and me. My hand hovered uncertainly over the telephone dial a minute. Boyne, he'd be the one to tell about it. He was on Homicide. He had been, anyway, when I'd last seen him. I didn't want to get a flock of strange dicks and cops into my hair. I didn't want to be involved any more than I had to. Or at all, if possible.

They switched my call to the right place after a couple of wrong tries, and I got him finally.

"Boyne? This is Hal Jeffries—"

"Well, where've you been the last sixty-two years?" he began.

"We can take that up later. What I want you to do now is take down a name and address. Ready? Lars Thorwald. Five twenty-five Benedict Avenue. Fourth-floor rear. Got it?"

"Fourth-floor rear. Got it. What's it for?"

"Investigation. I've got a firm belief you'll uncover a murder there if you start digging for it. Don't call on me for anything more than that—just a conviction. There's been a man and wife living there until now. Now there's just a man. Her trunk went out early this morning. If you can find someone who saw *her* leave—"

Marshaled aloud like that and conveyed to somebody else, a lieutenant of detectives above all, it did sound flimsy, even to me. He said hesitantly, "Well, but—"

Then he accepted it as was. Because I was the source. I even left my window out of it completely. I could do that with him and get away with it because he'd known me for years, he didn't question my reliability. I didn't want my room all cluttered up with dicks and cops taking turns nosing out of the window in this hot weather. Let them tackle it from the front.

"Well, we'll see what we see," he said. "I'll keep you posted."

I hung up and sat back to watch and wait events. I had a grandstand seat. Or rather a grandstand seat in reverse. I could only see from behind the scenes, but not from the front. I couldn't watch Boyne go to work. I could only see the results, when and if there were any.

Nothing happened for the next few hours. The police work that I knew must be going on was an invisible as police work should be. The figure in the fourth-floor windows over there remained in sight, alone and undisturbed. He didn't go out. He was restless, roamed from room to room without staying in one place very long, but he stayed in. Once I saw him eating again—sitting down this time—and once he shaved, and once he even tried to read the paper, but he didn't read it long.

Little unseen wheels were in motion around him. Small and harmless as yet, preliminaries. If he knew, I wondered to myself, would he remain there quiescent like that, or would he try to bolt out and flee. That mightn't depend so much on his guilt as on his sense of immunity, his feeling that he could outwit them. Of his guilt, I myself was already convinced or I wouldn't have taken the step I had.

At three, my phone rang. Boyne calling back. "Jeffries? Well, I don't know. Can't you give me a little more than just a bald statement like that?"

"Why?" I fenced. "Why do I have to?"

"I've had a man over there making inquiries. I've just had his report. The building superintendent and several of the neighbors all agree she left for the country, to try and regain her health—early yesterday morning."

"Wait a minute. Did any of them *see* her leave, according to your man?"

"No."

"Then all you've got is a second-hand version of an unsupported statement by him. Not an eyewitness account."

"He was met returning from the depot after he'd bought her ticket and seen her off on the train."

"That's still an unsupported statement, once removed."

"I've sent a man down there to the station to check with the ticket agent if possible. After all, he should have been fairly conspicuous at that early hour. And we're keeping him under observation, of course, in the meantime, watching all his movements. The first chance we get we're going to jump in and search the place."

I had a feeling they wouldn't find anything even if they did.

"Don't expect anything more from me. I've dropped it in your lap. I've given you all I have to give. A name, an address, and an opinion."

"Yes, and I've always valued your opinion highly before now,
Jeff—"

"But now you don't, that it?"

"Not at all. The thing is, we haven't turned up anything that
seems to bear out your impression so far."

"You haven't got very far along, so far."

He went back to his previous cliché. "Well, we'll see what we
see. Let you know later."

Another hour or so went by and sunset came on. I saw him
start to get ready to go out over there. He put on his hat, put
his hand in his pocket, and stood still, looking at it for a minute.
Counting change, I guess. It gave me a peculiar sense of suppressed excitement, knowing they were doing to come in the
minute he left. I thought grimly as I saw him take a last look
around: If you've got anything to hide, brother, now's the time
to hide it.

He left. A breath-holding interval of misleading emptiness
descended on the apartment. A three-alarm fire couldn't have
pulled my eyes off those windows. Suddenly the door by which
he had just left parted slightly and two men insinuated themselves, one behind the other. There they were now. They closed
it behind them, separated at once, and got busy.

One took the bedroom, one the kitchen, and they started to
work their way toward one another from those extremes of the
apartment. They were thorough. I could see them going over
everything from top to bottom. They took the living room
together. One cased one side, the other man the other.

They'd already finished before the warning caught them. I
could tell that by the way they straightened up and stood facing
one another frustratedly for a minute. Then both their heads
turned sharply, as at a tipoff by doorbell that he was coming
back. They got out fast.

I wasn't unduly disheartened—I'd expected that. My own
feeling all along had been that they wouldn't find anything
incriminating around. The trunk was gone.

He came in with a mountainous brown paper bag sitting in
the curve of one arm. I watched him closely to see if he'd

discover that someone had been there in his absence. Apparently he didn't. They'd been adroit about it.

He stayed in the rest of the night. Sat tight, safe and sound. He did some desultory drinking. I could see him sitting there by the window and his hand would hoist every once in a while—but not to excess. Apparently everything was under control, the tension had eased—now that the trunk was out.

Watching him across the night, I speculated: Why doesn't he get out? If I'm right about him, and I am, why does the stick around? That brought its own answer: Because he doesn't know anyone's onto him yet. He doesn't think there's any hurry. To go too soon, right after she has, would be more dangerous than to stay a while.

The night wore on. I sat there waiting for Boyne's call. It came later than I thought it would. I picked the phone up in the dark. He was getting ready to go to bed over there now. He'd risen from where he'd been sitting drinking in the kitchen and put the light out. He went into the living room, lit that. He started to pull his shirttail up out of his belt. Boyne's voice was in my ear as my eyes were on him over there. Three-cornered arrangement.

"Hello, Jeff? Listen, absolutely nothing. We searched the place while he was out—"

I nearly said, "I know you did, I saw it," but checked myself in time.

"We didn't turn up a thing. But—" He stopped as though this was going to be important. I waited impatiently for him to go ahead.

"Downstairs in his letterbox we found a postcard waiting for him. We fished it up out of the slot with bent pins—"

"And?"

"And it was from his wife, written only yesterday from some farm up-country. Here's the message we copied: 'Arrived okay. Already feeling a little better. Love, Anna.'"

I said faintly but stubbornly, "You say written only yesterday. Have you proof of that? What was the postmark date on it?"

He made a disgusted sound down in his tonsils. At me, not it.

"The postmark was blurred. A corner of it got wet and the ink smudged."

"All of it blurred?"

"The year date," he admitted. "The hour and the month came out okay. August. And seven-thirty P.M. it was mailed at."

This time *I* made the disgusted sound, in my larynx. "August, seven-thirty P.M.—1937 or 1939 or 1942. You have no proof how it got into that mailbox, whether it came from a letter carrier's pouch or from the back of some bureau drawer."

"Give up, Jeff," he said. "There's such a thing as going too far."

I don't know what I would have said. That is, if I hadn't happened to have my eyes on the Thorwald living-room windows just then. Probably very little. The postcard *had* shaken me, whether I admitted it or not. But I was looking over there. The light had gone out as soon as he'd taken his shirt off. But the bedroom didn't light up. A match fire winked from the living room, low down, as from an easy chair or sofa. With two unused beds in the bedroom, he was *still staying out of there.*

"Boyne," I said in a glassy voice, "I don't care what postcards from the other world you've turned up, I say that man has done away with his wife! Trace that trunk he shipped out. Open it up when you've located it—and I think you'll find her!"

And I hung up without waiting to hear what he was going to do about it. He didn't ring back, so I suspected he was going to give my suggestion a spin in spite of his skepticism.

I stayed there by the window all night, keeping a sort of deathwatch. There were two more match flares after the first, at about half-hour intervals. Nothing more after that. So possibly he was asleep over there. Possibly not. I had to sleep sometime myself, and I finally succumbed in the flaming light of the early sun. Anything that he was going to do he would have done under cover of darkness and not waited for broad daylight. There wouldn't be anything much to watch for a while now. And what was there that he needed to do any more anyway? Nothing, just sit tight and let a little disarming time slip by.

It seemed like five minutes later that Sam came over and

touched me, but it was already high noon. I said irritably, "Didn't you see that note I pinned up, for you to let me sleep?"

He said, "Yeah, but it's your old friend Inspector Boyne. I figured you'd want to—"

It was a personal visit this time. Boyne came into the room behind Sam without waiting, and without much cordiality.

To get rid of Sam, I said, "Go inside and smack a couple of eggs together."

Boyne began in a galvanized-iron voice. "Jeff, what do you mean by doing anything like this to me? I've made a fool out of myself, thanks to you. Sending my men out right and left on wild-goose chases. Thank God I didn't put my foot in any worse than I did, and have this guy picked up and brought in for questioning."

"Oh, then you don't think that's necessary?" I suggested drily.

The look he gave me took care of that. "I'm not alone in the department, you know. There are men over me I'm accountable to for my actions. That looks great, don't it, sending one of my fellows one-half-a-day's trainride up into the sticks to some godforsaken whistlestop or other at departmental expense—"

"Then you located the trunk?"

"We traced it through the express agency," he said flintily.

"And you opened it?"

"We did better than that. We got in touch with the various farmhouses in the immediate locality, and Mrs. Thorwald came down to the junction in a produce truck from one of them and opened it herself, with her own keys!"

Very few men have ever got a look from an old friend like the one I got from him. At the door he said, stiff as a rifle barrel, "Just let's forget all about it, shall we? That's about the kindest thing either one of us can do for the other. You're not yourself, and I'm out a little of my own pocket money, time, and temper. Let's let it go at that. If you want to telephone me in future, I'll be glad to give you my home number."

The door went *whopp!* behind him.

For about ten minutes after he stormed out, my numbed mind was in a sort of straitjacket. Then it started to wriggle its way free. The hell with the police. I can't prove it to them, maybe, but I can prove it to myself, one way or the other, once and for all. Either I'm wrong or I'm right. He's got his armor on against them. But his back is naked and unprotected against me.

I called Sam in. "Whatever became of that spyglass we used to have around on that cabin cruiser?"

He found it someplace downstairs and came in with it, blowing on it and rubbing it along his sleeve. I let it lie idle in my lap first. I took a piece of paper and a pencil and wrote six words on it: *What have you done with her?*

I sealed it in an envelope and left the envelope blank. I said to Sam, "Now here's what I want you to do, and I want you to be slick about it. You take this, go in that building five twenty-five, climb the stairs to the fourth-floor rear, and ease it under the door. You're fast—at least you used to be. Let's see if you're fast enough to keep from being caught at it. Then when you get safely down again, give the outside doorbell a little poke, to attract attention."

His mouth started to open.

"And don't ask me any questions, you understand? I'm not fooling."

He went, and I got the spyglass ready.

I got him in the right focus after a moment or two. A face leaped up and I was really seeing him for the first time. Dark-haired, but unmistakable Scandinavian ancestry. Looked like a sinewy customer, although he didn't run to much bulk.

About five minutes went by. His head turned sharply, profile-ward. That was the bell poke, right there. The note must be in already.

He gave me the back of his head as he went toward the door. The lens could follow him all the way to the rear, where my unaided eyes hadn't been able to before.

He opened the door first, missed seeing it, looked out on a level. He closed it. Then he dipped, straightened up. He had it. I could see him turning it this way and that.

He shifted in, away from the door, nearer the window. He thought danger lay near the door, safety away from it. He didn't know it was the other way around: the deeper into his own rooms he retreated the greater the danger.

He'd torn it open, he was reading it. God, how I watched his expression. My eyes clung to it like leeches. There was a sudden widening, a pulling—the whole skin of his face seemed to stretch back behind his ears, narrowing his eyes. Shock. Panic. His hand pushed out and found the wall, and he braced himself with it. Then he went back toward the door again slowly.

I could see him creeping up on it, stalking it as though it were something alive. He opened it so slenderly you couldn't see it at all and peered fearfully through the crack. Then he closed it, and he came back zigzag, off balance from the sheer reflex dismay. He toppled into a chair and snatched up a drink—out of the bottle neck itself this time. And even while he was holding it to his lips, his head was turned, looking over his shoulder at the door that had suddenly thrown his secret in his face.

I put the glass down.

Guilty! Guilty as all hell, and the police be damned!

My hand started toward the phone, came back again. What was the use? They wouldn't listen now any more than they had before. ("You should have seen his face." And I could hear Boyne's answer: "Anyone gets a jolt from an anonymous letter, true or false. You would yourself." They had a real live Mrs. Thorwald to show me—or thought they had. I'd have to show them the dead one to prove that they both weren't one and the same. I, from my window, had to show them a body.)

Well, he'd have to show me first.

It took hours before I got it. I kept pegging away at it, pegging away at it, while the afternoon wore away. Meanwhile, he was pacing back and forth there like a caged panther. Two minds with but one thought, turned inside out in my case. How to keep it hidden, how to see that it wasn't kept hidden.

I was afraid he might try to light out, but if he intended doing that he was going to wait until after dark, apparently, so I had a little time yet. Possibly he didn't want to himself, unless he was driven to it—still felt that it was more dangerous than to stay.

The customary sights and sounds around me went on unnoticed while the mainstream of my thoughts pounded like a torrent against that one obstacle stubbornly damming them up:

how to get him to give the location away to me so that I could give it away in turn to the police.

I was dimly conscious, I remember, of the landlord or somebody bringing in a prospective tenant to look at the sixth-floor apartment, the one that had already been finished. This was two over Thorwald's; they were still at work on the in-between one. At one point an odd little bit of synchronization—completely accidental, of course—cropped up. Landlord and tenant both happened to be near the living-room windows on the sixth at the same moment that Thorwald was near those on the forth. Both parties moved onward simultaneously into the kitchen from there, and, passing the blind spot of the wall, appeared next at the kitchen windows.

It was uncanny—they were almost like precision strollers or puppets manipulated on one and the same string. It probably wouldn't have happened again just like that in another fifty years. Immediately afterward, they digressed, never to repeat themselves like that again.

The thing was, something about it had disturbed me. There had been some slight flaw or hitch to mar its smoothness. I tried for a moment or two to figure out what it had been, and couldn't. The landlord and tenant were gone now and only Thorwald was in sight. My unaided memory wasn't enough to recapture it for me. My eyesight might have if it had been repeated, but it wasn't.

It sank into my subconscious, to ferment there like yeast, while I went back to the main problem at hand.

I got it finally. It was well after dark, but I finally hit on a way. It mightn't work, it was cumbersome and roundabout, but it was the only way I could think of. An alarmed turn of the head, a quick precautionary step in one certain direction, was all I needed. And to get this brief, flickering, transitory giveaway, I needed two phone calls and an absence of about half an hour on his part between them.

I leafed a directory by matchlight until I'd found what I wanted: Thorwald, Lars. 525 Bndct. . . . SWansea 5-2114

I blew out the match, picked up the phone in the dark. It was like television. I could see to the other end of my call, only not along the wire but by a direct channel of vision from window to window.

He said, "Hullo?" gruffly.

I thought: How strange this is. I've been accusing him of murder for three days straight and only now I'm hearing his voice for the first time.

I didn't try to disguise my own voice. After all, he'd never see me and I'd never see him. I said, "You got my note?"

He said guardedly, "Who is this?"

"Just somebody who happens to know."

He said craftily, "Know what?"

"Know what you know. You and I, we're the only ones."

He controlled himself well. I didn't hear a sound. But he didn't know he was open another way, too. I had the spyglass balanced there at proper height on two large books on the sill. Through the window I saw him pull open the collar of his shirt as though its stricture was intolerable. Then he backed his hand over his eyes the way you do when there's a light blinding you.

His voice came back firmly. "I don't know what you're talking about."

"Business, that's what I'm talking about. It should be worth something to me, shouldn't it? To keep it from going any further." I wanted to keep him from catching on that it was the windows. I still needed them, I needed them now more than ever. "You weren't very careful about your door the other night. Or maybe the draft swung it open a little."

That hit him when he lived. Even the stomach heave reached over the wire. "You didn't see anything. There wasn't anything to see."

"It's up to you. Why should I go to the police?" I coughed a little. "If it would pay me not to."

"Oh," he said. And there was relief of a sort in it. "D'you want to—see me? Is that it?"

"That would be the best way, wouldn't it? How much can you bring with you for now?"

"I've only got about seventy dollars around here."

"All right, then we can arrange the rest for later. Do you know where Lakeside Park is? I'm near there now. Suppose we make it there." That was about thirty minutes away—fifteen there and fifteen back. "There's a little pavilion as you go in."

"How many of you are there?" he asked cautiously.

"Just me. It pays to keep things to yourself. That way you don't have to divvy up."

He seemed to like that, too. "I'll take a run out," he said, "just to see what it's all about."

I watched him more closely than ever after he'd hung up. He flitted straight through to the end room, the bedroom that he didn't go near any more. He disappeared into a clothes closet in there, stayed a minute, came out again. He must have taken something out of a hidden cranny or niche in there that even the dicks had missed. I could tell by the pistonlike motion of his hand just before it disappeared inside his coat what it was. A gun.

It's a good thing, I thought, I'm not out there in Lakeside Park waiting from my seventy bucks.

The place blacked out and he was on his way.

I called Sam in. "I want you to do something for me that's a little risky—in fact, damn risky. You might break a leg, or you might get shot, or you might even get pinched. We've been together ten years and I wouldn't ask you anything like that if I could do it myself. But I can't, and it's got to be done."

Then I told him, "Go out the back way, cross the backyard fences, and see if you can get into that fourth-floor apartment up the fire escape. He's left one of the windows down a little from the top."

"What do you want me to look for?"

"Nothing." The police had been there already, so what was the good of that? "There are three rooms over there. I want you to disturb everything just a little bit in all three to show someone's been in there. Turn up the edge of each rug a little, shift every chair and table around a little, leave the closet doors standing out. Don't pass up a thing. Here, keep your eyes on this."

I look off my wristwatch, strapped it on him. "You've got twenty-five minutes, starting from now. If you stay within those twenty-five minutes, nothing will happen to you. When you see they're up, don't wait any longer—get out and get out fast."

"Climb back down?"

"No." He wouldn't remember, in his excitement, if he'd left the windows up or not. And I didn't want him to connect danger with the back of his place, but with the front. I wanted to keep my own window out of it. "Latch the window down tight, let yourself out the door, and beat it out of the building the front way, for your life!"

"I'm just an easy mark for you," he said ruefully, but he went.

He came out through our own basement door below me and scrambled over the fences. If anyone had challenged him from one of the surrounding windows, I was going to backstop for him, explain I'd sent him down to look for something. But no one did. He made it pretty good for someone his age—he isn't so young any more. Even the fire escape backing the apartment, which was drawn up short, he managed to contact by standing on something. He got in, lit the light, looked over at me. I motioned him to go ahead, not to weaken.

I watched him at it. There wasn't any way I could protect him now that he was in there. Even Thorwald would be within his rights in shooting him down—this was break-and-entry. I had to stay behind the scenes, as I had been all along. I couldn't get out in front of him as a lookout and shield him. Even the dicks had had a lookout posted.

He must have been tense doing it. I was twice as tense, watching him do it. The twenty-five minutes took fifty to go by. Finally he came over to the window, latched it fast. The lights went, and he was out. He'd made it. I blew out a bellyful of breath that was twenty-five minutes old.

I heard him keying the street door, and when he came up I said warningly, "Leave the light out in here. Go and build yourself a great big whiskey—you're as close to white as you'll ever be."

Thorwald came back twenty-nine minutes after he'd left for Lakeside Park. A pretty slim margin to hang a man's life on. So now for the finale of the long-winded business, and here was hoping. I got my second phone call in before he had time to notice anything amiss. It was tricky timing, but I'd been sitting there with the receiver ready in my hand, dialing the number

over and over, then killing it each time. He came in on the 2 of
5-2114, and I saved that much time. The ring started before his
hand came away from the light switch.

This was the one that was going to tell the story.

"You were supposed to bring money, not a gun; that's why I
didn't show up." I saw the jolt that threw into him. The window
still had to stay out of it. "I saw you tap the inside of your coat
where you had it as you came out on the street." Maybe he
hadn't, but he wouldn't remember by now whether he had or
not. You usually do when you're packing a gun and aren't a
habitual carrier.

"Too bad you had your trip out and back for nothing. I didn't
waste my time while you were gone, though. I know more now
that I knew before." This was the important part. I had the
spyglass up and I was practically fluoroscoping him. "I've found
out where it is. You know what I mean. I know now where
you've got it. I was there while you were out."

Not a word. Just quick breathing.

"Don't you believe me? Like around. Put the receiver down
and take a look for yourself. I found it."

He put it down, moved as far as the living-room entrance, and
touched on the lights. He just looked around him once, in a
sweeping, all-embracing stare that didn't come to a head on any
one fixed point, didn't center at all.

He was smiling grimly when he came back to the phone. All
he said, softly and with malignant satisfaction, was: "You're a
liar."

Then I saw him lay the receiver down and take his hand off
it. I hung up at my end.

The test had failed. And yet it hadn't. He hadn't given the
location away as I'd hoped he would. And yet that "You're a
liar" was a tacit admission that it was there to be found,
somewhere around him, somewhere on the premises. In such a
good place that he didn't have to worry about it, didn't even
have to look to make sure.

So there was a kind of sterile victory in my defeat. But it
wasn't worth a damn to me.

He was standing there with his back to me and I couldn't see
what he was doing. I knew the phone was somewhere in front

of him, but I thought he was just standing there pensive behind it. His head was slightly lowered, that was all. I didn't even see his elbow move. And if his index finger did, I couldn't see it.

He stood like that a moment or two, then finally he moved aside. The lights went out over there; I lost him. He was careful not even to strike matches as he sometimes did in the dark.

My mind no longer distracted by having him to look at, I turned to trying to recapture something else—that troublesome little hitch in synchronization that had occurred this afternoon when the renting agent and he both moved simultaneously from one window to the next. The closest I could get was this: It was like when you're looking at someone through a pane of imperfect glass, and a flaw in the glass distorts the symmetry of the reflected image for a second, until it has gone on past that point. Yet that wouldn't do, that wasn't it. The windows had been open and there had been no glass between. And I hadn't been using the lens.

My phone rang. Boyne, I supposed. It wouldn't be anyone else at this hour. Maybe after reflecting on the way he'd jumped all over me—I said "Hello" unguardedly, in my own normal voice.

There wasn't any answer.

I said, "Hello? Hello? Hello?" I kept giving away samples of my voice.

There wasn't a sound from first to last.

I hung up finally. It was still dark over there, I noticed.

Sam looked in to check out. He was a bit thick-tongued from his restorative drink. He said, "Awri' if I go now?" I half heard him. I was trying to figure out another way of trapping *him* over there into giving away the right spot. I motioned my consent absently.

He went a little unsteadily down the stairs to the ground floor, and after a delaying moment or two I heard the street door close after him. Poor Sam, he wasn't much used to liquor.

I was left alone in the house, one chair the limit of my freedom of movement.

Suddenly a light went on over there again, just momentarily, to go right out again afterward. He must have needed it for something, to locate something that he had already been looking for and found he wasn't able to put his hands on readily without it. He found it, whatever it was, almost immediately, and moved back at once to put the lights out again. As he turned to do so, I saw him give a glance out the window. He didn't come to the window to do it, he just shot it out in passing.

Something about it struck me as different from any of the others I'd seen him give in all the time I'd been watching him. If you can qualify such an elusive thing as a glance, I would have termed it a glance with a purpose. It was certainly anything but random, it had a bright spark of fixity in it. It wasn't one of those precautionary sweeps I'd seen him give, either. It hadn't started over on the other side and worked its way around to my side, the right. It had hit dead center at my bay window, for just a split second while it lasted, and then was gone again. And the lights were gone, and he was gone.

Sometimes your senses take things in without your mind translating them into their proper meaning. My eyes saw that look. My mind refused to smelter it properly. It was meaningless, I thought. An unintentional bull's eye that just happened to hit square over here as he went toward the lights on his way out.

Delayed reaction. A wordless ring of the phone. To test a voice. A period of bated darkness following that, in which two could have played at the same game—stalking one another's window squares, unseen. A last-moment flicker of the lights— that was bad strategy but unavoidable. A parting glance, radio-active with malignant intention. All these things sank in without fusing. My eyes did their job, it was my mind that didn't—or at least took its time about it.

Seconds went by in packages of sixty. It was very still around the familiar quadrangle formed by the backs of the houses. A sort of breathless stillness. And then a sound came into it, starting up from nowhere, nothing. The unmistakable, spaced clicking a cricket makes in the silence of the night. I thought of Sam's superstition about them, that he claimed had never failed to fulfill itself yet. If that was the case, it looked bad for somebody in one of these slumbering houses around here.

Sam had been gone only about ten minutes. And now he was back again, he must have forgotten something. That drink was responsible. Maybe his hat, or maybe even the key to his own place uptown. He knew I couldn't come down and let him in, and he was trying to be quiet about it, thinking perhaps I'd dozed off. All I could hear was this faint jiggling down at the lock of the front door.

It was one of those old-fashioned stoop houses, with an outer pair of storm doors that were allowed to swing free all night, and then a small vestibule, and then the inner door, worked by a simple iron key. The liquor had made his hand a little unreliable, although he'd had this difficulty once or twice before even without it. A match would have helped him find the keyhole quicker, but then Sam doesn't smoke. I knew he wasn't likely to have one on him.

The sound had stopped now. He must have given up, gone away again, decided to let whatever it was go until tomorrow. He hadn't got in, because I knew his noisy way of letting doors coast shut by themselves too well, and there hadn't been any sound of that sort, that loose slap he always made.

Then suddenly it exploded. Why at this particular moment, I don't know. That was some mystery of the inner workings of my own mind. It flashed like waiting gunpowder a spark has finally reached along a slow train. Drove all thoughts of Sam and the front door and this and that completely out of my head. It had been waiting there since midafternoon today, and only now— More of that delayed reaction. Damned that delayed reaction!

The renting agent and Thorwald had both started even from the living-room window. An intervening gap of blind wall and both had reappeared at the kitchen window, still one above the other. But some sort of hitch or flaw or jump had taken place right there that bothered me. The eye is a reliable surveyor. There wasn't anything the matter with their timing, it was their parallel-ness, or whatever the word is. The hitch had been vertical, not horizontal. There had been an upward "jump."

Now I had it, now I knew. And it couldn't wait. It was too good. They wanted a body? Now I had one for them!

Angry or not, Boyne would *have* to listen to me now. I didn't

waste any time. I dialed his precinct house then and there in
the dark, working the slots in my lap by memory alone. They
didn't make much noise going around, just a light click. Not
even as distinct as that cricket out there—

"He went home long ago," the desk sergeant said.

This couldn't wait. "All right, give me his home phone
number."

He took a minute, came back again. "Trafalgar," he said. Then
nothing more.

"Well? Trafalgar what?" Not a sound.

"Hello? Hello?" I tapped it. "Operator, I've been cut off. Give
me that party again." I couldn't hear her.

I hadn't been cut off. My wire had been cut. That had been
too sudden. And to be cut like that it would have to be done
somewhere right here inside the house with me. Outside, it
went underground.

Delayed reaction. This time final, fatal, altogether too late. A
voiceless ring of the phone. A direction finder of a look from
over there. Sam seemingly trying to get back in a while ago.

Surely death was somewhere inside the house here with me.
And I couldn't move, I couldn't get up out of this chair. Even if
I had got through to Boyne right now, that would have been
too late. There wasn't time enough now for one of those camera
finishes.

I could have shouted out the window to that gallery of
sleeping rear-window neighbors around me, I supposed. It
would have brought them to the windows. It couldn't have
brought them over here in time. By the time they had even
figured which particular house it was coming from, it would
stop again, be over with.

So I didn't open my mouth. Not because I was brave, but
because it was so obviously useless.

He'd be up in a minute. He must be on the stairs now,
although I couldn't hear him. Not even a creak. A creak would
have been a relief, would have placed him. This was like being
shut up in the dark with the silence of a gliding, coiling cobra
somewhere around you.

There wasn't a weapon in the place with me. There were
books there on the wall in the dark within reach. Me, who

never read. The former owner's books. There was a bust of Rousseau or Montesquieu—I'd never been able to decide which. It was a monstrosity, but it, too, dated from before my occupancy.

I arched my middle upward from the chair seat and clawed desperately up at it. Twice my fingertips slipped off it, then at the third raking I got it to teeter, and the fourth brought it down into my lap, pushing me down into the chair. There was a streamer rug under me. I didn't need it around me in this weather—I'd been using it to soften the seat of the chair. I tugged it out from under and mantled it around me like an Indian brave's blanket.

Then I squirmed far down in the chair, let my head and one shoulder dangle out over the arm on the side next to the wall. I hoisted the bust to my other, upward shoulder, balanced it there precariously for a second head, blanket tucket around its ears. From the back, in the dark, it would look, I hoped—

I proceeded to breathe adenoidally, like someone in heavy upright sleep. It wasn't hard. My own breath was coming nearly that labored anyway, from tension.

He was good with knobs and hinges and things. I never heard the door open, and this one, unlike the one downstairs, was right behind me. A little eddy of air puffed through the dark at me. I could feel it because my scalp, the real one, was all wet at the roots of the hair.

If it was going to be a knife or head blow, the dodge might give me a second chance; that was the most I could hope for. My arms and shoulders are hefty. I'd bring him down on me in a bear hug after the first slash or drive and break his neck or collarbone against me.

If it was going to be a gun, he'd get me anyway in the end. A difference of a few seconds. He had a gun, I knew, that he was going to use on me in the open, over at Lakeside Park. I was hoping that here, indoors, in order to make his own escape more practicable—

Time was up.

The flash of the shot lit up the room for a second, it was so dark. Or at least the corners of it, like flickering, weak lightning.

The bust bounced on my shoulder and disintegrated into chunks.

I thought he was jumping up and down on the floor for a minute with frustrated rage. Then when I saw him dart by me and lean over the window sill to look for a way out, the sound transferred itself rearward and downward, become a pummeling with hoof and hip at the street door. The camera finish, after all. But he still could have killed me five times.

I flung my body down into the narrow crevice between chair arm and wall, but my legs were still up, and so was my head and that one shoulder.

He whirled, fired at me so close that it was like looking a sunrise in the face. I didn't feel it, so—it hadn't hit.

"You—" I heard him grunt to himself. I think it was the last thing he said. The rest of his life was all action, not verbal.

He flung over the sill on one arm and dropped into the yard. Two-story drop. He made it because he missed the cement, landed on the sod strip in the middle. I jacked myself up over the chair arm and flung myself bodily forward at the window, nearly hitting it chin first.

He went all right. When life depends on it, you go. He took the first fence, rolled over that bellyward. He went over the second like a cat, hands and feet pointed together in spring. Then he was back in the rear yard of his own building. He got up on something, just about as Sam had. The rest was all footwork, with quick little corkscrew twists at each landing stage. Sam had latched his windows down when he was over there, but he'd reopened one of them for ventilation on his return. His whole life depended now on that casual, unthinking little act—

Second, third. He was up to his own windows. He'd made it. But something went wrong. He veered out away from them in another pretzel twist, flashed up toward the fifth, the one above. Something sparked in the darkness of one of his own windows where he'd been just now, and a shot thudded heavily out around the quadrangle enclosure like a big bass drum.

He passed the fifth, the sixth, got up to the roof. He'd made it a second time. By George, he loved life! The guys in his own windows couldn't get him; he was over them in a straight line and there was too much fire-escape lacing in the way.

I was too busy watching him to watch what was going on around me. Suddenly Boyne was next to me, sighting. I heard him mutter, "I almost hate to do this, he's got to fall so far."

He was balanced on the roof parapet up there, with a star right over his head. An unlucky star. He stayed a minute too long, trying to kill before he was killed. Or maybe he was killed, and knew it.

A shot cracked, high up against the sky, the window pane flew apart all over us, and one of the books snapped right behind me.

Boyne didn't say anything more about hating to do it. My face was pressed outward against his arm. The recoil of his elbow jarred my teeth. I blew a clearing through the smoke to watch him go.

It was pretty horrible. He took a minute to show anything, standing up there on the parapet. Then he let his gun go, as if to say, "I won't need this any more."

Then he went after it. He missed the fire escape entirely, came all the way down on the outside. He landed so far out he hit one of the projecting planks down there out of sight. It bounded his body up, like a springboard. Then it landed again for good. And that was all.

I said to Boyne, "I got it. I got it finally. The fifth-floor flat, the one *over* his that they're still working on. The cement kitchen floor, raised above the level of the other rooms. They wanted to comply with the fire laws and also get a dropped living-room effect as cheaply as possible. Dig it up—"

He went right over then and there, down through the basement and over the fences, to save time. The electricity wasn't turned on yet in that one; they had to use their flashlights. It didn't take them long at that, once they'd got started.

In about half an hour he came to the window and wigwagged over for my benefit.

It meant yes.

He didn't come over until nearly eight in the morning, after they had tidied up and taken them away. Both away, the hot dead, and the cold dead. He said, "Jeff, I take it all back. That damn fool that I sent up there about the trunk—well, it wasn't his fault, in a way. I'm to blame. He didn't have orders to check on the woman's description, only on the contents of the trunk. He came back and touched on it in a general way. I go home and I'm in bed already, and suddenly pop! into my brain—one of the tenants I questioned two days ago had given us a few details and they didn't tally with his on several important points. Talk about being slow to catch on!"

"I've had that all the way through this damn thing," I admitted ruefully. "Delayed reaction. It nearly killed me."

"I'm a police officer and you're not."

"That how you happened to shine at the right time?"

"Sure. We came over to pick him up for questioning. I left them planted there when we saw he wasn't in and came on over here by myself to square it with you while we were waiting. How did you happen to hit on that cement floor?" I told him about the freak synchronization. "The renting agent showed up taller at the kitchen window in proportion to Thorwald than he had been a moment before when both were at the living-room windows together. It was no secret that they were putting in cement floors, topped by a cork composition, and raising them considerably. But it took on new meaning. Since the top-floor one has been finished for some time, it had to be the fifth. Here's the way I have it lined up, just in theory. She's been in ill health for years, and he's been out of work, and he got sick of that and of her both. Met this other—"

"She'll be here later today, they're bringing her down under arrest."

"He probably insured her for all he could get and then started to poison her slowly, trying not to leave any trace. I imagine— and remember, this is pure conjecture—she caught him at it that night the light was on all night. Caught on in some way, or caught him in the act. He lost his head and did the very thing he had wanted all along to avoid doing. Killed her by violence— strangulation or a blow.

"The rest had to be hastily improvised. He got a better break than he deserved at that. He thought of the apartment upstairs, went up and looked around. They'd just finished laying the floor, the cement hadn't hardened yet, and the materials were still around. He gouged a trough out of it just wide enough to take her body, put her in it, mixed fresh cement, and recemented over her, possibly raising the general level of the flooring an inch or two so that she'd be safely covered. A permanent, odorless coffin.

"Next day the workmen came back, laid down the cork surfacing on top of it without noticing anything—I suppose he'd used one of their own trowels to smooth it. Then he sent his accessory upstate fast, near where his wife had been several summers before, but to a different farmhouse where she wouldn't be recognized, along with the trunk keys. Sent the trunk up after her and dropped himself an already-used postcard into his mailbox, with the year date blurred. In a week or two she would have probably committed 'suicide' up there as Mrs. Anna Thorwald. Despondency due to ill health. Written him a farewell note and left her clothes beside some body of deep water. It was risky, but they might have succeeded in collecting the insurance at that."

By nine, Boyne and the rest had gone. I was still sitting there in the chair, too keyed up to sleep. Sam came in and said, "Here's Doc Preston."

He showed up rubbing his hands in that way he has. "Guess we can take the cast off your leg now. You must be tired of sitting there all day doing nothing."

If you have enjoyed this book and would like to receive details of other Walker Mystery-Suspense novels, please write for your free subscription to:

Crime After Crime Newsletter
Walker and Company
720 Fifth Avenue
New York NY 10010